MW01048510

# SECRETS

*in*

# WATER

# SECRETS

*in*

# WATER

BARBARA SAPERGIA

COTEAU BOOKS

© Barbara Sapergia, 1999

All rights reserved. No part of this book covered by the copyrights herein may be reproduced or used in any form or by any means – graphic, electronic or mechanical – without the prior written permission of the publisher. Any request for photocopying, recording, taping, or storage in information  storage and retrieval systems of any part of this book shall be directed in writing to CanCopy, 1 Yonge St., Suite 1900, Toronto, Ontario, M5E 1E5.

This is a work of fiction. Names, characters, places, and incidents either are the product of the author's imagination or are used fictitiously. Any resemblance to actual persons, living or dead, is coincidental.

Edited by Jack Hodgins.

Cover image by Roberto Gonzales.
Cover and Book Design by Duncan Campbell.

Printed and bound in Canada.

Canadian Cataloguing in Publication Data

Barbara Sapergia, (date)
Secrets in water
ISBN 1-55050-157-7

I. Title.

PS8587.A375S43  1999     C813'.54     C99–920145-X
PR9199.3.S225S43  1999

COTEAU BOOKS
401-2206 Dewdney Ave.
Regina, Saskatchewan
Canada    S4R 1H3

AVAILABLE IN THE US FROM
General Distribution Services
4500 Witmer Industrial Estates
Niagara Falls, NY, 14305-1386

The publisher gratefully acknowledges the financial assistance of the Saskatchewan Arts Board, the Canada Council for the Arts, the Government of Canada through the Book Publishing Industry Development Program (BPIDP), and the City of Regina Arts Commission, for its publishing program.

THE CANADA COUNCIL | LE CONSEIL DES ARTS
FOR THE ARTS | DU CANADA
SINCE 1957 | DEPUIS 1957

SASKATCHEWAN
ARTS BOARD

Canadä

city of
Regina

*For April and Janice*

# CHAPTER ONE

Annie likes to sort the mail into piles on the dining room table: junk mail; bills; cheques from clients; real letters. There aren't many real letters these days — letters written solely for and addressed to herself or Charles. She blames the city. Toronto. Four years, and she hasn't made the smallest dent in it, while the people she knew before seem to have fallen away. She does know people here, but they're all connected with Charles's work. She glances at *The Globe and Mail*, open to the daily cryptic crossword, where she's only managed to solve a scattering of clues. She stares at the date: Thursday, March 12. The winter is interminable. It thawed last week, but the slush froze again the next day. Now the city feels bleak and dirty and cold.

Setting aside an envelope announcing on its brightly printed exterior that she, Annie Ransome, is almost certain to win one million dollars if only she will send in her registration documents immediately, she notices an envelope with some of the attributes of a real letter – her name typed in uneven letters on an old manual typewriter with a worn ribbon; a regular envelope with no printed messages. But there's no return address, and it's too bulky to be only a letter. She slits it open, taps the bottom, and its slick insides cascade out on the table. A half dozen or so black-and-white photographs.

They are old pictures, probably from the 1920s, judging by the clothes and hair. Several feature a stiff, uncomfortable-looking man and woman, he sitting in a wooden chair, she standing implacably beside him. The man wears a plain black suit and white shirt, the woman a starched-looking pleated shirtwaist over a long skirt tightly fitted over the hips. Her hair is drawn back into a bun, but not tightly, so that it flares becomingly around her face in a sort of loose pompadour. She could look soft and vulnerable, but doesn't.

There must be some mistake, Annie thinks. These images have nothing to do with me. She sits down at the table to examine them more closely and feels a tingle of recognition.

The remaining pictures show a boy and girl about seven years old, dressed in children's versions of the clothes worn by the man and woman, sitting side by side on a bench. With blue or grey eyes and fair hair, they are the sort of golden children who could be successful models nowadays.

She realizes she has seen the pictures before, or pictures like them, at the beginning of her mother's photo album, the part she always used to hurry past. Now she knows them. The man is her great-grandfather, Eamon Conal; the woman, his wife Maude. Maude Rowan Conal, she was always called. The boy and girl are their twin children, Robbie and Maisie. Maisie was Annie's grandmother. All of them now dead.

They seem much more *present* than people do in photographs these days; their eyes strike her with hard direct force. Eamon's eyes under the straight dark eyebrows suggest an intense desire for something – wealth, education, power, love? – no one will ever know. Maude's burn with determination. To endure? To keep Eamon from realizing what he desires? What is it about Maude that makes Annie think this? Something about the way she stands so close to him, so fierce, so possessive, without actually touching.

They make an arresting pair. Strong, satisfying faces. Maude's hair wavy and thick. She remembers someone, her mother it must have been, saying that Maude had the most wonderful hair, a very dark gold, reaching almost to her waist when she brushed it out.

Why have these pictures come to her now? She looks at the postmark, but it's blurred, unreadable. Who would have had the originals? Her mother, Allison, probably, in her apartment in Riverbend. Or her mother's cousin, Rita, the daughter of the boy in the picture. But why send them now? Annie's never expressed the remotest interest in old pictures. Of course, that wouldn't stop Allison or Rita, not if they wanted her to have them.

A final picture shows a baby in an elaborate starched dress, extravagantly ruffled and tucked and embroidered, propped up against a dark chesterfield. Her eyes, wide open and somewhat puzzled, gaze into the distance. The small hands, clenched into fists, are settled against the folds of the dress. There is an air of watchful unease about her, which Annie thinks or at least hopes must be uncommon for a baby, and a sense of inappropriate maturity in the gaze.

No doubt who this is. It's Annie herself, at five months, dolled up in the family christening gown and set down on her grandmother Maisie's plush sofa; on the back, her date of birth, January 17, 1968. The picture makes her feel uncomfortable; she slides it back out of sight and returns the pictures to the envelope. Time for work.

She sets the envelope on the table and moves to her nearby computer desk, one of those units that disappears behind folding doors when you have company; her work is already set up. She looks at the screen and feels a sudden dark wash of oppression. Why did she agree to type this dry, dull dissertation about the history of a small Ontario town? Somebody, a graduate student she has met only once, is going to get a doctorate in history for this, and Annie will come in for a small thank you among his many acknowledgements.

It's Thursday, and she's promised to have it done by

next Monday. After that, she's got two more jobs lined up, one an anthropology thesis and one a study of the novels of Carol Shields. She used to think the work was interesting, but for the last few months she's been having a hard time getting started in the morning and a harder time keeping it up as the day wears on. She's tired of typing other people's words.

She looks around the apartment, which seems to recede before her eyes. The second floor of a renovated brick house on Rose Avenue in Cabbagetown, it meets Charles's minimum definition of success at this stage of his career, but it's only a step on the way to the house in Rosedale he already anticipates. It's furnished with some fairly expensive pieces, sofas and chairs upholstered in neutral colours, occasional tables in exotic woods polished to a soft sheen by the cleaning lady, everything precisely arranged and a little too tidy for actual comfort. There are a couple of good abstract paintings, one by the dining table and one in the living room, by a Toronto artist Charles says is about to become "hot." The thought enters her mind that the apartment has no character, certainly nothing of herself. There's something a bit transient about it, like a well-appointed waiting room.

The impression is not dispelled by the muffled roar of traffic on Parliament that penetrates the double-glazed dining room windows. She could see the traffic if she wanted to, through these back-facing windows, sighting through a gap in the buildings, but she's schooled herself to limit her focus to the apartment and the surrounding yard. She can't quite deal with the sheer volume of people and vehicles in this city.

She stares at the words on the screen. Once again she asks herself why she keeps on working. Charles makes enough money now for both of them. And yet, she's always believed you had to have work. Some kind of work. People respect you if you have work. You respect yourself. Her mother told her that, and her mother has always had work, at least until very recently.

She scrolls to the end of the chapter she finished yesterday and begins to type. Like smoke against the flickering screen, she sees the ghostly images of Eamon and Maude, their burning eyes.

LATE THAT EVENING, the phone rings, startling Annie, who has dozed off in the middle of *Prime Suspect* on PBS. Charles is still at work, beavering away on some special report he thinks will impress his bosses at the network. The phone rings again, but the answering machine takes over, Charles in his official voice reeling off their message. *You have reached Charles B. Wilkins and Annie Ransome. We can't take your call at this time....* Then Rita's voice. Rita, her mother's cousin; but for Annie more like an aunt...or a mother. Annie mutes the sound on the television.

Rita, at home in Saskatoon, is asking her to call back as soon as possible. Annie hears the tone of her voice;

trying and failing to sound calm. She feels a sharp hit of adrenaline that gets her off the couch and over to the phone before Rita can hang up. Rita asks how she's getting along, asks if Charles is home, and Annie starts into a bit of a rant about all the overtime he's working, but she can feel Rita waiting, so she stops.

"I'm afraid I've got some bad news," Rita says.

"What?" Annie asks, knowing it's something terrible, but unable to think of a single thing it might be.

"It's your mother," Rita says. "I'm so sorry, Annie, I hardly know how to tell you this. Allison is dead."

Annie feels the words explode around her, disparate words that she doesn't want to come together. She needs to hang up the phone before more of them can be spoken. She sees the images on the television, now totally alien and incomprehensible – a frightened child, her breath ragged; a woman calling. A few moments ago she had nothing more important to do than watch them. Or fall asleep.

"No," she hears herself say, "she can't be. She was here at Christmas. She was fine." As if this is some kind of proof; as if Rita will realize her mistake.

"Annie…I don't want to say this…but it looks as though she committed suicide."

*"What?"* Rita can't mean it.

"I'm very sorry."

The woman detective on *Prime Suspect* is questioning a young girl. Annie watches the actor's eyes, the semblance of compassion in them.

"Tell me what happened."

"She was in Edmonton," Rita begins.

"*Edmonton?* Mother never goes to Edmonton. She hardly ever leaves Riverbend."

"Apparently she'd been travelling a lot lately. I didn't know how much until…." Rita waits a beat. "They found her in a hotel. She'd taken a lot of sleeping pills…and she'd had a couple of drinks."

"She must have made a mistake. She did drink too much sometimes, you know that – she must have lost track of the pills." Annie's voice is almost pleading. "It must have been an accident." Another silence; Annie hears only her own rapid breathing. "Rita?"

"She left a note."

Annie thinks of a car at a level crossing as a train slams into it. "Oh, my God."

"She said it wasn't anybody's fault. She said, 'No one is to blame.'"

"No one is to blame?" Annie asks. Then she's crying, big harsh sobs. Allison really is dead. She has taken herself away. She has ended all discussion, all debate.

"I don't know…" Annie struggles to stop crying, "I don't know what to do, Rita."

"I've agreed to fly to Edmonton tomorrow – to claim the body." Not *claim your mother*, Annie thinks, just *the body*. "If that's all right with you?"

"Yes, of course it is. If you don't mind."

"No, I don't mind. What am I saying? Of course I mind, but I think I'm the best person."

"Yes, thank you. Thank you, Rita, that would be –" Annie doesn't know what she's saying. "What about, you know, the funeral?"

"We'll take her back to Riverbend, of course."

"Yes," Annie says. "That's what she'd likely want." As if what Allison would want still matters. After what she's done to herself. Done to them.

"I thought we might have a service at the church. Maybe next Tuesday, the seventeenth. St. Aidan's. Shall I talk to the minister for you?"

"Yes, please, Rita."

"Listen, I'll call you again when I know more. Annie, is there someone you can get to come and sit with you?"

There's no one she knows well enough; no one she'd let near her now.

"That's okay, Rita. Charles will be home soon."

"That's good. I don't think you should be alone right now."

The pain in Annie's head is like the worst migraine. Her voice sounds thick, alien to her ears. "Rita, how could she do it? How could she do it to me?"

"I only wish I could tell you."

Annie realizes she has to get off the phone. Somehow she says enough to reassure Rita that she'll be okay. That Charles will come home. That he'll look after her, although she's not at all certain about that. Finally she is hanging up the phone. She goes to the sofa and curls herself into a ball, wrapping her arms around her shoulders. The room, the air, everything is changing around her, and she doesn't want to know anything about it.

She wonders how this can be her life. She hasn't chosen it, hasn't consented to it. And yet a voice, cynical and bitter, is saying that it was bound to come to this sooner or later. She doesn't know where that voice comes from, but recognizes it as her own.

She watches the figures on the screen. She has no idea what the story's about. It's very dark and people are running, desperate, down a street. There's a child, a terrified child, hiding somewhere. And then the woman's face, the detective's face, so determined to get to the bottom of things. Annie stares at the face, but it doesn't tell her what to do. She picks up the remote and turns off the big-screen television. She looks around the room for anything to hold onto, but it might as well be empty.

## CHAPTER TWO

"You'll have to go, of course," Charles says the next morning, as he spreads unpasteurized wildflower honey on his seven-grain toast.

"Of course I will," Annie says, irritated for no reason she can explain. "I've booked a flight Monday morning."

He spoons raw cane sugar into his espresso. He avoids looking her in the face. She realizes he probably thinks she looks like hell. Her eyes have big circles around them and her brown hair looks the same as when she got out of bed, even though she brushed it.

Annie pours cream into her decaf coffee. Despite his words, she feels that he doesn't want her to go. "Charles, if I could possibly avoid it, I would."

He stirs his espresso without speaking, his face guarded, but the lips pressed firmly together suggest words unsaid.

"I gather you feel you can avoid it?" She tries not to

sound bitter. She can't really afford to lose her temper just now.

"Well, it is unbelievably busy at work, and they're running my in-depth report on homelessness –" Charles is a news anchor now, but he likes to keep his hand in on the reporting side too. Probably thinks it gets him extra points with his bosses.

"Fine, you've convinced me." Of course he doesn't want to come. He couldn't wait to get out of Riverbend and he never goes back if he can help it. "I'll tell people you couldn't get away."

Charles squirms, but leaves it alone. "What about our dinner party next Friday? You'll be back by then, won't you?" He tries hard to look casual, but there's an almost imploring look in his eyes. He can't read the news, do special reports, *and* cook dinner for twelve. Not yet, anyway.

She almost laughs out loud. She'd forgotten all about it. Getting out of the dinner party will be the one reward for going to the funeral. She loathes giving dinner parties. Entertaining Charles's bosses, struggling to cook the sort of menu Charles considers necessary to a chic Toronto soirée, preferably something mentioned by Joanne Kates in one of her restaurant reviews. Charles even tries to talk like a restaurant critic. His entrées are always "napped" or "wreathed" or "blanketed" in sauces, his veggies come in "towers," and everything has to be *al dente*, even things that taste better fully cooked. And things that would taste good crisp have to be raw.

Things that should be raw, paradoxically, must sometimes be cooked.

Annie still remembers the disastrous grilled radicchio in balsamic vinaigrette that turned all limp and bitter and nasty. They had to throw it out, Charles hovering over the garbage pail with a stricken face. She'd had to turn away so he wouldn't see her laugh. Sometimes she overcooks the vegetables just to get to him. And he subjects her to endless quizzes. Are the eggs free range? Is the milk from contented cows? Is the pasta organic? Is the pesto fresh? Is the balsamic vinegar aged in oak casks? Is the oil extra virgin? Give me a break, she'd said once, it's hard enough to find one virgin these days, let alone an extra one.

Charles is watching her, waiting for her answer.

"Screw the dinner party, Charles. There's been a death in the family." He looks at her warily, afraid she's going to snap, not wanting to provoke her. He changes tack.

"Oh hell," he says, "I took your black dress to the cleaners with my suits."

"Who says I'm going to wear black?" Annie asks. This is how it's been for them lately. If Charles wants something one way, she suddenly wants it the other. And nobody's dealing with it.

"Well, it does look, you know, more...."

A red glare flashes through her brain and she's suddenly on her feet, looking down at him. "Oh, fuck off, Charles," she says, and it feels very good.

"What did you say?" he asks, tucking his arms close to his body like an offended chicken. An offended free-range chicken.

"You heard me," she says, unwilling to back-pedal now.

She knows she's not being fair. Charles didn't make her mother die. But Charles is here. She can get at him. She sees he's really hurt. She's sorry for what she said, but can't make herself take it back.

MONDAY MORNING Charles drives her to the airport through a city of shining ice. Trees sag under the weight, pedestrians edge along sheer sidewalks. A cold wet gale blows off the lake, the kind that cuts right through your coat. The kind that makes Annie eat her former words about easterners – that they don't know what real cold is. The storm raged all night and, for a while that morning, Annie, clinging to the warm cocoon of the bed, thought she wouldn't be able to go, she'd be storm-stayed. She savoured the words in her mind, enjoying the old-fashioned sound. You can't miss your mother's funeral. Except you can if you're storm-stayed. But this was only a fantasy; by eight o'clock the city had started to function again. Air Canada had assured her the flight would be taking off, only an hour late.

She glances at Charles's sculpted brown hair, his dark eyes steady on the road. He hasn't spoken since they left the apartment, but at least he's keeping the car on the road as the traffic skates and slips around them. As usual, he is perfectly dressed and groomed. She doesn't look that bad herself, in her fancy Linda Lundstrom parka that Charles insisted she buy, with fur trim dyed to match its teal green shell. They look like a couple in a glossy ad. Or almost. Annie never looks quite posh enough for Sir Charles Burford Wilkins, as she sometimes refers to him in her mind.

On the expressway, Charles manoeuvres around minor crashes; cars still move, slower than usual, but each making the same statement: all this can actually work, even now, as long as you know what you're doing. Annie has never got used to it, the speed, the paltry space available to each car, but it's second nature now to Charles. He loves to show his mastery of this way of driving, this way of living. But four years in Toronto have turned Annie into a non-driver, although she renews her licence faithfully each year.

She's almost surprised that Charles was willing to take the car on the road today. It's a very snazzy car – although she always forgets the brand name – and it means a lot to Charles. Still, it's not the car he really wants, the Bimmer. He had to tell her that Bimmer meant BMW.

Near the Air Canada terminal, Charles slots the car into a metered spot in the same section where they parked to pick up Annie's mother at Christmas. She remembers bending to kiss her mother's cheek and Allison somehow managing to turn awkwardly so that

Annie felt her lips brush the woollen collar of her coat. The whole holiday had been like that, a series of near misses.

Charles takes Annie's arm and sees her inside. He actually takes possession of her ticket, which is waiting for Annie at the check-in counter. He tries to take the boarding pass as well, but Annie's too quick for him, snatching it and giving him a "nyah-nyah" sort of look. He gives her a slightly wounded look back, as in, How can you be so childish? Then he reasserts control, herding her along corridors to the security control for her gate. He passes her the carry-on bag and emits a small sharp breath of completion. In his efficient way, he has delivered her safely to the checkpoint. Now it's up to her. A moment ago she'd resented his management of herself and her possessions; now as he lets go she feels a jab of panic.

He kisses her on the lips, then on both cheeks. "Call me. Let me know how it goes." He's ready to bolt, ready to front the next wind, the next story, the next challenge. But not before she sees for a fraction of a second an answering panic in his eyes. Charles? Panic? What else might he be hiding? She hands her boarding pass to the security woman.

She finds the waiting room for her flight with no trouble. But the plane, already delayed by the storm, won't take off for another two hours after all. They're still de-icing the wings. The thought of ice on the wings nearly undoes her, but there's no turning back, and not only because the ticket's paid for. She wouldn't give Charles the satisfaction.

The last thing she wants is two unstructured hours; two hours to think again about things that might have made her mother want to die. The loss of her own mother, Annie's grandmother Maisie, a year ago. Or the end of her job as manager of ladies' wear in a small department store in Riverbend. Allison worked there for nearly thirty years, almost all of Annie's life, until six months ago the store closed, driven out by big discount stores in the suburban malls. Annie remembers her mother's words about work and respect. And yet how can these events, painful as they were, account for what has happened?

When they're finally hurtling down the runway, which she knows has a ravine at the far end, she feels the acceleration in her gut and is certain they're not going to make it. She sees the wreckage in the ravine, the story leading the evening news. Charles won't know how to cope, she thinks; his driving skills and managing ways won't be any use this time.

At the last possible second, the clumsy bird claws its way into the smudged sky and climbs rapidly away from the storm-bound city and its tall trees heavy with ice. For a moment Annie doesn't care about anything. The man with the thesis has been put on hold till she gets back. She's got away from Charles and not yet been claimed by anything new. She hardly hears the flight attendant explain the safety features of the plane or the pilot's confiding chat about air speeds and cruising altitudes. Soon someone's given her a cup of hot, sweet tea.

The in-flight movie turns out to be not a movie but an episode of Mr. Bean, the one where he accidentally steals a baby. Annie has seen it before, but is charmed once again, almost brought to tears by the strange little fellow's frantic efforts at child care. As the episode ends, the baby's carriage floats up into the sky, buoyed by bright red helium-filled balloons, and Annie drifts into sleep. She dreams she's flying through sunny blue air; the baby is there too, darting like a fish in and out of clouds. Near by, Charles sits on a sooty little cloud, disapproving. Something like a giggle floats through her mind.

She wakens to feel the plane descending to snow-wrapped prairie, dull matte white broken only by straight roads and curving lines of creeks and brush. Five o'clock and night has already begun to leach the winter light from the sky. She feels the earth pulling them back and would give anything not to be part of this, not to be entering this once familiar world. She sees Riverbend spread out below, its winding creeks, the railyards splitting the city into two discrete parts, connected by the aging downtown with its wide streets and fine old brick and stone buildings.

She closes her eyes as the plane touches down, bounces a couple of times, and steadies. "Made it again," she thinks, and realizes she's put no faith in the idea of a landing. She gathers her coat and bag to her in the suddenly stifling plane as a vapid tune plays over the sound system and a voice advises them to stay buckled up until the plane stops in front of the terminal. She unbuckles anyway and realizes at once that it's just one of her pathetic and ineffective acts of defiance.

Walking through the passenger gate, she feels as vulnerable as a newly hatched chick. Rita is there, looking solid, respectable, and slightly apologetic in her fur coat. Maybe she thinks Toronto will have turned Annie into one of those animal rights people who throw paint at anyone in fur. Or maybe Annie's only imagining she looks apologetic; maybe she's only tired. In a moment Annie is gathered into those warm and reliable arms, the fur soft against her cheek. If only it could have been like this with Allison, an uncomplicated embrace without either of them worrying about whether it's too public or too emotional. Rita does look tired, has strands of white now in her wavy black hair and curved lines at the corners of her mouth; but Annie can see she's determined to do what must be done.

Rita rounds up Annie's bags, takes her out through the bitter air into the still-warm car. They drive to the rather grand old railway hotel through icy streets where road graders, like huge frantic insects, clear away a record fall of snow, more snow than Annie ever remembers seeing. Night is drifting over the city; she won't think about tomorrow. One thing at a time.

# CHAPTER THREE

Annie tries to focus on the flowers: pink and white freesias, filling with their exuberant sweetness the too still air of the old stone church, so much more run-down now than when she was young. St. Aidan's, the small neighbourhood church where Annie and Charles were married; where Allison once sang in the choir.

Annie couldn't recall, when Rita had asked her, what flowers her mother had liked, or even if she'd liked any. So she'd chosen her own favourites. Now they will always remind her of this day.

"We will never know what was in our friend Allison Ransome's heart the night she died." The Reverend Aubrey Bunting, "Bunty" everyone calls him, looks up from his papers. Hoping to make eye contact, no doubt, she thinks, stubbornly resisting his compassion. He must be over seventy now, his hair a silvery nebula around a thin face with still bright grey eyes, but he sometimes breaks his retirement to conduct weddings and funerals for families he knows.

"Allison was only fifty-four years old. We regret that no one was there with her. To show her the many things that might have tied her to life." Does he mean me? Annie wonders, engaging for a moment those clear old eyes. She doesn't think it would have made any difference.

Annie feels like she's at the bottom of a deep river, the pressure of the water almost more than her body can withstand, every slight movement requiring effort. Sounds are distorted, hard to make out.

"But no one passes out of this life without God's compassion, and we must believe Allison felt its presence on that night."

Annie tries to keep the words from touching her. Bunty couldn't have cared about her mother, couldn't possibly have understood her. She wants nothing to do with him or his god. He's an old fool, a twentieth-century Polonius.

"Each of us saw her in a different way – mother, friend, neighbour. None of us can say how she saw herself. But one thing is clear. Allison could be difficult at times."

Annie hears a collective sigh, a shifting of bodies in the oak pews – as if people are thinking, Ah, it's to be that sort of funeral; telling the truth about the dead. That kind is always hardest to bear. Lies are much easier. No need to confront the actual person. Now Bunty has brought Allison before them all: never satisfied; always wanting what she couldn't have; contemptuous of whatever came to her easily. Relentless, demanding, her dark eyes boring into you.

Annie, too, shifts in her seat, trying to hold her mind and body in some kind of equilibrium. Rita, seated next to Annie, turns to look at her, concerned. Rita, her mother's cousin, born on the same day, but another sort of woman entirely, as if their personalities formed in opposition to one another. And beside Rita, Edith Ashdown watches too, with that aloof superior way she always has, her fine-boned face still beautiful despite her seventy-some years. Her hair is totally white now, a strong contrast with her dark blue dress, but Annie remembers the deep, glowing auburn Edith carried into late middle age.

They're probably afraid I'll break down and make a fool of myself, Annie thinks. She gives them both a look that says, I won't, so mind your own business. And it's as if her mother is there beside her, the two of them glaring together. For a half a second, Annie wants to laugh.

"Sometimes one sensed anger or impatience in her manner, and Allison did not suffer fools, or those she took to be fools, easily. Perhaps I was one of those myself."

Another wave of surprise – that Bunty should admit this – flows over the pews like wind riffling water. Perhaps, Annie concedes, he's smarter than she gave him credit for.

"Finally, she decided to end a life that had become

too difficult for her." Annie feels shame flow through her. But of course everyone here must have known already. "Let none of us make easy judgements about that. We did not know her pain; we cannot know what fears and cares disturbed her mind." For the first time since Rita's call, Annie remembers that in the past suicides were denied church burial. Perhaps Bunty has decided Allison was not responsible for her own death, that she killed herself because of a disturbed mind.

"I think she must have been happiest as a child, exploring River Road and the wild abundance of the riverbank, with its chokecherries and prairie roses," Bunty continues, and she sees a glaze of tears in his eyes. "Let us remember above all that child, restless and always questing for beauty."

Questing for beauty. Was that how Allison was? Before she was anyone's mother? Annie has always known her as Mother, and has only lately begun to think of her as Allison, a person separate from herself. Now this man wants her to see her mother as a child.

"Our deepest sympathy goes to Allison's daughter, Annie." Bunty is looking right at her. For a moment, she's terrified that he'll mention her father, Clifford Winter, who abandoned her mother when Annie was a baby, but thank God he doesn't. "And our sympathy also to Rita Conal Fortowski, her cousin and lifelong friend. And to her neighbour and friend, Edith Ashdown."

Edith has nothing to do with Mother, Annie thinks.

She's almost twenty years older, and I'm sure Mother never even liked her. We were never good enough for Edith. She has nothing to do with any of it.

"In compassion for that long ago child, let us sing together a hymn long beloved of the children who come through this church, 'All Things Bright and Beautiful.' "

The organ begins to play. People stand and sing. Every word is a pain; all Annie can do is to face each one as it comes and try to send it spinning away from her. She can't let even these little words in or they will break her open like an eggshell and spill her onto the church floor.

"All things bright and beautiful...." Her mother never felt she was beautiful, but she wanted to be. "All creatures great and small....All things wise and wonderful...."

At last, Annie wins the battle and the words break into blurred, meaningless syllables. She keeps a small part of her mind on duty to tell her when they stop. Finally they do. It's all over. But no, she's forgotten something.

"Edith has asked for some music Allison greatly loved. Schumann's *Kinderszenen, Scenes of Childhood.*" A girl of about fourteen moves confidently to the piano, which must have been brought in specially from the church hall. The gentle notes begin, drawing Annie into their own self-contained world – not of words this time, but of feelings. Words she could deny, but not this seamless construction of sound. Why did Edith have to tell them about the music? How did she know about it?

*She sees herself as a little girl. She wears a short cotton dress and white leather shoes. She is looking at Allison, looking at Mother, trying to understand what she's supposed to do. If she knows what it is, she will do it and Mother will be glad. She watches Mother's face, but it doesn't tell her what to do. Mother's face blurs, turns away, and at that moment the child understands that she is not what Mother wanted. She is not good.*

The tears she has been trying to keep far away break through. Rita takes her hand and presses it. Annie slowly takes back her hand, trying not to do it ungraciously. Sympathy will undo her now. She lets the music pass through her, lets it play itself in her body until finally it too is over and the girl rises quietly from the piano.

There is no coffin to view. Allison has already been cremated, by her own wish and certainly by Annie's too. Allison dead is a sight Annie could not have faced.

Because she is the daughter, sitting in the front pew, she has to leave the church first. As Rita leads her along, Annie concentrates on the effort of moving her legs – as if she's pushing against a current. She feels the weight of all the eyes on her; people turn towards her like curious fish as she passes. Most of them middle-aged or old, people who knew her mother, but near the back she sees two serious-looking children, a boy and a girl, watching her intently. Who brings children to a funeral, she wonders?

She longs to be done with all this, but only the first

ordeal is over. They have to go to the reception, but before that Rita says they must stop outside the church so that people can talk to them. They must simply get through it. Wasn't that what her grandmother Maisie was always saying? *We must get through, child.* But now Annie is reluctant to leave the watery world of the church.

Outside the frozen ground is covered in deep snow, piled in huge mounds along the church walk. The air is a drier, flimsier element, harsh against her throat and lungs. Ice crystals spin in the weak winter sunshine. She imagines them piercing her skin, millions of shining needles. As she zips up her parka against them, she has to squint her eyes against the brightness of the motes of ice and the two rainbow fragments that flank the muted sun. Sundogs. It's more like January than the third week of March.

Rita stands by her as, one at a time or in pairs, the people approach her. Some take her hand in theirs, some hold her awkwardly against their breasts. Awkwardly, because she's been away too long; they can't tell any more how she feels about these common liberties. Mercifully, the chill air counsels them to be brief. *So very sorry...a shame to lose her that way...anything we can do, anything...splendid turnout....*

She doesn't know what she says back. Her face is brittle, as if the shards of ice have entered it. Pure pain to hold it calm, but there's nothing else to do. You can't run away from your mother's funeral. You can't scream and yell. You can't faint. Any of those things would feel better than this, but you can't do any of them. She says a few words to each, words immediately forgotten, and watches them scurry away to their cars.

NOW THEY HAVE TO GO TO EDITH'S HOUSE, that overgrown monstrosity on River Road, with its two front-facing bay windows that resolve themselves on the third floor into fake turrets, outlandish looking against the prairie sky. As if the Ashdowns had foreseen a need to defend some day, at least symbolically, their castle overlooking the river, built on the proceeds of Homer Ashdown's speculations in land. Annie remembers her mother, Allison, speaking of her attraction to this house when Edith was a young woman and Allison a child skipping along the public sidewalk, her feet tapping out the old rhymes. *On the mountain lives a lady, Who she is, I do not know.* Her rope whirling round and round, but her gaze always on the house and yard. And on Edith, the acknowledged queen of this privileged world. *All she wants is gold and silver, All she wants is a fine young man.*

Edith has insisted on having a reception. This makes Annie so angry. Edith has no right, it's none of her business. The Ransomes were never good enough for Edith when Allison was alive; why does she care now?

The anger is good. Edith is someone to blame. Annie knows this is not rational. She doesn't care.

"I don't understand why you gave in," she accuses Rita in the car.

"She called me up and offered –" Rita begins.

"Butting her way in, as usual. She had nothing to do with Mother. We should have rented the church hall."

"Oh, Annie," Rita says, suddenly looking tired, "try to be reasonable."

Annie immediately feels ashamed. She's making things worse for Rita. As if Rita had no grief of her own to deal with.

"I'm sorry," she says. "I guess I'm not coping very well."

"Of course, Edith *is* Charles's aunt," Rita reminds her.

"Only by marriage," Annie says quickly. Rita looks at her. "Oh. I'm doing it again, aren't I?" Rita doesn't push it.

As they near the street by the river, Annie tries to lighten the mood. "I guess I should be honoured Edith offered us the ancestral mansion. You know, I'm surprised she's never given it a name. Lady Edith Hall, for example. Or Ashdown Towers."

Rita smiles. "Edith's Little Acre." She turns onto River Road and slows as they pass an older single-storey frame house.

"There's my ancestral mansion," Annie says, looking at the little house. She feels depressed just looking at it.

"Maisie's Manor," Rita says, trying to keep it light.

"How about Bleak House?" Annie asks, and then

wishes she hadn't, because she's promised herself not to cry. Rita parks the car and waits for Annie to grow calm; then they walk past the last few houses to Edith's. Annie doesn't even glance at the place where she herself grew up, in a house almost identical to Maisie's. She perceives the spot only as an absence; their old house burned down a few years ago and has been replaced by a sprawling bungalow which almost fills the thirty-foot lot.

ANNIE'S SURPRISED TO FIND EDITH'S HOUSE not quite as imposing as she'd remembered. Compared with some of the more baroque creations of Cabbagetown, Edith's house is a modest enough affair. So it's not true she hasn't got anything out of Toronto, Annie thinks; it's given her a new perspective on the Ashdown place. Still, her stomach knots as she passes through the front door into the big verandah. She could count on one hand the times, none of them pleasant, she's crossed this threshold.

INSIDE, RITA TRIES TO KEEP CLOSE, to shield Annie, translate for her. People swirl around her in Edith's grand living room, the ones who didn't stop to talk at the church saying how sorry they are, how they hope Annie will be all right. They expect her to answer, and sometimes she does, but mostly Rita does it for her. Annie has all she can manage keeping track of her arms and legs, heavy and cumbersome and almost as useless as in dreams. The room is beautiful – apricot walls set off by cream-coloured mouldings; chairs and sofas covered in sapphire, amethyst, topaz; the old grand piano, with its polished ebony case; crystal wineglasses sparkling in lamplight the colour of golden wine; polished tables bearing flowering plants with cerise flowers and a heavy sweet scent. She feels a moment's pleasure in all the glowing colours. Until she sees Edith enter the room with a tray of glasses and all her resentment comes flooding back.

On a side table, she sees a picture of Edith's younger daughter and feels another flash of annoyance. Tira's flamboyant beauty, crowned by thick wavy red hair, always made Annie jealous, from first grade to the end of high school. Tira has Edith's imperious self-confidence, as if it's part of the natural order that things should go her way. Beside the picture is one of Edith's older daughter, Eleanor, the plain one, almost ten years older than Tira, the one Edith has never got on well with. Edith has even placed the photograph of this tentative, pinched-looking daughter in a plainer frame; was this unconscious or deliberate? As if Edith can't quite believe this woman can also be her daughter?

Although Annie has never known Eleanor well, they are related through marriage; Eleanor is the wife of Rita's younger brother, Johnny; but there's no photograph of him anywhere. Another one not good enough for Edith, Annie thinks.

Edith hands Annie a glass of sherry and she feels the sweet wine stab through her. Just give me a whole bunch more of this and I'll be fine, her brain is saying. But she can't allow herself to lose control.

Several people ask about her husband. She explains that he was too busy at work and couldn't make it. He's probably just afraid to face death, she'd like to say. But she wouldn't dare. The flash of malice might tear away the thin mask she's put on for these people.

She has a bad moment when Bunty comes to offer his words of consolation. How he remembers Allison from her confirmation class so many years ago, and how she'd been one of the brightest and always asked the most difficult questions. He was a young minister then and sometimes hardly knew what to answer. She'd told him once that she didn't understand the Trinity and he'd gone through it all as best he could, and she'd asked, "Why do they all have to be men?" And then one day, Bunty says, she stopped coming. He's always blamed himself. When he tells her how like her mother she is, Annie says, "I hope *not*," as if he means that Annie will do what Allison did, even though the sane part of her mind knows he couldn't mean that. He looks so horrified that she's sorry she said it. She reminds herself that he is not stupid and tries to smooth it over, not aware of quite what she says, only that he goes away soon, which is good.

Rita appears beside her, takes hold of her arm, and leads her towards the kitchen. Annie almost jerks her arm away, but she's just made a fool of herself once and isn't quite ready to do it again. Rita takes her to the sink. She runs the cold water tap, gets a glass, adds ice. She fills the glass and holds it out to Annie.

"I'm not thirsty," Annie says.

"Drink," Rita says, making her take the glass.

Annie takes a perfunctory sip, as if to humour Rita. The sip turns into a huge gulp. She takes a quick breath and drinks the water down without a pause.

"All right," she says, "maybe I was a bit thirsty."

"Annie," Rita says, "do you think you could let up a bit?"

"I don't know what you mean," Annie says, although she does.

"I mean, stop blaming everybody. I heard what you said to Bunty."

"What was I supposed to do? Saying I was like Mother, for God's sake. I thought they gave these people sensitivity training nowadays —"

"Annie!" Rita says.

"What?"

"Stop it. Just stop."

The pain of Rita's reproof hits her as though she's a small child who's done something unforgivable and she starts to cry, hard. Rita holds her. "It's all right," she says. "It's all right to cry." No, it's not, Annie thinks, it's not all right. She chokes back the sobs and takes deep breaths. She pours a glass of sherry from a decanter on the counter. She allows Rita to take out a brush and tidy her hair.

"I'm okay now," Annie says shakily, taking a drink of the sherry. Rita doesn't answer, just gives Annie a little time. Then they turn and go back to the living room, where Rita finds Annie an armchair and brings her some small sandwiches. Annie feels the sherry at work in her brain, not that she's had a lot, but it's affecting her more than usual. It feels good to be sitting, to have nothing much to do. She seems to be moving into a different space, as though the reception has changed gears. She's begun to be detached from it, to observe it as an intricate social puzzle.

She notices at intervals three old ladies, sisters they must be, their hair drawn back in old-fashioned buns secured by black combs, wearing hideous black taffeta dresses. Small veiled hats on their heads sport tacky black feathers. Real, serious funeral outfits. They sit in straight-backed chairs covered in flowered tapestry. They are knitting, busy as grackles, as though they may as well get on with it, funeral or no funeral, but Annie catches them more than once looking at her. She half expects Rita to introduce them as long forgotten great-aunts or cousins twice removed of Allison's, but nobody ever mentions them, nor do they ever come any closer.

At last there is a point where she can definitely see that people are leaving – a diminishing of the human mass, a wearing down of the engine driving them. All the rituals have been run through. The tea and sherry drunk. The dainties eaten. Oh, the dainties! Even in the midst of her numbness, Annie remembers eating three incredibly rich chocolate brownies, the sweet rush of chocolate blotting out everything for a moment. And thinking, How can I be doing this? How can I eat?

As if on some signal, the three old ladies exchange glances and gather up their knitting into big black patent leather handbags. As they pass, each one gives Annie a little pat on the arm or shoulder of what might be encouragement or comfort. They at least don't seem to expect her to say anything. In a moment they've pulled on long black coats and wafted out the door. The house shrugs off the crowd, settles back into itself and its usual sole duty of housing Edith Ashdown in the comfort to which she's always been accustomed.

It's almost over. Nearly twenty-four hours since she arrived and again the light is leaving the sky. Soon Rita will drive her to the airport and the plane will lift her away from all of this. She doesn't like plane rides, but she's going to like this one. She sees Rita and Edith standing together in a corner of the living room, Edith's hand touching the piano. Edith speaks and Rita listens. Rita turns and looks at Annie. She nods at Edith. What's Edith up to? How dare they discuss her as if she isn't even there! They come closer, Edith in the lead.

"Why don't you stay overnight at my house? It'll be very quiet, and you can sleep as long as you like in the morning." The calm, observing part of Annie can see how carefully Edith speaks, keeping her voice cordial but casual.

"That's all right," Annie says, "I'll be home before

midnight." She tries to sound certain, but she can see that for some reason Rita thinks she should accept.

"You don't look fit to travel," Rita says. "I'd feel better if you stayed over and got some rest. I can bring your suitcase in."

Annie glares at her. Why should Rita betray her to the enemy? Rita meets the glare but doesn't respond to it.

"In fact," Edith says, "you might even like to stay on a few days and look over the house."

"What?" Annie says. Why should she want to look over Edith's house? The showplace of River Road it may be, but it's not on her list of priorities.

"Maisie's house, I mean. Allison inherited it when Maisie died, and now it comes to you, of course. You knew that." Ah, Maisie's house. Annie did understand that it was willed to her, but has never even considered going near it. She never liked it when she was young and hasn't been inside it for ten years, not even when she came back for Maisie's funeral last year, so why would she want to see it now? And why does Edith want her to stay?

"I've checked with the lawyer," Edith goes on. "He'd be happy to pop round tomorrow. He's got a few papers for you to sign. There's only the house and a small savings account, I understand. Very straightforward, no question of probate. He sees no problem in giving you immediate access."

"I'm not interested in immediate access. All I want to do with that house is sell it," Annie says, glad to have something to sound legitimately annoyed about. "The quicker the better."

"I can understand how you might want that," Edith says, maintaining her carefully neutral manner, as if they're talking about what bus to take to go downtown.

Really? Annie is thinking. Can you really understand? Surely Edith is carrying all this quiet reasonableness too far. And what does she mean she's checked with the lawyer?

"But you might as well put a few things in order. You'll get a better price that way."

"Well, thanks for the suggestion. Mother's death has taken all my attention lately. Figuring out how to turn a fast buck on Maisie's place has somehow escaped my notice."

Annie can see Rita trying to keep her patience. She obviously can't believe Annie's talking this way. Neither can Annie. She's never been this rude to anyone in her whole life. But Edith deserves it. Doesn't she?

"It would escape your attention, of course," Edith agrees pleasantly. Why isn't she answering Annie back? What does she want?

"There might be a few things you'd want to keep," Rita says, obviously trying to relieve Edith of some of the burden of talking to Annie.

"I doubt it," Annie says. She feels the combined power of their eyes: Edith's bluer than Annie would have remembered; Rita's dark and full of loving kindness.

"I wish I could stay and go through things with you,"

Rita says, "but I have to be back at work tomorrow morning, and it's a three-hour drive."

Annie doesn't know quite how it happens, but somehow or other, by holding out against the idea of going through Maisie's house, she finds herself by degrees becoming snared into staying the night at Edith's.

"But I've got a plane to catch." Annie makes one last attempt, afraid she's starting to sound feeble.

"Oh, you'll have no trouble changing that," Edith says. "Airlines can be very understanding."

"Not in my experience," Annie says nastily. Edith is wearing her down, but that doesn't mean she's going to give in gracefully.

"In fact, I can do that for you," Edith says, and Annie realizes she probably can. Edith has always known how to make people and things answer to her wishes. "And I'll call Charles and let him know." Charles. She's forgotten all about him. Serves him right for not being here.

Finally, Annie's too tired to argue. They take her up to a softly lit bedroom. The coverlet on the walnut four-poster is already turned down, as if Edith has counted on her staying. Rita gives her a quick hug and follows Edith out the door. Earlier, Annie would have sworn she'd be unable to sleep, but that only goes to show how little she knew earlier. She slips off her shoes and lies down on the island of the bed, leaving behind the day and everything and everybody in it.

CHAPTER FOUR

A t noon the next day, Edith serves Annie the tea and toast which is all she has agreed to eat. Edith sits down across from her in the blue-tiled breakfast nook, intending to keep her company, but when Annie freezes in mid-bite she gets right up again. Maybe the girl doesn't like to have people watch her eat; some people are like that. Her daughter Eleanor for one. So Edith putters around the kitchen, wiping non-existent specks off the countertops.

Annie has signed the few papers the lawyer brought over and Edith has signed as executor. Now Annie has legal possession of the house and its contents and of Allison's meagre bank account, about twelve thousand dollars. Annie doesn't seem to understand that there really ought to be more, but she's bound to in time.

Annie looks calmer than at the funeral, but terribly tired and pale. And she's too thin, Edith decides. The naturally straight hair with the permed ends gives her a waif-like look. The eyes, shaded by dark circles, are too guarded; the olive skin looks smudged. She chews the toast furtively, as if she shouldn't be eating when her mother has died, or so Edith imagines. Why do people harbour such ideas? she wonders. It's not as though it will help the dead person. Edith herself has always believed in the importance of good diet; even during the most difficult times of her life, food was always there for her, something she could count on. In fact, that's probably what got her through it all. That and sheer bloody-minded determination. Well, why not? Other people can roll over and meekly die if they want to.

After Annie has finished eating, Edith helps her into her coat and gives her the key to Maisie's house. Annie practically grabs the key from her hand. As if I would keep it from you, Edith thinks. How like Allison the gesture is. As if neither of them could believe anything would be surrendered to them willingly.

Annie promises only to be back by dinnertime. Edith knows better than to offer to go with her. She opens the door on a day that is dull and cold, with a bitter north wind blowing. Snow is piled high along the sidewalks where people have shovelled their walks after the big storm, revealing sinister patches of black ice. Only a few days until the official beginning of spring, but winter shows no signs of giving up. Edith sees Annie out the door into the bluster and watches her down the street, until Annie turns and glares at her.

Edith almost laughs out loud. Allison left you more than a house, my girl, Edith thinks. Oh, how annoyed Annie'd be if she knew Edith was referring to her, even in her mind, as a "girl." Well, she isn't going to know.

SOMEONE HAS SHOVELLED THE FRONT WALK, but Annie doesn't even wonder about it or really take it in. She looks at this narrow house where her mother grew up, set back a scant ten feet from the public sidewalk. She remembers staying there with her grandparents sometimes as a child and, for a moment, she's scared to go in, lest she suddenly find herself once more trapped in those times, with those people.

In fact, why should she bother? There's no law says she has to. She's so tired, and it would only make her feel depressed. All that stuff in there, she doesn't have the strength to go through it. There's nothing here for her, nothing inside she could possibly want.

Annie turns to leave and takes a few steps back towards Edith's before she stops. She looks back at the house. If she doesn't go in now, she won't have another chance. She'll fly back to Toronto, and the house will become someone else's house. But she doesn't care about that, does she? It's an ordinary house, nothing special about it. Of course, if that's the case, she certainly isn't scared to go in.

Annie opens the front door and steps into the cramped entrance hall, taking it nice and slow. As cold air rushes in, the house exhales a musty breath of long-dead cigarette smoke, burnt grease, furniture polish, dusty carpet, and room freshener that may once have been "pine." When she feels its stale breath in her face, she knows the house has a life of its own. In the many months it's been sealed up – since her grandmother Maisie's death – the house has slept on, waiting. Now it needs someone to get it going again, get its lungs working. Under Maisie's rule, it probably had bronchitis. Maybe even pneumonia. She hopes it's not consumptive. At any rate, she won't be staying long enough to do much for it. She'll give it a good airing, but even Annie knows the past can't be cleared away as easily as that.

Not that it matters; she's selling the house. She's never much liked it, and she has no particular reason to spend any time in this small town, on this street of modest houses along the riverbank. Modest, that is, except for Edith's.

The place is fairly warm. Someone has left the thermostat at sixty degrees, but Annie needs it much warmer. She turns it up to seventy-four and leaves the front door ajar; she hears the furnace cut in. She takes off her winter boots and slips into the shoes she's brought with her. She hangs her fancy parka in the hall, on a brass hook like the ones in old school cloakrooms: three of them, screwed into a length of one-by-six board nailed to the wall. One each for Maisie, grandfather Phillip, and their only child – Allison, Annie's mother. Presumably they never had visitors. But no, the custom was to put visitors' coats on the parents' bed. The craftsmanship is no doubt Phillip's, and would have represented the high-water mark of his achievement in the home improvement line. Of course, what did she expect of him, working as he did from a wheelchair?

She feels a stab of pity for this grandfather she remembers as never really knowing how to talk to her, and shame for the ridicule she uses to defend herself from pity. They'd told her over and over that Phillip was in a wheelchair because he'd fought in the war to make the world safe for children like her. But she'd wanted an ordinary grandfather who could walk around and do things. She didn't want to feel grateful, or sorry for the damage the war had done. As a child, she'd often wished she could belong to some other family.

She suddenly wonders if her mother felt the same way growing up in this house, with its pervasive fears and its endless rules. Don't play in the street. Don't go to the riverbank. Don't talk to strangers. Don't break that. Don't spill that. Don't yell. Don't run. Don't whistle. The last one had driven Annie crazy. "A lady doesn't whistle," Maisie would say. Why not? Why doesn't a lady whistle? Annie always asked. What goddamned difference could it possibly make, that's what she'd ask now, if Maisie stood before her. Of course, a lady probably doesn't swear, either.

She's too hard on her grandmother, she knows she is. But the hardness armours her to pass through this place.

The paint in the hall is...what could she call the

colour? White with a faint undertone of puce? Yes, that's it. Puce. A real Maisie colour, it extends throughout the house. It drags her down. Leaves a bad taste in her mouth. She should put her coat back on and leave.

The living room needs light as much as it needs air. She opens the heavy maroon drapes to reveal tightly closed venetian blinds underneath. Not those narrow metal mini-blinds, but old-fashioned one-inch wooden slats. Charles, who cares about such things, recently mentioned that they're coming back into fashion. With the drapery down, who knows? The blinds might have a certain charm.

She decides to take down the drapes. With a bit of light coming in, someone might actually want to buy the place. She lifts the hooks out of the tracks and folds the panels into bulky squares. Dust embedded deep in the weave billows into the air as they compress. A spider darts out from the last panel and she squashes it with her foot, mildly surprised at her daring. For a long time, Charles has been doing this sort of thing for her. Maybe she's symbolically crushing Edith, she thinks, and almost giggles.

When she's folded the drapes into a shapeless heap of aged cretonne, she opens the blinds. Southern light streams into the room, touching every old object filled with her family's history, picking up every particle of dust as it floats through the air or adds its almost undetectably small weight to her arms and face, flows up her nose and into her throat and lungs. The thought almost makes her gag.

She tries not to think of dust mites. She's been reading articles about them everywhere lately, although she lived the first thirty years of her life without knowing they existed. It seems these microscopic louse-like insects are pretty well all over the place – her mattress, her bedspread, her clothes, and even, God help her, her eyelashes. They've also staked out her floor, where they munch happily on stray flakes of skin that fall from her daily without her knowing, in a gentle rain. She's been trying to get her mind around the idea of mites, but it doesn't particularly want to be got around. It's a fairly grisly item, her mind, but there are limits to the horrors it's willing to take in. The body doesn't much like the idea either. For once they agree on something.

Probably there aren't any mites here, only dust. After all, the house has been closed up for nearly a year, so whose skin would they have had to eat in all that time? They're probably dead, their filthy corpses abandoned in heaps against the walls and furniture, like dust blown into a ditch.

This is not helping. She holds the front door open wide. Air surges into the room in deep, cold waves. Air from the far north, clean, dry, and antiseptic. Mite-killing air. When she starts to shiver, she closes and locks the door. What to do next?

She takes stock of the furniture: too much for a small living room maybe twelve by fifteen feet. Two substantial wing chairs covered in a dull maroon cretonne to match the drapes. (Cretonne, she likes the sound of it.

So stodgy and unworldly; so like Maisie.) Two blue tapestry footstools; a soiled pink brocade chair; a hunter green plush sofa; tables, all shapes and sorts. In a corner, covered by old copies of *Life* and *Reader's Digest*, a small Queen Anne writing desk and chair; and, serving as a coffee table in front of the sofa, a graceful Duncan Phyfe table. The last two are antiques, she remembers being told, probably the only pieces in the house she could get real money for, if she had time to sell them. The floor is dark beige wall-to-wall broadloom, worn and soiled.

Annie feels overwhelmed. She doesn't want to have come out of this place, these dull old-fashioned colours; doesn't want this to be her tradition. She can almost see Maisie in the pink chair, wearing one of her dark wine-and-green print dresses, skirt arranged carefully over her knees, her steel-grey hair curled to within an inch of its life. She can almost see Maisie's disapproving look when Annie wore anything that showed the shape of her body.

"Really dear," she'd say, "that doesn't look very nice. You ought to wear a girdle." And Phillip, in his wheel-chair, which used to sit where the Queen Anne desk is now, might look at Annie for a moment, startled, and then turn away to look at the birds that came to the feeder on the other side of the window.

No wonder Allison never did manage to talk to Annie about sex. Growing up with Maisie must have made her want to avoid the whole subject. She'd fobbed Annie off with the same twenty-year-old booklet from the Kotex company she got from Maisie back in the fifties. After that, Annie was assumed to know everything she needed to know.

The narrowness of Maisie's life with Phillip strikes her like a physical pain. Why think of changing any of this? The thing to do is follow her first impulse – find a real estate agent and sell it as fast as she can. For whatever price she can get. The house is sick – dust mites are the least of it – but maybe somebody else can cure it. The thing for her is just to get out, before its grime and suffocating odours settle any further into her skin, her hair, her lungs.

She feels a burning at the back of her throat and a peculiar sensation in her stomach – like it's trying to levitate. She runs for the bathroom and spills her breakfast into the toilet. She flushes until there is only clear water in the bowl. Washes her hands with cold water and a hard dry shard of lavender soap. Splashes her face and dries it on a frayed linen towel.

Annie Ransome looks at herself in the plain single mirror of the medicine chest and sees a different person than she thought she was. Her thirty-year-old face, without make-up or any other disguise, looks young and scared. Her brown hair is shapeless, the curl almost grown out. She's been reminding herself to take care of it, but suddenly knows that she won't be getting another perm. She's tired of making her hair do things it doesn't want to do.

She only did it for Charles.

The doorbell rings, startling her. She walks on soft feet into the living room and up to the door. She doesn't want to open it, but feels implicated in some basic social agreement. Otherwise why does she have a doorbell? It rings again.

Why hadn't Maisie got one of those peepholes? Anyone could be out there, for all she knows. She thinks she hears breathing. That's ridiculous, not through the door. Really, this is stupid, she's going to open the door. Edith's expecting her back for supper, so if she is murdered, at least it will be discovered quickly. Oh, and what kind of consolation would that be, and for whom? Come on, she's not going to be murdered. This is Riverbend, not Detroit. There's a shuffling outside, then the crunch of retreating footsteps in the snow. Feeling foolish now, she flings open the door, but there's no one there.

She feels a sudden lightness in her head, an indistinctness to the boundaries of her body. She must have been holding her breath without realizing. She drops to the floor, a little faint; the floor feels good. After all, you can't hurt yourself lying on a floor. Except it's dirty. Something's spilled along the bottom of the wall, a spray of brownish drops, like blood. Why would there be blood at Maisie's front door? Why wouldn't Maisie have cleaned it up? Unless she didn't know it was there. The blood of the house, Annie thinks. Of course, it could just as easily be Coca Cola.

In the kitchen, she runs the tap until the tepid water

turns icy cold and drinks down a tall glass. She can deal with all of this, as long as she takes it slow and easy. She's a grown woman. She's left this place behind her. Soon she'll be back in Toronto and she'll wonder why it bothered her.

Annie notices some papers underneath the phone book on the kitchen table. She leafs through them and finds the return portion of an Air Canada excursion ticket from Riverbend to Edmonton. Her mother must have been in the house shortly before she died. Although Annie understood in theory that her mother committed suicide, the wasted ticket makes it more real. What, she wonders, was Allison doing in the house? How long had she been meticulously planning her death?

EDITH SPOTS ANNIE coming back down the street in late afternoon, pinched and white-faced and barely able to drag herself up the walk. A gust of wind follows her in before Edith can slam the door on it. A wave of sympathy takes Edith by surprise, a strong visceral impulse that makes her want to hold and warm this cold, luckless chick. Fortunately, it doesn't show, so Annie doesn't get her back up. Or maybe it shows, in another way, when Edith assumes the full authority of which she's mistress and orders Annie upstairs to lie down. This time Annie hasn't the strength to object.

"How could they live there?" she asks no one in particular. "How could they bear it?"

Edith doesn't even try to answer. Go, her eyes say. Annie turns and goes up the stairs, pale as smoke. When Edith looks in on her fifteen minutes later, she's lying on the bed asleep, her breathing rough and deep. Edith guesses Annie would hate to be seen so naked of defences or even of consciousness. She covers the girl with a woollen blanket and closes the door.

Why has she tried so hard to make Annie stay? Was it really such a good idea? Having failed to be of use to Allison, what makes her think it will be any different with Annie? Too late now for second thoughts. The die is pretty much cast and something or other, some process she hasn't a name for, is already under way.

CHAPTER FIVE

Annie finds herself opening the door of Maisie's house again the next morning, Thursday, a day briskly cold, but sunny, after another night of snowfall. She feels more rested, and Edith has convinced her, much as she hates to be influenced by Edith, to take one last look, one final inventory.

The place smells fresher than yesterday. Bright light flows in through the open blinds. The living room still feels crowded – with furniture and with the presences of Phillip and Maisie. But she's stronger this morning. Maybe she can go through this house and keep it at bay. See its spaces as a series of rooms not so different from any other small rooms.

Something's irritating her, however. The rug. It's giving off dust, and its awful dun colour is seeping into her pores. It's not a colour she wants to be. Along the baseboard near the kitchen doorway, someone has lifted up a corner of the rug and turned it back. It must have been her mother, when she was here last.

Under the rug, the floor is narrow oak boards, stained dark by ingrained dirt. Annie pulls on the corner of the rug, revealing a larger space, and plants one foot on the wood, her leg holding back the rug. She lifts one of the small tables onto the bare wood to prop up the end of the rug. Working her way around the edges of the room in this way, she frees more and more of the wood.

Finally, only the green sofa is still on the rug. Putting her weight into it, Annie is able to pull the rug away from the wall, the sofa floating along on top of it. Then she gets behind the sofa and manages to ease it onto the floor a corner at a time. Another spider explodes out from under the sofa, completely terrorized, no doubt, and she stomps it without a flinch. The rug is now bunched up in the middle of the room. She wrestles it into a lumpy uneven tubular shape. She opens the front door, grabs one end, and starts to drag it outside.

She has it pulled onto the front steps when a uniformed mailman appears, cocooned in a bulky blue parka, a man her own age with long black hair. He has a stack of mail ready in one hand, and, scarcely breaking stride, he takes the rug end from her in his free hand and pulls, dragging it off the path into the snow. He hands her the mail – several circulars addressed to "Occupant" and a hand-printed envelope marked

"Ransome, 39 River Road."

"Morning," he says and turns to go.

"Wait," she says. "How did you know there was anyone here?"

"Edith Ashdown told me to start the mail up. Nice to see someone in the house again."

"But I'm not staying," she says. He doesn't hear. He's already swinging down the path, expertly fishing in his bag for the next catch of mail.

Edith. Of course. Queen Edith. Anyone else, the mayor even, would have to go down to the Post Office and produce nineteen pieces of identification, but Edith speaks and it is done. That's the how, but why is she doing it? She can't imagine Annie will be staying long.

Annie drops the mail on the Duncan Phyfe table and surveys the oak floor, which is the closest thing to a marketable feature she's noticed so far. It really should be sanded and refinished, but in the meantime she could at least make it clean. Maisie's cupboards yield floor-cleaning gear and a tin of desiccated paste wax. Annie lugs everything but the sofa into the middle of the kitchen and sets to work. She scrubs the floor on hands and knees, until the water in the scrub pail is black and even the remaining dirt on the floor looks clean, then she applies the paste wax with a soft cloth, rubbing it into the wood like she's giving a massage.

When she's covered every square inch, she has a terrible moment of doubt. The floor looks completely dull.

She has nothing to show for all the work. Then she remembers the way Allison taught her to polish the floor, when they were too poor to own a floor polisher. In a wicker sewing box in Maisie's bedroom, she finds old woollen socks waiting to be darned. Waiting forever, because the only person who would have done it is dead. Annie knows how, Allison showed her once, but she's never darned a sock in her adult life and doesn't plan to start. She pulls the socks on over her shoes.

Slowly and carefully at first, she sweeps her feet across the tacky surface. The wool takes up the excess wax and, through some process she can't explain, something to do with wool and wax molecules and friction and heat, the wax begins to change form. It begins to shine and be slippery, and she glides across it like a skater. Round and round she goes, watching in wonder as the oak takes on sheen, refusing to worry about falling. Finally, she does slip and fall, but manages to land on the soft bulk of the sofa. She looks around her, and it's no longer the same room she entered in the morning. She's surprised to find she's been having something that feels a lot like fun.

She begins returning furniture to the room. Each piece finds a new place. There isn't room for all the tables or for the pink chair, but the Queen Anne desk with its matching small chair fits along the wall near the kitchen door. The television goes on one of the small tables. The wing chairs sit looking out the window, with the Duncan Phyfe table between them. When she eases the footstools into place in front of the big chairs, the blinds letting in wide slats of warm, buttery light, something clicks. The room isn't ugly any more.

SHE SITS IN ONE OF THE WING CHAIRS, feet tucked up on a footstool, finding it surprisingly comfortable, its firmness just what she needs. Maisie's cupboard has provided English Breakfast tea, with sugar and a tin of evaporated milk to go in it, and a box of stale Peek Freans Garden Cream biscuits. Only about a year old, she thinks, so they're probably safe. She's read that cookies nowadays are almost all made from the same mixture of white flour, beef tallow, and various flavourings and additives, all of it so refined that their shelf life is more or less infinite. Cookies made immortal. Unlike their owners. For the first time, she finds herself hoping this is true, because she is definitely going to eat these cookies.

This is a part of Maisie's heritage she doesn't mind. Tea in a lustrous pink china pot, sweet bland cookies like an emblem of innocence. Or is it wilful ignorance? People who eat these cookies have entered into an agreement to keep their lives within safe and comfortable bounds. They don't ask for exotic new flavours. No Thai cuisine, no Tex-Mex, no California nouvelle cuisine has ever invaded their kitchens. Only good plain English cooking. In Maisie's case, that meant cooking fresh peas until they looked and tasted the same as canned. *Still, you know where you are, don't you?* she can almost hear Maisie saying.

Annie takes an experimental bite of cookie and finds it good. She pops the rest of it into her mouth in one chunk. It's all she wants for the moment, the insipid sweet cookies with their creamy icing and the hot sweet tea. She eats until the cookies are all gone. Energy and warmth flow into her. The wing chair supports her tired back. The room is utterly quiet, except for the furnace cutting in and out, the house creaking and settling around her. She hasn't felt this peaceful in ages. Is she beginning to get over her mother's death already?

She picks up the remote control and flips on the television – the most up-to-date thing in the room, a thirty-inch model with stereophonic sound – a gift from Allison, who used her discount at the store. Maisie'd also got Allison to subscribe to every cable channel going. Annie is surprised to find that no one has ever got around to cancelling the cable – it must be one of those automatic debits, she thinks.

Channel surfing, Annie moves unerringly to the station with the face and voice she knows so well. A man in a beautiful grey suit and a tasteful red tie speaks to the nation in a voice that inspires complete trust, a voice only slightly less trustworthy than the voice of God. It issues from a perfectly moulded head topped by perfectly moulded hair, and is reading, in perfectly moulded sentences, the twelve o'clock news.

Charles. Her husband.

Charles explains that people who know about such things are beginning to see a tiny but perceptible growth in the economy. Housing starts are up marginally; domestic automobile sales show a slight upturn. Experts predict a small but measurable growth in the economy some time later this year. Hot damn, she thinks, there'll be dancing in the streets tonight. Actually, it sounds more like a horoscope than a news item.

Next Charles describes a devastating fire out of control in the hills around Los Angeles. After months of drought, fires have started and been spread by strong Santa Ana winds. Pictures on the screen show fantasy homes being swallowed by vast sheets of flame, arbitrary and terrifying as lightning, people clinging together on hillsides. As he talks, Charles lets a touch of concern seep into his voice, modulating his delivery from Knowlton Nash into Sandi Rinaldo without a visible gear change. And then without any warning, he departs from the script. He looks right at her, right into her eyes.

"Annie," he says. "What in hell do you think you're doing?"

Annie almost drops her teacup. He can't be talking to her. But he is. "I mean, I'm a patient man," he says, and guilt rolls over her in oceanic waves, "but how would you like it if *I* went off to my mother's funeral and didn't come back when I said I would?"

He makes the mistake of pausing, as if he really wants an answer. She discovers she has one.

"Hah!" she says. "If *your* mother had died, I'd have gone to the funeral with you. So there." But he doesn't hear. Besides, his mother's safe and well in Pasadena, California. Oh, he's starting up again. What in hell's going on?

"...anything at all wrong, I'm willing to sit down with you at any time to talk things through. Only I think you'll agree it's only fair that you come back home. As anchor of a major network's national news service, I can hardly drop everything and head out to some one-horse town my viewers barely even heard of and —"

Annie flicks the mute button and enjoys watching Charles flap his gums. So serious, so reasonable, so determined. So *Charles.* She starts mimicking every expression back at him. And there's not a thing he can do about it.

She touches the mute again, and he comes roaring back: "...will concede I have a point here. And by the way, the cleaning lady quit, and I can't figure out where you keep those little yellow bags for the vacuum cleaner, and I've even had to take my shirts to the laundry and...."

She feels laughter bubbling up from under her diaphragm. She makes a face at him, planting her thumbs in the corners of her mouth, pulling downwards at her cheeks with her index fingers, and pushing her nostrils up with her baby fingers. She wags her tongue and rolls her eyes, but he doesn't seem to notice.

"As a matter of fact, they made a big scorch mark on

the collar of my best Egyptian cotton."

He is so hurt and so truly outraged that she can't hold the laughter. It shrieks and snorts and spurts out of her, sprouts tears in her eyes. She gasps for breath. It feels so good.

"Oh, my God, Charles," she says, "I just didn't know. Can you ever forgive me?"

And then the television decides to behave normally again and Annie sighs with relief. Her imagination must be working overtime. "In a related story," Charles is saying, "a local family is learning the true meaning of charity...."

Annie turns him off. She feels a twinge of guilt for making fun of him. After all, everyone says he's very good. If only he didn't do authority so very well. Annie realizes she's never been entirely comfortable with authority. Suddenly she's incredibly tired. She decides to lie down on the sofa for a few minutes, but in mere seconds she's asleep. When she wakes up again, it's dark and time to go back to Edith's for supper. Oh well, she's worked enough on the house for today; but she finds as she pulls on her coat that she's almost reluctant to leave this room.

On the way back, she stops at the end of River Road, a cul-de-sac overlooking the earth cliffs of the riverbank, and leans on the wooden fence built to keep people from walking or driving over the edge. Thirty metres below the street, the river – a creek, really – is still frozen fast, the valley with its parks and houses and market gardens hidden beneath unmarked snow, worlds away from the grimy ruts of River Road. She has forgotten how pristine this valley can look, how clean and fresh the Riverbend air can taste, at least when the wind isn't blowing from the direction of the oil refineries.

She turns to Edith's house, perched on the edge of the cliff and reigning over the street in every way, speaking eloquently of money and purchased culture and family pride. Edith needn't think that Annie's intimidated. Edith's father may have cleaned up selling squeezed-looking lots for squeezed-looking little houses, but she's no better than anyone else.

Annie is puzzled by the fact that she's still here. She was going to fly back right after the funeral, and now she's got a house to consider. How has Edith persuaded her to stay on, even a few days, to put the house in order? She can't figure out what made her agree.

Edith's yard is narrower now on the side overlooking the river than Annie remembers. This is not simply a matter of things shrinking as you grow older; the cliffs are slumping and crumbling away, a little each year, and no one has been able to figure out how to stop them. This process had already started when Annie was a child, but she thinks it may be accelerating. Now the cliff edge is only half the width of the house away; surely the process will lead to certain inevitable consequences. Edith doesn't seem worried.

Perhaps she doesn't care, as long as the house lasts to the end of her life.


EDITH SITS ACROSS THE TABLE, her back straight, eyes steady, face composed. I may be old, her look seems to say, I may no longer be Edith Ashdown of the glossy auburn hair, but I do not give an inch to anybody. Her hair is perfectly groomed, her make-up subtle. She still has vestiges of the beauty Annie remembers, carries herself as if nothing's changed. Her eyes at any rate are still bright. Cornflower blue, an observer with a poetic eye might say. Her dress of heavy slub silk is the same colour. She wears it with careless ease, for all the world as though other people have prepared and served this complicated meal and not she herself in her big old-fashioned kitchen.

Edith is waiting for some kind of answer. Annie searches her memory and realizes Edith has asked about the house.

"It needs a lot of work," Annie says. "And it's so small. I can't think who'd want to live there."

Edith nods, the picture of sympathy. Like some helpful aunt. Well, of course she is Charles's aunt, as Rita pointed out. But she's never been particularly helpful before. Just the opposite, in fact. She even tried to prevent Annie from marrying Charles. And before Charles, Annie had dated Edith's son, Lockwood. They'd broken up before the question of marriage arose, or Edith would surely have objected to that as well.

"You'd like something a bit larger, of course," Edith says. "That's quite understandable." Annie doesn't answer. "If you were staying, I mean."

As they eat together, at opposite ends of the big mahogany table, Annie has to stop herself from telling Edith about her day. She wants to tell someone, but you never know what Edith will do with knowledge, what seemingly unimportant piece of information will suddenly give her power over you.

"This is delicious," she says, hoping to change the subject. Edith has outdone herself. Cream of leek soup. Veal médaillons in lemon and white wine sauce. Tiny new potatoes from some distant place where it's already summer. Fresh green beans with toasted almonds. Sautéed mushrooms with butter and garlic. Deep red tomatoes that really taste like tomatoes instead of dyed wet cardboard, in a dressing of olive oil, wine vinegar, and fresh basil with a faint licorice taste. Unsalted cultured butter. Nothing can be ordinary at Edith Ashdown's.

"My fruit and vegetable man came today. I thought we might as well have everything fresh."

"It's lovely," Annie says and addresses herself to her food, as if it's too wondrous even for conversation. If only Edith could be managed so easily. She raises her eyebrows in what Annie thinks of as her ironic look.

"I don't suppose you'll stay long then," Edith says after a long pause.

"No, probably not." But even as she says it, Annie feels a twinge of disloyalty to Maisie's house. Her second day there, and already one of the rooms feels like home.

"That's too bad. I would have liked a new neighbour." Edith lifts a piece of scarlet tomato to her lips.

"Someone's bound to buy it, I guess," Annie says callously, ignoring the oblique compliment, although she knows how rarely Edith pays a compliment of any kind.

"I meant I would have liked you as a neighbour," Edith says, her blue eyes boring into Annie.

"Well, thank you." This is really embarrassing. Is Edith implying that she likes her?

"Never mind," Edith says. "You would hardly move here on my account."

"There's Charles, of course, to consider," Annie says lamely.

"Is there?" Edith asks drily, almost as if she knows things aren't that great between Annie and Charles. How could she possibly know that? Before Annie can reply, she adds, "Oh, he called here earlier. I told him you couldn't be reached. I promised to mention it whenever I saw you. Did I do the right thing?"

"Oh, yes, certainly," Annie says, trying to be nonchalant. "I'll call him. Soon."

"Whatever you think best. Rita called too. I told her you were doing as well as could be expected. Are you through with that?" Edith asks, looking at Annie's plate, and before Annie can decide if she is or isn't finished, Edith whisks it away. Never mind, it's probably for the best. There's a substantial looking deep-dish apple pie for dessert.

Before Edith can return, Annie grabs a piece of tomato from the salad bowl and enjoys the pleasure of eating it without being watched.

"BY THE WAY," Edith says, as Annie goes up to bed, "the man from the funeral home stopped by with the ashes."

"What did you say?" Annie almost chokes on the words.

"The ashes. They always go to the next of kin." Edith hesitates. "Perhaps you're not ready to think about this yet."

"I most certainly am not," Annie says.

"I'll hang on to the urn then, for the time being," Edith decides. "You'll let me know when you're ready."

"Yes, thank you," Annie says stiffly, "I'll certainly let you know."

## CHAPTER SIX

Friday morning, Annie has no sooner hung up her coat than the doorbell rings, and this time she answers without a moment's hesitation. It's only two children, a girl of about ten and a boy of eight or nine. They seem familiar; Annie wonders if they might be the children she remembers seeing at the back of the church at Allison's funeral. The girl is blonde and skinny with long straight hair, none too tidy.

"Are you done with that rug?" she asks.

The boy looks at the rug lying in the snow as if it contains a secret message.

"I suppose I am," Annie says.

"Is it okay if we take it?" the girl asks.

"What do you want with it?" Annie asks.

The boy turns to her. He has light brown hair and bright red cheeks. Apple cheeks, Maisie would have said. "It's for our mom. She wants a rug. She told us she did."

Annie imagines their mother wondering who on earth would be stupid enough to give her children such a rotten old rug. "Are you sure she'll want this? It's pretty old. I was just going to get rid of it."

"We don't have much money," he says. "She wants a rug."

"Well, okay," Annie says, still doubtful, "but how will you move it?"

"Willy and I can carry it," the girl says, boldly watching Annie with her clear grey eyes. "My name is DeLinda," she adds, "and this is my brother Wilson."

"I'm Annie Ransome." Wonderful, now they're exchanging names. Why did she bother answering the door? She hasn't got time for these kids.

"We know," Willy says. "You're her granddaughter. The old lady's daughter's daughter."

"You knew the old lady, did you?" Annie asks.

"Of course we did," DeLinda says. "We visited here all the time."

"She said she would be our grandma," Wilson says. "Our other grandmas died."

Annie tries to keep the disbelief out of her face.

"Be quiet, Wilson," DeLinda says. "She might not like it. She's the real granddaughter."

"Don't be silly," Annie says. "I don't mind." But she does, in a funny way. It's one thing to resent your grandmother and quite another to have someone else claiming her. Anyway, why would Maisie have spent time with these children? Wouldn't she have found them "common" or maybe even, to use her strongest condem-nation, "vulgar"?

The sun is shining hard today, and it's warmed the town since yesterday, almost to the freezing point. Melting water drips from the eaves. The children look at her, wanting something. But they won't ask, appar-ently; she has to think of it. They couldn't possibly expect to be asked in, could they?

"What does it look like without the rug?" DeLinda asks.

"Quite nice, really," Annie answers. "There's a pretty oak floor underneath. I washed and waxed it."

"Can we see?" Willy asks, unable to keep the eager-ness from his voice.

"Wilson!" the girl hisses. "That's not polite." But no one is fooled.

"Would you like to come in and see?" Annie asks. "The living room, I mean. I haven't cleaned the rest yet."

It's as simple as that. They're in, standing in the entrance hall on the small mat Annie found in the back porch and placed there for boots. She wouldn't even have the strength to throw them out, if it came to that. Not that it would. They look solemnly around the room.

"It's very attractive," DeLinda says, stiff with disap-proval. "The floor is very nice."

"We'd do ours like that if we had a wood floor," Wilson says. "But we have linoleum. That's why she wants a rug."

"I see," Annie says.

"There's less stuff in here now," Willy says, his hazel eyes making a circuit of the room as if he's searching for old friends.

"Yes, I thought there were too many things in the room. You couldn't turn around without bumping into them."

"Where's the pink chair?" DeLinda asks, not troubling to hide her disdain.

"Sitting in the kitchen at the moment. I don't think there's going to be room for it."

"I suppose you'll be getting rid of that too?" the girl asks.

"Well, I hadn't thought –"

"Can we have it?" DeLinda asks eagerly, politeness forgotten.

"I suppose so," Annie says, feeling a bit trapped. DeLinda keeps looking at her, and Annie realizes the girl means right now. She goes to the kitchen and lifts the chair from the back, by its wooden arms. She sets it down in front of the children. DeLinda runs her hands over the dingy pink brocade, the carved arms and legs.

"It's pretty," she says.

"She always liked to sit in it," Willy says, and Annie feels ashamed. The fact that her grandmother always liked to sit in it is precisely the reason she doesn't like the chair.

"She was English, you know," he says.

"Believe me, I know."

"She said we could have tea even though we were a little young for it. And she gave us these cookies."

"Biscuits, Wilson. Garden Creams." DeLinda is nothing if not correct.

"Do you have any of those?" he asks.

"Not today," Annie says, feeling guilty about polishing them off. "Maybe another time." Oh God, does she want them to come another time?

"Are you going to live here?" DeLinda asks.

"I don't think so. I'm staying with Edith Ashdown while I get the place cleaned up." To sell, she doesn't add, not wanting to provoke DeLinda to further scorn.

"The Witch," says Wilson. "We know her."

"She's not a real witch," DeLinda says.

"Don't you sleep here?" the boy wants to know.

"No, I don't," Annie says. "It's not ready yet." What am I saying? she wonders. As far as she knows, she doesn't plan to sleep here at any time.

"I wouldn't stay with that Edith Ashdown witch," Willy says. "I'd be afraid to go to sleep."

"Don't be silly, Wilson," DeLinda says.

"Your sister is right," Annie says. "I'm perfectly safe." It occurs to her that she ought to have denied that Edith was a witch. Oh well, too late now.

"Why aren't you in school?" Annie suddenly thinks to ask.

"Our teachers have to do an in-service," Wilson says. "So they can learn to teach us better."

DeLinda is ready to move on. She signals her brother with a decisive look.

"Okay, Willy, you take hold of the legs and I'll grab onto the back. We'll take the chair first and come back for the rug."

Annie can think of no objection, and in moments the children are bearing away Maisie's favourite chair like treasure trove. Watching it go, she feels a pang in the area she imagines contains her heart. For a moment, she'd like the chair back, to examine it again, to see if it could live for her too.

But the children have been too strong. They tramp down the snowy sidewalk, holding the chair high. They begin to sing. It sounds familiar. A hymn Maisie tried to teach her long ago, the one Bunty chose for the funeral. "All things bright and beautiful…." The sun is warm on Annie's face and hair. The children's voices trail away on air that tastes of spring.

ANNIE GETS DOWN TO WORK on her project du jour, the kitchen, and doesn't even notice when the two kids come back for the rug, only that it's gone the next time she happens to look out.

The kitchen is only about ten feet square, with old-fashioned cupboards and appliances and a small eating table. The door to the back porch is extra wide; through its window she can see the long wooden ramp once used for Phillip's wheelchair. The back door, as if Maisie was ashamed at having a ramp. Probably a lady didn't have a ramp in those days.

By noon the kitchen is scrubbed clean. Glass panes in the wooden cupboards sparkle, worn linoleum countertops and floors reflect a faded but almost spotless blue. The small arborite table with plastic-upholstered chairs is banished to the back porch and a walnut gate-leg table, newly polished, set up in its place, along with a pair of wooden dining chairs Annie found in Maisie's bedroom.

On the table she spreads a luncheon cloth of cream-coloured linen with intricate open-work embroidery in pale blue. She found it folded away in a drawer, obviously something Maisie'd been saving for a royal visit or some other worthy occasion that never came. With it were a pair of candlesticks, plain silver columns flaring wide at top and bottom. Newly polished, they sit in the centre of her table as she eats a lunch of tinned mushroom soup and saltine crackers.

This is the only food left in the house, but there's plenty of it. She counts forty-two tins of cream of mushroom, stashed in various corners of cupboards, and thirteen cream of celery, along with five boxes of crackers of assorted types. Also eight boxes of cube sugar, sixteen tins of evaporated milk, and a package of dried-up raisins. Four kinds of tea: English Breakfast, Earl Grey, Russian Caravan, and Darjeeling. Four jars of red currant jelly, five of Scottish marmalade. Seven packets of cheap white paper serviettes.

Time to go shopping. How long can life be sustained on tea and mushroom soup and Garden Creams? Perhaps Maisie died not of a heart attack but of simple malnutrition.

She surveys the room. Damned if she hasn't done it again. A little fresh paint and she could almost think about living here. Since Annie's never been the home-maker type, she's amazed to discover how much she seems to know – no doubt by osmosis, because Allison never actually taught her anything – about cleaning and polishing and decorating. Yes, she's turning into quite the little chatelaine.

She remembers seeing *Calamity Jane* on television when she was a kid. In one scene, Calamity and her friend make over a grungy old cabin. Through the wonders of film editing, they scrub and mend and run up curtains in mere seconds, singing, if she remembers correctly, an offensively cheerful song the whole time. Maybe the movie is where Annie learned cleaning. That and the directions on the various boxes, bottles, and tins.

Wherever she learned it, she's amazed to find herself enjoying it. It certainly beats typing somebody's boring history thesis. Maybe she should become a cleaning lady.

Annie sips her soup and realizes she could angle the table holding the television so that it's visible in the kitchen. She adjusts it and takes the remote back with her. Time for more news.

Today Charles's tie is deep blue with a narrow diagonal red stripe at four-inch intervals. It strikes her how few ways a man in his position has available to vary his appearance. His shirts have to be white, or maybe cream or blue. He doesn't have the option to change earrings; in fact, he can't wear even a single gold earring. After all, does God or the Prime Minister wear a gold earring? Jewellery is limited to cufflinks and tie bars. Today Charles wears his gold tie bar, the one with the soft brushed finish. The one that cost him five hundred dollars, an elegant dolphin with a tiny turquoise eye. When he wears it, no one can touch him. He is simply perfect. Once upon a time, she thought the tie bar was too expensive, but that was before Charles explained it to her; for an effect like that, what's five hundred dollars? Nothing, that's what.

Charles reads the news, absolutely straight, and she can't believe yesterday ever happened. He does the intro for a health item on "the unseen danger that may lurk in *your* home, the hidden plague that could be making your family sick." On screen, a hugely magnified creature, with segmented legs and a back that looks like a crabshell, appears. Her old friend the dust mite, plying its way along the borders of some unsuspecting mattress. It has a rounded belly, as though it's getting lots of good quality skin and nail parings. Its waste products, Charles informs her, accumulate in huge ditches at the edge of the mattress.

Zap. She will not watch that. She will not believe

anything like that is living at the base of her eyelashes. Or anywhere else on or near her. Any flakes of skin falling off her are going straight into the vacuum cleaner and nowhere else. She is not personally sustaining vast ecosystems of brainless, purposeless, invisible animals. Of course, how does she know they're purposeless?

She feels a slight irritation along her eyelids and the impression of very tiny beings walking across her arms. And again there's the salty taste at the back of her throat as she dashes to the bathroom and throws up her pathetic lunch. She's got to stop thinking about dust mites; or else find something more substantial to eat.

Tea. She needs tea. The mere act of filling the high-capacity kettle is calming. She turns on the burner and sits down at the table to wait. The television now shows a bare room with foam mats on the floor. Men in white pyjama outfits are bouncing and pinging around the room in the lotus position. All she can think of is the terrible strain on their joints. A voice explains that the men are followers of "the Maharishi" and are practising yogic flying, which, contrary to appearances, is not simply bouncing and pinging while sitting cross-legged on mats. No, not at all. While it may be imperceptible to the viewer, there is a moment – a very brief moment – when the men are not merely jumping in a new and painful way but *levitating*. Flying, in fact. And if enough people can learn to do this at once, it will change the face of the world. It will turn people from lawless, irrational creatures into helpful, co-operative citizens.

Flying? This is surely not what Icarus had in mind. But they look so happy, bobbing about. They don't have the slightest idea how silly they look. She imagines them all twenty years later suddenly discovering they need hip joint replacements. And yet…what if there is a moment when they really do break free of gravity? For only a hundredth part of a second, but enough to show them what it means to be loosed from the earth's bounds.

But, she thinks, what good would that be? Where else would you go? And besides, how come they only have men doing it? Zap.

Charles is doing his sign-off. He's at the point where he performs a warm smile, thanks people for tuning in, and invites them to watch him again this evening on the network's Pulse Action News. Time for a quick cut to a commercial. No. It can't be. He's looking at her. Again.

"Annie," he says. "For Christ's sake, call me!"

She zaps the TV off completely. Invisible bugs in your eyelashes and flying men in white pyjamas are one thing. A haunted television set is something else again. A tiny whistle sounds and grows in power to a shrill blast. Saved by the kettle.

Over tea, Annie notices she hasn't read yesterday's mail, which sits on the table in the living room. She brings it to the kitchen table and gets a knife from Maisie's cutlery drawer for a letter opener. Most of it consists of glossy flyers for nationally advertised products, along with a few circulars from local tradespeople done on home computers. "House Painting, Interior and Exterior, reasonable prices, call Jacob." That's a keeper. "Al's Second Hand Store. Do you have Grandma's Old Dining Table or Mom's Old Four Poster and you don't know What to Do with them? They could be worth BIG $$$ to you. Give me a call, that's Al, or come see me in my store. Call now. That's Al – Al's Second Hand." She keeps it. The circulars for roofing, furnace cleaning, and triple-glazed windows she tosses out. She won't be staying long enough to need them.

At the bottom of the pile is an actual real letter, the one addressed by hand to "Ransome, 39 River Road." She'd noticed it the day before, but had forgotten it in the cleaning frenzy. Who could be writing to her when she doesn't even live here? Of course, it could be for Allison, or even for Maisie. Someone who hasn't heard the news. She holds the envelope in her hand and feels an electric sort of tingle from it. She puts it aside and pours more tea. She could do with some cookies, but for now there's only saltines. She tries dipping a saltine in the tea, but the effect is not good. The saltine immediately gets soggy and the tea tastes of salt. Maybe she should go out right now and buy Garden Creams.

Why not just give in and open the letter? She opens it and recognizes the handwriting, which closely resembles her own, at once. The letter feels heavy in her hand. She tries to put it down, but can't.

## CHAPTER SEVEN

"My dear Annie," the letter begins. "I don't know if you'll even get this letter. If you do, it will probably mean you're in the house."

Annie puts the letter down. Why should she have to read this? What good can it do now? But it sits on the table, daring her to ignore it. These are her mother's last words to her, superseding everything which has ever passed between them. She takes a deep breath to steady herself, to stop the words from dancing around on the page, and picks up the letter.

"Please do what you want with the house. I went through it after Maisie died, but I couldn't face sorting out her stuff. I hope you'll find something of value to keep, although you never cared much for old things. I would never have known what you'd want, so it's better you'll be doing the looking. Except, of course, I did send the pictures of Eamon and Maude – and the ones of

Mother and Uncle Robbie. I felt there was something special about them and I wanted you to have them.

"I don't know if you'll ever be there in the house, but I feel you will. I feel like I'm really talking to you." Again Annie puts the letter down, shaking with rage. How like Allison to leave her with a monologue that can never be replied to. How can she write so calmly, as if she's explaining a few details about doing the laundry or buying groceries?

"You no longer need me, haven't for a long time. I don't say that with any bitterness, young people are meant to reject their parents' advice. I don't think mine was ever much good anyway. You're much better off on your own. I wouldn't want you to end up like me."

Annie stops again as her emotions catch up with her. At first she'd imagined she'd dealt with them at the funeral, felt what pain she had to feel, but she sees now that the funeral was only a test run. The feelings have simply been waiting for her in the ocean of her chest and belly, picking their own time to stroke their way to the surface.

How could you think this way? she asks the letter. Mothers *want* their daughters to be like them. They don't kill themselves and leave their daughters alone. They help them.

How could she imagine Annie no longer needed her? Annie sees that she has always needed more than her mother could give. That Allison has always kept her at arm's length.

"They gave me ether when you were born," the letter goes on. "I don't remember any of it. When they brought you in, I could hardly believe you were mine. Could hardly believe I'd managed to produce a child. I was afraid there'd been some mistake, and you'd be claimed by someone else. Your real mother. But that never happened. In fact, the nurse said you were the only baby born that night. You had to be mine.

"In time I became a reasonable facsimile of a mother, but I was always convinced you saw through me."

Annie lets the tears come. The pressure inside is too much otherwise, but she finds it physically painful. Like the powerful forces of childbirth, she supposes, when something has to come out of you, whether you're ready or not, with its own way of working.

"I never saw through you. I thought you saw through me." She sees the terrible waste of it. A mother afraid to love her own child. Afraid she's not good enough. And the child sees her mother turn from her and thinks, I am not good, my mother doesn't love me. She feels a burst of rage at the stupidity, the betrayal, but she can't give way to that yet, can't begin to handle it. There's another half page.

"I don't want to leave for good without saying how much I did love you. How proud I was of you." Liar, Annie thinks. If you loved me, you couldn't have done this. "I don't mean your appearance or good work in school or anything like that. I mean I was just proud of you." This is something Allison has never said. Annie has never understood till now how much she's needed to hear it.

"Above all, I want you to know this isn't your fault. It all started long before you were born. I've known for at least a year that everything was coming to an end. Maisie's death and the loss of my job were only the final reasons, but I'd felt for a long time that I couldn't continue. No one is to blame. I ask your forgiveness for any pain my death will cause you. My very best love, your mother, Allison."

"No!" Annie shouts. "I won't forgive you. You don't deserve it. How could you? How could you do it?"

Her everyday self surrenders. Annie faces grief for what feels like the very first time. There's no stopping it, any more than you can stop a thunderstorm or a flash flood. It can only be endured. It's a hundred times worse than throwing up. It grabs her by the throat, the chest, the belly. It has to escape, it will pull her apart if it has to. She sees that it's been there inside her ever since Rita called to tell her Allison was gone, and she's been holding it in. She has no idea how she did it, how she could be that strong. Now it's coming out, no matter what.

It pulls her face into twisted shapes. Her breath is torn from her. She feels like something is trying to choke her. The pain is so strong she wants to run into walls or fall unconscious on the floor to get away from it. She wails out loud in a voice she doesn't recognize. She finds herself on the floor, rocking, her own arms around herself as far as they will reach. It goes on and on. There are colours in the dark behind her eyes. Everything is in motion. Only the floor is cool and clean and solid, holding her.

After a long time, she doesn't know how long, the flood of pain ebbs, at least for this time, leaving her tired beyond words or thought. Everything she believed she was for thirty years, a certain familiar shape she thought was herself, is swept away. There is no way she can pull the blind back down that was keeping all this pain and knowledge hidden.

And this anger. Allison has found the strength to arrange her own death. Why couldn't she have used that strength to live? Annie is tired of accusing her mother, but she can hardly bear the sense of waste. She can't bear it, but there's no choice.

What would have happened if she'd simply flown home to Charles after the funeral? These feelings would never have been expressed. Charles would never have understood, would never have allowed it. The work of keeping everything in would have consumed her strength until she no longer even knew she was doing it.

Wanting air, Annie cranks open the casement window over the sink. She hears the drip of melting snow off various parts of the house, hears or maybe feels water stirring in the eaves. The snowpack in the yard looks the same but different, as if it's shrinking inside itself. Spring is coming, whether she's ready for it or not.

She would like to take this as some sort of hopeful

sign, but it makes her bitter. She wishes she could be with her mother, talk to her, hold her, even for a moment. Today has been the first lesson in knowing that this will never again be possible. She doesn't pretend even to herself that she's learned it yet. She only knows it's waiting to be learned.

COMING UP TO EDITH'S YARD, she's startled by a rush of wings and keen cries, as clouds of waxwings wheel over her head then flow on some signal to the backyard to light on a towering mountain ash. They feed on the cold, half-rotted fruit, their cries a tangle of high-pitched sound that pierces and almost stuns her.

A second rush of birds streams to the great tree; she feels it move through her own body, senses the force of their will, their ruthless grasping of what sustains them. She enters Edith's verandah and the sounds are instantly muted.

LATER, with Edith, she can't keep up the usual guard, the usual pretences that ensure Edith can't hurt her or even touch her. She can't lie or conceal, because it takes too much energy. She tells Edith briefly about the letter, for the moment beyond tears. Edith doesn't try to comment on it, just listens. They sit down to dinner and Annie eats the delicious food, grateful to have it and grateful that Edith has prepared it, for whatever reasons. Reasons Annie can know only if Edith chooses to tell her. Tonight she is not afraid of anything Edith can say. Or almost not afraid.

Later, she calls Charles from the kitchen after Edith is in bed. "Sorry I haven't called. I've never been through anything like this." She wants to say, It takes all my strength, but he would think it melodramatic. Or maybe that's what she would think.

"I'm sorry," he says, "it must be hard. I know I'll have to face it some time, but I can't even imagine it now."

"No, you can't imagine it," she says. "You can't prepare. All you can do is try to cope."

"When do you think you might be coming back?" he asks. She hears his uncertainty. There should be a way to handle every situation; but in this case he has no idea what it is.

"I don't know." She hears a flatness in her voice. Fatigue, and an inability to dissemble.

"What about me?" he says. "Don't I count for anything?"

"Of course you do," she says, but it sounds hollow. "Would you like to come down for a bit?"

"Don't be ridiculous," he says. "I'd ruin my chances for L.A."

For what? What did he say? The phone goes suddenly quiet.

"I applied for a job in Los Angeles. I didn't mention it before, because I knew you had a lot on your mind."

Her body goes cold and the walls of the kitchen seem to waver. "Did you think I'd go to Los Angeles?"

"Well, you would, wouldn't you?" He sounds so suddenly unsure, so un-Charles-like, that any other time she would pity him.

"I don't really know, Charles, but it's the last thing on my mind right now."

"We'll talk when you get back," he says soothingly. "Don't worry. What do you do all day, anyway?"

"Work on the house."

"Why? You're not going to live there." She doesn't respond. "You're not, are you?" Until this moment, she's never acknowledged to herself that she had a choice.

"Annie? What about me?" He means this to sound assertive, even demanding. But she hears an apprehensive note in his voice she's never heard before. Or did she only fail to recognize it?

"What about you, Charles?"

"I can't believe you're talking this way."

"I can't believe you didn't mention L.A."

"I was going to – Annie, just come home and we'll talk about it."

Any other time, she'd agree to be on the next plane. But not today. Today her sense of duty, or whatever it is, is not functioning. "I can't right now."

"You're trying to drive me crazy."

"I have to go. The little yellow bags for the vacuum cleaner are in the linen closet."

"What?"

"The little yellow bags for the vacuum. They're in the linen closet."

"Why do I need to know that? The cleaning woman came today."

"Oh." So the cleaning lady has not quit. "Well, I have to go. Goodbye, Charles."

"Annie, wait."

She sets the receiver gently onto its rest.

# CHAPTER EIGHT

Saturday, March 21. Cold again today, as if yesterday's melting was only a cruel joke. Hah! Got you again. You people fall for this every time. And she does too.

Harrison's Grocery is almost empty this morning. No doubt the crowds have flocked to the new Superstore, forgetting this small, locally-owned relic of the first wave of supermarket building. Here she tracks down the source of Maisie's food cache. Down this aisle, Maisie got her mushroom soup. Over here are the saltines. The Garden Creams are harder to find, but she finally spots them in a small section of "fancy foods." And the fresh produce and bakery sections are surprisingly good for a small independent store.

She likes this store; it's small enough to simplify her choices. Never has she felt less need for twenty brands of laundry detergent or ten kinds of toilet bowl cleaner. She replenishes her supplies of cleaning products and floor wax, buys silver polish for the first time in her life. She may not be staying long, but she owes it to Maisie to get the silver sparkling one last time. Owes it to Maisie? She can't believe she's thinking this way.

At the checkout, she notices the woman cashier looking at her. As if she wants something. To be recognized? Annie really looks now and finds she does know the woman. Blue eyes, dark red hair, probably coloured now.

"Mrs. Thompson?" Her memory kicks up the name just in time.

"That's right," the woman says. "Corinne. You're Annie Ransome, aren't you? I'd know you anywhere."

Corinne Thompson hasn't changed much since Annie went to school with her daughter, except for a few more lines around the mouth and eyes. Of course that's only twelve years ago, what did she expect? A little old lady with white hair and a cane?

"We were so sorry about your mom," Corinne says. "So many sad things happening these days. It makes you think, it really does."

"Yes," Annie agrees, not trusting herself with more words.

"I hear you're staying on awhile in your grandmother's house. It'll be nice to have you around."

"Thanks," Annie says, feeling she must now ask how Sylvie is doing, but dreading the possibility of having to see her again. Sylvie married right after high school, an older man who owned a small chain of hardware stores.

Harold Borebank, the name said it all. Sylvie, who'd shared Annie's teenage rebellion, done the usual stupid, dangerous things with her. Annie'd wanted to scream at her, "You've sold out! For three hardware stores and a fancy house!" She hadn't said it, but Sylvie'd known anyway. She'd asked Annie to be her maid of honour, but after that they'd never spent an hour alone together.

"How's Sylvie?" she makes herself ask.

Corinne's face tightens. Annie sees the lines left by pain, by the forces that have tried to pull the face to pieces.

"Oh, you don't know. Sylvie's gone." Gone, Annie thinks. Does Corinne mean she's left Harold? No, more than that. "It was breast cancer. They kept telling her it couldn't be, she was too young."

"Oh, no," Annie says.

"She put up an incredible fight, but it spread so quickly. She had chemotherapy and radiation, but none of that helped. It only made her feel worse. You know how it is."

Annie nods, but she doesn't know. She's never thought about it, never had any reason to.

"Harold was so good to her." The simple words break through Corinne's control and her eyes fill with tears. "And I must say, he's wonderful with their son Donnie."

Annie is afraid to let herself feel anything for Sylvie yet. "I really am sorry," she says. "I've got out of touch with Riverbend since I moved away."

"You should give Harold a call," Corinne says. "I know he'd be glad to see you. You were at their wedding." As if that qualifies her as a friend. Someone who was there when they were happy, even if she hadn't wanted to be there. Corinne smiles, pleased to have thought of the suggestion. Trying to salvage happiness where she can.

"I will, I'll do that," Annie lies through her teeth. She would never voluntarily call Harold, even if it meant doing without telephone service. She wants only to get out of here as quickly as she can, before the news about Sylvie hits her.

Like delivering angels, two customers with loaded carts appear behind Annie and Corinne begins ringing Annie's purchases through. A teenage boy appears out of nowhere and starts bagging them, and in moments Annie has paid and escaped from the store.

She loads the groceries into Edith's car, gets in the car and fastens her seat belt, and starts to cry. Sylvie's dead, and Corinne has to deal with that every day. It must be terrible to have your daughter die before you do. Corinne is not that old herself, maybe still under fifty. She must have been so pleased when Sylvie married Harold, to know her daughter would never want for anything. She must have looked forward to old age, grandchildren, an orderly life.

Sylvie, Annie's old friend, is gone. No way now to take anything back. The image of Harold who was so good to Sylvie forces itself upon her. She doesn't like to think that she might have been wrong about him, that she acted like an intolerant fool. But she was eighteen years old when Sylvie married. She hadn't wanted life to get that serious that fast, and she'd always believed Sylvie felt the same.

BACK AT MAISIE'S, Annie unloads the groceries and packs them away in what are now her cupboards. In the cupboard over the sink devoted to canned goods, she decides to rotate her merchandise, bringing Maisie's soups to the front to be used first. Reaching to the back of the cupboard, she finds a piece of folded paper wedged into a small crack where the side of the cupboard doesn't quite join the back. She almost throws it away, before she notices it's in Maisie's handwriting. She smoothes it out and reads:

> He was a good man and kind to me always,
> certainly he was, but he would not learn to con-
> trol his thoughts and at the end did not know
> God. So his works ought to be destroyed, but this
> is a great burden and perhaps should be left to
> other hands. There is no one to speak to about
> this. Perhaps it is safer to just wait and see.

What does it mean? Presumably "he" must have been Grandpa Phillip, but what were his works, and why must they be destroyed? Maisie can hardly be talking about

Phillip's woodworking projects. Annie folds up the note and tucks it away in the tea towel drawer where she's stashed Allison's return ticket.

Annie treats herself to Earl Grey tea and Garden Cream biscuits and turns on the news. It's Charles, filling in on Saturday again; always filling up his time with work. He reads the noon news without deviation. If anything is bothering him, he gives no sign of it. Today his blazer is navy blue and his tie is grey with a dull gold stripe through it. He has a fresh haircut – one hundred bucks, but worth it, because it sets him off from ordinary men who don't know the news.

Charles gives it to her straight. The reports of an economic upturn, recently made by a bunch of people who should know, have now been questioned by another bunch of people who should know. Unemployment may not be down after all, but merely hiding. It appears there are people who have simply given up looking.

And the fires in the Los Angeles hills are now completely out of control. In Albania, an earthquake has killed three hundred people. In Egypt, a man has cut off his daughter's head because she married without his consent. In Mexico, a bus has plunged off a mountainside, killing all the people aboard. In Detroit, a junior high school student has been stabbed because another boy wanted his running shoes. And in England, the first women priests have been ordained, and a vicar in Lincolnshire is displeased. "I would burn the bloody bitches," he explains to a reporter. "I would shoot the bastards if I was allowed, because a woman can't represent Christ."

Annie knows that if she's patient and waits till the end Charles will reward her with a pleasant or humorous bit of news. An act of kindness or heroism, a story about a cute child or a cute dog, or something weird but non-threatening, or something about a movie star. But today she can't wait for it.

"Goodbye, Charles," she says, and flips him off, wondering for the first time how he can stand it, this endless repetition of death and disaster, day after day.

So Charles has applied for a job in Los Angeles. She refuses to think of it. It's not only the fires or the racism or the crime or the smog or even the earthquakes. She has never learned to drive on freeways and doesn't plan to. Therefore she is the last person who should ever consider living in Los Angeles.

The doorbell rings. She's getting a lot of attention for someone who doesn't even live here. A bit nervous, she opens the door. Rita. Wrapped in a bright blue fleece cape and looking much more rested than at the funeral. Carrying a bottle of red wine.


MAKING LUNCH, Annie finds she doesn't really hate cooking, just arguments about cooking. They drink red wine in crystal glasses while Annie makes a beautiful salad of butter lettuce, fresh tomatoes, and avocado. Dessert is Wensleydale cheese with thick slices of whole grain bread. Edith's mania for fresh things must be rubbing off on her.

Afterwards, Annie shows her the letter. She knows it will make Rita cry, but this time Annie herself is able to put her arm around Rita.

"She was afraid to touch me, Rita," she says. "I always thought there was something wrong with me."

Rita shakes her head as if to dispel memory. "She used to hold you like you were made of glass. Always afraid she'd make some terrible mistake, harm you in some way."

"That's ironic, isn't it?" Annie asks. A memory surfaces, one she's kept hidden for a long time. "I ran away once, when I was little. I was angry because she said I couldn't play on the riverbank. They were always saying that, all of them. So I did, to show them."

"You would have to do that, of course," Rita says. Annie tries to smile.

"It was steeper than I thought, and when I tried to come back up, I slipped way down and I could hear the water, really close. Every time I tried to climb up, the dirt and stones crumbled away, like an avalanche. I was afraid to move, but it was getting darker, and I was also afraid I might slide the rest of the way down into the water. They'd always warned me that would be the end, because the current was so bad." Rita nods, but doesn't interrupt.

"I thought I'd have to stay there all night, until I heard Mother calling me. Suddenly she was standing over me, shouting my name. She grabbed my arms and pulled me to my feet. She was shaking me…she was so angry. She dragged me up the bank. And I knew right then…Rita, I thought she didn't love me."

Annie finds she's given up the idea that she mustn't cry. Tears stream down her face almost without her notice.

"Of course she loved you." Rita speaks with utter certainty.

"She hurt me," Annie insists.

"Yes, and you've hoarded your pain like treasure. And never looked for the reason."

"Reason?" Annie is indignant. "What reason could there be?"

"Didn't anyone ever tell you about Edward?" Rita asks gently. "He was Allison's best friend when she was little."

"No," Annie says, "I never heard of him."

"Allison really loved him a lot. I remember being jealous of them. Anyway, one day they played by the river and Edward fell in. The river carried him away. Allison ran to get help, but there was no use. I don't think they ever found him."

"That's terrible." Annie feels achingly sorry for the little boy, but something begins to lift from her spirit. His death makes sense of something in her life.

"It scared Maisie and Phillip, and they used it to scare her. Not that anyone needed to scare her more, after what she'd seen. But they thought they were protecting her."

"God," Annie says bleakly. "What awful parents."

"I suppose the hospital forgot to pass on the owner's manual when she was born," Rita says wryly.

Annie laughs a little. "Same thing happened with me."

"You have to give up the pain," Rita says. "Give up being the child."

Is that what she's been doing? Hoarding pain? Like Bunty, Rita has shown her Allison as a child; breaking down the idea of "mother" and putting someone else, much less familiar, in her place.

RITA POURS ANNIE A GLASS OF WINE. "You've probably been wondering about Allison's apartment," she says.

"No," Annie says, "I haven't." How could she have forgotten her mother's apartment downtown? Will she have to clear that out too? And why didn't Edith remind her?

"And I imagine you must have been surprised at how small the balance was in Allison's savings account," Rita continues.

"No," she says, wondering what Rita's getting at, "I had no idea how much it should be. Whenever we asked about money, she always said she had enough."

Rita takes a deep breath and goes on. "When Worthington's closed down six months ago, they were more or less bankrupt, but they did pay severance to a few long-time staff."

"Of course," Annie says. "I knew that. Mother got something."

"Allison got fifty thousand dollars," Rita says.

"Fifty thousand!" Annie says.

"And before that she had saved about fifty thousand more, mostly in the last ten years or so. She expected to have a pension from the store and use the savings to top it up a bit." Rita waits for Annie to speak.

"So where is the money?" Annie asks. "In the apartment?"

"No. She gave up the apartment. Two months ago, Allison sold or gave away every single thing in it. She took her severance money from Worthington's and most of her savings and she travelled." Rita pauses. "All over North America."

"What?" Annie doesn't believe it. "She never said a word. I've had letters from her during that time."

"She was back here a few times. Maybe she wrote you then. But most of that time she travelled. I only found out after she died. I mean, I knew about a couple of the trips, and Edith knew about several, but we only pieced it together when we talked to Len Beach, her travel agent." Rita sips her wine, watching Annie take it in.

"She went to Winnipeg, San Francisco, Edmonton, Albuquerque, Halifax, Phoenix, Victoria, Seattle, Whitehorse, Chicago, Vancouver, Minneapolis, you name it – she even spent a week in London. Near the end, she went on a cruise ship to Alaska. All this in no particular order, with no particular attention paid to logical itineraries."

"My God," Annie says, "it's like some kind of fairy tale. I can't believe anyone connected to me did this."

"I couldn't either, at first. But it happened. She used to send postcards to Len, with brief observations about the places she saw, the grand hotels she stayed in, the dinners she ate, the dresses she bought."

"Dresses?" Annie asks, bewildered.

"Some of the money went for clothes. As you know, she was a buyer for twenty years and she liked good stuff. She must have decided to have whatever she wanted."

"But where are these dresses?"

"Well, she died in one of them." Rita lets this sink in. "And the others she must have left in hotels all over the continent. Because they don't seem to be anywhere in Riverbend."

Annie cannot reconcile any of this behaviour with her mother. Allison must have been somebody different than or more than she ever imagined.

"They're obviously not in the apartment and they're not in this house."

"How do you know that?" Annie asks.

"Edith and I took a quick look when I brought the body back. We couldn't find anything."

Annie goes to the kitchen and fishes the return ticket out of the tea towel drawer. "I guess we missed that," Rita says. "We weren't looking for papers."

Annie doesn't know what on earth to think. She's considered herself a reasonably grown-up person with a reasonably sophisticated idea of the kinds of things people do. Clearly, this image must be radically revised. Clearly, she doesn't know a damn thing.

"We're sure she used this place as a base between trips," Rita says. "Edith did run into her a few times, but Allison was very cagey about what she was doing. Edith didn't feel she could push. Now she's sorry, of course."

Annie tries to shuffle all these facts into something she can grasp. The part about Edith being sorry, for anything, is especially startling.

"Len Beach feels bad too. He kept telling Allison she could go so many more places with the money she spent, or go to the same places for far less money, if only she'd let him plan her trips properly. But Allison just took off, paying full fares, going wherever she felt like going, until the money ran out, most of it anyway."

All Annie's life, her mother has given her lessons in the best way to spend money. To make it stretch as far as possible. To get value for the work you did to get the money. What is she trying to tell her now?

"Rita," she says, "I need to be by myself for a bit. I'll go into Maisie's room."

"No need," Rita says, getting her fleece cape, "I've told you everything I can. I thought I'd drop in on Edith for a moment. Then I have to drive back."

"But you can't go yet," Annie says. She only wants to be alone for a short time, then she wants Rita to be there.

"You don't need me to hold your hand, you know," Rita says.

"Yes, I do so," Annie says. It sounds so childlike that she starts to laugh.

"Oh, there is one more thing." Rita takes a ring from her finger, an opal set in gold. Before Annie knows what's happening, Rita takes her hand and puts the ring on her finger. "There," she says, "fits perfectly. It never quite fit me."

"What is it?" Annie asks, looking at the play of colour in the stone.

"Allison gave it to me, must have been twenty years ago. She said it should be yours some day. We both knew 'some day' meant when she died."

Annie tries to take it off, but Rita takes hold of her hands. "Just accept that she wanted you to have it." Annie stops trying to take off the ring, although the gold band feels hot on her skin. "It doesn't mean you have to be like her."

Annie takes the words at face value. The ring is hers now and symbolises her mother's love, however badly flawed it was. Her mother was different in many more ways than Annie knew, made terrible mistakes, but her love can no longer be in doubt.

LATER, Annie stands on her step and looks towards Edith's. As she expected, Rita's car is gone. Maybe Rita was right. Tonight she's beyond the desire or ability to talk. She gets her coat and heads back to Edith's. When Edith opens the door, Annie can see in her face that Rita has told Edith about their talk. Edith doesn't expect her to say anything. She hangs up Annie's coat and ushers her into the kitchen, brings her supper on a tray, and leaves her alone to eat.

## CHAPTER NINE

Sunday morning, Edith feeds Annie a brunch of egg and salmon pie and coffee with hot steamed milk. She drifts in and out of the kitchen, leaving Annie to her own thoughts. Annie feels that sometime in her long sleep she's turned a corner and the thought makes her tingle with exhilaration – shot through with trepidation. Normally, trepidation makes her cautious, makes her draw back, but now it's balanced by the need to find out what her new path is going to be. She thanks Edith for the food and heads for her house.

TODAY ANNIE HAS RESOLVED to work on the bedrooms. If she's going to stay in town much longer, she has to start living in the house. And is she going to stay much longer? If Edith asked, she'd probably say no. If Charles asked, she'd say, I don't know. Does that mean she is? Until she decides, she wants some place to sleep, a place of her own choosing.

Which bedroom could she imagine sleeping in? If she chooses Allison's, would it be like choosing her mother's life? If she chooses Maisie and Phillip's room, which is larger and holds a double bed, will she feel out of place, a usurper of Maisie's power? It dawns on her that she's been given this power, all of it and such as it is, whether she wants it or not. She is all that's left of them. The last of the Conal Ransomes. They have surrendered everything to her. So she can certainly sleep in any of their beds if she feels like it.

She begins with the small bedroom, the one her mother grew up in. She's not afraid of it now. It has a dainty girlish look that must never really have suited Allison. An elaborately finialed and curlicued wrought iron bedstead painted white, covered with a shell pink chenille bedspread that matches the pink priscilla curtains. A pretty wooden dresser with a scalloped top, carved with a border of flowers. A round walnut-stained night table with another round shelf underneath piled up with old *Reader's Digests*. The carpet is the same as what used to lie in the living room and the walls are of course white with an undertone of puce, although she's starting to wonder if she only imagined the puce.

On the wall, an anorexic-looking ballerina wears the filmiest, gauziest silver skirt, her long legs displayed at an unbelievably wide angle to each other. She has an ecstatic look on her face, but then, Annie thinks, so did the faces of medieval flagellants. Allison, who could never dance and who never looked thin in her life, must have hated the picture.

By now Annie is skilled and efficient. She tears up the rug and pitches it outside in the snowbank, strips the bed and takes down the priscillas and throws everything in the washer, dusts and polishes the wooden furniture, and washes and waxes the light maple floor. She kills two more spiders and cleans the panes in the window.

Time again for the ritual of the wool socks, and this floor too begins to shine softly. Once again, she's claiming a space, not so that everything is erased, but so that it has her mark on it, clear and certain.

If she wants to sleep here, she'll need a curtain. From the linen cupboard where she piled them, Annie retrieves one of the maroon panels that used to hang in the living room. On the bedroom window the panel has a new life, contrasting pleasantly with the polished floor. The room actually seems more spacious than before. In fact, it needs something more. A chair to sit in. Too late she realizes that Maisie's pink brocade would have been perfect. Now she'll actually have to buy something. But that's ridiculous, she's not staying that long. Maybe if there's something cheap at Al's Second Hand Store.

The doorbell rings. She holds back, wanting to remain in the peace and safety of the small bedroom. But she's not afraid any more. She makes herself answer.

It's the children, Wilson and DeLinda. DeLinda's hair is done in French braids so tidy they resemble carved wood, and both their faces look freshly scrubbed. But today Annie's aware of the worn look of their cheap clothes. The girl holds out a package.

"Our mother sent this for you." She shoves it into Annie's hands. "It's a housewarming present."

Loosely wrapped in tissue paper is an old-fashioned biscuit tin. Annie lifts the lid and sees round, plump, peanut butter cookies.

"They look wonderful," she says, but it's not enough. "Would you like to come in?" she asks.

"For tea?" Wilson asks.

"Sssh, Willy, that's rude," DeLinda says, but looks glad the idea's been broached.

"Yes, why don't we have tea?" Annie shepherds them in, hanging their coats on the two remaining hooks and placing their overshoes on the mat. She sits with them while they wait for the kettle to boil, Wilson on the green couch, DeLinda and Annie in the wing chairs.

"It's not the same," DeLinda says.

"It's nice, though," Wilson says, as if he hates to admit it but is determined to be fair. They both seem to be struggling with their loyalty to Maisie.

"I suppose it is quite nice," DeLinda admits, "but it had more in it before. It was more complete."

"This is more my style," Annie says. "I find it quite complete." Except for the pink chair, she doesn't add.

"Where's our pictures?" Willy asks.

"What pictures?"

"She used to have our pictures on the little desk," DeLinda explains. "The Queen Anne desk," she adds importantly.

Annie goes to the desk and opens its single drawer. Sure enough, there are photographs, one of each child, in round mahogany frames. The pictures look oddly old fashioned, not only because of the dressy clothes the children wear, but more because of the intensely serious way they gaze out at the world. They remind her of Eamon, in the restless demanding look of them. She'd better watch out, or they'll be demanding things of her.

Annie gets the dishcloth and wipes dust from the glass and even cleans the frames with furniture polish. She sets the pictures on the desk. They look good there, as if they really are part of the family. The room is more complete.

The children settle into their seats, satisfied now that some measure of justice has been seen to.

The kettle whistles. DeLinda picks up a couple of *Reader's Digests* from the floor where Annie has forgotten them. She passes one to Wilson and settles in to read Humor In Uniform, after giving Annie a mildly reproving look, presumably at the shabby way she's treated Maisie's reading materials.

Annie brings tea on a tray and the peanut butter cookies on a blue Wedgwood plate. She pours tea in real china cups, passes milk and sugar. They stir the tea with great seriousness, take one cookie each on their bread and butter plates. They wait for her to fix her own, but even after she takes her first sip, they still don't make a move.

"You don't have a cookie," Wilson says.

She puts one on a plate and balances the plate on her lap. They watch. They actually want to see her eat it. But her stomach's been so bad lately – and peanut butter, she can't predict what it'll do. They wait. She tries a small bite. For a moment the salty taste's there, and then it ebbs and she can swallow and it's utterly delicious. Has she really been eating store-bought cookies and thinking them good?

"It's wonderful," she says, and now they eat too.


OVER DINNER, she tells Edith about the children. "Oh, yes," Edith says, "they were over there a lot before she died."

"They said Maisie told them she would be their grandma," Annie says.

"Very likely," Edith says. "She seemed genuinely fond of them."

Whatever opinion Edith may have on this situation, she keeps it to herself. Annie contemplates telling her what the children call her: The Witch. She decides to save it. With Edith, she thinks, it's nice to have a little something in reserve.

Annie addresses herself to the ginger shrimp stir-fry.

Nothing old fashioned about Edith's tastes. As if she's trying to make it clear that being old is not the same as being out of it. Annie has doubts about introducing ginger into her stomach, but it actually feels good once it's down there.

"I thought I'd drop back to the house after dinner," she says. "I've been working on Mother's bedroom and I'm nearly finished. And I've got laundry in the dryer."

Later, when she's ready to leave, Edith appears at the door with an armload of folded linens. "I would like you to have these," she says. "They were Eleanor's, but no one uses them now."

"These" are a set of cream muslin sheets with blue open-work embroidery along the hems. Annie can feel on her tongue the words she was trained as a child to say – "Oh, I couldn't possibly" – but her teeth won't let the words out. Edith places the linens in her arms.

"Thank you, Edith," she says. It's as easy as that.

Maisie would have been absolutely shocked. The sheets are too good, do not belong to her. But Maisie is dead and the sheets are beautiful; Annie wants them and Edith wants her to have them. End of story.

Under the sheets is a printed Indian bedspread, deep indigo blue on white woven cotton, in a pattern that makes a circle contained in the bedspread's square; inside the circle, gaily decorated elephants march round and round. She can't wait to have it on her bed.

Tonight is the first time she's walked down to Maisie's house – no, to her house – in the dark. It's perfectly quiet, but she finds herself running the last few steps and urgently thrusting her key into the lock.

TUCKING IN THE SHEETS with perfect nurse's corners, Annie feels the smooth cotton under her fingers, smells the scent of rose sachets. The deep blue circling elephants delight her. How lovely it will be to sleep in this room.

She's avoided looking inside the dresser. Now she decides to take a quick look. The top drawer is filled with Allison's girlhood treasures. A pink satin jewellery box with assorted trinkets. An old book with a real leather cover: *Songs of Innocence and Experience* by William Blake. She glances at the flyleaf. "To Allison, on her tenth birthday, from her grandfather, Eamon Conal." She sets it out on the bedside table.

She arranges the pillows against the head of the bed, kicks off her shoes, and lies down, breathing the faint emanation of roses. She realizes the unpleasant smells are gone from the house. It's growing younger, opening to new possibilities.

She picks up the book, its leather cover worn and soft against her fingers, trying to imagine Allison doing the same thing. Did she wonder why her grandfather was giving her a used book? Could she understand anything of the poetry? Annie opens the book and reads:

> Tyger! Tyger! burning bright
> In the forests of the night,

> What immortal hand or eye
> Could frame thy fearful symmetry?

The tiger is a perfect animal spirit for Allison, who would never have realized it.

The book falls open to the centre, revealing a sheet of folded paper. She opens it out, expecting another of Maisie's notes from beyond the grave. But this sheet is in the same hand as the inscription on the flyleaf: great-grandfather Conal's. She reads:

> When I see my children I marvel. The girl with her barleystraw hair – the boy with eyes the colour of bachelor's button. How could these two come from me? I am stopped up, blocked. I lead nowhere. Yet here they are before me. So alive I can almost feel their blood moving in them.
>
> I am afraid to touch them. Not only because of the sickness in my blood. I fear I will contaminate them with my thoughts – dam the flow of spirit in them. They know nothing of doubt – are sure to shake from life what they want of it. Is this what every generation of parents sees – and sees no choice but to stop – because it is too much alive? But I say we must not stop it! If they can but carry this with them!
>
> How can I help my dearest Maude? To understand that they are the best of us. Born

anew and not to be betrayed. Not to be bound like every old generation by rules and evasions. And deprivations which recreate the punishments and disappointments we ourselves knew. I know the children drive her at times near distraction. And yet – if we can but keep them free.

Annie replaces the paper in the book, seeing the young man staring out of the picture, feeling the passion in him. What made him write all this down, and what was the sickness in his blood? She is touched by his desire to protect the children. She sees Maisie as she actually turned out and her great-uncle Robert, Maisie's twin, as he turned out. Between the intention and the realization, something very powerful has intervened. How did the vibrant girl with barleystraw hair become the grandmother Annie remembers most for her prohibitions and restraints?

The only answer she can think of is Eamon's wife, Maude Rowan. And if she was the author of the harm, what made her betray the children? Or did she not see it as betrayal? Annie searches her memories of Maisie for any trace of the child Eamon hoped would shake what she wanted from life, but she finds none.

Except for the children. DeLinda. Wilson. A girl and her brother. Children full of desires and already beginning to suffer from real deprivation. Did Maisie see them as a re-creation of herself and Robbie? Her chance to make different choices?

Suddenly weary, more than she has been through the last few days of cleaning and arranging, Annie returns the book to the table, the pillows in their scented cases supporting her, buoying her. Her arms and legs drift away from her; she thinks of babies and the moment when they fall asleep in their mothers' arms, totally limp.

*Two children stand at the end of the street, looking out over the river. Their shoes loosen pebbles underfoot which make a small avalanche down the bank, a soft drumming like gusts of rain or sand against a windowpane. The avalanche grows, pebbles and grains of dust sucked into whirls and eddies that fall away and fall away. The children step back to avoid being taken. A deep current of stones plucks at the boy's ankles. The sister grabs his hand and leads him away from the bank. Below, swift waters foam against sharp rocks.*

*Now they stand on a sidewalk in front of an ornate Victorian house, all towers and verandahs and gingerbread shingles. Great trees shade the street; the air is warm on their arms. The children have got hold of an enormous wooden chair covered in deep rose brocade. They wrestle it down the street, inch by inch almost, it's so large.*

*A tremendous wall of water flows over the bank and races down the street. It sweeps down on the children, lifts them into its current as they leap for the chair, for its brocade lap and a desperate grip on its large wooden arms. They whirl and tumble in the wild current, clinging to the chair, which is really a chair but is also the body of an old woman. The chair is sinking now, pulling them down deeper in the water.*

*And then the girl lets go. She pries the boy's fingers from the chair. Holding his hand in one of hers, she uses the other to stroke to the surface and the air.*

"Annie," a voice is saying. She gulps the air, her heart pounding. She opens her eyes, and Edith is standing over her. "I was worried when you didn't come back. I had a key, from when Maisie was ill. Are you all right?"

Annie can't stop the surge of joy at being out of the current, at the enormous amount of air available for breathing. Edith peers at her anxiously. "Oh, Edith," Annie says. "If only you could have seen."

Edith holds her. It can't be possible, not Edith The Witch, but she's doing it. Annie is still the girl in the dream, with a girl's body. Edith is not her mother, just a benign presence. Of course Edith isn't really harmless, but she has made herself harmless to Annie tonight.

Then there's that salty taste at the back of her throat, and she breaks from Edith's arms and runs for the bathroom. Edith comes and supports her over the toilet until she's through, then sponges her face and hands with a washcloth dipped in cool water. They both know what it means. Annie realizes she's known for some time, but hasn't let what she thinks of as her "forward" self know, the self that stands between the world and her inmost needs. What an idea, a forward self that can't be allowed to know the whole truth, and an underneath, further back self, in touch with absolutely everything.

Is this where the child Maisie dwelt in the old grandmother, pushed so far back that no one knew she was there? Not even Maisie herself?

But oh, the joy, when the two selves can merge, when the forward, outward person can know the other – the one that's so much more feeling, seeing, and hearing that Annie thinks human beings must have got their concept of omniscience from it. Not God, but ourselves – knowing so much more than we let ourselves realize.

"How long have you known?" Edith asks.

"Maybe a few minutes, maybe a few weeks."

Edith seems to find nothing odd about this statement. "Will you be coming back to sleep?" she asks.

"No," Annie decides, "I think I'll stay here."

Edith accepts this without a word of protest. Annie has nothing with her to sleep in, but Edith helps her off with her clothes, neither of them bothering to be embarrassed about her nakedness. Edith pulls back the covers and tucks her in the bed. She turns out the lamp on the bedside table and moments later Annie hears the key turn in the lock.

For a moment she thinks of being alone and naked in the house, thinks of Charles alone and angry, thinks of Edith walking alone down the empty street, but none of these thoughts has any power over her. The dark air around her is warm and welcoming. She gives way to sleep, releasing herself into it like a bird taking flight.

Sleep. Sleep. Oh, sleep.

CHAPTER TEN

Edith stands by the railing at the end of River Road, looks out across the valley, washed in moonlight reflected off snow, the old railway trestle barely visible in the soft light. At wide intervals, street lamps glow – and lights in the houses where people are still awake. Below her, snow melts and the earth grows warm; she can smell moisture in the air. She can almost hear the river coming back to life, and it makes her feel old. Too many winters, she thinks; too many springs. She's overlooked this valley for so many years now and so little has visibly changed, as if it's an enchanted place cut off from the forces that shape the world. In truth, she understands that everything has changed, it just doesn't show yet.

She thinks of Annie sleeping, and of how she's being caught up in the girl's life, beginning to want things for her. She's puzzled that this should be happening; she's kept herself unentangled for so long. Even her children have little claim on her anymore.

There is so much she could do for Annie, so much she could tell her. Maybe she should simply tell her everything at once, all the things she knows about Annie's mother and her family, and be done. No, she won't do that. There's one thing she's learned from raising her own three children – if raising isn't too ambitious a word for what she did – and that is, that you can't tell anybody anything, no matter how much you may need for them to know, if the person doesn't think it's something they want to know.

Besides, she doesn't know quite how this process with Annie works. She's got the girl to stay in Riverbend, but maybe Annie has to take it from there. And it could be that Annie's staying had little to do with her. For how could she have kept her, if Annie had really been determined to be gone? Unless Annie knew there was work she had to do here. Why should I want to help her? Edith wonders. A slight smiles forms on her lips. Annie looks so childlike in sleep, with her small breasts and slim arms and legs, that even a worse person than herself would surely feel some compassion, some urge to protect her.

No, you can't tell a person anything, especially a son or daughter, at least after a certain age. Unless they come to you. Maybe that's beginning to happen. She sensed such joy in Annie tonight, something that wasn't there before. She wishes Allison could have felt joy, but doesn't think she ever did. Edith knows she can't change the past, but she hopes that knowledge of the past can change or help Annie.

Edith looks at her house. For the space of a single breath, she's afraid to go back in. Afraid danger or contagion has entered in the short space she's been out in the dark. Back straight, eyes unwavering, she stares the fear down. Then it's as if a cloud lifts and she feels only confidence that once more the house will shelter and protect her, as it's always done, even in the worst of times. Acts of will are something Edith has always been good at.

In any case, she's never really alone in the house.

She goes in through the unlocked front door and closes it after her.

CHAPTER ELEVEN

The rumble of distant thunder pulls her from sleep. Usually she wakes frightened and disoriented after the first night in a new place. This time she is comfortable and aware of the boundaries around her. She enjoys the smooth touch of the muslin sheets, the pleasure of moving her arms and legs without getting tangled up in pyjamas or nightgowns. Her body is warm, fluid. Her bedside clock says 11:15. She has slept the clock around. In the distance, she hears the horn of a diesel locomotive.

"Thy belly is like an heap of wheat." The words of the Song of Solomon, so archaic, so agricultural, give her a warm, smug pleasure, what Maisie called feeling "chuffed." Her belly is full of something better than wheat. Secret treasure. Is pregnancy a miraculous event or a last straw before disaster? It all depends on your point of view. Today she can almost feel her blood whirling through her veins. Staying alive is such a complex set of choices, but today, so far, everything seems simple. Even the question of herself and Charles seems capable of some kind of resolution.

The rumbling reverberates through the valley. Winter thunder, she thinks, how lovely.

Her fleece sweatshirt is folded on the night table where Edith left it. She pulls it on. There is also a leaf green tea plate with half a dozen saltine crackers arranged on it. Edith must have come in some time this morning and put them there. Annie remembers reading that crackers eaten first thing before getting out of bed are supposed to help prevent morning sickness. She really has to pee by now, but fires off a message to her stomach. Are you prepared to accept crackers at this time? The stomach considers and reports; not exactly thrilled, but willing to chance it.

The crackers taste dry and lifeless, but stay down. She pulls on the underpants and jeans folded neatly on the dresser and sprints to the bathroom; she uses the toilet and washes her face and hands with a new bar of Pear's soap she found in the linen cupboard.

Granola and milk tastes good and stays down. Today she should get on with the cleaning; she should do Maisie's room. The weather channel tells her it's warm again – just above freezing. And a couple of channels over, Charles is finishing an item about a ferry boat sinking off the coast of Madagascar and drowning four hundred people. He segues into his final item, his daily "good news" tidbit.

According to an expert in human genetics, he explains, we are more closely related to other people than we realize. Any two people on earth, no matter how geographically separated, no matter how unlike in stature or skin colour or any other characteristic, are no more distantly related than fiftieth cousins. "What a small world it is," he confides, "one big family of man." Annie doesn't think Charles really believes this. As a person who knows the news, he sees himself as set off from ordinary mortals.

Today Charles looks very serious. He's wearing a brown jacket she's never seen before and she doesn't think it suits him. It's a misconception that people with brown hair and eyes necessarily look good in brown. She makes a mental note to tell him he should get his colours done. Or do people still do that? She's lifting her index finger to shut off the power when he stops in the middle of his sign-off and looks right into her eyes.

"What does it mean, Annie?" he asks. "Do you ever plan to come back?" This gets to her. It's more reasonable and calm than she'd expect from him, and the slightly plaintive quality affects her more than anger or impatience could. "A lot of people have called wanting to get work done. And that guy with the history thesis is really nervous. Frankly, I'm running out of things to tell them."

The sarcasm is back. She zaps him right off.

It must be her own guilt doing this. Charles would

never say these things. Would he? And she *has* left him holding the bag with her clients. He'll handle it, though; he's good at making arrangements.

Anyway, there's no time to worry about it. She's going out. Before she can think of any of the chores waiting to be done, she pulls on a windbreaker Edith has lent her, an old one of Tira's. Cheered by its bright red fleece, she escapes out the door. At the bottom of the street, by Edith's, she looks out over the valley, with its market gardens and neighbourhoods of tidy old houses and, looming over them, the sugarloaf form of Robin Hill, where she used to toboggan. Beyond the valley, the prairie resumes – real prairie, unbroken grassland stretching away to the distant Stony Hills.

Annie folds herself between the rails of the fence and carefully picks her way down the steep bank.

It's unbelievably warm in the full southern sun, the air heavy and moist, snow wet and slippery with melting. Near the bottom she loses her footing and slides the last ten feet on her bottom. The physical sensation is wonderful. She hasn't felt anything like it in years.

She notices a deep depression in the bank where much of the snow has already melted, revealing muddy clay and gravel. She recognizes it as one of her childhood places. She and her cousin Kate, Rita's daughter, used to come here. They called it their hideout, and they needed a hideout because they were robbers. But the only places they ever robbed were their own houses. They took small objects that their mothers would search for with puzzled frowns and eventually forget about. Things that weren't big enough or expensive enough to occupy their attention for long. Annie and Kate wrapped their loot in plastic bread bags and stashed it behind rocks in the cave. Summer nights, they'd sneak down the bank and unwrap their treasures in the moonlight, bursting with wicked joy.

There was an oddly-shaped silver spoon with a cross on the handle; a huge black paper clip; a pair of dangly rhinestone earrings; a choker of shiny jet beads; a set of jacks, their shapes mysterious as runes, covered with peeling silvery paint; a pair of pink net gloves; old keys that no longer opened anything; a gold-link expansion bracelet with a smashed watch face which Annie'd worn turned to the inside of her wrist; and a magic wand of clear plastic, with sparkles suspended in it, from Woolworth's. It wasn't stolen, but the money was, from Allison's and Rita's purses, nickel by nickel and dime by dime.

Once they'd even kept a dead mouse in a plastic bag, fascinated by owning something dead. When it developed a terrible smell, they'd sealed it up again and buried it, bag and all. If I poke around a bit, she wonders, will it still be there?

Annie moves out on the ice, enjoying the idea of standing on what will soon be rushing water. The ice is durable and thick, but somewhere below it the water must be running free. Are there creatures alive and moving under the ice, even in winter? Are there fish? It astonishes her how little she knows. What good was all her schooling, if she doesn't even know these simple things? She resolves to borrow Edith's library card and bring home books about the life of a river.

She crosses the river and strikes out across the valley – territory she claimed as a child. She remembers it in summer, the wide market gardens, lush in the river bottoms, dense with vegetables and berries. Potatoes and carrots, squash and vegetable marrow; glowing ripe tomatoes; sweet golden corn. Hiding in the tall corn with Kate, laughing because no one could find them, no matter how hard they looked; smugly pleased to think how everyone would cry and feel bad if they were lost in the cornfield, or if they died; until they scared themselves enough to return to the safety of their own yards.

The land is still covered in deep snow, hard enough to walk on in most places, and crusted over with a shiny glaze of ice where it's melted and frozen again. Annie tries walking on it, but it gives way and she finds herself up to her thighs in snow. A road has been blown out to the farmhouse at the centre of the gardens; Annie decides to follow this.

There isn't anyone home at the farmhouse. A dog sits tied up on the front step, but it doesn't seem interested in Annie. In a split-rail paddock, a brown Shetland pony, with a cream-coloured mane like the froth on a glass of dark ale, stops to watch her. Annie leans against the rails and the pony trots over. When she reaches over to stroke its head, it stands contentedly.

She's amazed. She's not good with animals. But the owners of this place must be, the pony is so tame. Without planning it, she leans forward and touches her face to the pony's, thrilled by the warm rough hair against her skin, the sense of another kind of life.

The pony is off again. It frolics around the paddock as if putting on a show for her, trotting in a wide circle. The sun shines down on the two of them.

## CHAPTER TWELVE

Annie parks Edith's '67 Cadillac on the main drag, known simply as Main. Although it's a bit like trying to park a living room or maybe a small cruise ship, she has no problem, because there are plenty of angled parking spaces – she could have two or three of them if she wanted. Parking costs a quarter for two hours, up from a dime when she and Charles were married.

The days are getting warmer, the snow turning to slush; the streets run with water. The moist air promises that summer will come to this place again. This should make her happy, but the changing season reminds her that Charles is waiting, more patiently than she could ever have imagined. She's played hooky long enough now. Time to get back to the serious business of life.

The downtown gives her the oddest feeling of familiarity, combined with the uneasy sense that this couldn't possibly still exist, so little altered from her childhood.

She decides to walk a bit. The downtown buildings are handsome, old-fashioned, foursquare structures. Some have fancy carved facades, or gracefully arched windows; a couple of banks are miniature Greek temples. The principal office blocks, which she recalls intimately from childhood visits to doctors and dentists, are substantial eight- and ten-storey edifices, smaller versions of the classic Chicago skyscraper. Built when Riverbend, with its railroad divisional point, oil refineries, flour mills, and meat packing plants, thought it was destined to be the next Chicago. Annie's never really looked at the downtown before, not with an outsider's critical eye. She has to admit, they knew what they wanted, and they went after it.

Worthington's, the locally-owned department store where Allison worked all her adult life, rising from clerk to buyer to manager of ladies' wear, owned one of these imposing buildings before closing it in the wake of big-box chain stores. Its windows are boarded up, a series of blind eyes framed by elegant stone arches. She remembers when the windows were full of bright displays; when her mother was inside helping to keep it all in motion. Now the downtown feels way too quiet. Even Harold Borebank's main hardware store, across from Worthington's, seems to have drawn in on itself. The action is in the suburban malls now, although it seems odd to talk of suburbs in a city of fifty thousand.

Edith has explained how the industries are slowly dying. The meat packers have mostly withdrawn to consolidate in bigger cities; Annie passed the boarded-up buildings on the way downtown. The railroad has closed most of its branch lines, although it still has a round-house for repairs, the same one she visited with her fifth grade class. Only the army base, set up to train pilots during World War II, still remains more or less intact, one of the lifelines of the city. But everywhere she feels a sense of shrinkage, of something no longer growing but turning back in on itself.

She wanders down a side street and finds herself in front of a once grand and still solid apartment building, a U-shaped building set down around a central court-yard. Florida Court. Where Allison spent the last ten years of her life – after she sold the house on River Road where she raised Annie. The apartment is one of the subsidiary puzzles of Allison's suicide. Annie wishes she could go in and see it, for a moment not believing what Rita told her – that Allison disposed of everything in the apartment before she began her travels. At first, Annie was simply grateful that she wouldn't have to go through the apartment. Now the enormity of the deed strikes her, her mother getting rid of every single thing that made up her everyday life. Annie feels in her gut the emptiness of those abandoned rooms.

She finds her way back to Main and her original des-tination. Al's Second Hand is a classic downtown store. An old two-storey painted building with large plate glass windows in front; the sign a painted wooden hand two metres across, complete with pink fingernails and a diamond signet ring. The hand is attached to a mechanism which makes it revolve. The mechanism sticks as Annie approaches the front door, seems to point at her as she stands, fascinated at being the apparent object of interest of something so large and inanimate. "Who, me?" she wants to ask. Then the hand gives a shuddering lurch and moves on.

In the window, Annie sees a large printed sign: "BIG SALE, THIS WEEK ONLY." And a smaller hand-lettered square, reading, "Part-time Help Wanted." Inside the store, a stocky middle-aged man with light hair and piercing black eyes is making eye contact with her, big time. He beckons her in, and she can't summon up whatever it would take – courage, determination, or even just common sense – to disappoint him. This is strange, because she's had no trouble lately disappointing her own husband. Disappointing, frustrating, infuriating, confusing, and God only knows what else. She's really going to have to deal with it.

She goes in. The man steps forward on crepe-soled shoes and announces that he's Al. The impression is of sand. Sandy suit, sandy Hush Puppies, bushy sandy eyebrows and nose hairs. A slightly gritty buff complexion. He holds out his hand, on which she spies the original of The Hand's diamond signet ring. She takes the hand with misgivings, hoping he isn't a crusher; but no, she gets a nice, firm, dry handshake. She doesn't run into the perfect handshake that often, but she does recognize it when she encounters it.

He asks if she's looking for anything special. She says she just wants to look around. After all, everyone knows you won't get a good deal if they know what you want. Better to sneak up on whatever it is. He urges her to feel free.

Annie browses, trying to ignore him watching her. The place is filled with the most amazing stuff, nine-tenths of it what she'd call junk, or at least she would have up to a few days ago, when all she could see was blistered paint, scratched wood, broken legs and fractured joints. Now she finds herself creating the rooms that sheltered this stuff, the people who depended on its support. She even finds herself imagining bits of it in her own house.

She stops by a kitchen cupboard with many small drawers and a small built-in counter for mixing things. Al scoots up behind her and informs her it's called a Hoosier kitchen, all that grandma ever had in the way of kitchen workspace. It's real oak and in good condition. He wants eight hundred dollars for it, but she can hear in his voice that he would bargain.

Beside it is a round wooden table, about eighteen inches in diameter, in some nondescript wood. Someone with not a bad eye has stained it pale slate blue and painted a border of flowers around it. She tries not to look excited as she hunts around for a price tag.

"That's done by one of our local craftspeople," Al says. "It's not antique, of course, but people do seem to like them."

"It is pretty," Annie says in an offhand sort of way.

There's no price tag on it anywhere. "What do you charge for it?"

"Hundred and twenty-five," Al says. "There's a lot of craftsmanship in it."

Annie considers. She has her credit cards, of course, but doesn't feel comfortable using them for something like this. She also has her bank account, arranged by Edith and the lawyer, containing $11,585 from the savings Allison left her. It was over twelve thousand, but she's spent a little on this and that. Groceries, jeans and sweatshirts, odds and ends for the house. She still has lots of money compared to the cost of the table. But very little for a woman who's more or less run away from her husband and has no idea what's happening next. Could she bargain? She's never bargained in her life.

"I'll give you ninety," she says.

"Ninety-five and you've got a deal."

"All right," she says, "but that includes delivery."

"Sold to the little lady," Al says, then looks alarmed. "'The little lady' is something I heard an auctioneer say once. No offence." He must think he's insulted her.

"None taken," Annie says.

"Well, I'll let you browse," he says, looking relieved. Maybe he thinks I'm a radical feminist, she thinks, whatever that means to him, who would cancel the deal in her outrage. Annie smiles. Of course, he did say crafts*people*. He's covered himself there.

Annie browses. This is fun. The thought of the blue table in her house is giving her a warm glow in her belly.

She settles down to look for a chair for her bedroom. She finds straight-back dining chairs, colonial and Shaker style. Overstuffed easy chairs covered in maroon or forest green plush, carved in huge palm frond shapes. And then, in a back corner, she sees it. The chair. Not the perfect replacement for Maisie's chair; Maisie's chair itself.

But that's not possible. She examines it up close. There's no mistaking the pink brocade, still faintly soiled, although someone has taken the trouble to polish the legs and the carving on the arms. For the first time, she notices the pattern of roses in the brocade.

"I can let you have that for two hundred and fifty," Al is saying. "It's worth more, but the demand for occasional chairs hasn't been that strong lately, so I'd be glad to give you a bargain. That would include delivery, of course."

This must be Al's idea of humour, since he already has to deliver the table. She tries to smile, but all she can think of is how she's fallen for the lies of two seemingly innocent children who pretended to love her grandmother. How she's given them tea in real china cups, put up with their criticism, spoken and unspoken; how she's polished their framed photographs and given them a place of honour on her best and only Queen Anne desk.

How can she possibly pay good money to buy back what was so recently hers? How can she not? Some people would think she was a fool to do it. Or is the wisdom in realising a mistake and correcting it?

"Two hundred," she says.

"Sorry," Al says, "but I think I'm already rock bottom on this one."

"Two twenty." Al shakes his head.

Annie realizes he's not going to budge. "All right," she says, "but can you do anything about those stains?"

"Most of our customers prefer to take care of that sort of thing themselves," he says, "but I could ask a dry cleaner friend of mine to take a look."

"Fine," Annie says.

"Of course, it might cost you an extra ten or twenty," Al says.

"Fine," Annie says. No use pretending to haggle now. They both know she wants this chair and might have paid even more for it. Al seems to be taking it quite philosophically – after all, he's made two sales on what must have been a dead afternoon before she came in – so Annie decides she may as well do the same.

She has only got back something beyond price. She has only had the chance, rare enough at any time, to correct the past.

But that doesn't excuse the children. Pretending they loved the chair, when all they wanted was to sell it. Let them try coming around again to cadge tea and biscuits now, she thinks. I'll give them more than they bargained for. Pay attention, Annie, the guy's talking.

"I see you have a good eye for old furniture," he's saying.

"Oh, so-so," she says modestly. "I like nice old pieces." She can't believe she's saying this. All her life she's rejected "old junk."

"Don't suppose you noticed the sign," he says hopefully, "but I could use someone two or three afternoons a week. Guy I had quit on me. Think you'd be interested?"

The correct answer is, No, thank you, I won't be staying in town that long. The one Annie hears spilling from her lips is actually, "Well, I don't know. What are you paying?"

The job, four hours each afternoon, three days a week, pays only minimum wage, but Al will give her a twenty percent commission on any items she sells over seventy-five bucks. Annie quickly calculates what she'd have made if she'd sold someone else the pieces she just bought. Ninety-five plus two-fifty is three hundred and forty-five, times ten percent is thirty-four fifty, times two is sixty-nine dollars. Not bad for a half hour's work.

"So whattaya think?" Al tries to sound casual, but she sees he wants her to accept.

"Could I have twenty percent off on anything I buy?"

"Sure, why not?"

"Okay," Annie says, "I'll give it a try." The sandy face lights up. It's a deal.

Annie can't believe it. She's got things to deal with in Toronto. Her husband wants to move to Los Angeles and he's taken to lecturing her on television. She's been here a week, she's tidied up Maisie's place for sale. She has no reason to stay any longer, not that she could articulate to a sceptical person. And now she's gone and got a job.


ANNIE CAN'T FACE EDITH RIGHT AWAY. She needs to think. She drives right by River Road and down the steep old lane into the river valley, crossing the iron bridge and passing under the old railway trestle.

The road winds along by the river and the old public beach where the river swells out. Hundreds of tons of sand have been dumped there over the decades, change huts and concession stands built. She remembers swimming there with Kate when they were children, drifting in the warm muddy water under the shade of overhanging poplars. The beach would have been scorned by people accustomed to Florida or California or the Caribbean, but they hadn't known that. What it did have was shade and the wonderful way the leaves broke up what light did reach the water. So you didn't get a headache squinting into the sun all the time, your face slowly settling into those nasty little lines.

She drives a little further, to the Swing Inn, where they used to go for ice cream, a rustic looking piece of architecture, a cross between a log cabin and a Swiss chalet. Somebody's fixed it up and turned it into a riverside restaurant. It's not open for the season, but she sees a woman inside, cleaning up. Out back, the snow has melted off a patio of clay paving stones. A middle-aged man in dark green overalls is sweeping up the debris of dead leaves and gum wrappers, dusting off the plain white plastic lawn chairs and the tables with their green-striped umbrellas.

Annie goes around to the back. The man looks up from his work.

"We're not open yet," he says.

"Could I look around?" Annie asks. "I used to come here when I was a kid."

"Oh sure, have a seat. The wife might even have some coffee inside."

The wife appears at the back door, also middle-aged, but trim in her matching coverall, her pleasant face framed in short blonde hair.

"First customer of the year," he says. "Do we have anything to offer?"

"I couldn't get the coffee maker working," she says, "but how about a float? Orange soda and ice cream?"

"Sounds great," Annie says, hoping the flavour won't be artificial, or if it is, that it won't hurt the baby. No doubt it's going to be like this the whole rest of the pregnancy. Eat or don't eat? Every morsel a moral minefield. But millions of pregnant woman must have had orange soda and ice cream at one time or another.

The woman brings out a tall glass, filled to the top with vanilla ice cream and frothy soda, with a straw and a large plastic spoon for the ice cream. "There you go," she says, "guaranteed to make you think of summer. On the house."

They leave her alone in the warmth of the sheltered patio. All around she hears the music of snow melting: high-pitched drippings and tinklings from the eaves; deeper gurglings from the drainpipes; and on the river the most amazing sound, like thousands of tiny violins played pizzicato on a hundred different pitches, as wind and sun finger a lacy pattern of ice on the river's surface.

The float is wonderful, sweet and cold and full of memories. Kate always had ginger ale with double ice cream and Annie would have orange. A soda and ice cream froth builds up on the sides of the glass, and she wishes she could read the future in it, the way some people read the tea leaves in a cup.

What am I going to do about Charles? she wonders. She has tried for eight years to make their marriage work, but for at least the last year she's been thinking it may be a lost cause; she's been thinking about leaving.

He'd seemed like quite a prize when she first got him. Brown eyes and wavy brown hair; great teeth; a good body. The sense that he was one of those people for whom things happen. He'd told her straight out, he was going places. And he'd told the truth. He'd started doing television news right here in Riverbend, which was what his father had done for a living all his life. But Charles had never for a moment planned to stay in Riverbend – he'd always known he'd be an anchor in a "real city." Even so, she'd never imagined he wanted to go anywhere as big and as dangerous as Los Angeles.

She'd actually taken him on over the objections of Edith Ashdown. She'd started going out with Charles in university, after her failed romance with Edith's only son, Lockwood. As things had grown more serious with Charles, Annie had somehow forgotten that Charles was Edith's nephew. So she'd been amazed when Edith summoned her one day to afternoon tea. They'd sat, tête-à-tête, in Edith's living room, while Edith tried to explain why it wouldn't be a good idea for Annie to marry Charles, tried to indicate, discreetly but clearly, that Charles was cold, self-centred, and filled with a craving for power. That he'd been that sort of little boy and was now that sort of man.

Annie'd been shocked, embarrassed. She'd heard of mothers who couldn't let go of their sons. Who thought nobody was good enough for them. Except that Edith was Charles's aunt, not his mother, and she seemed to be saying that *Charles* wasn't good enough for *Annie*. Annie'd thought it must be some kind of trick, a falsely polite way of putting her down. A last-ditch effort to keep the Ransomes from marrying into Edith's precious family. For the first time, Annie wonders if Edith really did mean to warn her.

Of course, Annie had known Charles when they were children, when she'd been completely immune to him. They'd pushed each other into mud puddles and fought over prizes in the school spelling bees, and mostly Annie had won. Later, she'd foolishly thought that "landing" him was another such victory.

At first she'd worked at being the good wife. Working part time, starting the computer typing and printing service out of their apartment so she'd have time to support Charles in his work. And she'd assumed that she'd soon be having children.

She'd been a little surprised when the children didn't come and more surprised to discover how much Charles cared that they didn't. Three years ago they'd submitted to every fertility test devised by modern science. Charles had his sperm counted, no mean feat when you considered that they came not by the hundreds or the thousands, but by the millions. Annie had tiny bits snipped out of her uterus and examined under powerful microscopes, had dye shot up into her fallopian tubes to see if they were clogged up like old drains. She even had a cervical swab after sex to find out what happened to Charles's sperm as they stroked their way through her slippery inner seas. All without a single clue as to why there'd been no babies.

When Charles had suggested *in vitro* fertilization, which he knew all about from a news item he'd done, something in Annie had balked. She was tired of the interferences and measurements and small scientific assaults on her body. She refused to undergo any further invasion. She would wait and see what happened. Charles hadn't been happy about it, but for once he hadn't had much to say.

Now it seems they've done it. She feels the same as

before and yet utterly transformed, as if every single cell, every molecule in her body, has changed into a new substance. Her belly is filled with the sensation she calls "angel wings" because she first felt it as a girl making snow angels. Angel wings is a feeling of lightness and a rush of power, as though her body's kicked into some kind of cosmic overdrive. Yes, cosmic. Her body, with a staggering disregard for common sense and good timing, has gone and got in touch with the cosmos. She should have known it would come up with something like this. The most difficult, the most inconvenient moment for anything to happen, let alone having a baby. She can't imagine what the body was thinking of. But then that's its trouble. It doesn't think.

All those years of waiting and trying so hard to believe everything was okay between herself and Charles, and nothing happened. So why all of a sudden, when she's thinking of dumping him, should one of his sperm take?

Maybe they knew, deep down, what she was thinking. Maybe they felt their biological clocks running out, at least with her. So they girded up their slender loins and ran their best race, climbing her inner ladders like maddened, thrashing salmon. They knew that, if they didn't succeed soon, there might be no more river. No more Annie Ransome Creek.

It was probably their last Christmas that made her want to call it quits. Christmas always brings out the worst in Charles. He believes it's about fashion and it's all done with money. His trees have to be silver or gold or white, decorated in coordinated colour schemes. He actually expects her to buy a complete new tree "decor" each year. Annie would rather get a real live tree and decorate it with strings of popcorn and cranberry and old-fashioned glass balls.

To be fair, Charles did allow this the year they did the Country Christmas, but he would never agree to have The Same Thing over again. It all has to look fresh for the annual Christmas party, when he invites his co-workers and bosses from the television network. At The Party he wears a suit and tie and spends hours fussing over some undrinkable punch recipe from one of his gourmet magazines. Presumably he doesn't notice the men furtively applying to Annie for rye and coke.

His gifts are the worst part. He's got a talent for finding the perfect object, usually something small, expensive, and shiny. His gifts are so perfect it's impossible not to resent them. Annie has never been able to match them, nor even come close. Now, when Christmas approaches, she finds her brain seizing up in a wash of icy fear, because she knows that once again she will fail; once again she will see the brief flash of disappointment as Charles realizes that she has been unable to discover the thing he most wants.

It's like the tests the fairy-tale prince has to undergo to prove himself worthy of the princess, only the roles have somehow been reversed.

In fact, though, the gifts aren't truly the worst part.

The worst part is his ability to get his way by exhausting her; with logic, with order, with inexorable, humourless persistence. The latter is key, because Charles has a very rudimentary sense of humour and reacts with pained disapproval whenever Annie's pops out. Lately it's been popping less and less often. In fact, it's starting to shrivel up.

If only she'd had "sense of humour" on her pre-nuptial shopping list. Yes, but you can't "shop" for men in this way, not like you would for, say, a shirt of 100% combed cotton. It doesn't work this way.

Oh, and why not? If she'd had the sense to think in terms of fabric in the first place, she might have saved herself a lot of grief. Charles, for example, is clearly a wiry worsted wool, very durable, but abrasive to the skin. Assertive, hard-twisted. Scratchy. The colour may change from day to day, running a mad gamut from grey to brown to navy, but worsted is what he is, every day of the week.

What she really needed was a nice cotton flannelette man. Bright red flannelette, maybe, a sort of human nightshirt. Silk would also be good; for instance, midnight blue silk satin. Or linen; how about a man of soft, absorbent cream-coloured linen?

What she's got, however, is worsted wool. It's rubbing her the wrong way and has been for quite some time.

She tries to be fair, to think of the positive things about him. He's good to his mother. He's a considerate lover. He's never lied to her, that she knows of. He works hard and is good at his work. He's also good in an emergency; knows how to organize people and things. He's smart, at least about some things. He doesn't often lose his temper. He makes good money. There must be more, but she's had enough of fairness for the moment.

## CHAPTER THIRTEEN

Maisie's bedroom is about ten by twelve feet and contains a double bed facing two windows overlooking the street. Annie enters through the doorway, widened after the war to accommodate Phillip's wheelchair. At the foot of the double bed is a pine blanket chest. On the south wall, a wide dresser with a matching mirror is crammed with family photographs settled on fussy crocheted doilies. Annie avoids focusing on the pictures. Beside them is a silver tray with a brush, comb, and mirror set with elaborately embossed silver handles. Worth money, she tries not to think, in her new role as a seller of second-hand plunder.

The walls are the usual puce-white, the rug the ubiquitous tan stuff, curtains dingy white lace. The bedspread is a hideous salmon-coloured chenille that looks like row on row of pink toothpaste squeezed out in long undulating worms writhing their way across the bed.

There is little sense of Phillip in the room. A pair of silver cufflinks with a matching tie bar in a china dish, untouched since his death over fifteen years ago. His photograph in his air force uniform, hair close cut, eyes looking somehow bewildered, which is how Annie remembers him. Bewildered; benign.

She has to do something with the pictures; even without looking directly at them, she feels the pressure of their eyes. Always demanding, hoping, wishing, praying for something. She finds a shoebox and stacks them inside. Part way through she loses control and looks.

There's one of Allison with Clifford Winter, Annie's father, on their wedding day. Clifford rather good looking, but with something stiff and awkward about the way his arm goes around Allison's shoulders. Clifford left them so long ago that Annie can barely remember him or the few years she carried his name. Maybe he touched her cheek once, or maybe he rolled a big blue ball towards her. She can't tell whether these things happened or whether she made them up. She used to wonder, but she doesn't care any more.

She did care once. When she was about thirteen, she'd hitchhiked to Saskatoon, where Clifford, now a successful doctor, lived with his second wife. He hadn't even let Annie in the door. He'd installed her in the back seat of his long black car and driven her back. He hadn't said a kind word the whole time. When they got back to River Road, he'd reached for his wallet and given her a hundred dollars. Annie'd felt the most terrible shame. She never tried to call him again.

There's a photo of Allison as a young girl of ten or eleven, wearing a pretty flower-printed dress. Her long hair hangs to her shoulders in rippling waves. Maisie once told Annie the story behind this picture. One day Allison had asked for curly hair instead of the usual braids. Maisie told her not to be silly, which was Maisie's usual response to anything unusual, but when Allison kept asking, she reached into some unsuspected reservoir of ingenuity. She washed Allison's hair and, when it was still damp, braided it tightly. When the hair dried, Maisie brushed out the springy waves and was pleased enough with her efforts to take a picture. From this picture, in a plain silver frame, Annie reads in Allison's face the hope that on this day she is beautiful.

It feels odd to see her mother this way, as if she might be a little sister or a younger version of herself. Or even a child of her own. She thinks of the wide array of possibilities that might have opened for this child and the knowledge of their loss. This day of wavy hair and possible beauty was an isolated moment. Common sense returned in a day or so, along with common restraint and common doubt.


ANNIE DRAGS THE MATTRESS and box spring into the living room. She uncovers the wooden floors and cleans and sock polishes them. She polishes the wooden furniture; washes and re-hangs the lace curtains over clean windowpanes. She washes and dries the chenille spread and folds it away in a box, to be given to some not-too-choosy charity. She replaces it with a faded but still pretty patchwork quilt made by great-grandmother Conal. She brings in her new blue table as a bedside table and places Allison's picture on it.

As she straightens up, she happens to look out the window. The two children, Wilson and DeLinda, stand on the sidewalk looking at the house. She pulls the curtain aside and the children see her. DeLinda takes Willy's hand and leads him away down the street.

Time for lunch. Breakfast has not stayed down, but she feels a keen appetite for lunch. A cheddar cheese sandwich with sliced tomatoes and bread and butter pickles tastes good and stays put, the plain fare a pleasant glob in her stomach.

Only when she's through eating does she allow herself to turn on the news. Charles is there, in the most atrocious outfit – a brown plaid suit and a hideous mustard yellow shirt with a damson plum tie. His hair is dishevelled; he looks unshaven. He holds a paper in his quivering hand, but doesn't look at it. Tears roll down his cheeks, one from each eye.

"Please, Annie," he says, "what are you trying to do to me?" She sees the fatigue in his face, the near desperation in his eyes. She feels a pang in the region of her heart. "Please tell me what –"

She zaps him off and quickly stacks her few dishes in the sink. Really, she must call him. But she'd have to go over to Edith's, and she's doing so well in the bedroom that she should finish the job. Finish what you start, isn't that everyone tells you? Well, then.

She has shoved the blanket chest aside to get at the bed and now realizes there must be something inside. She finds two new white woollen blankets and, underneath, a set of white cotton sheets and cases, clean and pressed and scented faintly by lavender. Each has a blue and gold band appliquéd across the hem, with the initial "C" embroidered above it. More of Maude Conal's work, no doubt.

Rage tears through her chest and belly, rage at the waste of gifts. Maisie has kept these sheets untouched all her life, as if she wasn't worthy to use them. Annie will be damned if she'll keep this tradition. If she isn't good enough to use them, who the hell is? The Queen of England? Elizabeth Windsor's got her own goddamned sheets and billions of dollars to buy more if she ever runs short.

She's going to break this cycle of self-denial right here and now. She'll sleep on Maisie's sheets this very night.

These things are hers now, all of them, by right. None of it is too good for her. She will use anything she likes. She will throw out anything she doesn't like. Nobody can stop her. They may not have intended it, but one way or another, by suicide or by default of old age, they have put her in charge. She imagines Maisie's horror at her seizure of these family treasures, imagines what she'd have done or said to the child Annie had she dared to propose anything like it. Forget all that, she thinks. I'm not the child anymore. I'm going to have a child of my own.

She makes the bed with great care, finishing with the pillows on top, the blue-banded cases overlapping the quilt. She's amazed at the beauty she's created or at least revealed in this room; saddened that Maisie lived so close to it all her life but couldn't let herself have it.

Annie saves two more framed pictures, one of Maisie and one of Phillip, and places them on the blue table beside the picture of Allison.

Exhausted, she lies down on the bed. In a moment she's lost in sleep, although still somehow aware of the room around her. The two of them, Maisie and Phillip, are there with her, looking exactly as they do in their pictures. Phillip, free of his wheelchair, walking normally, just as though he was never a gunner in a bomber, was never hit by the shrapnel that severed his spinal cord. Maisie looks relaxed, as if she's having a bit of a lark. Her hair is softer than Annie remembers. They amble about the room examining the changes, pointing at the bed, the dresser. They crowd in close, vying for her attention. Phillip takes her hand in a childlike, trusting way and offers her an object, a beautiful turquoise egg. She holds it in her closed fist and feels it grow warm. Maisie points to it and smiles. Whenever Annie tries to move, they get in the way, smiling sheepishly at their own clumsiness.

Annie doesn't mind. They are not troublesome to her. She feels friendly and helpful towards them. She accepts them, even when they insist on climbing up on the bed and lying down with her, one on either side. She doesn't mind; in fact, it feels good.

SHE FINDS THE PAPERS in a carved wooden box in Maisie's hankie drawer. They make a stack an inch thick, yellowed with age and oxidation and slightly warm to her touch. The whole thing has a wide rubber band around it, and then it's sorted into smaller bundles secured with paper clips. Some are five or ten pages long, some single sheets. Taken as a whole, the stack has a weight and solidity to it; a presence.

It's more stuff from Eamon Conal, her great-grandfather, all of it handwritten. There's no question she's going to read it. Like everything else here, it's part of her inheritance. But she knows so little about Eamon; whatever fact she tries to pin down about him tends to squirm away when she gets up close to it. He was Irish, she's sure of that, or at least his father was. His wife, Maude Rowan, was English or maybe Scots. And there was a farm, but for some reason that was gone fairly early in the story, because Maisie always talked of it as something she could barely remember.

They'd had to sell the farm at some point (after the war?) and move to the city. Eamon had worked at some sort of manual labour. "The outdoor life was good for him," she remembers hearing. Did that mean farm work had not been good for him? Something about breathing? Asthma? But then how could he work outdoors? And Maude had worked in a store, she remembers hearing that. Things had been "hard, very hard," Maisie had never tired of saying – the sort of statement guaranteed to bore a grandchild in a slightly more affluent time. Who could really care about hardships they couldn't imagine, inflicted on people they'd never seen? And yet, she wishes now she could have Maisie back for even five minutes to ask her a few questions.

She picks up one of the single sheets from the top bundle.

For three years I have not seen the sky
except through this fine metal mesh. It stills
and deadens the air. Shatters the sun's rays to
weak fragments – with no power to warm or
cheer. Every man should be able to see the sun.

Ah, Sun-flower! weary of time,
Who countest the steps of the sun;
Seeking after that sweet golden clime
Where the traveller's journey is done.

Here is a kind of pit deep below the prairie
– with hills arching around us like a horseshoe.
We are in an offshoot of this wide valley
gouged into the earth thousands of years ago –

by meltwater from the glaciers which once covered all of this land. If I could climb these hills I would stand once more on the plains – and once more contend with my thoughts about this matter of the sky.

Sometimes the sky seems to press close upon me, on my face, my arms, my chest. Other times it is more distant than I can imagine. All in the way you squint your eyes at it. Sometimes it is solid dense blue like water set without freezing. Other times so thin and transparent I could almost see through – to the blackness of space. To the planets and stars numerous beyond counting – which yet populate space but thinly because as Dr. Nugent says it is so vast a place.

So much time to think. And never any word of whether I will leave this place or when my traveller's journey shall be done. And so all these ideas crowd into my mind – and sometimes I see one thing and sometimes another – depending on how I squint my eyes at the sky.

And then it stops, as if he ran out of steam or interest. The poem fragment she recognizes as William Blake, but where is the pit below the prairie? Why has he not seen the sky for three years? There is a sadness or oppression in his words, yet he seems so curious too. She turns over a few pages and all of them look the same, densely written sheets interspersed with more snippets of poetry. Part of her wants to get right into reading, but she realizes in time that the moment isn't right. The writings of Eamon Conal, which are surely the "works" referred to in Maisie's hidden note, will require the fuller concentration of a new day. She replaces the works in the box and puts it back in the drawer, concealed under a lifetime supply of small white linen handkerchiefs.

She has reached a stopping place, or at least a resting place, and tea is required.

The ritual is now a familiar pleasure. Water to a rolling boil, scalding the pot, measuring the loose tea into the pot, and pouring the dancing water in. Steeping.

For some reason she becomes aware of the phone, an off-white wall phone near the table. She picks it up; after all, who knows when a phone may decide to turn itself on? A dial tone purrs in her ear, ready to do her bidding. She hangs up, feeling off balance, vulnerable. The phone has come alive. How? But then, how else? Busybody Edith, of course. If Annie had wanted to connect the phone, which in fact she hadn't, she would probably have had to pay a whopping big deposit. No doubt Edith simply told them not to talk nonsense and to turn it on at once or else.

As Annie stands watching the phone, it shocks her by ringing in a loud, peremptory way. She glares at it, daring the smooth plastic thing to do it again. It does it again. Probably Edith, making sure her orders have been obeyed. Let her wait. But it keeps ringing.

"Hello?"

"May I speak to Annie Ransome?" It's a man's voice; baritone, well-mannered, slightly diffident. She doesn't know any men like that.

"This is Annie Ransome speaking," she admits, against her better judgement.

"I don't know if you'll remember me," the voice is saying, "but you went to school with my wife...Sylvie. Sylvie Thompson she was then."

"Harold Borebank?" she asks. "Of course I remember you."

"That's right," he says, encouraged. "You were part of our wedding. Maid of honour."

"Of course," she says, fumbling for something non-committal to say. "It's good to hear from you. I was very sorry to hear about Sylvie. I didn't know until I ran into Corinne at the store."

"Yes, she told me you'd met. She was really glad to see you."

"I was glad to see her too," Annie says lamely.

"She thought it would be nice if you and I got together – you know, for coffee or something. Oh, and I'd love to have you meet my son."

My God, he wants to see her. "That would be nice," Annie says, "but I'm awfully busy right now. You see, my mother left me my grandmother's house, and I'm working really hard to get it in shape before I sell it."

"I understand," he says, sounding smaller.

"But later, when I'm further along," she says, "let's have coffee some time." It sounds forced, but she can't help it.

"Sure thing," he says, not fooled, "I'll give you a call. Or better yet, why don't you call me when it's convenient? I'm in the book." She can tell from his voice that he doesn't expect it will ever be convenient. He thinks he's being brushed off. Well, isn't he?

"I'll do that," she says, "and it was good of you to call."

"Any time," he says. "Bye now." He hangs up before she can even say goodbye. Too late she thinks how hard it must have been for a lonely widower to call up a much younger woman who was once his wife's best friend. She thinks of all the stand-up comedy routines about the agony of asking a girl out. When Annie was young, she'd always thought how easy it must be for the boys. Of course, this isn't exactly a dating situation.

She wishes she'd been kinder. And yet what is there for them to talk about? What is the point of meeting?

Talking to Harold has warmed up her own phoning muscles, however. Without giving herself time to think, she grabs the phone and dials the apartment in Toronto.

"Hello?"

The voice is like nothing she can remember. Soft. Hesitant. None of the newsreader's assumed authority. No male bravado, no aura of power. She has expected to be lectured, but in an instant understands this will not happen. Because he isn't in the mood. And because she won't let it happen. Not any more at all ever.

"Hello, Charles, it's me. Annie."

"Annie? How are you?" She can hardly believe it. He's asking how she is, as the first order of business.

"I'm fine," she says, "but I'm going through something really strange."

"You and me both," he says. She wonders what he means.

"It's hard to explain on the phone. I've been looking through some of the old stuff here. I found out some of it's important to me."

"Furniture? You could bring some of it home."

"I'm not sure yet. Maybe it belongs here. Charles, I think I'm starting to understand them more. Grandmother. Mom."

"Understand why she did it, you mean?" His voice is different; huskier somehow.

"Sort of," Annie says. "A little."

"Well, do what you have to do." It's the most extraordinary speech she's ever heard him make. Magnanimous – but without making a show of it. Modest magnanimity, wow. A Charles first. Now she's being sarcastic. Stop it.

"Thank you, Charles," she replies. "Oh, I wonder if you'd mind calling the guy with the history thesis. I don't think I'll be able to finish it."

"No problem. I already gave it back to him."

"Oh. Well, thanks. That was good of you."

"I do miss you." There's no edge to his voice, no attempt to make her feel guilty.

"I miss you too," she says, but it's a lie. She may come to miss him, but so far she hasn't started. "What about the L.A. job?"

"I don't know yet. I sent them a bunch of my stuff. News anchor and reporting. Even a bit of print journalism."

"You really want it, do you?" She tries to keep her voice as neutral as possible.

"It would be an exciting opportunity," he says. "The way I figure it, I can't stay in this job too long. Either I'm going to move up, or I'm going to fail."

Is that how he sees it? Is that how his bosses see it? Doing the job he does, doing it well, is apparently not the point. You can't ever stay the same. You have to be moving up. You have to want more all the time. Or you fail.

"Of course, we'd be closer to my mother." Ethel Wilkins lives in Pasadena. Every year she invites them to come for the Rose Bowl game, and every year Charles is too busy.

"You never have time to see your mother."

"Maybe I would if we were closer."

"Maybe you would."

"You'd come, wouldn't you?" he asks. "You wouldn't have to live in the city. There's dozens of pretty little places around L.A."

"And you'd commute?"

"Sure. Everybody does. Nothing to it."

"So you really want it?" she asks again.

He hesitates. "I don't want to go alone, if that's what you're asking."

"Listen," she says, caught by a generous impulse which begins to alarm her even as she speaks, "you want to fly down for the weekend? We could talk about it."

"I don't think I can get away. Things are pretty hairy here."

She should tell him about the baby, she knows she should. It's his baby too. But it's inside her. She has to get used to it. She wants to know if they're going on together before she tells him.

"Oh, the cleaning lady up and quit," he says.

"Did she?" Annie asks.

"Didn't you say something about vacuuming on the phone last time?"

Annie doesn't want even to consider the possibility that Charles's anomalous television performances are predicting the future. "I don't know," she says, "I was in a pretty confused state. Did you find the yellow vacuum bags?"

"Oh, yeah, no problem. In fact, a woman from work even offered to do it for me."

Annie waits for the rush of jealousy to hit. Nothing happens.

"But hell, I guess I can manage a little vacuuming on my own. After all, Mother taught me all that when I was a kid."

Well. A day of revelations. All these years she's

believed the vacuum cleaner was as foreign to him as manuscripts in ancient Sanskrit. "I'm glad you're coping," she says. "Listen, I have to run. Edith's invited me for dinner."

"Aren't you at Aunt Edith's?"

"No, I'm at the house. Edith must have hooked up the phone."

"So I can call you there now? What's the number?"

"No idea, but it's a fair bet Edith will tell me. I'll let you know."

"Yes, let me know."

"We'll talk soon. Goodbye, Charles."

"Bye."

She hesitates a half-second, in case he's not done, then quickly hangs up.

Time to get ready for Edith's. But something feels different. The weight on her shoulders. It's lighter.

Outside, the street is slushy, the gutters running with water, a miniature river system rushing to join the creek below. The air is soft and moist on her face, an invitation to deeper breathing. She can smell mud.

Her belly, where something is growing, radiates warmth. Her limbs have some new kind of feeling, some new kind of consciousness.

She can't keep living this way indefinitely. But she's not prepared to stop yet. Her life here has a lot of things in it she didn't have before. She doesn't know what choices she's going to make about her life, and she isn't going away until she finds out.

## CHAPTER FOURTEEN

*Hazy, pearlescent light, swirling like smoke; atmosphere heavy like a weight. Sitting up in a narrow bed, covers pulled tight pinning his legs. Windows down the length of a long narrow room. Light outside bright, hurtfully bright. Screened windows, a fine metal grid overlaying the things outside: trees heavy with green leaves, beds of scarlet-red tulips. He longs to be out there, to touch the glowing petals. His forehead is hot and his chest aches as if filled with a large metallic object. The air is heavy on his skin. He feels immensely sad.*

*Rumbling in the distance. A tremendous crash of thunder, then two more in quick succession. And yet the sky is the same, bright and blue. The tulips burn red, the trees are still. But a storm is coming....*

Annie wakes once more to thunder, in Phillip and Maisie's bed. Light floods the room, broken up by the white lace curtains. The dream's feeling of sadness is still with her.

She looks down at her body, a little puzzled at the way it looks. She remembers the dream and has a sharp pang of desire to go back inside it. To be in that place again – the long narrow room with the swirling golden light, the trees outside and flame-red tulips. To be in that body again, a man's body, larger than her own. Some part of it is familiar; is there a photograph somewhere like this? But the dream also has a taste and an odour she has never known. She tries to fall back into this space, but thunder peals again, shaking the bed, vibrating in her belly. The dream drifts away like smoke.

Something about the thunder is wrong. The quality of sound, the specific gravity of the air. The timing! The something wrong has a very familiar feel to it.

She sits up in bed to hear better. It's like the sound of shelling in a war movie. Dynamite. Now she understands. The snow is melting too fast, and the narrow, winding creek is clogged with jagged chunks of ice that catch and lodge in the riverbends. They have to dynamite to break up the ice and get the water flowing, or the valley will be flooded. The valley with its woods and market gardens. With the quiet old dog and the pleasant pony in the paddock.

Her stomach flips and the room turns around her. She takes a deep calming breath and makes it settle down again. She nibbles at the plain crackers she now keeps by the bed. Nice trick, it's working again.

The sound of shelling stops. The feeling of sadness slowly ebbs. She finds she wants to get up.

The TV weather tells her what her body has already guessed. It's a beautiful day. April second. Ten degrees, bright sunshine, no wind. As soon as she finishes break-fast, she grabs her parka, pulls on her boots. Before she leaves she goes to the refrigerator and grabs a carrot. She breaks it in half and puts it in her pocket.

Outside everything flows. She hears water dripping, sees it running away in streams to the river. The warm air in her face excites her. Choosing the lane into the river valley, wide enough for only one car in each direc-tion, requires no conscious decision. Today she doesn't dare cross on the ice, visibly melting with two inches of water on top of it, but chooses the old iron bridge. Soon she's nearing the paddock by the house. The pony is there again; it trots over to her when she leans against the rail. Its eyes startle her, so different from human eyes, but seemingly friendly, or at least not hostile. She strokes the horse's head, runs her fingers through its creamy tangled hair.

Why has no one told her how pleasurable this could be? How could she be thirty years old and know nothing about animals?

She has never had animals to play with. Allison (and before her, Maisie) thought pets were foolish. Just an extra expense and likely to give you some disease. She looks at the coarse hair of the pony and hopes it won't give her a disease. Or if it does, that it won't be serious. Or if it is, that she won't suffer long.

This is a game she'd been playing with herself in Toronto. Weighing the dangers around her. Trying out possible outcomes. I hope that isn't a mugger behind me. Or if it is, I hope he doesn't have a gun. Or if he does, I hope he doesn't shoot me. Or if he does, I hope it isn't fatal.

She discovers she doesn't seriously believe the pony will give her a disease. She reaches into her pocket for the pieces of carrot. She holds one out in her open palm and the pony takes it, its mouth soft and warm against her hand. She offers the second piece. The pony eats that too. She gives herself to the moment, to the pony crunching the carrot and the sun on her face.

"Annie?" she hears someone say with surprise. She turns to see the man she thought she was avoiding, a tall balding man with a lanky body. It's hard to look into his face because of what pain has done to it. Lines deeply scored on either side of his mouth; grey eyes hurt and defenceless.

"Harold," she says. "Is this your place?"

He nods. "We moved here when she got sick. She liked it down here. That's her pony."

"He's wonderful," Annie says. "He let me pet him."

"He likes you," Harold says, "because you're like her." Annie starts to deny it – she and Sylvie never looked that much alike – but understands in time that Harold is right. The pony has been waiting for a woman to come and has decided that this one will do.

She can't think of anything to say. It's all she can do to meet his eyes, which seem to have the power to transmit his anguish into her body. She understands how he must have loved Sylvie and wonders what it would have been like to receive that love.

She sees him start to break down. All her life, such situations have horrified her. She has avoided them wherever possible. She feels more than sees Harold make a slight move towards her.

"I know you never thought I was right for her," he says. His body shakes. His eyes demand that she understand.

Annie goes to him and holds him, amazed that she can do it, feeling the weight of him against her, almost as if she's carrying him. Somehow she knows to hold him tight, to give him the feeling of something solid around him.

"I just loved her," he says, through heavy sobs. Apparently no one has ever told him that a man mustn't cry.

"I know," she says. "I didn't understand. I was a stupid kid."

"I'm sorry," he says, but it's too late for him to stop.

"It's all right," she says, for all the world like somebody's mother. After a while he quiets, seems to become aware of the strangeness of it, but still he clings to her. Annie sees a boy about eleven years old approach them.

"Dad?" he says. He looks at Annie, trying to figure out what's happening.

Harold pulls away and smiles at the boy. Annie's amazed to see that he's not ashamed of his tears.

"Donnie," he says. "This is Annie. She was your mother's friend when they were young. We got talking about her."

Donnie nods. He looks like Sylvie, all right. Freckles and red hair, and pale green eyes studying her as if he has to make sure she's not going to hurt his dad. Harold is blowing his nose on a tissue.

The boy appears to come to some judgement. He relaxes. The pony is still standing around companionably. Donnie reaches over and strokes its face.

"This is her pony," he says. "Charlie."

"We've met," Annie says, "only I didn't know his name." Quite a coincidence. Only she can't imagine anyone ever calling *her* Charles by the diminutive form. Did Sylvie do it on purpose, she wonders? Probably she just liked the sound of it.

"Want to go for a ride?" Donnie asks.

"I don't know how to ride," she says.

"He's really quiet," Donnie says. "Hang on, and I'll get a bridle." And he's off before she can decide what she wants.

"It'll be okay," Harold says.

Donnie bridles Charlie and helps Annie mount. Her thoughts are instant confusion. Amazement that Charlie puts up with it. That it feels like she's up high, when it's only a Shetland pony. That there's nothing to hold her on if Charlie happens to run off with her.

Donnie hands her the reins, but sees that she has no idea what to do with them. He takes them back and leads Charlie in a circle around the paddock. Harold watches, looking proud that his boy has known what to do and done it with simple generosity.

Afterwards, Donnie leads her back to Harold. She slides off, enjoying the new way her feet encounter the ground, the strangeness of once more bearing her own weight. She strokes Charlie's forehead and, as far as she can tell, he seems to enjoy it. Donnie takes the reins and, in one smooth movement, lifts himself onto the pony's back. They canter round and round the paddock. Is it possible the pony enjoys carrying the boy on his back? That's how it looks to her, anyway.

"He's a wonderful boy," Harold says.

"He looks like Sylvie," Annie says.

"Yes," Harold says, "it's strange to have lost her and yet to have her face in front of me all the time."

"I'm surprised he offered me a ride like that."

"He'd remember your name. She used to tell him about all the trouble the two of you would get into."

Annie hopes this isn't true. She remembers their escapades only too well, though she's wanted to forget; they don't fit with the person she's tried to be since she got married.

*Dark water and moonlight, her head spinning from too much rum and coke, and when the boys dared them to take* their bathing suits off and come into the deep water, she and Sylvie did it, throwing the flimsy bits of stretchy nylon onto the bank.

Moonlight bathing them in cool silver, sending ripples over the water. Breeze against their nipples, hair, tickling between their legs. Plunging into the water together, the water, entered earlier, now warmer against their skin than the air. Sylvie reaching the boys, laughing and splashing.

Annie dives deep into the water in the middle of the creek, where it's ten or fifteen feet deep. She's never done this, always stayed where it's safe. A rush of pleasure going down so deep, water flowing over her skin, her legs kicking, insinuating trickles of water entering her vagina. Then she opens her eyes to blackness, the current pulls at her legs. She touches bottom and her fingers dig into formless slimy mud that sticks to her, and all her joy dies. A universe explodes in her mind, wild atoms streaming out into space. She doesn't know who she is, a girl in a river, doesn't know how to save herself or that she needs to be saved. Just an organism operating below the level of words or ideas, filled with terror and recognition and without the desire to change anything.

A hand grabs her ankle – what she begins to understand is her ankle. A hand pulling her away from the mud and darkness, up into the air. She feels the air on her skin, but doesn't breathe. They carry her to the riverbank. Sylvie turns Annie on her stomach and forces the water from her lungs. Annie feels herself choking, retching, and sees Sylvie now too, sees the terror in her eyes; and beyond her the boys stand watching, forgetting for a moment their nakedness.

Annie begins to cry with a sorrow that feels endless, inconsolable.

Sylvie kneels and holds her as she begins to shiver. "There, there," she says, "it's all right." Annie feels that it isn't all right, but loves Sylvie for trying to make it so. She is cold. The boys bring the blanket, rough and sandy, from the beach and Sylvie wraps it around her. Only Sylvie can touch her now, only Sylvie can hold her till she's warm again.

"Annie?" Harold is saying. She can't imagine what her face looks like, but tries to pass if off lightly.

"Funny, having a kid know about your wicked past," she says.

"Oh, we decided even before we were married, we were going to raise our kids differently than other people."

"Really?" she asks.

"You bet. We were always going to tell them the truth, and we weren't going to pretend that grownups never made mistakes, and we weren't going to lie to them about sex."

Annie is amazed. Radical theories of child-rearing are not what she'd ever have expected from Harold. "Did you stick to it?" she asks.

"Pretty well," he says. "And so when Sylvie died, Donnie knew it was okay to talk about it."

"I suppose that must be important," Annie says.

"When my mother died, it wasn't like that. My dad made me feel it was something shameful that couldn't be mentioned."

Donnie is stopping beside them, slipping off the pony. Annie suddenly feels like an intruder, or at least like a guest who has stayed quite long enough.

"I'd better go," she tells Harold. "I'm clerking part time at the second-hand store downtown. Starting today." To Donnie she says, "Thank you for the ride."

"That was just Charlie," he says. "He doesn't mind."

"Well then, for showing me how," Annie says. "I never did that before."

"You can come again," he says. "I could show you some more."

"Thanks," she says. "I hope I can."

ANNIE WALKS DOWN THE ROAD. When she looks back, Harold and the boy have gone into the house. Only the pony is still there as proof she didn't imagine the whole thing.

She does see some other people though, in the field to the left of the yard. Three old women in bright coats, red, green, and blue, crossing the field. Their hair is completely white. Perhaps they are sisters. They walk arm in arm, not in the way people walk when they are weak or sick, but straight and upright, companionable. The one in red gestures with her free hand, and Annie hears the others laugh.

She wishes that one of them could suddenly turn out to be Maisie, but knows that's impossible. She bends, pretending to adjust her boot, so she can see them go by.

As they come close, they smile and nod in her direction. I've seen you before, she thinks. But something is off key. Three old women – the ones from the funeral, that's it, in stiff black taffeta like charred onionskin. Now they are transformed; they seem so alive, with the resilience and intimacy of sisters who get on well. They move fluently, full of knowing. She remembers them leaving the funeral and half expects them to touch her again as they pass, but they only smile with a sort of generic good will, absorbed in their own concerns, giving no sign of knowing her in any specific way.

Annie watches them over the iron bridge. She will not be sad. Maisie is dead now, and whatever she lost during her lifetime is lost for good. But the women are alive and have revealed themselves to her.


HER AFTERNOON at Al's Second Hand is pure fun, start to finish. Al tells her things about the furniture – what things are valuable, what people like these days – and he tells her where he and his wife went on their winter vacation (Taos, New Mexico). He's a hoot to be with, and treats her somewhere between a daughter and a babe. But he never steps over the line he's drawn for himself.

A woman comes in and Annie almost sells her the Hoosier kitchen, before realizing she wants it for herself. She summons all the guile of which she's capable to steer the woman away from the Hoosier, then redoubles her efforts and sells the woman a complete dining room suite worth twelve hundred dollars and a dinnerware set for one seventy-five. Al is so pleased he agrees to cough up the commission as soon as the woman leaves the store.

Annie bargains Al down to six hundred including delivery on the Hoosier kitchen and reminds Al of her twenty percent discount, which brings it down to four eighty. Less, of course, the commission he's just paid her. She writes out a cheque for two hundred and five dollars and hands back the commission. She wants to laugh out loud. It's the first time in her life she's had fun in any sort of job. Is it only because she doesn't really have to do it?

She decides not to look a gift horse in the mouth. And besides, how does she know yet whether she really has to do it?

Later, as she finishes a hasty supper of macaroni and cheese, it all catches up with her. She manages to brush her teeth and put on a nightgown before she falls into bed. Tonight she chooses Allison's bed. She thinks dreamily of the elephants circling over her all night. She picks up the *Songs of Innocence*. "Little Lamb, who made thee? Dost thou know who made thee?" The words blur in front of her eyes. She remembers Eamon's papers and feels again the desire to read more of them. Tomorrow, she promises herself, putting the book down.

As her limbs drift away from her, she remembers her

dream and understands that it was about Eamon, in some sort of hospital, and that she will dream of him again. The thought frightens her, but she also feels a strange eagerness.

## CHAPTER FIFTEEN

How sweet I roam'd from field to field
And tasted all the summer's pride,
Till I the Prince of Love beheld
Who in the sunny beams did glide!

Once again Annie recognizes Blake, copied out in Eamon's hand, in assertive black ink; his own words continue beneath the quotation:

I love to read these lines and think of my dear children. Yesterday they came with Maude on her visit so that I was able to wave to them through the screen windows – and I reckoned that it is three years since I touched them or even saw them face to face.

Between the war and this place I have spent less than a year under the same roof with them. I think I am no longer quite real to the children but more a storybook figure their mother makes up for them. I might be a good and wise king who would be with his young prince and princess if he had not been bewitched by a wicked magician. Or I could be the friendly woodsman who saves Red Riding Hood from the wolf. And who are they? Hansel and Gretel in danger of being eaten by a witch? No. Today they are Jack and Jill.

They set off hand in hand to climb the big hill to the west of my pavilion. By wheeling the bed nearer the windows we are able to keep them in sight the whole time. Something of me at least goes with them. How I wish for the simple pleasure of climbing a hill with ease – or even with difficulty – but I know it is unlikely I will ever again do so.

Maude observed them closely and I felt she wanted to speak. I pressed her as to what was wrong. She asked if I thought the children should be encouraged to spend more of their time with other children. A friend of hers had suggested they be sent to different schools – but Maude had not liked to do this as it would mean Robbie would have to walk two miles to school – and through a rough part of town.

I asked why all this should be necessary when the children are so happy together, so absorbed in their own charmed circle. And she said, That is just the point, Eamon, perhaps they are too close. When I protested she said, It's all very well now but what about when they're older? And besides, the other children are beginning to tease them.

So what does it come to? Because they have the closeness and quick understanding of twins, they are to be forcibly separated and constrained. Can she not see this will make them unhappy? I long to intervene – but seem to be losing a father's rights as Maude is the one who must see to everything for them. She must be strong because I am not. Beneath it all is what cannot be said. She is afraid of such closeness of body and spirit – afraid it cannot remain innocent as they grow into men and women. I don't believe this. Their closeness is their nature and I do not believe we can change it without doing harm.

Annie begins to see Maisie as a child, a joyful, favoured child with sunlight in her hair. This child has no outward resemblance to the woman Annie knew, but somehow they must be connected.

They came to a small rise on the hill and as they clambered over the top Maisie tripped on something and pitched down the short slope.

Robbie was right behind and couldn't stop so he fell after. Their bright images falling were captured in my eye like a tinted photograph. But they fell into a hollow where I could not see them. I watched for them to come out again higher up – but nothing moved and I was afraid. I felt the muscles tighten in my chest – and the pain of the lower ribs which are no longer there but retain the ability to give pain. I feared they had fallen into cactus – the prickly pear Doctor Nugent tells me grows up on the hill. I saw in my mind's eye Maisie holding her hands to the light and trying to pull out the sharp spines. Or Robbie.

And then I spied them higher up – climbing hand in hand now. I knew they would not fall again. I envied them the fierce charge up the hill, their certain knowledge that they will have what they want.

> He show'd me lilies for my hair,
> And blushing roses for my brow;
> He led me through his gardens fair
> Where all his golden pleasures grow.

I thought of all the things I knew that they did not yet have to know, all the things I would rather not have known. I envied them the not knowing.

Watching them on the hill gave me joy and sadness both. I had no real fear for their safety – and yet for me the hills are almost fearfully high. I am really only comfortable on the prairie. My father told me many times of the green hills of Ireland – but they are real to me only as fairy tales are real. The Sleeping Beauty. Jack and the Beanstalk. I always wanted to climb the Beanstalk – but I was afraid of it too.

Annie puts the papers down. Eamon is coming so close now, not as a great-grandfather she never knew, not as an old shadow-man, but as a young one full of passion. He is becoming as real to her as any man she has ever known.

People from the east say how flat the prairie is. I feel so exposed, says old man Bainbridge, the man who bought the homestead near our farm. I don't see that – I see the prairie from the inside – the hollows and rises of land that can shelter or even hide a man's body. Except when the tornadoes sweep down like the hand of God – then there is no hiding. Although of course I do not believe they are the hand of God. God or some force has perhaps set all of Nature in motion a long time ago – but I cannot imagine any God worthy of respect getting up some fine summer morning and deciding to raze a man's barn or mow down his crops.

But many still think this way. It is God's punishment on us – so said old Mrs. Price when we had no rains one spring. Aye, said Bainbridge, that it is. I did not think it worthwhile to offer any comment – but it hurt my mind to imagine the time they must waste relating the weather of each succeeding day to past events. For how long might a man infer that he has been good on a day when the weather is fine? Or how long bad when it is cloudy? And does the badness of some close neighbour spill over onto the surrounding farms?

This last is a favourite speculation – for of course such people do not confine their examinations to their own behaviour – but cast about among the country for examples of unrighteous living – which they are sure has caused the hail or the drought or the howling blizzard. It never seems to occur to them that while one farmer may be deep in sin another close by may be leading a blameless or even a laudable life. But careful thinking is not the province of the old man Bainbridges and Mrs. Prices of this world. I would like to tell them what I prefer to believe – that every sunny day has been brought about by the warm bright spirits of my Robbie and my Maisie.

Of course when I am feeling low the possibility will at times occur to me that they may be right. What if it be unfair? What if it be irrational? Perhaps the God who formed us has remained in some primitive state – full of capriciousness and longing for vengeance. When I fall into this frame of mind I am more ready to listen to the priest and to reach out for whatever absolution he can give. But it does not satisfy my mind.

So I will say now for myself alone – for now and forever – that I will not be part of such demeaning notions – unworthy of beings endowed with reason. I, Eamon Conal, stand for a new life – grounded in truth and compassion – eschewing ignorance and superstition as far as I am able.

The children reached the top of the hill. I could feel Maude's eyes on me as she sat in her wicker chair by the bed – and I knew what she wanted. She could never say it in words. It must always come from me. In such matters the husband should always lead. God forgive me – she has become a better Catholic than ever I was. I was so tired that I only wished to remain still – but her eyes could not be denied.

So I told her I had had enough of the sun and asked her to wheel the bed back into the room. The other men on the verandah looked away – only Jimmy who is sixteen and shares the room with me couldn't help watching us with his curious young eyes. Maude opened the door between the room and the verandah and wheeled me in. She plumped up my pillows behind my back. She pulled the blind on the window that looks onto the verandah. And she said, No one will come, will they Eamon? I said, No sweetheart, no one will come. I wonder – did she realize I had no way of knowing if they would or wouldn't come?

She has made me promise never to tell another soul what happens at such times – and I will not, but some time or other will write it down. Simply for myself – because that is a useful work if a person wishes to understand a thing and have clear thoughts about it. But I am weary. This is enough for now. I have been brought to this place to rest and that is what I do – until it seems my blood slows and almost stops. And that, says Doctor Nugent, is what slows the bacilli and lets the lungs heal.

But my mind is never still.

Annie runs her fingers over the pages handled by Eamon Conal so many years ago, which still seem touched by his restless spirit. She feels no fear of contagion; surely all this happened too long ago. She thinks of his still-young body attacked by tuberculosis, for that

is surely what was wrong with him, and the only treat-
ment prolonged rest in a sanatorium. Like Annie here
in her grandmother's house, he was given a time-out
from life. Most lives are wound up tight as clockwork
and jolt and lurch their way along as they can or as they
must, until the mechanism slows or stops. The only way
out of this mechanical process, for most people, is death
or illness. For Annie it has been death, although not her
own. She feels a kinship with Eamon because they have
both been given this chance.

Allison's death has given her a freedom she never
knew before, at least not since childhood. A home of
her own, money to live on for a space. It can't go on forever, this space, but it is still comfortingly large; she
can't yet see to the end of it. She thinks of the weeks
ahead as fat oranges, each filled with many sections,
each section crammed with sacs of juice ready to burst
against her teeth, releasing sweetness.

She has always believed she was not a person who
could live alone. The only time she tried, when she was
in university, she'd felt so cut off from other people that
she was afraid she was slowly disappearing. But there's
nothing lonely about this life. Her home is filled with
presences who slowly yield their secrets; through the
medium of the house ceding truths they could never
have faced in life. Maisie and Allison are increasingly
at ease with her; they are losing their defences, their
everlasting prickliness, to reveal the spirits who lived
inside them. Annie is gathering from them a kind of

blessing. It seems you get your inheritance only if you're willing to take it.

Time for tea. Annie puts the papers back in the hankie drawer. She can only take them in short bursts. In fact, she approaches everything in short bursts now, because she gets tired so quickly. All her energy is going to her uterus, or at least that's how it feels. Her uterus in turn is taking up a huge amount of space in her mind. Sometimes she sees herself as a rather small woman connected to a gigantic uterus. Other times the uterus seems small and contained, and she reaches down and gives it a little pat. She feels as if she's discovered two or three new gears on her car. Sometimes she's in overdrive and that's a new thrill, but a lot of the time it's bull-low.

It's all process. She can't foresee the end. A baby, warm and alive and kicking its heels, nestled in her arms, in about seven months. She has no sense of that. Just the thing inside her, still very small and far from looking like her or anyone in the family. There is only her body and the way it is now, this very day.

She takes tea in her living room, choosing the pink brocade chair, which she's decided to cram into the room after all. Al's friend has done a great job of cleaning the upholstery, so it looks almost new. Better than new, actually. Full of a history that gives it subtlety and depth you wouldn't see in anything new. And it's unexpectedly comfortable, its wooden arms propping up her own in a pleasant and familiar way.

So much has changed in the three weeks she's been

in the house. Life has a new rhythm to it. She's inside the house and part of it in a way she'd never dreamed possible. She must always have had this need to possess and be possessed by a place. If she'd ever suspected she had this need, she'd probably have gone and picked something totally different. But she didn't pick this place, it picked her. Or maybe she did pick it, but couldn't let on what was happening, or the everyday sensible Annie Ransome would've stepped in and put a stop to it.

The doorbell rings. Annie gets up to answer, no longer really remembering the time when she found it difficult. She opens the door on a beautiful spring day. The sidewalks are bare, the snowbanks turning rapidly to slush. Everything sparkles. On her front step two children stand, Wilson and DeLinda in light spring jackets, their cheeks red with moving around in this delicious air.

She looks into their faces and seems to read their guilt. But they've no reason to think she knows anything. No way of finding out she's working at Al's Second Hand.

"Hi," Wilson says. "It's us. You know."

"We came to see how you're doing," DeLinda says.

"I'm doing all right," Annie says. "Would you like to come in?"

"Yes, please," Wilson says, but DeLinda hangs back as if something doesn't quite add up.

Annie lets them in, but makes no move to take their

jackets. She steps back into the room, allowing them to see all around it. Of course they see it at once.

"It's the chair, Lindy," Wilson says. "She's got the chair."

"Be quiet, Willy," his sister says.

"Yes," says Annie, "it's a lot like my grandmother's chair, isn't it? I decided I was wrong about not wanting another chair in here, so when I saw this one in a second-hand store, I bought it right away. It looks nice, doesn't it?"

The children don't say a word.

"What do you think, DeLinda?" Annie goes on. "Don't you find it a lot more complete?"

Willy looks at DeLinda as if she's got to find some way to get them out of this, but she just stands there. Her eyes go to the Queen Anne desk, where two portraits in polished mahogany frames no longer take pride of place. She begins to cry and, seeing her, Wilson cries too, both of them looking at the chair as if it's an old friend they'll never see again.

Annie feels the hurt, self-righteous feeling inside her breaking up. For the first time it occurs to her that they mightn't have wanted to sell the chair, but needed the money.

DeLinda takes her brother's hand. "Come on, Willy," she says. "We have to go." And out they go.

*Wait*, Annie wants to say but doesn't as she watches the door close. Now she sees that she could have talked to them, asked what happened. She doesn't know what their life is like, but it's probably harder than hers. She should go after them, call them back.

Annie opens the door. The children are standing outside the gate, still hand in hand, looking back at the house and crying. They remind her for all the world of all the paintings she ever saw of Adam and Eve right after they were chucked out of the garden. When they see her, they turn and run.

"Wait!" she does call this time. But they keep running, DeLinda almost pulling Willy off his feet, almost yanking his arm out of its socket.

Annie goes back in and sits in a wing chair, this time avoiding the pink brocade as if she's no longer worthy to sit in it. She's uncomfortably aware of her body and especially, as usual, of the place where the zygote or the embryo or whatever it's called at this stage, is growing. She doesn't feel too pleased with herself. She now believes that what she did was far worse than their selling the chair. After all, they're children. She wishes she could make it right with them, but realizes she has no idea where they live or even what their last name is. Perhaps Edith will know, but she's so oblivious to anyone she thinks is beneath her.

The phone rings. Annie runs to the kitchen to answer.

"Hi, it's me. Charles. Got your number from Directory Assistance."

Amazingly, she's glad to hear his voice. If only he won't start in about her coming back.

"Hi, Charles. How are you?"

"I'm well," he says. "You?"

"I'm feeling well," she says, trying not to think *uterus, pregnancy, baby,* in case the truth leaks across the phone wires; she's still not ready to tell him. God, she really is mean.

"You sound different," he says.

"Oh? Maybe I'm getting a cold." Well, it could be true.

"I've been thinking about you a lot," he says. "Trying to imagine you in that stuffy old place of Maisie and Phil's." Can it be he's finding her more interesting now that he's not seeing her every day? Is this happening to her too?

"Actually, it's not stuffy anymore," she says. "I've cleared out a lot of the junk and washed and waxed the floors to where you really wouldn't recognize the place."

"Do you ever go walking in the valley?" he asks, which is the last thing she's expecting.

She decides to trust him a bit. Or maybe she's testing him. She tells him about the market garden and the pony and the three old women in bright coats. She tells him about Harold and Donnie. She tells him about Sylvie and the breast cancer, the unfairness of it.

"It's good she got to live in the valley like she wanted. I always thought it was something special."

"You did?" Annie is surprised.

"Sure – I used to go there when I wanted to be alone. I liked the woods along the creek. I used to pretend I was the only person in the whole valley."

"You did?" is all she can say again.

"Yeah – I did. You don't have to sound so surprised."

"It's just, I don't usually think of you and nature in the same breath." The same universe, she doesn't add.

"Yeah, well," he says, a little hurt, "people make too much fuss about nature nowadays. Back then, it was just going down in the valley. Going to the crick. You know, I even camped out some nights, at the foot of Robin Hill. I used to pile thick grass under my sleeping bag and I'd make a little fire and roast potatoes in it for supper."

Wonder upon wonder. How well does she really know this man? "Weren't you scared at night?"

"Not really," he says companionably. "Not as long as I was outside while night was falling, so I could feel part of it."

Amazing to hear him say all this. "Sounds lonely, though," she says, to keep it going. "I'm amazed your parents let you go alone."

"Oh, it was pretty safe. There used to be a hobo jungle down there back in the Depression. But when I was a kid there were only the rabbits and gophers."

"Still…."

"And I think my dad used to walk down and check on me in the night, but I never really saw him and we never talked about it."

"I would never have thought your mother would agree."

"I think he talked her into it. He'd gone there as a

boy, and he wanted me to have that too."

"So if you had a son, would you let him do that sort of thing?"

"Oh, no," Charles says. "It's much more dangerous nowadays. Maybe in Riverbend you still could, but not in any bigger place."

"I suppose not," she says. She remembers the job Charles was trying for. "Heard anything about L.A.?" she asks.

"Not much. They're reviewing the tapes. If they like them, they'll give me an interview."

"When would you go down?"

"Actually, their station manager would come up here. They're also talking to a guy at CBC."

"Oh, that's unusual. But at least you wouldn't have to go to a lot of trouble." Of course, he might have been looking forward to the trip.

"Well, I should go," Charles says. "Have to get ready for the six o'clock news. But it was good talking to you."

"You too," she says, meaning it. In the last few minutes, Charles has seemed more real to her than he has for years. He hasn't said anything about missing her and it's such a relief. It almost makes her feel like she's missing him. "I'll look for you on the news," she says.

"Aw," he says, "I bet you watch Peter Jennings."

"No, really," she says, and then realizes he's kidding her. Score one for Charles. "What're you wearing?" she asks.

"Oh, you know," he says. "The usual uniform. Gets

pretty boring, doesn't it?"

My God. He does know. This *is* a day of revelation. Better quit while she's ahead.

"Thanks for calling, Charles. Goodbye, now."

"Talk to you soon," he says and is gone.

Annie pours more tea. Has this amazing conversation really taken place? And why is it so amazing? Because it's the first time in such a long time when neither has been trying to get the other one to do or not do something. Charles has been talking to her as to another independent person who might be interested in his experiences. Could it ever be like this all the time?

Annie remembers the children and the tears raining down their faces. She starts to cry herself, remembering the heartbreaks of childhood, which are never funny to the people experiencing them and which feel as though they will never, ever end or be made right. Pregnancy is making me more emotional, she thinks, but knows it's more than that.

# CHAPTER SIXTEEN

A man in a sort of space suit walks through trees into a clearing filled with wooden boxes on stands, their height roughly the same as the man's. The man approaches the boxes. On the chest area of his suit is an octagonal black area made of some stiff material, like a small black stop sign. The man speaks, his voice slightly muffled by the suit.

"I'm in the clearing now. They've seen me, I think. They've started to mill around. They're moving towards me."

A dense black cloud, a writhing swarm, appears and bears down on the man, accompanied by a loud humming. The cloud divides itself into hundreds of individual insects. They hurl themselves repeatedly at the man's protective suit, especially at the black octagon.

"I can feel them through the suit." There's amazement in his voice. "They don't just land and sting, they hurl themselves at me. Hard. I can feel it through the suit."

The man must want to run away, must be thinking, What if they break through the suit? He is clearly shocked by this thorough, concerted violence of mere insects, but stays in the clearing as the bees continue to launch themselves at him like living bullets. Angry buzzing is such a cliché, but not to these tiny creatures, which, according to the announcer – Charles – feel something akin to human rage, only more concentrated, more enduring. Their rage is provoked by the mere sight of the man and intensified by the black patch on his chest, which researchers have noted seems to particularly set them off. Charles draws her attention to the fact that they sting the black sign much more frequently than any other part of the suit. Unceasingly. They are not trying to scare the man away, Charles explains, they are trying to kill him. Without the suit, he would already be dead of anaphylactic shock.

The man's voice when he next speaks reflects this knowledge. "I'm going to begin moving off now."

Charles's voice interrupts again to explain that the next phase of the experiment, which is designed to learn more about the habits of killer bees, calls for the man to retreat slowly from the area of the hives and into the forest. The man is seen moving off. Ordinary bees, Charles explains, would gradually lose interest, but these stay with the man, their fury unabated. They pursue him through the forest. They sting. The man is killed over and over.

Next the bees are subdued by smoke and left overnight. The experiment resumes in the morning. The man appears again in his suit, and immediately the bees begin to mass.

"The bees have not forgotten their anger," Charles is saying. "They attack again and again." He goes on to conclude the item. Killer bees are moving inexorably north every year. They mate with ordinary bees and transform them, because killer bees are always domi-nant. Nobody quite knows how far they are likely to penetrate. Nobody quite knows what's to be done about them. People continue to die, not many, but a few more each year. Most people are lucky enough not to be where killer bees are, which is actually the only way to prevent them from killing you. (That or a protective suit.) People have died because they don't know this. The best news is for people in the northern United States and Canada. With any luck, the cold winters will prevent the killer bees from surviving there.

And then he moves on to something completely vac-uous and calming, about a new industry that's turning what used to be thought of as garbage into beautiful works of art that tourists snap up as if they were gold nuggets. Already this new industry is having a rejuve-nating effect on the economy of the tiny New England village where this modern economic miracle is taking place. Charles continues in this fashion, never once mentioning that the so-called works of art, which all the viewers can see, are mass-produced and of a startling ugliness and crudity, tiny statues of beavers and bears moulded from recycled paper and rag fibres and hand-painted garishly. What kind of culture could allow a man to refer to these things as art? Who could be so unfamiliar with actual art as to be fooled? But it doesn't matter; it's Charles's job to end the news on an upbeat, to get the viewers out of the mood of anxiety or despair that might be engendered by too much thinking about insects of mass destruction.

Annie zaps off the television. How many such items does Charles absorb each year, and what's it doing to him? How many murders and kidnappings, how many ferry sinkings and bus plunges? How many plane disasters and train derailments? How many stories of disease and homelessness and hunger? How much stolen plutonium, how much toxic waste? How many tales of torture and oppression?

What on earth is it doing to him? He never talks about it. He talks about the technical side, the way they covered a story. He talks about getting to an important story first, before the competition. But where in all of this is *he?* She doesn't have the foggiest idea.

# CHAPTER SEVENTEEN

What's Edith up to, Annie wonders? It's not her nature to ask for favours, yet that's exactly what she's done. The arthritis in her hands is acting up, she says – all the humidity caused by the melting snow – but Sunday's her day for calling, and she's promised to see an old friend. Would Annie mind driving her? Well, of course she's not going to refuse, not after the way Edith looked after her those first few days after the funeral. No doubt about it, Annie's been summoned to the palace, and it makes her uneasy.

They sit in the dining room, which looks disused now that Annie isn't sharing meals with Edith. Everything is dusted and polished within an inch of its life, even the carved silver frames of the photographs on the buffet. A picture of Edith and Arnold at their wedding, Arnold with the nervous look of a man who's taken something that doesn't belong to him. Close by, their three children, Lockwood, Eleanor, and Tira. And at a slight distance, there's one of Allison, in a smaller frame. Now where did that come from? It wasn't there before. Is Edith testing her, to see if she's noticed?

Edith is fanning through some colour photographs. Her finger joints don't look much different than usual, and they're certainly not slowing her down any. Edith looks up and sees Annie watching.

"I don't have trouble with pictures, because they're so light. It's anything to do with weight or pressure that gives trouble. Even something as slight as turning a tap. Or a steering wheel."

Annie feels like a bit of a swine, caught out thinking these thoughts, but she doesn't apologize. Around Edith you either grow a thicker skin and hang on to your ego or you pack it in and go under.

"Of course," she says. "It must be very annoying."

"You have no idea," Edith says. "Now, I hope you won't think it insensitive, but I had someone taking photographs at my place the day of the funeral and I thought you might like to have a set."

"What?" Annie asks, astonished. "You took pictures?"

"Had them taken," Edith says. "The man was very discreet; a real professional. Oh, I know, you probably think it's a preposterous idea. I did too, at first, but then I thought there should be some kind of record." No doubt she sees the outrage fighting with curiosity on

Annie's face. "You never know when they might interest you. Do you?"

"I suppose not." It galls her to say it. But she has to see the pictures.

Edith hands them over. They are surprisingly interesting. Lots of them include Annie, although she has no memory of a camera or flashbulbs. She notices how tight and controlled she looks, as if she'll be damned if she'll break down and cry in front of any of these people. The pictures are a fairly complete record of the funeral, a sort of visual guest book. Edith, of course, plastered all over the place, and there's Rita, and Reverend Bunting, probably waxing eloquent about having Allison in his confirmation class. And the three old bats in black taffeta. The pictures are proof that she was really there, along with all these people. For the first time she sees some truth in something Rita told her at the funeral: that the people came to be with her. She turns away, not wanting Edith to see the tears in her eyes.

Her eye catches a photograph of Tira on the sideboard, smiling radiantly, and she feels instant hostility. Unlike her sister Eleanor, who has only managed to be called attractive through rigorous attention to dress and grooming, Tira is effortlessly and almost excessively beautiful. Bountifully beautiful. Insultingly beautiful. *Much good it's done her*, Annie can almost hear Maisie muttering. Or is that herself?

Annie always got along fairly well with Tira, but resented her all the same. Annie considers herself to be somewhere in the middle ranks when it comes to looks and feels perfectly happy there as long as people like Tira aren't hanging around rubbing her nose in their beauty. In fact it was Tira's excessive beauty that prompted Annie and her cousin Kate to formulate what they called their Compensation for Beauty laws, under which people with an inordinate amount of beauty would have to make up for it in various ways before being allowed out among the general population. Kind of like handicapping in golf. Tira, for example, would have to wear a big smudge of soot on her forehead and have one of her front teeth blacked out. Edith would have to glue a big red wart on her nose. Annie sees Edith watching her and almost laughs out loud.

"Tira looks beautiful in that picture," Edith is saying.

"Really, no kidding," Annie says. "When doesn't she? She should have to wear a paper bag over her head, that's my opinion." Wow, she can't believe she said that. She always has all these sarcastic comments in her head, and damn, if she hasn't gone and said one out loud. And to Edith, for heaven's sake.

"I beg your pardon?" Edith says urbanely, her eyebrows rising a millimetre or two.

"Well, all that beauty can be rather blinding," Annie says. "She has to think of her responsibility to society." Say, this is really fun. She's never had the guts to act this way with Edith; maybe nobody has. It has definite possibilities.

However, Edith has tactics of her own. She begins to

pick up the photographs. "So I gather you don't want the pictures," she says.

Annie is sorry now. She forces herself to tell Edith that she does want the pictures. Edith hands them over. Annie grits her teeth and thanks her.

"Oh, and I had this picture of Allison copied for you," Edith says. "I didn't think you'd have it."

She picks up the black-and-white portrait of Allison from the buffet, Allison as a young woman in her twenties, looking as happy and as pretty as she ever would in her life. She wears a wine-coloured velvet dress that sets off her dark hair and the dark eyes looking expectantly at the camera. "It was taken just before she married that –" Edith hears the malice in her own voice, stops, and regroups. "Before she married Clifford Winter."

Annie takes the photograph from Edith, almost rudely. How did Edith get hold of it anyway? Suddenly she's certain Edith stole it from Maisie's house. After all, she had a key, and the house sat empty so long. But why did she want it? And what else has she seen? Eamon's papers? These are for Annie's eyes only. Family things.

"Did you ever know Maisie's father, Eamon Conal?" she asks, watching Edith's face for signs of guilt. Which is a ridiculous idea, because Edith never feels any guilt, or not as far as anyone has ever discovered.

"I can't say I knew him," Edith says. "But I used to see him around when I was a girl. He did some work for my parents." What kind of work? Annie wonders, willing Edith to tell without being asked. "He designed our flower beds, I think. Planted a lot of the trees. A very fine looking man. Lived to be seventy-eight, in spite of all the dire predictions."

"So he recovered fully then?" Annie asks, hating to reveal her ignorance before Edith, but needing to know anything Edith can tell her.

"Oh, you were never really cured in those days," Edith says, "before antibiotics. More like a remission – I think that's what it would be called now."

"But the tuberculosis never really went away?" Annie asks. "It was lurking down in his lungs waiting to pounce again?"

"Something like that," Edith says. "By the by, none of the family ever said it was tuberculosis. You didn't, because people would avoid you like…well, like the plague. They talked of 'an attack of pleurisy' or 'the year Father broke down.' If Maisie were standing here right now, I expect she'd still correct you."

"Who did they think they were fooling?"

"You'd have to ask them that. Oh, look, here's a good one of Rita. She looks so *well*, doesn't she?"

Something in Edith's voice nettles Annie. Something condescending. As if Rita looks good *in her way*. (Not like Tira, for instance, who is beautiful in anyone's way.) Rita, Allison's cousin and Kate's mother. If only Allison could have been more like her. Instead she'd spent a lifetime trying not to be like Rita. "There's something common about Rita," she once said, and Annie'd been so angry she'd slammed out of the house.

"Yes, she does, she looks very well," Annie says. "I've always loved Rita's looks."

"I should think so," Edith says, making Annie want to reach out and slap her.

Annie has always liked Rita's style, her warmth and sensuality, things Allison lacked or was afraid to show. Rita has always seemed comfortable inside her body, while Allison inherited Maisie's mania for brassieres and girdles and straight seams on your nylons. They were probably the last two women on earth to mourn the dropping of seams from nylon tights. Whereas Annie refuses to wear tights at all. She can't bear the elastic around her waist, can't stand the binding and pulling.

In the photo, Rita wears not black but jade green knitted wool that shows off her dark eyes and still dark hair and her lovely rounded figure.

"You called her Aunt Rita, didn't you?" Edith asks.

"She's like an aunt," Annie says. "Anyway, I could hardly go around calling her 'Cousin-Once-Removed Rita,' could I? It didn't sing to me."

"I would imagine not," Edith says, examining the picture. "Oh," she adds, "if only Allison could have been more like Rita."

Annie stares at her, caught without anything to say, so Edith sails right on. "I know they had parents who were twins. But it's the mother who's most important, I think. And of course Maisie married Phillip, and I don't think he questioned any of her ideas. Whereas Robbie, with some sort of inner wisdom, chose a woman who could counter the worst side of him. I honestly think it's Sophie who made the difference in those two girls."

Edith's probably right, but Annie isn't in the mood to receive pearls of wisdom about her family from Edith.

"Yes, no doubt," she says rudely. "Hadn't we better be going?"

"Certainly. I'll get you a big envelope for those pictures," Edith says. "Oh, and I wasn't patronising Rita, you know."

"Weren't you?" Annie asks.

"No," Edith says. And a big hole in reality opens up right before Annie's eyes, almost as if Edith had said "I wish I could have been more like Rita."

The hole closes up again before they leave the house, but now Annie's seen it, she can't quite *not* see it ever again. As Edith puts the funeral pictures into the envelope, Annie suddenly realizes the picture of her mother is also in one of Edith's silver frames, which must be quite valuable. Edith picks it up and goes to put it into the envelope. Annie makes a strangled noise.

"What?" Edith asks.

"Well," Annie says. "The frame....I mean...." She is too embarrassed to go on.

"Of course I meant you to have the frame as well," Edith says. "Even without it, I have enough silver frames to last me my life. Not that that's such a long time anymore."

It's so easy for Annie to think of reasons not to accept the frame, but she also remembers the night

Edith gave her the embroidered sheets. Can't she just accept this as well? She manages to say, "Thank you, Edith." Edith answers with a terse smile and a little shake of the head.

THEY TAKE THE OLD WINDING LANE into the river valley. Today it's muddy and slippery and more than a little dangerous. April twelfth and there's still lots of snow left in the valley, and in places the melting water threatens to wash out the road. The big old scow of a Caddy slews around in the mud, its ponderous rear end trying to waddle off the road, but Annie keeps it going straight. Edith was right to ask for help. And of course if they get stuck, she'll have someone to send for help. Someone young and strong.

Edith's friend lives on an old street that follows the twisted course of the river and boasts a strange combination of architectural styles and income levels. The houses are of two sorts: simple frame bungalows too small to pass today's building codes and the grand old homes of those of the town's wealthy who preferred a woodland setting and the grace of the river going by their doors. Some of the latter imitate the chalets or castles of Europe or the ornate elegance of Victorian England, while others are sprawling wood and stone bungalows of undoubted splendour but no known provenance.

Annie expects to be directed to one of these great

edifices, but Edith bids her stop in front of a very plain white house, maybe six hundred square feet in all. The grey Cadillac must look impossibly strange beside it. Is this really where Edith meant to come? Maybe she's getting forgetful. Not likely.

Their knock is answered by a man Edith's age or maybe slightly younger, wearing carefully pressed blue jeans and a teal green work shirt. His surprisingly luxuriant hair is medium brown, grey only around the temples, neatly trimmed in a sort of modified pompadour, like an old matinée idol's. The slight wave in his hair is the only deviation from the utter plainness of his clothing and grooming.

"Hello," he says. He seems surprised to see them, but it's not the sort of surprise which produces action. Again, Annie wonders if they've come to the right place.

"Good morning, Tom," Edith says. "I thought I'd drop by and see how you're keeping. And as it was rather wet, I thought I'd get some help with the car. This is my niece, Annie Ransome. Annie, this is Tom Bradley."

The man looks a little baffled by this long speech. "How do you do?" he says finally, without making any attempt to shake hands. Edith actually has to make a move in his direction before he steps back to let them enter a large central room that is living room, dining room, and kitchen in one. It's relentlessly neat, except for the dining table where woodworking tools and assorted bits of wood are strewn about. Everything about the room is as unassuming and unadorned as can be, except for the homemade shelves on the wall, filled with his work: miniature versions of the big houses in the neighbourhood, the chalets and castles and Victorian monstrosities, each finished in perfect detail – painted wooden trim, leaded windows, stone fireplaces, chimneys of tiny bricks he must have got from a child's building set.

He invites them to sit down and offers them tea. Edith accepts for both of them, and produces from her large handbag a foil-wrapped loaf shape.

"I brought banana bread," she says. "I thought it would go well with tea." Tom looks at the silvery shape for a moment, then takes it from her and places it on the kitchen counter. He puts water on to boil and begins to set out a pretty china tea service. Edith chats to him as he works.

"How have you been feeling?"

"Oh, I'm quite well, mostly. I still get pains in my chest, but the doctor gave me those nitroglycerin pills."

"And that helps with the pain, does it?"

"Oh, yes," he says. "And I'm careful not to do too much. Of course, you can't stop living either."

"No, I suppose not," Edith says. "Well, I wanted you to meet Annie," she says. "She's my nephew Charles's wife, and once upon a time she even went out with my son Lockwood."

What is Edith doing? Why would this man care whose wife Annie is or what mistakes she made in her foolish youth? Locky, for godsake, she never thinks of him if she can help it. Next to him, Charles is a regular Prince Charming.

"And I knew Annie would like your houses." She turns to Annie. "Tom has been making these model houses for several years now," she says. "Aren't they a marvel?"

"They're wonderful," Annie says, thankful to have anything to say. And they are wonderful. It's not only the meticulous attention to detail, either. Each house seems to have a life to it, an emanation of feeling she's not sure she saw in the houses themselves. As if this man, Tom, has seen to the secret heart of each one. The houses draw you to them by the power of his vision.

"Tom's working on something for me just now," Edith says. "He's doing a model of my house." Ah.

"That's it on the table," Tom says, as if he's giving them permission to go look. Annie goes to the table and, sure enough, she can see the beginnings of the shape of Edith's house, with its bay windows and turrets and tower rooms and its spindly rooftop widow's walk, like a giant puzzle he's assembling.

"It'll be a challenge, all right," he says, growing more talkative now that he has this ready subject. "It's the hardest one so far."

"I can imagine," Annie says. "So many windows and all that wooden trim."

"Oh, I like doing the trim," he says. "You can have fun with that."

One part is already finished. He's done a perfect replica of Edith's backyard gazebo, all pillars and railings and fancy fretwork. Annie is delighted.

"Oh, look, Edith," she says. "Isn't this lovely?"

Edith comes to the table and looks at the gazebo. She can't seem to resist picking it up in her hands. Her eyes fill with tears as she examines it.

"It's perfect," she says, turning to Tom. "But I didn't know you were going to do the summerhouse."

"It's part of the place, isn't it?" he asks. "I thought you'd like it."

"I do like it. It was always one of my favourite places. I just didn't expect it."

He brings the tea and banana bread to the coffee table and they all sit, Annie beside him on the sofa, and Edith on the matching chair, with the gazebo on the table in front of her. Tom glances questioningly at Edith, who immediately begins to pour the tea. He passes banana bread to Edith and Annie. He looks hard at Annie as if trying to place her.

"You must be related to Maisie and Phil Ransome, I suppose."

"They were my grandparents."

"I used to do a few odd jobs for them," he says.

"Tom worked in the old greenhouse for Mr. Hayashi," Edith says. "And he did a lot of gardening and building jobs for people. In fact, he looked after my garden for a while. And of course Maisie and Phillip needed help after he was in the wheelchair all the time."

"I always liked their house," Tom says.

"Annie's been fixing it up," Edith says. "It's looking lovely."

"Oak floors inside, I think it was?" Tom says.

"Oak in the living room, maple in the bedrooms," Annie answers.

"You take care of that," he tells her. "Wood is always worth taking care of."

Annie nods, as if it's suddenly important to agree with this strangely serious man. They sit a while longer, sipping the incredibly strong tea and eating Edith's banana bread until Edith decrees that it's time to go.

Tom Bradley stands in the doorway watching them as Annie backs the car into the lane, but he doesn't wave. Edith sits companionably beside Annie, apparently pleased with the visit. The Lady of the Manor, Annie thinks. Lady Bountiful dispensing largesse to the worthy yeomanry. The deserving poor. Annie is a little dismayed to feel her sarcasm dying away; she's enjoyed the afternoon too much. Better watch out, she thinks, you'll turn into a regular little Pollyanna.

## CHAPTER EIGHTEEN

He is on the hillside. Thick tangled grass pulls at his ankles. Parched yellow grass. He climbs, calves aching, lungs straining, heart thundering in his ears. Birds clamouring. Bees loud in the wildflowers. His chest on fire, but still he climbs. Above him the sun hangs just above the horizon of the hilltop. How can it be so big and so near, almost near enough to touch? Like a colossal egg yolk. That bright colour egg yolks are in spring.

He stops to rest. At his feet he sees the fleshy leaves of prickly pear, the only moist thing in this dry world, their flowers with thick waxy petals, yellow and cream with a flush of crimsony pink; inside, a single drop of water that catches and reflects the sun. He peers into a flower, drawn to the delicate flushed centre.

He looks down the long, long slope and far below sees a group of extraordinary creatures all in white bounding up the hillside like Mexican jumping beans. Ping, ping, ping, *they vault and bounce erratically upwards with amazing speed, converging on the place where he waits and watches. Surely they are all going to land on the very square of grass he stands on. They will knock him to the earth, push him away from his centre. But no, they fly on past him like human grasshoppers, the sashes on their white pyjama tops flying in the golden air, humming and whirring like tops or like windmills. Their teeth flash in mirthless grins or maybe it's grimaces of pain because of their crossed legs.*

*The last one hurtles past, moving up, up. They near the top, gathering strength for a final burst of power that flings them high in the air; and one by one they shoot up and into the startlingly near yellow sun where they disappear like rocks into water.*

*He longs to follow, but his legs are stone. The last man explodes into the sun and is taken in. The sun bulges and strains around these new shapes it has absorbed. It grows larger and heavier until it tips and begins to roll down the hill. He cannot climb to the sun, but the sun is coming to him. He feels the heat as it comes closer, searing against his hands, his face, the sun gathering speed....*

Annie wakes, fighting to stay in the dream until the sun reaches them, but she can't do it; she feels on her face the tears of desire and of its loss. And thirst, desperate thirst. First, for water; but also for learning more.


CAROLINA ATWATER, a fifty-something woman in a bright magenta dress, magenta-trimmed glasses, and hair dyed a patently false shade of burgundy, is in charge of the Local History Room at the Riverbend Public Library. She is clearly one of those whose nature it is to help others and, yes, she does know of a sanatorium in the area. It's beside a lake in a deep valley carved by the last retreating glacier, about eighty miles from Riverbend, near a town called Perdue, which means "lost" in French and was named for a trapper from Québec who disappeared in a blizzard.

This sanatorium was built in 1914 and operated into the early fifties, Carolina explains, only closing down when all its patients had been cured by the new wonder drugs that came out after World War II. It's been turned into a summer camp for handicapped children, but one of the patient pavilions has been preserved as a museum.

"It's an amazing place," Carolina says, pulling a bulky file from a drawer. "A deep valley carved out below the level of the prairie." Annie feels a surge of excitement, remembering Eamon's description of the valley gouged into the earth thousands of years ago.

"My parents had a cottage there, on the lake, and we could see the San from our road. It had its own power plant, vegetable gardens, bakery, its own skating rink for the staff." Carolina holds up photographs from the file as she talks. Long narrow pavilions set in wide lawns, a power plant with a huge stack, a thriving garden with what looks like acres of potatoes and corn. The last picture shows a graveyard in a narrow valley, the graves marked with small standard-issue gravestones. "I guess the people in Perdue didn't want all those germs in their nice town graveyard," she says.

"I thought I might go take a look," Annie says.

"Did you know someone who spent time there?" Carolina asks.

"My great-grandfather, I think. He came back from World War I with tuberculosis."

"What was his name?"

"Eamon Conal." Annie feels a tiny stab of disloyalty at naming her great-grandfather as the man who had tuberculosis.

"Eamon Conal! Why didn't you say?"

Carolina leads Annie to the back of the Local History Room, set up to look like a turn-of-the-century parlour. On the wall, an ornately framed photograph shows an old man with a long white beard standing in front of a bed of tulips. Annie recognizes the burning eyes at once; they seem to look right into her brain. If the picture has such force, what must the man alive have been like?

"Everyone knew Eamon," Carolina says. "He did all the landscaping for the city. Started as a gardener's assistant and ended up running the show. They couldn't make him quit till he was over seventy."

"So that was what he did. I remember hearing my grandma saying he always worked outdoors and how the fresh air was good for him."

"I can remember him still," Carolina says. "I was just

starting out with the Library – I was the Story Lady in the Children's Section – and we could see him from the windows. He'd wear a dark jacket and trousers – an old suit, I suppose it was really – and a white shirt. And it was like he belonged out there. He was truly a man of gardens."

A man of gardens. Annie sees a black and white movie in her mind: Eamon trimming hedges, setting out bedding plants, pushing a wheelbarrow. Always outdoors until he became part of the plants and the earth.

Eamon writing his papers late at night when everyone else was asleep.

THE DROP INTO THE VALLEY is unexpected and breathtaking, the narrow highway winding its way into a long valley surrounded by hills and deeply scored by ravines. The hills, almost bare of snow, are covered in pale buff grass, with a hint of green from spring runoff. Brush, a dark rusty red, chokes the still snow-filled ravines.

Perdue in the valley bottom is at first just another forgotten small town, although Annie notices a few lovely old houses. The main street businesses are shabby now, many of them boarded up. Beyond the town, the road leads north between two small lakes; a sign points west, reading "Children's Opportunity Camp, 2 miles." Annie turns west.

She parks in the lot that fronts the property and follows a boardwalk to a map. The surrounding hills thrust arms forward on either side of the San and curve around at the back. This horseshoe formation shelters a huge complex, many smaller structures clumped around a larger central building, which the map identifies as the administration building. To the east, nestled into the hillside, is a building labelled "Veterans' Pavilion and Sanatorium Museum, Tuesday to Friday, 2:00-4:00 p.m." Luckily, it's a Tuesday, a little after two.

She strolls up the hill on another wide boardwalk through beautifully landscaped lawns. The air is warm and moist and somehow soft. Winter has been so hard this year that she's almost forgotten air can make you feel this way. It takes her by surprise, makes her want to jump or maybe shout. This must be what happens to calves and lambs in the spring. Only they can't know how remarkable it is. They've never been anywhere but spring.

At the administrative building, the boardwalk turns right and leads to a cluster of patient pavilions. The one with the sign in front is clearly the one she wants, the Veterans' Pavilion. Eamon was a veteran. Perhaps this is the very building he stayed in. She sees a long building with a screened porch running the length of it; the porch faces southwest to allow a view of the grounds and the lake below and also, to the west, of the great hill that rises over the complex.

The door at the west end of the building is open and Annie enters. There's no one sitting at the small table, just a printed card with the hours of operation and the name "Veterans' Pavilion Museum, Perdue Historical Society." Annie moves down the long hall with doors leading off to the right, looking into a series of identical rooms, each furnished with a pair of single beds and a hodgepodge of dressers and bedside tables in every known style. Some pieces have neatly-typed cards attached. "Donated by the family of Major Edward Dreaver." "Donated by Miss Elsie Howes."

Annie enters a room near the centre of the building. Two neat beds, as before, each with its own bedside table bearing a covered cup with a pile of folded gauze squares beside it. A chest of drawers for each man; one of them is very like the one in Allison's bedroom in the house in Riverbend. Perhaps Eamon had seen the resemblance and bought the piece as a memento of his time in the San. She thinks this might well be the room he shared with the much younger Jimmy. It has windows looking onto the long porch. The door to the porch is between the two windows.

The beds are covered in coarse grey wool blankets with black stripes along the bottom. At the foot of each bed is a cylindrical object in rust-coloured pottery. There are a couple of framed prints on the wall, one of a sailing ship being tossed in a terrific storm and one of sheep safely grazing on a wide green hill. No doubt this covered the gamut of emotions considered appropriate for patients.

On first glance it all seems distant enough, but when

she looks closely at one of the beds and imagines Eamon lying there, it suddenly becomes personal. Annie is unprepared for the rush of feeling that hits her. It's as though the walls, long steeped in memories and pain, yield an impression or scent of these events. She feels a great sadness in her chest and a desire to weep. At the same time she has the sense that there is no use in weeping. The sadness is too vast and full for tears ever to be done with.

She steps into the porch, almost empty except for a couple of beds and some dark wicker chairs, and she's in the long narrow room of her dream. The walls actually are yellow, but more vivid than in the dream. Someone, sometime, must have described this to her. The floors are wide maple boards. Screened windows run from ceiling to waist height along the length and sides of the porch. It should be a lovely space but isn't quite. Maybe because it's so obviously institutional. She sits in a chair beside one of the beds, looking up at the magnificent hill to the west.

This is where they sat, she's almost sure of it. She looks up the hill to where the two children climbed until they were outlined by the sky, as Eamon watched, longing to be with them. Maude on the chair beside him, wanting something from him, only he must think of it. The husband must lead. The younger man, Jimmy, watching, only dimly understanding.

Annie feels like a flush over her entire body the most astounding, the most pervasive sexual desire she has ever known, not in any part or parts of her body, but diffused into every bone, every muscle, every cell, every positive and negative space of her. She wants to reach out and embrace someone, but at the same time the sadness is there, almost choking her. Eamon's words echo in her ears as if they are her own.

She thinks of the clump of cells forming itself into a more and more complex being inside her. She thinks of her baby being born and sees herself in this chair, trying to soothe the crying child into sleep. She can almost feel its weight in her arms. And it seems that there is no point at all in bringing a child into this world; that no good can possibly come of it; that she will not make a proper mother.

She sits in the chair, hands clasped to upper arms, rocking herself. She thinks of the words Maisie used to say in prayer, in a dull rote voice that used to make the child Annie want to scream. *We have done that which we ought not to have done, and we have left undone that which we ought to have done, and there is no health in us.* An Anglican prayer, Maisie had turned Anglican when she married Phillip.

"Are you all right?" someone is asking. Annie sees an elderly woman, very spry looking in a red sweatshirt and blue jeans and heavy-soled sneakers. Her long grey hair is braided and wound around her head. A pin on her sweatshirt reads "Vi Tripps, Volunteer Director."

Vi Tripps pulls up another wicker chair and sits by

Annie, patting her gently on the back. "There, there, now," she says. "It can be a sad place. I know." Annie sees that the woman does know. She doesn't look unhappy now, but as though she has been in the past.

"Did you have someone in the San?" Vi asks. "You look so young."

Annie tries to determine whether she can speak calmly. Vi Tripps looks at her encouragingly out of wonderfully steady blue eyes. She doesn't seem the least bit embarrassed by any of this and, oddly, neither does Annie. In any case, Annie has no energy available for dissimulation.

"My great-grandfather was here, a long time ago," she says. Vi hands her a tissue and Annie blows her nose.

"What was the name?"

"Eamon Conal. He was here at the end of World War I."

"Before my time," Vi says. "I didn't come to the San until the Second World War. I was fifteen years old."

"They had kids here?" Annie asks, horrified.

"Oh, yes, lots of us."

"It must have been awfully lonely," Annie says. "Away from your family."

"Yes, at first. And then the others became my family. Only closer."

"Closer?"

"Yes. I met my husband here. And I figured out what sex was here. I was even married here, in a little chapel on the grounds. We were two of those who went home. A lot didn't."

"That's terrible."

"It was very sad, but you had to get used to it. They tried to take them away at night, so we wouldn't know, but we always did. We'd say, 'The Bone Wagon's hauled another one away.' But the Bone Wagon never got Billy and me."

"It sounds a bit…." Annie doesn't want to offend the woman.

"Callous?" Vi grins. "I suppose it does. But it wasn't healthy to feel sorry for ourselves. And I hardly ever did, except sometimes when I'd read stories about girls on the outside who could ride horses and play tennis and go out on dates. No, the ones I pitied were the babies."

"Babies had TB?" Too late Annie wonders if she should have said "broke down."

"The babies didn't have it. Their mothers did, and they'd be brought in before the delivery. Usually the babies would be okay, but if they stayed around the mother, they'd be infected, of course."

"What happened to them?"

"They were whisked away as soon as they were born – to the Preventorium as they called it." Vi points to a square frame building surrounded by trees. "They were raised right here, by the nurses."

"Their mothers never even got to hold them?"

"Oh, no," Vi says. "Far too dangerous with an active case. Now, the lucky ones, their mothers got better and took them home, but sometimes the mother died. And a lot of times there wouldn't be anyone on the outside to look after them. Some of them stayed for their whole childhood. We even had a little school for them."

Listening to the story gives Annie a painful empty feeling in her womb. The mothers never got to hold their babies. She knows instinctively that this is the one thing that would definitely make her crazy. All those months of carrying the child inside you, and then not being able to touch it when it came out.

"I've just made tea," Vi says. "I'll get us each a cup and then I'll show you around."

The tea is hot, strong, and sweet, and there are two homemade ginger cookies on the saucer. Annie savours them as though cookies have only that moment been invented. Being here with Vi Tripps – two women drinking tea and chatting on a verandah – feels so comfortable, and also seems to validate for Annie the changes that have been working their way through her life.

Annie's eyes stray to the nearby bed and the round clay vessel at its foot.

"Oh, you're looking at the pig," Vi says. Annie looks blank. "The clay thing. It's called a pig. Because of its little round belly."

"What's it for?"

Vi shows her the plug in an opening on the side. "It's sort of a pottery hot water bottle. They'd fill these up and tuck a few of them into your bed and they'd keep you warm for hours."

"Were you cold?" Annie asks. "I thought there'd be a fever."

Vi laughs. "No, of course we weren't cold in general," she says. "This was for when we went to sleep. Out here, you see, on the porches."

"Oh, you slept out here," Annie says. "I suppose that must have been nice – kind of like camping."

Vi laughs even harder. "It was nice, all right, when it was thirty below and the snow was piling up on your covers."

"What?" is all Annie can say.

"We didn't only 'camp' in the summer, you know. We did it all year round, no matter what the temperature. If it was really bad, they gave you a couple of extra blankets."

"But why? Was it some kind of weird punishment?"

"All part of Chasing Cure. You see, there was only so much they could do for us. Basically, there was good food, bed rest, and fresh air. Oh, you wouldn't believe the food. Four squares every day. Steak and pork chops and chicken and ham, and three kinds of vegetables dripping with butter, and soup and pickles and buttered rolls. Every meal there was a big glass of milk with extra cream in it. And you had to eat it all, no mistake about that. Good thing we'd never heard of cholesterol."

"Didn't you get fat?"

"Not like you'd think. Oh, we tended to be nicely rounded, but I guess it really did go to fighting germs.

Now, bed rest was bed rest, not much to say about that, so that brings me back to fresh air. They figured you couldn't get too much. We spent part of each day and all of each night on the porch."

"But our winters are so cold. You wouldn't do that nowadays even with healthy people."

"Ah, but we weren't healthy. You see, the bed rest and the cold air had just one purpose. To slow the body down – they thought that would also slow down the progress of the disease. Then the resting body, fuelled by all that food, would have the best chance to fight the disease."

"Eamon – my great-grandfather – wrote of his 'slow blood,'" Annie says.

"That's how it felt. As if your blood, your mind, the whole world, had been slowed right down."

"When did you get out of here?" Annie asks.

"I was eighteen. They told me I would never be able to have children and I'd have to take it easy all my life, or I might break down again. Well, I had four children, and if they thought I could take it easy looking after that bunch – You know, they tried to keep Billy and me from getting married. But we knew better."

"Didn't you hate living here?"

"A lot of the time, yes. But you kept it to yourself. Because people were dying all around you, and you believed you had this one chance to live."

"What chance?"

"Chase Cure. Do everything they said, and do it with

enthusiasm. I believe the term used today is 'attitude.' You had to do everything with attitude, even if it was only lying around all day. You had to fight every single moment."

"Did it work?"

"Who knows? Maybe we'd have got better anyway. But if we ever broke down again, we always went back to it. You might say Chasing Cure became a religion with us."

"Eamon wrote about feeling pain in the ribs that were no longer there. Why weren't they there?"

"That was one of the treatments. Remove some of the lower ribs around the infected lung so it could collapse and rest. They did the surgery right here."

"And when the person was better?" Annie feels a bit faint. "How'd they get the lung un-collapsed?"

"Oh, they didn't. It stayed down. Better that way. Kept the bacilli walled off from the rest of the body."

"For a lifetime?" Annie still can't believe it.

"That's right. It's one of the ways you can spot an Old Crock. The operation throws the body out of kilter. They almost always have one shoulder higher than the other."

"Old Crock?"

"That's what we call ourselves."

"So Eamon spent his working life doing outdoor labour, on one lung?"

"Well, what was the alternative?"

Annie thinks about it. "None, I guess."

"What made you start looking into Eamon's life now?" Vi asks. "Most young people don't seem to have time for the past."

Annie smiles. Up until recently this would have described her perfectly. "My mother died. I've been staying on in the house she left me, getting it in order."

"I see," Vi says.

"My mother committed suicide," Annie finds herself saying, although she's almost certain she never meant to tell.

Vi is paying close attention. "Are you all right?" she asks.

"I don't know," Annie says. "I think so."

"This is a dangerous time for you," Vi says. "You know that, don't you?"

"What do you mean? That I might do the same thing?"

"No, but you have to deal with all that darkness, or it will take hold of you. Do you have someone taking care of you?"

"No," Annie says, "not really."

"Are you married?"

"Yes, but my husband's not here."

"I would feel better if you had someone watching over you," Vi says. For some reason, this doesn't sound bossy or officious.

It comes to Annie that she hasn't spoken the whole truth. She thinks of Edith, insisting she stay on for a while and cooking her wonderful meals. Making Annie confront the house, giving her the lovely sheets, holding her head when she was sick. Starting up the mail and the telephone. Maybe someone is watching over her.

"There is someone," she says. "My husband's aunt. I think she's keeping an eye on me. I didn't realize it till you asked."

"That's better then," Vi says. "More tea?"

Annie is suddenly exhausted. The bed with its coarse dark blankets looks incredibly inviting. The pillow slip looks clean.

"If I could just lie down here for a moment. I think I've got to sleep a little before I drive back." Annie is sure the woman will not deny this simple request. In fact, won't she even stay and watch over her while she sleeps? Annie starts to rise.

"No," Vi says sharply. "Don't do that. You will not lie down where Eamon lay. He's another of your dead ones, and you can't let him take you over either."

The woman is right. To lie in this bed, where people have suffered and died. Where Eamon lay and wondered if he would die. Isn't she having enough of his thoughts and dreams already? She feels a physical coldness go through her, as if she's been dropped into an icy lake. Or a grave. Cold to her toes and to the roots of her scalp. She must have been crazy to think of it.

"Where, then?" Annie asks. "Is there a hotel in town?"

"Hotel, nonsense," Vi says. "You'll come to my house."

"Won't Billy mind?" Annie says, although she's

already made up her mind to go.

"Billy passed away last year," Vi says. She holds out her hand. "Come."

"What about the museum? It's not four yet."

"Well, they'll have to come back another day, won't they?"

"I guess they will," Annie says.

THE ROOM HAS PALE BLUE WALLS. A plain white quilt on the pine bedstead. Paintings of Vi's three daughters, done as young women in their twenties, each with a flower in her hand. Striking paintings, constructed of thousands of minute jabs of paint. Taken together they give an impression of bristling energy. Marianne, a brunette, holds a huge scarlet poppy; Rosemund, with auburn hair, has a magenta peony; and Diana, a dark blonde, holds a tiger lily like a small flame flowing between her hands.

"Your paintings are wonderful," Annie says.

"My best work," Vi says. "My hands were better then."

Annie looks at Vi's hands. The knuckles are enlarged and knobbly, like Edith's. Arthritis. She hadn't noticed before. "Do you still paint?"

"Yes, but the technique has changed. Less fine detail. More sweep. More impatience. I'll show you sometime."

Vi holds her hands well apart and brings them slowly together, until they almost touch. At the last moment they seem to repel each other and move apart again. She repeats this movement several times, as if there's some kind of energy flowing between them.

"I'd like to try something to help you," Vi says. Annie who doesn't usually trust strangers, nods. "Lie down and get comfortable then." Annie takes off her shoes and lies down on the bed.

"Close your eyes," Vi says. "I'm just going to hold my hands over your face to begin with." Annie senses the hand shapes in front of her closed eyes. "Do you feel anything?"

"Warm," Annie says. It's a pleasant feeling, like the sun hovering close.

"Good," says Vi. She begins to move her hands, still not touching. Some kind of energy flows over Annie, like a helpful electrical current. The muscles in her face seem to melt and flow in the stream of radiant energy.

"Okay, and turn over." Annie turns onto her stomach and Vi goes to work on her back. It's like a massage, but Vi never touches her. Once more the muscles warm and grow fluid, as if she's lying under a hot sun.

Vi works down the buttocks and legs to the feet, her hands moving in long sweeps to the toes, following through into the air to complete the stroke. Annie feels as if all tension and pain are being carried out of her body through her deliciously warm toes. Vi does the same along Annie's arms and hands, each stroke sweeping past her fingertips. In the middle ages this would surely have been seen as some species of witchcraft and this woman would have been burned. Medieval Christianity would have mistrusted anything that felt this good.

"What is it?" Annie asks.

"Turn over again," Vi says. Annie turns, and Vi moves her hands over Annie's torso in the same long sweeps. They linger for a moment over the abdomen and then abruptly stop. Annie waits, but nothing more happens. Annie opens her eyes.

"Reiki," Vi says. "A Japanese healing therapy. I discovered I had a talent for it."

"Why did you stop like that?"

"You're pregnant, aren't you?" Vi asks. "How many months?"

"I'm not sure," Annie says. "A couple, probably."

"May I take it you haven't seen a doctor?"

"Well, no," Annie admits. "I haven't quite got around to it." Vi looks at her reproachfully. "I guess I didn't want some guy in a white coat bossing me around."

"Nonsense," Vi says. She leaves the room and comes back in a moment with a leather-covered address book and a piece of paper. "Dr. Margot Summers, Family Medicine," she writes, with an address in Riverbend, and hands it to Annie.

"Go see her. She won't boss you around. Not much anyway. Still want to sleep?"

"Maybe a half hour or so," Annie says. "And then I think I could drive home."

"All right," says Vi. "I'll talk to you later."

The next thing Annie knows, sun is flooding the sky-coloured walls, the glowing paintings, and Vi is there by the bed with a cup of tea. "Sleep well?" she asks.

Annie's body feels as if it's grown into the bed during the night, her flesh adhering to the soft covers. "My clothes look like I've slept in them," she says.

"They certainly do," says Vi. "Drink your tea."

## CHAPTER NINETEEN

*F*alling now, falling. No, floating. And landing. Smooth,
*resilient. Warm. Some kind of room. Soft trickling
sounds. Walls curve and flare around her. Light flows
through, deep pink shading to crimson where the walls fold in
on each other. It's like being in a rose. She laughs without
making a sound. She's got small somehow, and she's got
inside a rose. Petals so smooth and fine you can't see any texture, only a sheen of colour like rosy pollen. Annie, Annie,
how does your garden grow? It grows and grows, that's all I
know.*

Then the wind-up alarm goes off and Annie's big
again. In fact, she's bigger than yesterday or the day
before, although she can't see each day's change.
It's nice to have her own dreams again. Today,
Tuesday, April 28, she's going to see Vi Tripps's doctor friend.

She decides to walk. It's only a half mile or so and the

sidewalks are quite passable, though the streets are thick with slush. She sets off through the neighbourhood she grew up in, called River Heights, though only the few houses along River Road – including her own and Edith's – have any view at all of the river. The rest, small frame or brick or stucco bungalows, could be anywhere. But somebody once named the place River Heights, and all the streets have been named after rivers.

Nile Avenue boasts a rundown old shopping centre which, before the Sunset Mall was built on the edge of town, had a drug store, a butcher shop, a greasy spoon café, a ladies' dress shop, and a service station. Now it has a small chain grocery store with attached gas bar, what Annie calls an inconvenience store. Orinoco Street has several blocks of Victorian-looking row houses that, in a bigger city, would long since have been renovated by yuppies, but in Riverbend are simply wearing out. Danube Crescent is a curving row of stucco bungalows with small dark front porches that once had – but seem now to have misplaced – a certain sturdy charm.

As Annie walks down St. Lawrence Boulevard, she feels the freshness go out of the morning. Surely the neighbourhood was never this shabby a mere twelve years ago? Or did she just not notice it? No, it really is different, although the process must have started by then. Twelve years of economic depression have meant twelve years without money to paint houses, fix gates, or shingle roofs. Not all of the houses are like this; some still have brave front gardens alive with poppies and daisies and iris, but many of the owners have given up. Too many yards are overgrown with weeds. Too many fences have broken or missing boards, like poorly tended teeth. The place that used to be proudly working class, everything modest but comfortable and shipshape, has lost its focus.

The sign on the old brick house on St. Lawrence reads "Rainbow Women's Clinic," with the names of Dr. Summers and two other women doctors written below. The wainscotted living room has become a waiting room furnished in bright primary colours and mainly filled with pregnant women, some with small children playing in and around a playhouse built into one corner of the room. Although the majority of the women are white, at least a third are aboriginal or black. This is a change from Annie's childhood when the neighbourhood was almost totally white. A poster on the wall, showing women of many races and ethnic backgrounds, invites women to join a co-operative daycare operating in the clinic's basement.

A nurse takes Annie's history in painstaking detail. Shortly after this ritual, she's in the consulting room in a blue cotton gown waiting for the doctor.

Margot Summers is a fiftyish woman with long greying hair in a bun. The impression as she enters the small consulting room is of tremendous energy.

There's a pleasant look of irony about her mouth, as if she's seen a lot but tried not to make too many judgements. When Annie admits that she's known she's pregnant for at least a month before arranging to see a doctor, Margot Summers gives her a look, as she pumps up the blood pressure cuff, that says, "Well, we both know that's foolish, so I won't give you hell."

The really unnerving thing is that something in the shape of the doctor's eyes reminds Annie of her mother. Allison also had the same restless energy as this woman, never seeming quite comfortable or quite satisfied, but this woman seems to have found a way to put her energy to good use.

For the pelvic exam, the doctor warms the speculum in water and moves it into position without causing any noticeable discomfort. The words "in good hands" go through Annie's mind. Dr. Summers keeps up a flow of questions throughout the pelvic exam, about nutrition, exercise, and the date of Annie's last period.

"I'd say you're about fourteen weeks. Everything looks favourable for a healthy pregnancy. I see from your history that you don't smoke, and you only drink the odd glass of wine, is that what you said?" Annie nods. "Your blood pressure's excellent and your cervix looks beautifully healthy."

No doctor has ever said anything like this to her before. No doctor has ever committed himself (they've all been men) beyond saying he could see nothing obviously wrong with her. Now, for the first time, someone who should know has told her there is something obviously right.

Annie takes a different way home, along the margins of the neighbourhood, bounded by railway tracks and various industries, many of them now boarded up. On the other side of this no man's land is the downtown and, beyond that, the more prosperous side of town: Prairie Heights; Annie's always been amused by the paradox contained in the name.

The streets are quieter than she remembers. Occasionally she passes a mother with a baby in a stroller or a man who looks like he's been too long without a job. She turns a corner and everything changes. A block away is the last remaining meat packing plant. The rumours are it's going to close too. Annie's heard about it on the news – how the company has offered the workers a fifteen percent pay cut. If the workers accept, the company will keep the old, badly-equipped plant going. No guarantee of how long.

Men and women walk up and down the sidewalk in front of a steel mesh fence around a long low building which has already begun to look abandoned. They carry hand-printed signs: "Don't Relocate – Renovate!" and "Chop the Managers, Not the Workers." They walk in orderly lines. One of the strikers, a rather gaunt black woman in her forties, tries to pick up the pace by leading a chant of one of the slogans, but after a few repetitions it dies away. Annie stops as the woman begins to sing in a strong, clear contralto.

> When the union's inspiration through the workers' blood shall run,
> There can be no power greater anywhere beneath the sun,
> What force on earth is weaker than the feeble strength of one?
> But the union makes us strong.

For a brief instant they all come together; the old song is new once again. But when the chorus ends, there's a deadness in the air, a sheepishness; strength now seems like a cruel illusion. The marchers slow their pace. A tired young woman about Annie's age stops for a split second before turning at the end of her circuit and looks Annie right in the eye.

"Who are you staring at, bitch?" she asks. She turns and marches on. Annie waits a moment, as if to show she's not being scared off, although nobody's watching. Then she moves on, fighting back tears.

She tries to understand the moment of irrational anger, to see herself as the woman must see her. Not working because some man is supporting her? Out for a stroll? Gawking at other people's misery? Of course she doesn't see it as gawking, but maybe the woman has, in some way, a point. She doesn't share their fear, their danger.

She imagines women cutting up chickens and wrapping the parts in plastic, their hands growing numb with cold. She probably saw this in one of Charles's news items. And the smell. There will be a pungent smell, even with the cold they must work in, of animal flesh and hair and blood, that follows you home at night on your own skin and hair. This work will go on day after day, always the same, and never end. Except that now it looks like it will end.

These are the kinds of jobs she's always feared, the ones she'd do almost anything to avoid. The woman is right. She's a tourist here. Marrying Charles has given her a freedom from all this, if it's given her nothing else. Freedom from the jobs which make you feel all but powerless, the logical structures which underlie them. But what happens if living with Charles becomes more difficult than dealing with the world? What happens when she has to raise a child? What happens if she has to start saying what she really thinks?

Could she spend all her working days cutting and packaging chickens, endless bodies of chickens – wings, legs, thighs, breasts, backs – until she gets old and has arthritis in her hands? Could she do this in order to raise her child? Could she do this while her child is in daycare, a friendly co-operative daycare if she's lucky, or a cramped, dark, understaffed one if she's not? Could she do all this and call herself fortunate to have a job of any kind?

Annie walks home through the diminished streets with their faint echoes of rivers, the streets that seemed full of hope and possibility in her childhood. She has escaped them with apparent ease, without even much conscious thought. Now they're being offered back to her, dead end or opportunity, she doesn't know which. With an enormous head start: her own house on the outskirts of this defeated neighbourhood. Her own little nest egg.

But who is she to say the neighbourhood is defeated? The women at the clinic aren't defeated. They have come together to create the daycare, something the women all need. When has Annie achieved anything remotely as important as that?

Maybe she could make a living at Al's Second Hand, dealing with the discarded or sacrificed artifacts of these people's lives. Sometimes the selling seems like cannibalism, herself and Al scavengers living off the bones and teeth and fallen hair of generations. Yesterday someone brought in a load of baby things. A cradle, a battered bassinet, a crib with rails set too far apart for today's safety standards. Stacks of clean and neatly folded baby clothes; blankets; an old quilt.

There was something wrong about it, and Annie hadn't wanted to touch any of it. The cradle looked a hundred years old at least, the sort of thing handed down from generation to generation. Only something had stopped that process. Somebody had to have the money, little as it was. Or there was nobody left to pass it on to.

ANNIE'S ROUTE has brought her to her old high school, River Tech. A long low factory-like place built in the twenties to provide a practical high school education for the children of workers. Where boys could learn trades and girls could learn nice clean indoor professions like secretary. This is where Annie dawdled her way to a sort of education, on her way to university.

Annie stops on the sidewalk to look in at a ground-floor classroom where girls sit in front of computers. Most of them look bored out of their minds. Suddenly behind a girl with Day-glo orange hair a gaunt figure pounces. The girl jumps about a foot as the hawk-like person bends over her. It can't be. Surely Miss Marshall must be dead by now, or at least retired. But it's her, all right. Annie can hear her like it was yesterday.

*Girls will be attired in a neat and respectable manner at all times. Their blouses will be clean and pressed, their skirts well fitted but not tight. Hair will be tidy and clean, hands well groomed. This does not mean blood-red polish. Lipstick will be tasteful and unobtrusive. Eye make-up is quite unnecessary.*

*Girls who are comfortable and confident of their appearance free their minds to learn; they prepare themselves for the business world and the demands of employment. Learning becomes a pleasure as well as a duty.*

Annie had been quick to learn the things Miss Marshall and the others had expected her to learn at River Tech. She would take it in and give it back to them on exams and then let it flow away from her again. She had seen how the school operated and made herself function in that world. And they'd praised her, called her a good student.

*If you learn your lessons here well, girls, you will gain skills which will stay with you for life. You will not be forced to grasp at the first job that comes your way – clerking at the corner confectionery, waiting tables at some greasy spoon, or,* and here she would pause to add gruesome emphasis, *scrubbing floors on your hands and knees in some rich woman's home.*

Annie and Sylvie had laughed at these speeches, and Sylvie had made no real attempt to gain any skills that would stay with her for life. But Annie, who had grown up with the fear of poverty, had listened, knowing she would need to work her way through university. And she'd actually liked the typing drills, where she could let her mind go and observe from a distance as her fingers developed speed and power. *Sometimes we try too hard to do what should and can be done with ease.*

Three solid, unquestionable skills she had learned – Typing, Shorthand, Introductory Bookkeeping – and she'd learned them quite well, although she'd never been the very best. There'd seemed no reason to be the very best when she could be better than average by barely trying. But in grade ten, a girl called Carolann Pfister got her certificate for typing one hundred words per minute. Annie, who'd been pleased with her own sixty words per minute, had wondered for the first time if she might be missing something. In the end, she'd simply put it from her mind. She remembers Miss Marshall looking at her sometimes – with reproach or maybe just disappointment.

She sees that being the best was never her mission. Being independent was never her mission. She has lived a life of cautious avoidance, using her few skills and her marriage to Charles to plot a course of safety and withdrawal.

Something else was going on inside her all that time and is still going on. Even now, after the years of high school and university, she finds it hard to put words to it, because it doesn't fit into any of the subjects she had to learn. But her education has at least given her words to approach what is going on. *Intuitive. Anarchic. Volatile. Inarticulate. Subversive.*

The woman who must be Miss Marshall happens to look out the window. When she sees Annie, her whole body seems to fuse with aggression. Nobody is allowed to disrupt her classes by any means. Annie finds herself slinking away, obscurely hurt that Miss Marshall is dismissing her as a common nuisance.

She stops by an iron statue of Winston Churchill, out of sight of the school and the militant Miss Marshall. Created by a post-war metalworking class, it bears the names of the school's World War II dead, names that were represented among her fellow students. Without warning, Annie feels her arm jerked behind her back, a hand grab her breast, hard. She hears something breathing behind her.

"Gimme your purse, you whore." It's a male voice. He twists her arm, turning her body so she can see his face. It's only a teenage boy, she thinks. But he has a pinched red face, pumped up with hatred and something like lust.

"What?" she says.

He pulls at the strap of her purse, which is worn over her shoulder. Her wallet and credit cards are in it, and the keys to her house. Without thinking, she hangs on to the strap. The boy lets go of her and yanks at it.

"Hey!" a sharp male voice calls. She hears running footsteps. The boy lets go of the purse and tears off down the street. Annie feels herself sinking into the sidewalk and almost immediately being helped to sit up by a man in jeans and a windbreaker.

"Are you all right?" he keeps asking. He helps her sit on the base of the statue. "Damned punk," he says. "Broad daylight too. I don't know what this town's coming to."

He insists on helping her walk back to the school, takes her to the office where they sit her down in the same waiting room where she used to sit when they sent her to the principal for some infraction of the rules. Annie starts to shake. The school secretary brings hot, strong tea. The principal calls the police, who arrive within minutes. She describes the boy to a russet-haired young policeman and his woman partner, but it sounds vague even to her. This can't be happening in Riverbend, she thinks. But it's not true. It can happen anywhere.

The principal, Mr. Eggerton his name is, drives her home through streets so calm she can hardly believe any of it happened. Except, her breast hurts, and she won-ders if that can do any damage. Didn't Charles do an item once about trauma and breast cancer? And what's happening inside her, as the harsh chemicals generated by fear circulate through her blood to the baby? The baby. She definitely thinks of it now as the baby.

Mr. Eggerton drops her off and drives away. Standing on her own walk, she hesitates, as if wanting proof the house harbours no intruder. Near the front step, she sees green shoots pushing through the soil. They must have been doing this for some time, judging by the size of them. Tulips. Irises. Spiky, thrusting. Deep green insis-tent beings shoving their way into the light. Why is it so easy for them and so hard for people? If only the right moves could be programmed into people; instinctive, powerful, unquestioned.

ANNIE SITS IN THE WING CHAIR, exhausted now that the adrenalin has ebbed away, her muscles aching. Oddly, she can now see the boy's face clearly. She tries to tell herself that she's safe now, that she's home. After a while, being in the house she has made her own has a calming effect; her breathing becomes slow and regular. Her body relaxes and passes into sleep. She wakes up some time in the afternoon, feeling restored to herself and ravenously hungry.

Over toast and baked beans, Annie watches a local television news bulletin. Spring runoff pours into the river, which has reached its highest level in fifteen years and is still rising. There's been too much snow the past winter, and it's melting too quickly. People are down in the valley filling burlap bags with sand and passing them to others standing in a long line. The last people in the line lay the bags along a dike.

Annie recognizes the place all this urgent activity is going on: in the valley, down the banks from her house, on the other side of the river. On Harold Borebank's acreage. Annie wonders how high the water can rise. Surely it can't ever fill the valley, can't ever reach her own house? But just as surely it will reach Harold's – and all the other places in the valley – unless it's stopped.

SHE FINDS A SPOT in the middle of the human chain; she neither has to fill the bags nor place them on the dike, she only has to move them along from one set of hands to another. She notices Tom Bradley, the man who makes the model houses, working further down the line. From time to time, she glances towards the dike, but of course there's no visible difference in it. After a while the dike begins to feel like an assembly line – but a voluntary line, operating with a shared purpose. Her arms ache.

"You look like you've had enough." Harold has come up behind her.

"I'm fine," Annie says, but suddenly realizes her strength is almost gone.

Without a word, Harold picks off Annie's oncoming bag and hands it to the next person in one smooth movement. Annie is no longer in the line. The sand-bagger army.

"Get some rest," Harold says. "You can always come back tomorrow."

"All right," Annie agrees. She would normally be offended, but he's right. It's only that she hadn't wanted to seem like a deserter. But the line has already absorbed her replacement. For the moment, nobody needs her.

It takes all she's got to get back up the hill, in her front door – this time without a moment's thought about intruders – and onto the closest available bed, Maisie and Phillip's. The boy's face flickers across her sight, and the doctor's and the women's in the clinic; she sees the strikers marching up and down in front of the plant, like wolves in a zoo, pacing out the limits of their enclosure.

Annie hasn't lived in Riverbend since she was eighteen years old. She's never been an adult member of this community, but today she wants to know she's made some sort of contribution. As she falls asleep she asks herself: "I have done something useful, haven't I?"

## CHAPTER TWENTY

She pulls down the blinds to the windows that overlook the verandah. I move to one side of the bed and she moves into that space beside me. The head of the bed is cranked up to make a back rest.

It makes me sad to look at her. She has lines now at the corners of her mouth and is surely too thin – I seem to see the bones under her blue crepe dress – which is a texture and colour that revolts me. I dare not say so – for she has worn it for me. Once I said, Wear colours, please, we don't see enough colours here. Now there is no way to tell her how I hate this colour. It has too much grey – it pulls my spirit down – this cheap artificial silk. The colour makes her skin look yellow. As if she were the sick one – while my cheek has the rosy glow of fever.

She lays her head against my shoulder – my
fallen shoulder – carefully so as not to hurt me.
She can't know how tired I am – how the sheet
lies like a weight on my skin. She touches my
cheek, she runs her fingers through my hair.
Her hair and eyes are still beautiful enough to
lift my mind for a moment. Her eyes are a sort
of amber colour and her hair is a dark slightly
tarnished gold – like brass – pulled back in a
single braid. She undoes the braid and pulls the
strands free to hang upon her shoulders. That is
a sight I never tire of seeing.

I touch her face and then her shoulder and
she presses closer – but always careful to place
no weight upon my chest. I let my hand slide
along until I stoke her breast – through the
crepe blouse – even against the resistance of
this wretched cloth with its tiny blisters and
muddied blue. Weariness burns through me
like flame – as passion for her body used to
burn.

No one will come in, will they? This is what
she asks every time. And every time I tell her,
No love, they will not come in. I want to give
her whatever love I can. Because of me, she has
had to sell our farm and go to the city and work
at the Woolworth's store – on her feet all the
day long. She has got the children ready and
come to see me on her one day off. I am such a

shameful failure – but I must not fail her now.

I make my fingers move faster. I reach into the opening of her blouse and under her brassiere where I feel for the small brown nipple. She would not want me to say it but this is what I do. She likes me to hold the tip with my fingers and roll it gently back and forth. She doesn't know how difficult it is. I wish she could kiss me on the lips – but we must never do that.

I know where she wishes me to touch next. She must never ask – it must be something I want. The priest has told her it is right to yield to your husband's desires. She has now made this her rule – but I know there was a time when there were no such rules between my Maudie and me. I move my hand lower – to touch the place between her legs that gives her so much pleasure. It is all I can do for her now.

Every time I wonder – does she sometimes do this herself those long evenings alone? She must do so – I cannot bear that this should be all there is for her. I want to ask her – but I can almost see the fear and shame in her face if I should do so. Perhaps she would even lie – because it would be yielding not to her husband's lawful desires but to her own unlawful ones. The flesh is for procreation. The man is the head of the household. That is what they teach.

Sometimes I think I am a fool – to believe

she is always alone – that she never has a man
in for the night. But then I feel ashamed and
truly a fool. For if Maude takes other men to
her bed – why should she come to me for this?

I reach beneath her skirt. I stroke her belly
and thigh. I move my hand to the place she
wants to be touched – I feel her legs tighten.
Dear Jesus – does she not understand how tired
I am? She breathes more deeply and her hips
twist – and for a moment something happens
in my own body.

Annie feels again the flush of desire that came over
her in the room at the sanatorium. She wonders if it's
wrong to listen in on this man's thoughts and feelings.
But she can't stop until she reaches whatever end his
story will have.

My cock seldom grows erect now – except
sometimes as I wake from sleep – or when I
read poems filled with passion for the beauty of
the natural world – and the beauty of desire
itself. Ah, Sun-flower, who countest the steps
of the sun. Once I surprised myself when Nurse
Willet rubbed my back – it came unexpectedly
to life and I felt so foolish – because she would
see it when she turned me. But she passed it off
as a joke as nurses must learn to do. She said,
Now, now, we mustn't overtire ourselves, must

we? That wilted it quick enough – and I felt disgusted at something so useless. It terrifies me how sometimes those feelings turn in me to shame and disgust. This I know must not be – and I wish I could tell Maude that it is all right to touch herself – no, it is more than all right – it is good. The church is surely wrong about this.

I remember Confession when I was a boy and the priest whispering, You must not – it is a sin. And I believed him – but I also believed that if I should suddenly die some day unconfessed I would go straight to hell – because I knew I was not going to stop. Now I will not believe such tales – for if I did I think I would become a crazy man.

Lying here day after day I must at least try to see clearly. Does the priest never wake with a hard cock – never stroke it even for a moment – never go off in his sleep – never so much as touch himself when he passes his water? Surely these things must sometimes happen. I am a man – I know what a man is. Now according to what they have always told us, the best a priest can manage is that he will always be on guard against himself – always trying not to touch himself there – always guilty if it gives him pleasure when he does. Such thoughts would drive me mad. They are against nature. I do not believe God made us as we are as a cruel game. I believe he meant us to know pleasure. I believe it is good.

This is what I must tell Maude. It is all right to love yourself. Don't be afraid. When I begin to speak of it she looks afraid – as if she believes I will hurt her. But I will tell her soon. I must tell her.

The page ends and, when Annie flips it over, she finds the next part is about something totally unrelated and is filled with loss. She wants him to go on, this great-grandfather who is younger than herself. She is thrilled by his desire to work things out for himself, his determination not to be stopped by what he has been taught; but she is afraid to know the outcome, afraid he will not succeed with Maude and the children. More than afraid, because she has seen the evidence.

Annie reads the next few pages. They describe his latest talks with Dr. Nugent, who besides being a physician and the head of the sanatorium, seems to be an ardent amateur botanist. They have been discussing prairie plants. Native grasses with roots over six feet long that can reach water even in a dry year. The cactus on the hillside, a succulent that stores its own water supply in its heavy prickly leaves. Dr. Nugent has brought in a specimen and Eamon has drawn a lovely pen-and-ink drawing, all neatly labelled, with the note that in the desert a person may survive on the water from cactus leaves. A drawing in cross-section shows a single drop of water along the cut edge. Farther along Annie discovers more drawings. Western red lily. Purple coneflower. Yarrow.

Then there's a passage about the death of Jimmy, the boy in the next bed, who turns out not to have been a veteran at all, which isn't surprising since he was only sixteen years old – but the Veterans' Pavilion was the only one with a bed open when he was brought in. It's clear from the way Eamon's words skirt around it that the boy's death is deeply shocking. His tone becomes increasingly pessimistic. She can hardly bear to read the words.

> I must tell Maudie she is to divorce me and forget me. This will give her at least the chance of meeting someone who can care for her properly – and be a true man to her and a father to the children. I am sure they have mainly forgotten me by now – so it will be all the same to them – only it will be better because they need someone with them.
>
> I have tried Confession. It does no good. Father, it does not help. There is no forgiveness. He says, No my son – it's the sickness. You will not always feel this way. But to me this is the true state – those who believe they are either happy or healthy are simply mistaken. The doctors say I caught the sickness in the war – but perhaps it was always there.
>
> I am so damnably useless – worse than no

husband at all. She deserves so much better –
my Maude – my Maude – my darling Maudie.
This is ugly and senseless – only I can put a
stop to it. But how can we divorce? I have
brought her into my church. How can I lead
her out of it? Or perhaps the solution is much
simpler. Perhaps I am going to die in this place.

No, you won't die, Annie wants to tell him. Don't
give up.

Annie imagines the face of Vi Tripps watching her
and knows she must stop reading. She plans to read
through to the end, but she's being more careful now.
Keeping her distance, taking it slow. She refuses to
dream his dreams.

THE DOORBELL RINGS. Annie hesitates, again feeling anxiety about what might be on the other side.
She makes herself open it. It's a woman, a dark-
skinned black woman in her forties, plainly dressed in
a yellow blouse and navy-blue slacks. She looks tired
but determined. She's the woman from the picket
line, the one who sang.

"Yes?" Annie says. What can this woman want with
her?

"You're Annie Ransome?" the woman asks.

"Yes," Annie says, surprised. "What can I do for you?"

"I'm Doreen Waters," the woman says. "The children's mother. Well, stepmother, actually." Annie looks totally confused. "You know – Wilson and DeLinda." Annie feels a rush of guilt and confusion. "Look, I need to talk to you. May I come in?"

"All right," Annie says, stepping back to let the woman pass. "I mean, yes, certainly, come in."

Doreen Waters follows her in and looks around the living room, plainly taking note of the pink chair. Amid a wave of negative feelings – anger, betrayal, guilt – Annie remembers her manners.

"Will you have a seat?" she says.

"Thank you." Passing by the pink chair, the woman sits in one of the tapestry wing chairs. Annie also avoids the pink brocade, settling herself in the matching wing chair.

"I may as well get right to the point," Doreen Waters says. "I've come about that damned chair. The one you gave the kids. I assume that's it there." She nods at the pink chair. "How is it you have it again, by the way?" Annie is a little amazed at the woman's direct manner, as if Annie is bound to answer her questions.

"I was in a second-hand furniture store," Annie says. "I'd realized I was sorry I'd given it away, and I was looking for a replacement."

"And there it was, staring you right in the face."

"That's right, it was. I was more than a little surprised," Annie says, hating the note of self-righteousness that slips into her voice.

"Naturally you assumed they cashed it in for a few

lousy bucks." The woman looks at her inquiringly.

Annie feels the ground shifting under her, or maybe it's been shifting since this woman entered the house. She suddenly wonders if there's some other obvious explanation why the chair was in that store. Something any other reasonable person would have guessed at once.

"Well, yes, I did," she admits. "And after they'd told me how much they liked it."

"They did like it," Doreen says. "They loved it."

"So why did they sell it?" Annie asks. Surely Doreen must admit that she had a right to be annoyed.

"They didn't, of course," Doreen says. "They would never do that. I'm surprised you could ever have thought that."

"Well," Annie says, wanting to defend herself, "What was I supposed to think?"

"Look, what you need to know is, their dad's a complete jerk. I'll tell you that for free, and it took me four years to find out for sure. That's how long I've been married to the guy. Since a year after the kids' mother died. Do I look stupid to you?" Annie looks embarrassed for a second until she realizes no answer is expected. "Well, I didn't think so either, but apparently I am, because I fell for this guy, but no more, believe me, the guy is out for good." The woman stops momentarily for breath, but Annie can't think of anything to say. She's never met anyone this candid before.

Doreen gets up and goes to the window. "Sorry," she says, "I don't normally go on like this, but I'm trying to get it over with, quick as I can. The point is, they bring this chair home and I'm at work and he gets it in his head, into his tiny, over-excited, under-developed brain, that it's this priceless antique. I could've told him different, but as I said, I wasn't there. And he starts seeing all the great stuff he could buy with it, such as beer and dirty magazines, so he waits till they're at school and he sells the thing."

Doreen stops for a moment to get control of her anger. Annie wants to hang her head like a bad dog. She has made the kids feel terrible and it wasn't their fault at all.

"He wouldn't tell me what he'd done with it," Doreen continues. "He made out like some people from out of town had bought it. And I was dumb enough to believe that too.

"So then they were afraid to come around here, because they thought you'd find out and you'd blame them. Then they did come one day and you had the chair back, and they could see you thought they sold it. And they didn't think you'd ever believe any different."

"I'm so sorry," Annie says. "But how could I know?"

"I suppose you couldn't *know*," Doreen says. "But look, everything about Wilson and DeLinda tells you they're good kids. So you decide to trust them. And then you see something makes you think they betrayed you. And you feel like a fool for trusting them. What it boils down to is, you stopped trusting your own instincts."

"I did feel hurt," Annie says. "I thought they'd tricked me."

"They said you'd taken their pictures off the Queen Anne desk," Doreen says. "That was just about the end for them."

"Oh, no!" Annie remembers their pride at seeing the pictures on the desk. "How can I make it up to them?"

"I've got a couple of ideas about that." Doreen comes back from the window and this time slips naturally into the pink chair, gives a little pat to one of its arms. "I was thinking, there's nothing bigger in their minds than those tea parties they used to have with your grandma, and of course with you."

"Of course! I could give them a tea." Annie hesitates. "If you think they'd come."

"I was thinking more like we'd give you a tea party. The point being, they could give you something for a change. I could just manage it this Saturday. Can you come?"

"It's going to be hard facing them now."

"Yeah, but that'll pass pretty quickly. Then you'll all feel a lot better. So can I count on you? Three o'clock sharp, and you have to dress fancy." Doreen's eyes crinkle at the corners when she smiles. "Sort of like the queen, only don't expect us to curtsey. Okay?"

"I'll be there," Annie says.

"Great," Doreen says. She looks much more relaxed now that she's got things settled. "Here's where come." She hands Annie a scrap of paper with an address on Orinoco Street written on it. "Our visiting card," she says, amused. "Well, I have to get going, they'll be home for lunch, and I want to get them fed before I head off to the picket line."

"I saw you the other day. It looks like hard work."

"Bloody waste of time. They're sure to close it down one of these years no matter what we do, but what the hell, sometimes you have to fight, eh?" Doreen moves to the door.

"I guess you do," Annie says. She remembers what Doreen said about the children's father. "Did you say their father's gone for good?"

"I sure did. I sent him packing." Doreen laughs. "I've got this brother, Frank, he's a huge guy and real quiet, the kind of quiet makes you think he's brooding on doing something to you. Now Frank wouldn't hurt a fly, but Rance never understood that. Funny name, eh? Sounds like rancid fat. He was fat too, although that was one of his good qualities."

Annie laughs.

"So I had Frank talk to him. He explained that Rance shouldn't come around anymore, or he'd take it very personal. Nothing threatening or anything, just really quiet and reasonable. Of course Rance wouldn't know how to interpret that. He couldn't imagine being big and not using it against people. Anyway, we haven't seen the guy since, and nobody misses him."

"Couldn't he get custody of the children if he wanted?" Annie asks.

"He'd have a fight on his hands," Doreen says, and her voice gets really hard. "I adopted them soon after we were married. Let him think he was talking me into it. Anyway, I don't think he'll bother. He wouldn't know how to look after them on his own."

She gets up. "You really have done a lot with this place. I don't know if Maisie'd be pleased, but I was always bumping into stuff before."

"So you used to visit too?" Annie asks.

"Oh, yes, we'd have our little tea-fests now and then. I got to really enjoy it."

"I wish I could have seen that," Annie says. "She was always so stiff with me."

"Some people are like that, aren't they? Better with strangers than their own family." Annie considers the possibility. "Are you surprised she'd ask a black woman to tea?"

"A little," Annie admits. "Knowing Maisie."

"She was too, I think," Doreen says. "But she liked the kids, so that made it easier for her. And I think she was kind of pleased with herself. Like she'd stepped out of her rut. Well, I've seen it lots of times. It's a bit of a bore, but what the heck, if I can contribute to anybody's consciousness raising, I'm only too willing."

"She probably never saw a black person when she was growing up here," Annie says, feeling some obscure obligation to defend Maisie.

"Oh, I think she did," Doreen says. "My dad was a railway porter and they used to stop over here in Riverbend between runs. They weren't welcome in the cafés or the beer parlours, so what they did was go for walks around River Heights. My husband too, my first husband, I mean, was a porter."

"Did you come up from the States?" Annie asks.

"Oh God," Doreen says, her face caught between pain and amusement, "if I had a dollar for every time I've heard that question. No, my people are from Alberta. Amber Valley. They came there from Alabama nearly a hundred years ago. The whole pioneer bit, believe me."

"I'm sorry," Annie says, feeling stupid.

"Not to worry," Doreen says, "it's par for the course. White people never seem to think a black person could be born here. Well, I must be off. I'll see you Saturday."

"Wait a moment," Annie says. "I don't know what to do. Should I give them the chair again?"

Doreen considers. "It's been done and then undone. Better leave it at that."

"I suppose you're right."

"You could always give them some other little thing later when this is all blown over, but I think the chair should stay with the house."

Annie realizes there is one thing she can do now to help set things right. She gets the photographs of the children out of the drawer, gives them a quick dust against her shirt, and puts them back on the desk.

"That's nice," Doreen says. "I'll tell them."

"Thanks for coming," Annie says, realizing how much she's starting to like Doreen.

"Well, I did it for the kids. But it's good to meet you."

"You too. Good luck with your strike."

"Thanks." Doreen shakes her head. "But we need a miracle."

Doreen takes a last look around the room and then she's out the door. Annie watches her stride off down the street. Doreen's visit has eased something in her, and she feels the desire to return to Eamon's story. She's sure she can handle it now. And after all, she knows how it comes out. It's not as though he doesn't go on to become the Chief Horticulturist. And to live longer than anyone ever expected him to.

ANNIE GATHERS THE PILE OF PAPERS and carries them to the kitchen table. She brews fresh tea and sorts through to where she left off. Another gap in the narrative occurs, filled with terse descriptions of doctor's visits and of a gradually worsening left lung. Eamon's sense of despair works its way off the page and into the air of the room. The very handwriting is more jagged and heedless, as if there's no importance to the way it looks. As if he doesn't expect to come back and read these pages again. She doesn't let herself do more than skim these parts.

And then a passage reaches out and demands her full attention – a section done in a very careful hand, as if he's written it at a leisurely pace, in retrospect. Or maybe he's rewritten or at least recopied it.

Maude was with me again last Sunday – having left the children outdoors at their usual task of climbing the hill. No one has yet been brought in to take the boy's bed – so we were able to be alone in the room without the usual pretences. And as so many times before Maude sat by me on the bed. I have to admit that for some time a despair had been on me – which I had no real thought of getting the better of. I knew that I had been happy once – when Maude Rowan was young and upright and the life in her strong as the magical tree her name recalled. Now I could no longer feel that happiness – and did not expect to again. But as before I was resolved at least to attempt to give her pleasure.

Suddenly another face was there beside hers – and almost as real. A young man with hair and skin that were the spit of hers. I knew him at once – he was Douglas Bonnycastle – a young man I served with in the war. He was killed one day by a sniper's bullet – as the two of us moved between foxholes – a bright cold day when everything had been quiet for hours – and we must have convinced ourselves they had all gone away. The boy turned to me with a look of disbelief – wanting me to unmake the day or the bullet or the ridiculous mistake of his being in its way. As if I must surely have

the power to do this. Then he fell in my arms –
I had to drag him the rest of the way to safety –
although I would rather have left him and run
– and although he was now beyond safety. His
blood was on my hands that day and for a long
time afterwards.

His face slowly faded away again – leaving
only Maude beside me. My hand had found the
way to the entrance to the most hidden, the
most female part of her – without my conscious
thought. And then she moved to my touch. I
felt her warm slippery moisture on my fingers.
And a kind of miracle began – although not
one the priest would recognize. I felt my hand
grow warm and tingling as if filled with some
kind of electrical power. This power moved up
my arm and flowed down my chest and lungs
and thence down to my legs. It was a warming
and vital power – flowing into every part of my
body and every drop of my blood.

Once again I saw my Maude as beautiful
and her skin tinged with rosy life. My fingers
moved and entered that warm and moist place
that had a power for me like the sun's. It
seemed to me as if joy was at that moment
invented for me and for her.

I was filled with amazement. How could I
have thought of dying? If I could but manage
to live I might have this feeling again and

again. Perhaps this is what my Maudie has been trying to show me all these months. For the first time in a very long time I began to think I might get well again. She felt the change in me. She pressed closer to me. She did not ask, Will anyone come?

Suddenly there came a confusion of voices in the corridor – and a racket of feet pounding along the wooden floor. We heard Nurse Willet's sharp call – No, children, no! Then Maude was on her feet – pulling down her skirt as the door swung open.

Robbie and Maisie, my dear children, burst into the room – out of breath from running and hot from the sun. Their lips and tongues were stained purple – they held something fast in their tightly closed fists. For a moment Willet was silent – deciding I suppose to let them have their moment now the damage was done.

The children were suddenly shy and solemn. Maisie said, Hello Father. Are you feeling better? I thanked her and told her I was. And the boy held out his hands to show crushed saskatoon berries – his eyes with their intense blue colour never left my face. I shall never forget his voice. We brought you saskatoons. Because you couldn't go up the hill. I thanked him and promised to eat them later.

Now Willet moved to clear them from the room but not before they emptied their hands of the sweet burden onto Maudie's handkerchief. Not before they left something of the open air and the sun on the hillside in that room – and forced back the walls holding me there.

I held my Maudie's hand. I told her how beautiful the children were and herself too. I told her I believed I might get well – and leave this place and live with them again. There is so much more I wanted to say – but cannot yet. Will I ever be able to explain it all? About the books I have read – and the thoughts I have about so many things – and the new way I would like to live. That place the poet imagined –

> Where the Youth pined away with desire,
> And the pale Virgin shrouded in snow,
> Arise from their graves, and aspire
> Where my Sun-flower wishes to go.

Annie longs to be there with him, to let him know that someone else understood. She knows him so well, although he can never know her. This must have been his moment of greatest joy and triumph. And he did get well and come home to them all. He spent a lifetime working with plants out in the sun. So much is explained now.

But not what happened to the children.

CHAPTER TWENTY-ONE

May 15th is Charles's birthday and one of Annie's working days at Al's Second Hand, a gorgeous warm day of soft golden sun. Al surprises her by closing the store for the afternoon so they can go and work on the dike, temporarily leaving the citizens of Riverbend without access to quality used furnishings. They drive down in his lumbering old '57 Chrysler, a perfectly preserved gas-inhaling remnant from the days when a man's worth was measured by the size and splendour of his car's fins. On the way, he stops at an ice cream stand and treats them both to double-decker Dutch chocolate cones. It feels like a holiday.

When they reach the valley, Al, who worked as a bricklayer as a young man, joins the line as a dike builder; Annie finds her usual place in the middle of the line. Soon she's absorbed in the physical motion, enjoying the growing strength in her muscles; she likes being aware of her surroundings but not really having to think. Charles, the baby growing inside her, Edith, the two children, and all the other people both living and dead who have been demanding her attention, are all comfortably remote as she works, distant planets in her personal solar system.

Today she has the delicious feeling of doing something plain and useful and finding herself more than up to the task. She sees people she's worked with here before. Teenage boys, Tony and Greg, who've skipped out of school, and who seem as friendly and harmless as the boy who attacked her was hostile and malignant, showing off their muscles in cut-offs and sleeveless T-shirts. Two old men in dark pants and shirts. Reverend Bunting, looking surprisingly athletic in a track suit. A couple of middle-aged women she remembers from the picket line. Harold is here filling sandbags and Donnie is off school helping him. Tom Bradley is here again, working near Harold.

On the other side of the dike, the water moves faster than the day before, bearing along twigs and other debris at a startling rate. Annie finds her eyes pulled to the river, to its immense power. She imagines herself in the water, helpless against its indiscriminate violence, and has to force herself to look away.

The dike still seems not to have risen, but this is because the river has kept pace with their efforts. In fact it's done more than keep pace, it's gained on them. Nobody mentions this, but she can feel that everyone's trying to work a little faster. Because they've all been listening to the radio. The prediction is, the crest will be eighteen inches above the present height of the dike. They expect it to come in the late hours of Sunday night. Today is Friday. Just over two days left to prepare.

Annie avoids the television crews wandering around disrupting the line and asking people what working on the dike means to them.

Mid-afternoon a group of "volunteers" is trucked in from the army base, fit young men who are given their orders and immediately begin to infiltrate the line from beginning to end. Annie again finds herself displaced and turns to see Harold approaching her.

"Time for a break," he says. "Let the kids take over for a while."

In the area behind the workers, which used to be Harold's cornfield and has now become a makeshift parking lot, a miracle of sorts is taking place. Annie stops to watch as a venerable grey Cadillac pulls up and Edith, in a sporty periwinkle blue corduroy dress, gets out. She pulls a couple of card tables out of the trunk and sets them up. Reverend Bunting hurries over to help as she throws a large flowered tablecloth over the tables, creating one long surface, and places on it plates of sandwiches, urns of coffee, pots of tea. Assorted dainties. Wow, Annie thinks, Edith's brought real china plates, cups, saucers, there's not so much as a crumb of styrofoam in sight. Spoons are real silver. People approach eagerly, heaping sandwiches onto plates as

Edith pours them cups of tea or coffee. "One lump or two?" Annie can almost imagine her saying.

Annie realizes how tired she is and thinks of joining the queue, at the front of which Tom Bradley is this moment receiving the sacrament of tea, when Harold touches her arm.

"Let's get out of here for a while." When Annie hesitates, he adds, "We could have a bite at Swing Inn. I just have to corral Donnie. Okay?"

Sure, why not? Annie thinks. She nods, and Harold goes to get the boy. She watches them talk. There's a change in Harold. He seems younger, more purposeful. His face has more colour, his eyes and lips seem more distinct, more firmly outlined. As if he's been dragged out of the lethargy of his grief. Donnie looks up for a moment, but his body language says it all. He won't leave the line. Harold shrugs and leaves him to it. For a second, Annie considers changing her mind, but doesn't like to renege.

Harold's car is at the house, less than a quarter mile away. Charlie is in the paddock and comes trotting over to be patted by Annie. Again she enjoys the touch of his coarse hair, the energy of another kind of life. She remembers Donnie's offer to teach her to ride.

When they reach Harold's station wagon, she stops and looks back at the dike. For the first time she understands in her bones how vulnerable this place is and always has been. She gets in the car beside Harold. They don't talk much in the car.

Swing Inn has come to brilliant life since Annie's previous visit. Poplar and birch emit small leaves of an amazing brilliant green. Each one looks freshly cut out, painted, and lacquered. A tall poplar makes her think of green flame shooting into the sky.

They sit on the patio, the air soft on their faces, and eat bacon and tomato sandwiches on toasted bread with chocolate ice cream sodas. Things kids ate on dates in Riverbend when Annie was a teenager. Annie feels uncomfortable. Is this turning into a date? she wonders. But the moment fixes her with its beauty; time and the speeding torrents of water seem momentarily suspended. The sun on their faces is tempered by the filtering leaves. It feels like a tiny pocket of Eden.

The river's high here too, halfway up the hill on which Swing Inn is built. The rental canoes have been lifted out of the racing brown water and turned over on the ground.

"Sylvie and I used to rent canoes down here on weekends," Harold says. "That's where we did our serious courting."

"I didn't know that," Annie says. Of course, she hadn't wanted to know.

"We used to sing. 'Cruisin' down the River.' 'Oh Shenandoah.' Every song we could think of with a river in it. I asked her to marry me right out in the middle of the river, only a few hundred yards downstream of this place. She said yes, and we came back here and had hamburgers. I had Double Cheese and she had a Mushroom Burger."

Annie watches him closely, half afraid he might break down the way he did before. Up close, his face has the same vividness she noticed when he was speaking to Donnie. His blue-grey eyes seem to have more colour than before. She catches a faint scent of crabapple trees somewhere near by, just beginning their annual flowering.

"I can talk about it now," he says, although there are tears in his eyes. "That's because you're here. It's helping me understand things better. I feel like I'm coming alive again and you're part of it."

"Because I was her friend?" Annie tries to steer the conversation in what she hopes are safe directions.

"We both had somebody die, but we're still alive. I think I've finally stopped feeling guilty about that." Annie turns away from him. The scent of crabapple is intoxicating. "What about you?"

"I don't think so. Not yet." Slow down, Harold, she thinks.

"I'm healthy, I have a wonderful kid, I have money for us to live on. I don't want to betray Sylvie, but I'm glad to be alive. I'm glad to be here right now with you." Annie feels herself pulling back from him. "That's not only because I feel drawn to you, because I realize you probably don't feel drawn to me in the same way. But it feels good to be with you."

So matter of fact, so unassuming. The one pickup line in the world that could work with Annie, and he knows it by heart, by instinct. She sees how Sylvie must have fallen for him. Just love me now, his eyes say, and I wouldn't ask another thing of you. Although he'd try, of course he would. He reaches out and touches her hand, and it's warm, like sun. If she wants to stop this, she should do something now. Robins sing in the poplar, very near. Harold leans across the table and kisses her on the lips. Not demanding, but definitely inquiring, warm and so very pleasant that she finds herself kissing back. The kiss calls up desire in her like the current in a river and she can immediately see a whole possible relationship unfolding with this man. She sees a blurry version of Charles's face, his lips moving, admonishing her, but her own voice overrides his. You never gave me this, it says, and I have a right to it. Harold looks at her, questioningly. She wants to kiss him again and again. What am I doing? she thinks. The place is enchanted, it must be. She wasn't planning anything like this. Was she?

The young waitress is placing the bill on the table. Harold grabs it before she can move a muscle, reaches for his wallet.

"We'd better go," he says.

"Yes," she agrees.

The ride to Harold's house takes what feels like about ten seconds flat. She is aware of his glance, questioning, her silent confirmation that he hasn't made a mistake, this is what she really wants, what she's really planning to do. Then they're in the yard, parking under the poplar trees. The river is so close, but for now the dike will protect them.

She loses her courage as she enters Harold and Sylvie's house for the first time, a house full of dark-toned woods and old brick, impressed with their life together. It brings tears to her eyes, makes Sylvie's death real at last. How can she intrude here? Does Harold think she's the only one who can? Because she and Sylvie were so close? Does he think he can get something of Sylvie back that way? That would be sick. Wouldn't it?

He sees her hesitation. He looks at her with desire that is surely for her alone. She pushes back the negative thoughts, moves into the house. It's warm and has a more lived-in feel than her own house, which is only inhabited by herself and a pack of ghosts.

She looks into the bedroom, panelled in rough cedar and warmed by a free-standing cast iron stove, now sitting cold. It looks like a secret clearing deep in the woods. The bed is king-sized. She can't help seeing Harold and Sylvie in it, making love in front of a crackling fire. Sylvie, her best friend, and this man.

"Please," he says, "it's you I want now." He holds out his hand and she takes it; they go into the bedroom. They pull off their clothes and lie pressed together on top of the bed. Nobody needs any foreplay. She feels her body warming, opening to him. She loves the way her body moves in the warm air as her arms go around him, as if she's swimming in a warm pool. His penis is hard against her belly, his nipples tense against hers.

When he enters her, Annie starts to cry. Not grief,

but something else. She has enjoyed sex before, has had orgasms before, hundreds, maybe thousands of them, but it's never felt like this. This is her body, the same one she's always had, but it's never felt so capable, so functional, so finely tuned. When he moves in her, she wants to laugh out loud at the wonder of it. She doesn't have to ask him to do it again, he does it again. And again. She only hopes he can wait for her, although he won't have to wait long.

"Annie," he says, "Annie." A part of her brain registers the fact that he's said her name, not Sylvie's. It doesn't matter, because Sylvie's with them all the same. Annie is herself and Sylvie too, Sylvie who held her on the night by the river. Annie misses her terribly, wants in turn to hold Sylvie and take away her pain. But the pain is all over for Sylvie, and it's only those who stayed behind who mind now. Harold moves in her, and they are both so hard and yet so silky smooth.

Annie comes first and then in seconds feels the tension burst in him, feels him pulse with pleasure, as she takes deep gusts of air into her lungs.

Afterwards he cries in her arms, kissing her lips, her cheeks, her breasts, as if to make up for some earlier omission, or to stake some sort of claim while she's still there willingly in his bed.

"Thank you," she says to forestall him. "Thank you for giving me this."

He doesn't even try to speak. She is grateful to him for not trying to draw conclusions or ask questions she can't answer. After a while she gets dressed.

"I'm going back to the dike," she says. She folds the quilt from her side of the bed over to cover him. "Bye, Harold," she says.

"Goodbye, Annie." He watches her out of the room.

Annie leaves the house and heads across the field. Back at the dike, Edith is gathering heaps of dirty plates into boxes and stashing them in her car.

"Like a hand with all these dishes?" Annie asks.

"That would be very helpful," Edith says. "If you're finished your business with Harold Borebank."

"I am."

"He seems to be taking quite an interest," Edith says.

"I'm as free as a bird," Annie says. And she is, at least for now.

"Come along then." And Annie hops into the driver's seat of the Caddy, where Edith has left the keys in the ignition.


BACK IN EDITH'S KITCHEN, Edith washes, hands almost fluorescent in yellow rubber gloves, and Annie dries. Annie offers to wash, but Edith explains that the heat is actually good for her hands. With remarkable speed, she piles up rinsed and steaming dishes. She has supplied Annie with a mound of freshly ironed linen tea towels.

Edith has something on her mind. She pitches right in, under cover of dishwashing.

"I know you thought I was an old busybody, wanting to have the reception for Allison's funeral."

You're damn right, Annie thinks of firing back at her. Only she can't keep that sort of thing going these days. Can't keep the biting edge she used to have towards Edith.

"I was surprised," she says.

"You were more than surprised," Edith says. "I could read it in your body. 'Edith is butting in. Edith didn't have anything to do with Mother. Edith always tries to take over.'"

"Well," Annie says, without rancour, "I suppose that's a pretty good translation." Edith hands her a delicate cream jug, holding on till she's sure Annie's grasped it firmly. "Jeez, Edith, that's genuine Limoges."

"I'm perfectly aware of that."

"You didn't take that to the river!" Annie now understands something of the value of such pieces.

"Didn't I?" Edith says. "I take pleasure in using my things. You can't hoard them, you know. Those people worked hard. I wanted them to have a nice lunch."

"Well, I'm sure they did."

"Now, regarding Allison." Edith hands Annie a deep blue Wedgwood teapot with a border of grape leaves in white. "It's true I was twenty years her senior, so you would naturally think there could be no connection between us. I thought so once myself, and I found out how wrong I was. It began when she was a child, before she was even in school."

"Right, and she used to come and stare through the rails of your wrought-iron fence at the beautiful garden of Edith Ashdown." Annie feels the edge coming back.

"Ah, she did talk about it, did she? She always wanted this place. My house, my garden. She was always worming her way in. Visiting, she called it. Always trying to play the piano when I wasn't looking."

Annie considers dropping the Limoges sugar bowl in her hand onto the Battleship Linoleum floor, imagines the elegant china shattering into irreparable small pieces.

"Couldn't you ever just let her play – when you *were* looking?" Annie feels a terrible tightness in her chest; she wishes her mother could have had what she wanted.

"Frankly, it never occurred to me," Edith says. "I was caring for my father in what I believe is aptly called a 'final illness.' Only his took twelve years and I had to hold things together all that time. Had to keep control of myself and this place."

"You had to control a little child?"

"Believe me, she wasn't your usual little child. Stubborn, wilful, ruthless, that's what she was. We were like enemies. Crazy as that sounds."

"You can say that again." Annie fires a volley of dried silverware onto the counter.

"Ah, but I paid her the compliment of taking her seriously as an adversary, didn't I? All her energy was bent on getting in and all mine on keeping her out. I was bigger and older, so mostly I won, but sometimes she did."

"What did she want?" Annie asks. "Once she got in."

"Well, of course, to play the piano, that was part of it. But you know, I think she wanted to come and live here. I think she really believed she could make me let her."

"But she wasn't strong enough? This serious adversary?"

"She might have been, ultimately, I suppose. She might have got the better of me, and who knows, she might even have got Maisie and Phillip to go along with it. Except one day she got more than she bargained for. She was always trying to get to the heart of this place, and one day she got her chance."

"Oh?" is all Annie can think to say. She does want to know more, but she hates having to encourage Edith.

"One day she wheedled her way into the garden by offering…no, insisting on, watering my roses. And after she'd almost drowned them, I felt I had to ask her in. I gave her cookies and milk here in the kitchen. In the nook there."

Edith nods towards the blue-tiled nook with its white table top and Delft blue seat cushions. Annie tries to see this stubborn, wilful, ruthless child, in the smocked dress and white boots and socks she wore in her preschool days. She imagines the child's eyes darting here and there in the room and beyond into the living room and the hall. Casing the joint.

Through the living room doorway, the piano, an upright grand, stands in solitary dignity, its case a beautifully polished dark walnut. Allison stares at and into its dark depths, needing to touch it, absorb it into her world. To the child it's not an inanimate object but a living creature waiting for her to awaken it. Annie feels the pain of her longing to touch it.

"You should have let her play that piano, Edith. It was just sitting there."

"Nonsense. The piano was doing my bidding. Which was that it just sit there." Edith drains the dishwater and starts again with fresh hot water and soap.

"God, you were mean." Annie lets the statement drift out between them. This feels so good. Finally, having it out with Edith.

"I wasn't mean. I was an ignorant, frustrated, young woman confronted with a bossy, bloody-minded little girl. And she did not kill herself because I didn't let her play the piano, if that's what you're thinking. Of that I am certain."

"I never said she did," Annie says a trifle smugly. "I was only talking about simple kindness." Edith refuses to be drawn, expertly stacking a flurry of Royal Crown Derby tea plates in the dish drainer, forcing Annie to prompt her. "So what happened that day?"

"I had to go outside for a moment because the pump had stopped. We had this pump to bring water up from the river – for the garden."

"Wasn't there a city bylaw against that?" Annie stacks the tea plates and carries them to the breakfast table, carefully placing them alongside the assorted cups and saucers, dinner plates, cutlery, and Limoges, all waiting to be put away.

"I wouldn't know," Edith answers. "But while I was outside, the little girl who was going to be your mother...Allison...crept stealthily into the living room and began to play on the piano. Or at least that's what she thought she was doing."

"How do you know it was stealthily?"

"I don't. But that's how I see it." Actually, it's how Annie sees it too. "My father, Homer, he was over eighty by then, heard the sounds and called out. Allison went upstairs, to his room. When I came back in, I found her up there, mesmerised by his terrible blue eyes and his wrath like unto the wrath of God, while he railed at her. 'Women are all bitches. You can't trust any of them. And you're another one of them,' he said, 'just like your bitch of a mother.'"

"That's horrible. What on earth was wrong with him?"

"Part of it was probably Alzheimer's disease, although we didn't know about that then. But a lot of it was just him. He was never a kind man, especially after my mother left."

"Then what happened?" Annie prompts.

"I called out her name and told her to go downstairs and wait for me. And then I made her finish the cookies and I made her promise not to tell anyone."

"Edith, how could you?" Edith doesn't answer. "And Maisie, for godsake – why did he call her a bitch? What could Maisie have done to him?"

"Maisie helped my mother run away from my father."

"You must be joking. She was always dead set against divorce."

"Maybe so. But she helped my mother escape from this house. And my brothers went away to university and never lived here again. I nursed Homer until he died. I was thirty years old by then. Your age. I never heard from my mother again, and I never forgave her."

"Oh, Edith." Something like pity or sympathy grabs Annie for a moment. "Maybe she'd died herself."

"And he left the house to Roderick, my older brother, and what was left of his money to my other brother, Arthur."

"But you're still here."

"Yes. I went a little crazy at the time. I made them give it all to me. Which, believe me, they would never have considered of their own accord, although Roderick was a stockbroker in New York and Arthur was a successful corporate lawyer in Toronto."

"Well, good for you," Annie says, although it's hard to say nice things to Edith.

"Yes." Edith can't keep the satisfaction out of her voice.

"Why did your mother leave?" Annie almost adds, "if that's not too personal a question." But she sees it's already way too late to worry about that.

"He thought she was having an affair."

"Was she?"

"Possibly, I was too young to know for sure. But certainly not in the way he imagined. I used to hear them quarrelling at night. He'd accuse her of being with every man they knew, countless times, indiscriminately, without regard for time or place or friendship or his good name. At first I thought it must be true, but over the decade or so I took care of Homer, I had a lot of time to think. I began to realize it couldn't possibly be true."

"It must have been awful. Did you ever talk to anybody about it?"

"I started to a little with Maisie before she died. She told me how Mother would come over to her place and cry. And when she'd come home again, Homer would claim she'd been seen with some man. That made me see it couldn't all be true."

"I can't imagine Maisie as anybody's confidante."

"Not everybody has a choice, you know," Edith says drily.

"I suppose not," Annie says. "Here you are talking to me." Edith looks annoyed. "Did Allison stop coming after that time with Homer?"

"She didn't come as often and she stopped trying to get into the house. I'd see her looking up at his window."

"How terrible it must have been for her. And to lose the piano too."

"Never mind. Maybe she hasn't lost it in the end."

"How do you mean?"

"I mean that I hear her playing all the time. Right now, for instance."

Annie stares at Edith in disbelief. Edith meets her gaze steadily. "What do you mean?" Annie asks.

"Playing the way she did as a child?"

"Well, it's changed, as you'd expect. It's not actual musical pieces, you understand, because of course she never had any lessons, but it's quite rhythmic and expressive. Very percussive at times, very gentle and lyrical at others."

"So what's it mean? Is your guilt making you hear it?"

"Certainly not. I'm perfectly comfortable with her now. I don't mind her playing at all. She plays and plays until she's satisfied."

"Edith? What are you trying to say?"

"I'm *saying* that I feel her presence here all the time. Not in some supernatural, dish-rattling poltergeist way, I just feel she's here with me. And she's welcome, at last. She's a bit like a daughter, a bit like a friend. I enjoy the company."

"I don't know what to say." Annie tries to hide her embarrassment.

"You think I've gone off my rocker, don't you?" Edith asks. "Annie, I'm old. I have enough to live on. Just. I rarely see other people. So I do what pleases me and I believe what pleases me."

"Okay, Edith. That's your business, I guess," Annie says. "Now, you said Mother didn't kill herself because you wouldn't let her play. 'Of that I am sure,' I think you said."

"I'm tired now, Annie. Thank you for all your help." Edith walks into the hall.

"Wait!" Annie says. "You can't stop now!"

"We'll talk about it another time. Let yourself out when you're ready." Edith wafts up the stairs like pale smoke and there's nothing Annie can do to stop her. For the first time Annie sees that arthritis has left her with a slight limp.

Annie remembers that it's Charles's birthday and that she should call him. How can she, after Harold? What would he think if he knew? Is it significant that it happened on Charles's birthday? Surely not, she couldn't know the opportunity would arise. The opportunity. Was that all she was waiting for? Surely not. Surely she never went down to the dike in search of Harold.

When Charles answers the phone, he sounds as if he's been into the Scotch – not drunk, but loose. He doesn't ask when she's coming home. "Annie," he says, "I'm thirty-three years old, and what have I achieved?"

For a moment Annie can't think of anything either.

CHAPTER TWENTY-TWO

She has only the one dress, her funeral dress, with her. That and a trunk full of old things of Maisie's, which no one in their right mind would wear, and even older stuff of Maude Conal's, which is prettier and infinitely better made, but which seems to have an air of sadness about it. Anyway, it's a tea party she's going to, not a costume party. Nothing for it, she'll have to ask Edith for something.

Edith turns out her closet. From what Annie can see, the woman has never got rid of anything she ever owned. Of course she doesn't have to, because she has an enormous closet built down one entire wall of her big front bedroom, with dresses arranged by era and colour. Edith pulls out dress after dress, draping them carelessly across the bed.

What lovely things Edith has chosen – silks, linens, cottons, in every kind of blue from turquoise to cornflower, in green from dark jade to bright emerald, in shades of rose and ruby and garnet and here and there a clear lemon yellow. Edith evaluates them coolly, holding some of them up to Annie's olive complexion or against her dark brown hair.

Annie is amazed to find herself coveting these dresses as she has never coveted clothes before. Of course, you don't have to be able to explain cold fusion, she thinks, to know that the fabric and cut of Edith's things is better than she has ever been able to afford in her entire life. Mind you, Charles is making good money; maybe she only made herself think she couldn't afford them. Because she doesn't see how you could spend money that way when there are people who don't have enough to eat.

While Annie is admiring a gorgeous midnight blue velvet cocktail dress, Edith suddenly makes a decision. The dress she helps Annie into has a flared skirt, button front with a scoop neck, and gathered sleeves to the elbow. The fabric is cream-coloured glazed cotton printed with extravagantly gorgeous periwinkle blue flowers. It fits beautifully, except that it's a little tight from bust to waist. Edith plucks a small metal tool, a seam ripper, from her sewing kit and calmly slashes the darts front and back.

"I expect you'll need maternity things soon," she says. "I could help you with that." Cripes, Annie thinks, she even kept her maternity clothes.

"But you wouldn't want any of my stuff," Edith says.

"Maternity clothes are much better nowadays. We'll get you some of those bright knit things that hug the body – no more trying to conceal it like we did."

Edith is not done; Annie must be accessorized. Edith rummages around in her late twentieth-century shoe and hat sections. Finally Annie is kitted out with off-white flats and a matching handbag and a jaunty straw hat with half-veil to the eyebrows. Very ladylike, and Annie has never felt so complete, at least as to clothing, in her life.

THE CHILDREN ARE PLEASED. They greet her at the door of the run-down row house, washed, combed, and pressed to within an inch of their lives. DeLinda's hair has been left unbraided and combed out in waves. A single daisy has been pinned to the waves. The children wear old-fashioned clothes, which must have been given to them by Maisie, because Annie recognizes them from old photographs of Robbie and Maisie as children. Are they reminding her that they had a place in her grandmother's world before she came barging in? Or are these just their favourite clothes? Doreen wears a pretty printed dress which is a kind of negative image of Annie's – deep cornflower blue ground printed with white flowers.

"Hi, Annie," Wilson says.

"Thank you for coming," says DeLinda. "Please come in." Doreen exchanges a look with Annie, but neither of them smiles.

Annie follows the children into a cramped living room filled with the most amazing mishmash of stuff. Fat overstuffed armchairs, an elaborately carved walnut sideboard, a graceful old pump organ in mahogany, an antique carved oak mantelpiece covered with all manner of things. Elegant china things; tiny clever mechanical things that wind up and move; carved wooden animal things (a zebra, a giraffe, and an elephant); curious small brass and silver things polished to high lustre; and photographs in wood and shell and silver frames of the children and Doreen. On the dark linoleum floor, steam-cleaned into a new lease on life, is Maisie's beige broadloom. With so much to look at, Annie almost forgets she was ever nervous about coming.

"I hope you like our antiques," Wilson says.

"They're very unusual," DeLinda says. "They were handed down to our mother from her great-great-grandmother, who brought them up from Alabama in the olden days. The organ and sideboard are very old."

"I can see that," Annie says. "They're lovely old pieces." The children look pleased by this acknowledgement. Their thoughts are clearly written on their faces. *We may be poor, but we have some very nice things.*

"We thought, as it's such a lovely day, we'd have our tea outside," Doreen says, leading Annie through a tiny kitchen and back porch to a backyard framed by a white picket fence. It's a narrow yard, about twenty feet wide, but deep, maybe eighty feet of grass sloping down to the back fence, planted with a maze of trees and clumps of tall, old-fashioned looking flowers. Tea is set out in a sort of clearing near the house paved with flat river rocks. A bright blue cloth rides a dilapidated table with mismatched wooden chairs arranged around it. A vase of spring flowers and trailing green ferns in the middle of the table is flanked by tall beeswax candles in silver holders.

DeLinda brings out a tray with a rounded loaf of Irish soda bread, followed by Wilson with small pots of jam and a plate of elegant butter balls, the two of them moving with the dedication of acolytes. They sit in the sunny clearing and Doreen pours tea. The children pass cream and sugar. Doreen cuts the soda bread into thick slices and the children hand them round with butter and jam.

Everything tastes so good in the clear warm air that praise flows naturally from Annie's lips. The fresh steamed loaf, the sweet strawberry jam. This green glade might be the whole world today – everything might end just beyond the back fence. She feels Wilson and DeLinda begin to thaw.

"Thank you," she says. "This is a splendid tea."

*We know,* their faces say. But still they're pleased. Something remains to be said, however. Somehow Annie finds the grace to say it. "Wilson. DeLinda. I'm very sorry I doubted you before. I was wrong. I should have talked to you. I hope you will forgive me."

The children hold their breaths the whole time Annie speaks. As she finishes, they let it all out and Wilson gives a brief sob.

"Our mother explained it to us," DeLinda says rather stiffly. "You didn't know what to think. It was understandable." She can't help adding, "I suppose."

"She said we should all get over it," Wilson says. "That's what I think too."

"So can we be friends again?" Annie asks.

"Yes," Willy says, looking happy and relieved.

"I think so," DeLinda says, more cautiously.

"Want to know how we got our names?" Wilson asks. Annie nods. "Lindy picked 'em. We used to be called Lynn and William, but Lindy said that sounded too ordinary. She said anybody could have names like that. So she made up our new ones. Our mother said we could too. I like 'em a lot better, don't you?"

"Yes," Annie says. "They have more style. More individuality." She sees them enjoying the big word being applied to them. DeLinda relents a little more.

"What name would you choose?" she asks.

Annie considers. "Actually, I think I'm meant to be called Annie."

"You're really lucky," Wilson says.

"I believe I am," Annie says. For a moment no one speaks, as if in awe of the delicate process which has taken away pain and misunderstanding. Annie sees DeLinda's face relax, as she lets go of the last trace of her resentment, sees her look at Doreen and smile.

"We're going back to work," Doreen says. "At the plant."

"The strike's settled?"

"You could say that. We took the company's offer."

"Oh." The offer to settle for less than they had before.

"Yeah," Doreen says, bitterness and humiliation in her face. "What can you do?" But she holds her head proudly, all the same. "May I pour you more tea?"

Annie holds out her cup and watches the steaming tea swirl in the white porcelain.


ANNIE WALKS THE FEW BLOCKS HOME, eager to change and head down to work on the dike, full of the surging energy of release from guilt, free to discard negative things and move forward. In Maisie's room, she hangs Edith's dress in the closet, realizing as she does so that Edith will not expect to have it back. She puts on blue jeans and a fleece sweatshirt, in case it gets cool later. She looks at the solid wide presence of Maisie and Phillip's bed and realizes she needs to lie down for a few minutes before she goes down to the river. After all, she is three and one-half months pregnant.

She falls asleep in moments, something she could never do before she was pregnant, and sleeps through the afternoon and evening and into the night. When the first drops of rain strike the window an hour or so before dawn and then settle into a steady drumming, the sounds are taken effortlessly into a dream of a chubby baby boy sitting on a blanket in a clearing among trees and playing, with serious joy, a battered tin drum. He has Harold's eyes and lots of wavy brown hair, like Charles. For a baby, she finds herself thinking, he's pretty good. Oh, a voice which must be her own says, is this a dream then?

# CHAPTER TWENTY-THREE

Annie hears the rain a moment before she realizes that the insistent ringing is the telephone. She sits straight up in bed, panic singing in her veins. Someone's died. That's the only reason anyone calls in the middle of the night.

Can't be Charles, she was only talking to him Friday night. Edith? She's all right. The children? Everyone she can think of is okay, more or less. In her family, the worst has already happened. Terror ebbs from her mind and blood, leaving her off balance, wondering if there's something she's forgotten to do.

She half expects the ringing will stop before she can make it to the phone. "Hello?" she says, prepared for the metallic nonsense of the dial tone.

"Annie? I'm sorry to wake you, but I need your help." How like Edith not to bother to identify herself.

"Edith? What's wrong?" The bedside clock says 4:00 a.m.

"I haven't time to explain. I'll pick you up five minutes. All right?"

"Five minutes?" It must be one hell of an emergency.

"Please come."

"All right. I'll be ready."

When Annie steps out of the warm house into hard rain, the Caddy is like a shadowy submarine lurking at the curb. At the wheel, Edith, in scarf and trenchcoat, stares straight ahead. Annie gets in and offers to drive, but this time Edith declines.

"I know where I'm going. And I'm more awake." As Annie does up her seat belt, Edith steps on the accelerator and quickly, expertly, turns the car around.

"Your hands?"

"My hands don't give me a moment's trouble at times like these." Ah. Times like these. The windshield wipers at top speed can't handle the sheets of water as the headlights clear a dim tunnel in the darkness. But there's no mistaking the feeling of descending, of falling into blackness, as Edith takes them down the old lane into the valley, completely dark except for weak pools of light from the widely-spaced street lights. Annie keeps the silence Edith has set for them until they pull up, skidding a little, at Tom Bradley's small frame house. Lights blaze from the windows. He must be expecting us, Annie thinks, as they get out of the car. Edith produces a key that unlocks Tom's front door. Annie follows her inside.

Tom, dressed in his usual work things, lies on the

floor near the kitchen table. The telephone receiver in his hand is silent, as if someone waits patiently for him to speak. Edith kneels beside him, feels for a pulse.

"Give me the phone," she says. Annie hands it over. Edith presses the button over and over before it yields a dial tone. Tom lies quietly, apparently unaware of them. He looks surprisingly boyish beneath the thick brown hair.

Edith dials 911. "This is Edith Ashdown speaking," she tells the dispatcher. "I need an ambulance at 2451 Riverside Drive immediately.... Yes, I know that's down in the valley.... Yes, I know it is.... Listen to me, a man is lying here unconscious. He's had a heart attack and he's probably dying. So you get an ambulance down here, and I mean at once.... Thank you." She sets the phone down and checks Tom again.

"Damn it, I never learned CPR."

"Neither did I," Annie admits.

"Watch him. Call me if you see any change." Edith gets up and goes to the bedroom.

Annie can't imagine why she's rooting around in there, what she could possibly be looking for. Tom Bradley looks so small and helpless, so absent, that she can't help feeling touched. He's so like a boy now, as if his life had been arrested at some point long ago and set in a pattern that shut out everything beyond his narrow world. She reaches out and touches his cool cheek. He opens his eyes and looks at her.

"Edith?" he says.

Edith comes back into the room in the act of closing her purse on some papers she's jammed into it.

"Edith, come here," Annie says. "He's calling for you."

Edith kneels and Tom looks up at her. At first he seems puzzled, as if she's not what he was expecting. He looks at Annie, as if comparing the two of them, then back at Edith.

"Edith," he says. "For a moment I forgot we were old."

"Hush," she says. "The ambulance is coming. Of course we're old." She takes his hand and holds it lightly in hers. She glances at the table, where the model of her house sits, perfect in every detail.

"I've finished your house," Tom says. "That's why I was up late."

"It's lovely," Edith says. And it is. He's made something new and better out of it, a house alive with laughing spirits. Windows and walls feel less stuffy and precise than the original, and the turrets have a comical, slightly exaggerated look that undercuts their pomposity. "Annie will take it home for me when we go."

"Do you have to go, Edith?"

"We all have to," she replies. "But I'll come to the hospital with you."

"That's all right then," he says. "I didn't like to go alone."

Annie hears a siren echoing through the valley, unbelievably loud in the still night; then the sound of brakes, bright flashing lights, and two male paramedics enter. One of them gets an oxygen mask on Tom and sets up an IV in his hand while the other questions Edith.

She has little enough to tell. Tom is sixty-seven years old and has had a heart condition for years. He takes nitroglycerin for angina. He has no living family in the town. He called her for help, but stopped talking. She didn't know what was wrong, so she came down right away. She has a key he gave her in case of emergency.

They have Tom on a stretcher and are loading him in the open back doors of the ambulance.

"I'm coming with you," Edith says.

"Okay," one of them yells. "Let's go then."

"Annie, you can lock up. And take the car back to your place." She tosses Annie the keys. She peels off her trenchcoat and flings that at Annie as well.

"She better come with us. It's a real mess." One of them already has the engine running. "She'll never make it up the hill."

"Yes, she will," Edith says. She looks at the model on the table for a fraction of a second and then hard at Annie. Annie sees that Edith really does expect her to take the model house. She knows she should protest, but it's all moving too quickly.

"Suit yourself then," the man says, as if Annie isn't involved in the decision, helping Edith in and shutting the doors. The ambulance takes off, fishtailing wildly. Annie can't imagine how she'll keep the Caddy on the greasy road. She considers staying in Tom's house until it's light. She looks at her watch and realizes it would be light already if it weren't raining so hard. She's really afraid to go out there, but Edith has commanded her and the road is only going to get worse.

All she can find to carry the house in is a big black garbage bag; at least it's waterproof. She pads the bottom and sides with a woollen blanket from the linen cupboard and lifts the house into its makeshift carrier. She notices the gazebo Tom showed them on their previous visit and gets another bag, this time lined with tea towels, to accommodate it.

Feeling like a thief in the night, Annie moves them out to the back seat of Edith's car. She goes through the house one last time, grabbing Edith's coat, putting the phone back on the table, and, in the bedroom, squaring up a drawer which Edith has failed in her haste to close properly. Then she turns out the lights, locks up, and gets into the Caddy.

As she heads down the winding road, she can no longer ignore the danger she's in. She thinks of the mud-greased hill ahead and of the vast quantity of water behind the dike. She thinks of the hard rain.

Her heart is all but frozen by these things. But she can't stop to analyze or plan, she just has to make it up the hill. For that she's glad she's got the Caddy, its power and weight.

She's on the hill, skidding all over the place, expecting to go off the road every moment, but just driving and hearing the whole time her own personal survival rap. *Come on, goddamn you. Come on, you bitch. Come on, damn it, come on.* A small hysterical part of her wanting to giggle, wondering who the bitch is: the Caddy, or herself? And so many things whirling in her mind all at once. The road, the lights hardly penetrating the dark, the rain, the blood roaring in her ears, the feel of climbing. Skidding and correcting for the skid. The thought of the thing inside her, the creature, the embryo, the baby. Have to keep the baby safe.

She feels the road level out and keeps driving into the rain and the beautiful straight street lit by amber sodium vapour lamps, drives until she feels her hands loosen their mad grip on the wheel, until her dry sobs stop and her breath slows. She pulls the car over and sits for a long time without doing any sort of thinking. When she notices her hands and feet are cold, she starts the Caddy and turns back for River Road. By the time she parks the car in front of her house, she can barely move for weariness. Somehow she gets the models inside and sets them on the kitchen counter in their dripping plastic shells.

All she wants is sleep. She heads for Allison's bed this time and crawls in under the indigo elephants. She dreams of Tom Bradley growing younger and younger until he is nothing but a baby in her arms, a vigorous baby kicking his legs. She holds him to her breast. She feels she's on the verge of some major discovery about babies. Something about all of us being babies and older people being nothing but larger babies projected a little distance forward in time and space, but still at their heart and essence nothing but babies.

She wakes again to rain, hating to leave the warmth of the bed, but realizing she must if she wants any tea. Why is it, she wonders idly, they can put a man or woman on the moon, but they can't design a simple robot butler to bring a person morning tea? Or a replicator, like they had on *Star Trek*, where the Captain had only to utter the words, "Tea. Earl Grey. Hot," and it was done.

Soon Annie has hot tea and toast, which she takes out to the living room. She brings the house and gazebo from the kitchen and sets them up in the centre of the Duncan Phyfe table. The house floats like a moated castle, an enchanted castle after an evil spell on it has been broken. Annie stares at it as the tea warms her.

She barely hears the thump of a car door closing outside and the revving motor as it takes off. She does hear the doorbell and discovers Edith on her front step looking wet and slightly shrunken. Annie ushers her in, makes Edith change the pullover sweater she's wearing for one of her own, then settles her in a wing chair.

Edith looks intently at the house. Annie brings her tea and Edith drinks, warming her hands around the bowl of the cup. She takes a small pill case from her pocket, tips out two pills and swallows them with the tea.

"It's this rain," she says. "It hits every bone and joint in my body. Old, old, old, that's what rain says to me."

She puts down the cup and tries to flex her fingers. Annie sees that she can barely move them.

"Well, he's dead. Tom's dead. You guessed, I'm sure."

"I didn't let myself think about it."

"His heart, of course," Edith says. Her face looks tired and, in spite of the rain and humidity, dry, as if it would be rough to the touch.

"Did he ever become conscious again?"

"No. But we'd said everything we had to say already."

"I see," Annie says, in a way she hopes Edith will construe as either encouragement to go on or willingness to continue in ignorance.

Edith doesn't appear to construe it any way at all. Her attention is on the model.

"That's not my house, of course," she says. "It's the way it would look if people had been happy in it." Annie nods agreement. "Except for the summerhouse. That's where we used to meet, you know. Tom and I."

"What?" Annie says, startled. Well, what did she expect? What else have Edith's actions and manner been telling her?

"He came to me one spring wanting to do work in the yard. It was the second year of Arnold's illness, and nobody knew what was wrong with him. Do you remember Arnold?"

Annie nods. "A little." Edith's husband was the older brother of Charles's father, John Wilkins. Somehow his name has never adhered to Edith; she has always been known in the neighbourhood simply as Edith Ashdown. Now that Arnold's been dead for fifteen years, people have almost forgotten Edith was ever married.

"I was just turning forty and beginning to feel old. How little I knew about it then. It was only ten years since Homer died and there I was looking after a sick husband." A bitter anger twists her mouth for a moment, but she controls it. "Arnold at least was pleasanter company," she says, as if that must have been some consolation. "I had the two children to look after as well. Locky and Eleanor were in school by then, of course."

"I see," Annie says cautiously, not sure whether she wants to know more.

"No, you don't. Do you have any scotch?"

"Yes, I'll get it." Annie goes to a kitchen cupboard where somebody, Allison probably, has stashed a bottle of single malt. Talisker. She pours a generous measure into a crystal glass. She fetches a woollen blanket and tucks it around Edith's legs, without hearing a sound of protest. She hands over the whiskey and Edith tastes it.

"Very good, Annie. Such character. You'd almost think it was alive. You'd join me, of course, but you have to think of the baby." Edith takes a deep drink of the whiskey, as if it can provide her with strength or supple hands or even youth.

"As I said, he offered to take care of my yard and, when I tried to send him away, he stood his ground. Before I knew, he was trimming my trees and digging my garden. I came outside myself to show him the roses that needed pruning, and I never questioned why I put on a yellow dress that set off my figure and tortoise-shell combs in my hair."

Annie can't think what to say, so she keeps quiet. If Edith wants to tell her this story, and it appears she does, nothing Annie can do is going to stop her. Nor does she seem to need any encouragement.

"Pretty soon I was meeting him in the summerhouse at night. We never talked about what we were doing. It was a silent compact between the two of us, and between us and the garden as it came into bloom." Edith's eyes are faraway, seeing the man and woman in the garden. "That was a perfect warm summer, rain when you needed rain and an abundance of sun that made everything grow, tree or bush, vegetable or flower, as I've never seen it before or since...the scent of roses and peonies heavy on the air, the trees like guardians around us.

"I was forty years old, but that didn't matter. Arnold, two children, might never have happened. It was the first time I really knew anything about being with a man. Why a woman might want to – aside from having a husband for respectability and children and looking after the bills."

Annie can hardly believe she's hearing this. She promises herself to stop underestimating people.

"It made me so glad I'd kept up the garden, glad I'd made Arnold sell his house when we married and move into mine. I kept my garden fair and one day Tom came into it."

Edith's face has grown softer, the cornflower blue eyes dark with memory. "All the summer long we heard the river below us. Sometimes we crept down the bank and bathed in the river. The river flowed around us and through us. We had the rhythm of rivers, the wisdom of rivers. All spring and summer of that year the river was high. We had to be careful in those currents, I can tell you. By the time fall came, it began to shrink back into itself; the current slowed. I could see the day coming when it would be covered in ice. And when the cold came, everything ended for us."

Edith's eyes fill with tears. Annie sees for a moment the younger Edith, hair glowing red-gold in the sun, or bathing, silent and secret, in the dark river.

"He never came back again?" Annie asks. "Not the next summer?"

"Oh, he stopped by the next spring, wanting to look after the garden. Wanting me to love him again. But I couldn't. The moment was gone, even though he didn't want to believe that."

"You never got together again?"

Edith shakes her head. "No. I suppose I could have after Arnold died, but the truth is, there seemed so little in common between us, except that brief season of pleasure. I didn't think we could bring it back. I was afraid of what might happen if we tried."

Annie sighs. And yet Edith has the memory; perhaps she spends a part of her life inside it. "But you were seeing him before he died," she says.

"A few years ago, he came to my notice again when he started making the houses. There was a story on the television news. He told the reporter he would make it the work of the rest of his life to build models of all the fine houses in the river valley."

"Did he succeed?"

"Oh, no. He might have, but I asked him to do my house. We were meeting by then, at his place, for tea. We were very decorous, not alluding to the past, although it was always there between us. After a while, he asked me to keep a key to his place. In case of emergency. I expect he didn't want to die alone."

Suddenly Edith's matter-of-factness can't be sustained. She weeps, without bothering to cover or turn away her face. Annie keeps her eyes on Edith's, determined not to slight her confidence.

"He mistook me for you," Annie says. "Back at his house, when he was conscious. I think his mind was back in the past for a moment."

Edith finishes the last of the whiskey. Annie pours her another. Edith drinks.

"I lied to you just now," she says. "He did come to himself for a few minutes in the hospital. I didn't want to admit to myself what he said. He said, 'Thank you, Edith, for loving me.'"

When Edith lets go of her usual iron control, it's as if what holds her up has been taken bloodlessly away; as if she's been gutted and boned. She slumps in the chair and doesn't bother to control her weeping, maybe doesn't even know she's doing it.

Annie kneels and puts her arms around Edith, who feels old and frail, like dried winter stalks of tall proud flowers, the bushy kind that rattle in the wind. It's her turn now to watch over Edith. For a while Edith permits it; then she begins to collect herself.

"I'm sorry," Edith says. "It's just the damn pain. I've had this for ten years now, and sometimes you get so sick of it."

Annie lets it pass. "Nobody's strong all the time," she says. "Not even you, Edith."

"Not even a mean bitch like me, you mean?" Edith asks, her usual self rebounding.

Annie smiles. "If you like. I don't know that I'd have used those exact words."

"Ah, but there was a time, when I was with Tom, when I was different. When everything seemed to work and my body was something besides a burden. Then you wouldn't have described me that way. Well, never mind," she says.

"So when was all this going on?" Annie asks, suddenly curious.

"Oh, it was the late sixties, I forget what year," Edith says with feigned casualness.

"Late sixties." Annie feels something click in her mind. "Wait a minute! Edith?"

"That's right," she says, looking Annie straight in the eye, "he was Tira's father. Eleanor and Locky were

Arnold's, of course, but Tira was Tom's child."

"So that's why she's so different. Does she know?"

"No, and I don't know whether to tell her. She can never meet him now, can she?" Edith looks really perplexed. And guilty? "Do you think I should?"

Annie tries to imagine how it would feel; having to relearn the most basic facts about yourself. "She'd probably want to know."

"I suppose you could tell her yourself now. But you'd have to know why you were doing it. You'd have to believe it wasn't simply to hurt her."

"And how would I know that?"

"I can't imagine," Edith says drily. "But I think you would know." Edith picks up Annie's tea and starts drinking it, for all the world as if she's simply mistaken it for her own, resuming by tiny increments her everyday demeanor of confidence and command.

"Thank you for listening," she says, trying to sound nonchalant. But the attempt irks Annie; Edith can't just pretend nothing much has happened.

"Did I have a choice?" she asks, rather nastily.

"No, but you did listen," Edith works to keep annoyance from her voice, "so I'm thanking you."

Annie decides to let it go. "You're welcome then, I guess," she says.

"Do you mind if I check the noon news?"

Edith picks up the remote and zaps on the television. The first image is almost unreadable: hard slanting rain pounding into water; pulling back to the blueblack swollen river running at ungraspable speed; then an aerial shot of the place where Annie has worked so many days moving sandbags down a human chain. Only there are no more people down there. The dike has given way, water pounding over and through it with a force beyond her imagining. Annie feels as if she's been struck; had the breath knocked out of her. The dike is broken. She remembers that she failed to work on it that one last time.

The shot changes to a view from the riverbank. Dark water shoots by, bearing boards and branches and unrecognizable junk on its back. A man speaks over the sound of rushing water. "The river valley was evacuated at dawn this morning after hard rain fell all night in Riverbend and points upstream." It's Charles, his voice so thick with emotion she hardly recognizes it. "Finally, at 6:47 a.m., Sunday, May seventeenth, the dike was breached, flooding hundreds of acres of prime agricultural land, as well as some of Riverbend's loveliest old homes." These words accompany shots of Harold's place, the river licking at its rooftops, the old poplars around the house just crowning above the flow, and shots of the wealthy riverside homes awash with mud and water.

Annie thinks of Harold and Donnie and the Shetland pony. They must have made it to safety, far away from the crushing weight of the water.

"This is not just another isolated natural disaster," Charles goes on, "it's a genuine tragedy in the history of this small but proud prairie city that has received so many blows in the past decade. A place I used to call home." The camera is on Charles's face now, as he looks over the drowned valley. His hair is wet; there are tears in his eyes. She's never seen him like this, not in their life together and certainly not on television.

"Edith! Did you see? Charles is here!"

"Oh, didn't I mention? He called yesterday to say he was coming in to cover a possible flood. The network picked it up from the local station. Apparently Charles asked if he could come out." Annie looks Edith straight in the eyes, thinking *bitch*, her mind trying to fight off panic. "He tried your place, but you must have been out."

"I was out for tea," Annie says, marvelling at how remote the children's party now seems. "It was a beautiful sunny day, not a cloud anywhere." How did he know there'd be a flood? The crest wasn't supposed to come until late Sunday. There should have been a whole day more to build up the dike. The rain, she thinks. The rain changed everything. If only she'd watched the news. If only she'd thought. And now Charles is here, and there's no way she's ready to see him.

"That's as may be," Edith says, and in spite of everything they've now been through together, Annie feels the old anger.

"You might have told me."

"I just did, in my way." Edith removes the blanket from her knees and folds it. Annie takes it from her and throws it on the couch, revelling in the anger surging through her.

"Or did you think it'd be more fun to let him surprise me? Yes, that'd be more entertaining, wouldn't it?"

"Must you overdramatize everything?" Edith says calmly. "Have you considered that I may simply have forgotten?"

"Not that seriously, no."

"You should consider it," Edith suggests. "You should be more trusting."

"What? With you?" Annie tries not to sound outraged.

"Why not?" Edith raises an eyebrow with delicate irony. "I've trusted you."

The woman has a point. "I suppose you have," Annie says, grudgingly. "When it suits you. God knows why."

"I doubt even God knows why," Edith says. "Don't you think we're rather on our own these days? Why don't we just find out if either of us knows why?"

Annie starts to laugh, but chokes it back. The damn woman is learning how to get round her. She feels a jolt of panic.

"Edith, I have to get ready for Charles. He could show up any minute."

"Oh, I think he'll be busy for a while." Edith says. "But I won't keep you. I'll come back for the house."

Edith is at the door, her usual veneer back in place. Except that she's still wearing Annie's sweater and doesn't seem to realize it. She slips on her now-dried trenchcoat.

Annie remembers other unfinished business. "You didn't tell me why Mother killed herself," she says.

"Didn't I?" Edith opens the door into the still beating rain and steps out.

CHAPTER TWENTY-FOUR

Maybe Charles is still busy gathering news; maybe she has a few hours left. Annie sets out the remaining stack of Eamon's papers on the kitchen table. No time anymore to read each one through. Now she must simply look for anything significant, but this batch of pages seems all out of order. Her eye is caught by a joyous phrase.

Blessed be the day! Going home to Maudie and the children. A biting cold day, January 15, 1920 – thirty degrees below zero. I cannot believe they will send me out in such cold weather. But apparently it is to be. They have done everything for me for over three years – commanded my every move. Now the bond of care is broken. No more armies of doctors and nurses – to watch the food I eat – the wastes that leave my body – the exact amount and sort of sputum in the metal cup by my bed. We have done all we can, they seem to say. Time for you to go.

Maudie cannot come down – they didn't give her enough warning. You would think they must have known I would be leaving soon. But apparently these decisions can be quite sudden. They will arrange for someone to drive me into town – and put me on the train. All by myself – I will ride a train again. I will have my ticket and five dollars for any emergencies that may arise. The only one I can think of is a sudden haemorrhage leading to death. For this five dollars will avail me but little.

I do not see how they can simply disown me in this way. They have claimed me as their own. How can that change in a single day? They feel nothing about this, as far as I can see.

They brought me a suit of clothes that isn't mine. And a white shirt with a stiff starched collar. Perhaps they mean to show me that I will only be fit to be a clerk in some stuffy office. After all these years of fresh air. I wonder whose clothes these are. Is he someone they have decided will never leave here? Or has he already fallen to the Bone Wagon?

That's it, I know – but I must thank my silent benefactor for this excellent thick and warm Irish tweed. Irish tweed for the Irishman who has long ago lost Ireland.

Nurse Willet brought it in – all brushed and pressed. She has always been brisk – but now takes it to new heights. As if she will sweep me from this room like dust – by the sheer force of her will.

Oddly enough, she helps me with everything one last time. She brings hot water and a soapy brush and shaves me. She helps me wash and dress. How is it that one day I can do nothing for myself – and the next day will have to do it all?

Will she miss me? Buried inside me is the thought that she will. I remember that day when she saw something she should not have seen. It means nothing – but I will never forget it or her either.

Perhaps it is right I leave this place in a dead man's clothes. That way I will never forget. It is strange to put on the guise of the outside world. Each button – each sleeve and trouser leg – reminds me of the many duties each body part must now remember how to perform. They speak to me of daily work – unceasing effort. The world is a busy place and now I will be required to mix in – as if I am part of it. I wonder if I can fool them. If I can fool myself. Is this the way a convict feels?

Maudie will be at the Riverbend station. Doctor Nugent has actually telephoned to the store – and arranged for her to be given the time off. It seems he knows the manager – a Mr. Ristage. He does not think the man will dock Maudie's pay. I put it to him as a humanitarian, the doctor said, I think he will do the right thing.

Doctor Nugent has given me a parting gift, a book on medicinal plants, illustrated with watercolour pictures. Unlooked for treasure. Lavender, eyebright, feverfew. Sea buckthorne, lady's bedstraw, hedge hyssop. Goldenrod, rowan, yew.

Oh God – I am so afraid of what is waiting for me out there. I seem to move from one theatre of war to another. Hard to say which is most frightening. I hope the children will be glad to have me home. Surely Maude will be glad – but it will be strange for her all the same.

I must be brave. I have prevailed thus far over death and trust I will not be defeated now. My blood has begun to move again – has grown new pathways through my body. My lungs have sealed off the contagion – like a wall built around the past. Part of my strength

must go to keeping it sealed. From this time
forward I must be on guard.

The next passage has been crossed out until nothing
can be deciphered of it, with no indication of who did
the crossing out. When the narrative resumes, the writing is hurried and ragged looking, as if he hadn't much
time or had grown impatient with the task.

At the end Willet did relent a little from all
her briskness. She gave me a present – a small
leather bound book for copying one's thoughts.
She must have sometimes seen me at my writing. I hope she has never read a word of it. I
will copy into her book one of William Blake's
poems. I am now too poor to give anyone a gift
– but perhaps in time I'll find a way to remember her too. They're coming soon. Willet says
Doctor Nugent has made a last minute decision
– to drive me himself. An unexpected honour. I
will miss him and our quiet talks about the
plants of the prairie. It has been a pleasure to
share his conversation. I wish I could be an
educated man.

It's taking too long. She has to speed things up. The
entries after Eamon arrives home are sketchy, sporadic
notes, the handwriting careless and uneven. There has
been no attempt as there was earlier to embellish or

even to tidy and re-copy them. Pieced together they tell the story of his quest to find a job and his gradual understanding that he must not speak of having had tuberculosis. He learns to speak of a "bout of pleurisy" after the war, which has the added advantage of introducing his war record. He hates to trade on it, but he has a family to look after and must use whatever advantages he has – and they are few enough.

Eamon begins to study plants; at first it's for pleasure, but gradually it becomes part of a plan that will allow him a means of support. His drawings of plants become more skilful and he begins to experiment with watercolours. One shows a branch of the rowan tree with a spray of bright berries. Beside it Eamon has copied an entry from his herbal: "For the wood of the Rowan is proof against all evil and should be planted close by the house. Better still if a cross of Rowan wood be placed over the door. And no boat whether great or small should be launched but that there be some small part made of the Rowan's wood. A man will do well to keep a small piece in his pocket at all times."

The papers tell also of Eamon's struggle to build strength and endurance through long walks and increasingly demanding calisthenics, always pushed just short of the point where his body will "break down" again.

There is the triumph of the day Eamon is chosen to work as an apprentice groundskeeper with the city. Nobody can know he will work his way up to the lofty position of City Horticulturist, a position which probably didn't even exist until he had prepared himself to merit it by dint of hard work and constant self-improvement. But the germ is there. Already he is studying plants and their cultivation in every spare moment. In those days it was almost a religion. *You can better yourself if you try.* And for many it became true. People worked their way up. Formal qualifications were not so necessary.

The papers also speak of Eamon's attempt to get to know his children and to be the father he dreamed of being when he was ill. Outwardly they are docile, respectful, and proud to have a father at last like other children. But between the lines Annie reads the difficulties. They continue to make strange with him, letting him into their lives only so far. There are secrets implied, sometimes by the children, sometimes by Maude, baffling to Eamon. After a few months, he reaches a conclusion. The entry has been carefully recopied.

> I can no longer delude myself. Something
> fearful has taken place. I have returned too late
> to prevent it. The first idea I had of it was
> Maude's continual watchfulness around the chil-
> dren. She always seemed to be looking for some-
> thing – and too often she seemed to find it. All
> this without consulting me or even confiding in
> me. I saw that Robbie and Maisie would become
> aware of her watching and would become utterly
> still and do nothing – until she looked away or

left the room. There was a constant communication between the children that needed no words. It was clear that they were not so carefree as I had believed. They no longer ran and played together.

I observed Maude constantly arranging outings for them with other children. Or sending one on an errand without the other. She had already without my knowledge or consent arranged for them to go to different schools. I remembered she had suggested this to me when I was in the hospital. I was angry when I discovered it had been done – but it seemed too late to make another change.

Maude insisted her choice was right. Already Robbie was becoming more like other boys. She was even oddly pleased that when a boy at Robbie's new school had started a fight our Robbie had bloodied his nose. To her this was evidence of improvement. I was very displeased. For a time there was much unpleasantness between us – with questioning from me and her constant assertion that she did only what was best.

When we know something is there to be found and never cease to look for it – the truth cannot remain long hidden. At last Maude told me all of it. During my illness – at least from the time she sold the farm and moved to town –

Maude had become friendly with a Mrs. Mabel Varens – an older woman she met at St. Mary's Church, and the sister of the priest. This woman came many times to tea at our house and often took care of the children when Maude did not bring them to the sanatorium.

At first this woman was delighted with my children. But the more she saw – the more she found to censure. Before long she infected Maudie with her fears. She did not like to see them so much together. She told Maude it was not the rule in other families where she visited. That it would be wise to encourage them to have different interests. She also said they should not be sharing a bedroom.

Maude having no other place to send him – since she occupied the only other bedroom herself – set up Robbie's cot in the kitchen. This the boy hated and stoutly resisted using – saying that he wanted to keep on sleeping with Maisie. This only worried Maude and her self-styled helper further.

One morning Maude rose and went to call the children. Robbie was not in his cot in the kitchen, nor was he in the bathroom. She found him in Maisie's room – the two of them in her bed nestled together. I fear that my wife lost her judgement. All her friend's direst warnings seemed confirmed. She had not wanted to tell me this part, hoping, as she said, to spare me.

I asked her what there could be in all this – beyond the innocent affection of two children always close from their birth. She asked how I thought I could judge – since I was not there to see. These were bitter words to me – because there have been too many times I was not there when they needed me.

She admits she behaved intemperately. She raised her voice – told them they were bad. She pulled Robbie from his sister's bed – told him he was never to do that again. I can only imagine his confusion, wondering what he had done wrong. In all this Maude did not trouble to hide her fear. I am sure she frightened them badly.

Thus does fear weaken judgement – and bring more harm than the thing feared. How Maude's acts on that morning will be worked out in future is unknown. But I am filled with foreboding.

Now she takes notice of their every movement – and the smallest physical contact. They are learning that they must not touch each other – or be alone together. They are learning to be ashamed of something they don't understand. This may lead to permanent alienation between the two children. Or will it in time create the very thing she wishes so much to prevent? By making them overconscious, may she not be showing them the way? She has us all thinking the most morbid thoughts. She has made us afraid of each other.

This is not all. She has altered her own ways with them – she is now most sparing of any sort of touch. This from a woman who had been warm and loving – to my certain knowledge.

Nor am I to touch them except in ways Maude considers harmless. I am not to take Maisie on my knee to read her a story. I am not to kiss the boy – not even at bedtime. Every day it seems less is permitted. I came home expecting such joy – but it is not to be allowed. This poisons my times alone with Maude as well. She has grown suspicious of all bodily pleasure. I in turn have let my anger corrode my love for her. How true the poet's words have become – *And priests in black gowns were walking their rounds, And binding with briars my joys and desires.*

This binding has come into our home without my wish or consent and may take many generations to unravel.

Now Annie understands it all. Of course, the understanding has been growing for some time. There's one last sentence, crammed into the corner of a messily written sheet and partly crossed out.

I cannot believe my eyes. For a moment I saw Robbie touch Maisie where he should not. She looked at him for a moment – I felt they both knew it was wrong. Then Maisie saw me watching and left the room. Has Maude been right all along? No – this is her doing.

After this the writing is less personal. The remaining entries become sparser in number and in the amount of detail. Gradually the passion for his work replaces Maudie and the children as the centre of Eamon's life and remaining memoirs. In the realm of plants, he can still find the harmony and joy he longed for in his human relations. He can pursue knowledge as far as it will take him and no one will be frightened, for no one has yet delineated decencies and indecencies in the couplings of flowers. At least not so long as they are clothed in the Latinate remoteness of scientific language.

The final page is a letter to his son Robbie some time before Eamon's death, offering him the papers "because I fear I've failed you as a father – yet still hope these words of mine may be of help. I send them to you rather than your sister – because I think you will at least read them before you burn them. I want you to know how much I loved you both and desired your happiness. This question haunts me still – Why are we so much less than we could be?"

Robbie did read the papers. Attached to Eamon's note by a paper clip is a short one from Robbie to his sister.

Maze –

I wanted you to see Father's papers. He sent them to me before he died, being certain, no doubt, Mother would destroy them if she found them. You know I have them, but you've always refused to see them. I think you should read them now.

I remember the early part of our childhood as a happy, beautiful dream. That all seemed to change when Father came home and for a long time I thought he was the reason. He gave me these papers so I could understand.

I'm sure you know I'm dying. I'm passing Father's words to you so you'll have at least the chance to look at them. You're my twin, Maze, and in some ways still the one closest to me. Only that all got buried as we got older. So – do this for me, or if not for me, to know your father better. I promise you it's not like any-thing you can imagine. I believe it's immensely valuable and, for you and me, necessary.

He signs it, "Love, as always, Robbie" – Robbie, in some final way a boy's name, not a man's. True in that way to the essential spirit in him, Annie thinks, remem-bering the slightly diffident charm of this dimly remembered great-uncle. She wishes she could have the three of them back, Eamon, Robbie, Maisie. She imagines them before her, now that death has removed so many false ideas and trappings, with their bared spirits revealed and able to speak openly. "Yes, I see how that was." "How beautiful we were, at times." "How I longed to see clearly." "Never mind, it's done." "I loved you." "Yes."

Annie sifts the papers. She has missed or skimmed over many pages in her haste, and she could go back and read them all, except that the impulse is dying in her even as she has the thought. It's complete. Or complete enough. Funny how that word keeps turning up. The satisfaction of completion is something aside from the joy or pain, a sense of triumph at having made it to the end of a journey. Annie has experienced the most important feelings and ideas of her great-grandfather's life, almost as a contemporary, his spirit grafted now onto her own. Perhaps she's even a little in love with him.

A folded piece of paper has slipped out onto the floor. Annie picks it up. It's in Allison's hand.

My dearest Mother, you never read them,
did you? Why couldn't things have worked out
differently? Each generation has denied the
next. Eamon's question haunts me. Why are we
so much less than we could be? I feel the loss
and waste of it. And my own daughter, Annie,
I can almost hear her voice accusing me. Why

couldn't you make it better? Why couldn't you let me be whole? Not that she ever did accuse me, but she should have.

Annie feels an ache in her throat and the impulse to weep. But these things, she discovers, are not going anywhere this time. They dissipate, they ebb, they are not part of her now. She is passing through some kind of barrier beyond grief and pain. Like breaking the sound barrier. Again she considers what would have happened if she'd flown home to Charles right after the funeral. Was it only Edith's intervention that made her stay, or did she herself have some part in it? She'd like to think she did, but daren't count on it. It's so hard to give Edith any credit, but she must.

She looks at Allison's note. *Why couldn't you let me be whole?* She thinks of Blake's mind-forged manacles, which Eamon tried so hard to break. She wonders if she will be able to do better. If her child will one day in turn accuse her. If she will reach the end of her life wondering, *Why are we so much less than we could be?*

She considers Allison's opening words. *My dearest Mother, you never read them, did you?* Of course Allison was wrong. Maisie certainly did read Eamon's "works," although she may have rejected their ideas, if the note Annie found in the kitchen is anything to go on. But did she entirely reject them? There is always the evidence of Maisie's times with Wilson and DeLinda.

Annie gathers up the papers, but does not take them

back to the hankie drawer. She sets them neatly in the centre of the kitchen table. She can't stay here now, waiting for Charles, waiting for him to come and pass some kind of judgement on her. The old Annie might have been that passive, but this one has a lot to do and no time for waiting.

She writes on a piece of paper, "Charles – Read this – Annie," and puts it on the top sheet of Eamon's papers. She gets Maisie's flowered umbrella from the bedroom closet, pulls on a jacket, and goes out into the rain. The phone starts to ring as she closes the door, but she feels no obligation to answer it. It should have tried ringing earlier, if answering was what it wanted. Outside everything looks murky. It's only about 5:00, but the rain makes it seem more like twilight.

Walking to the cul-de-sac at the end of River Road, she picks out dark figures against the rain. People stand quietly, two or three deep, looking down. As if being a resident of the street gives her special privileges, Annie pushes her way to a space along the railing.

Beside her she notices the three old women from the funeral, the ones who passed her in their walk, back when there was snow on the ground. Wearing bright orange slickers, they gaze out across the valley, as if taking the measure of the waters.

The top of the cliff has never been so close to the river. Water drowns the willows by the creek and laps against chokecherry bushes higher up. The whole valley under water is so much bigger than anything that could be shown on television. She is appalled at the amount of water. Only roofs, and treetops like sprigs of broccoli, break the surface. Bits of river flotsam streak past like tracer bullets in a war movie. The grand homes Tom was copying are reduced to suggestive details; a turret here, a widow's walk there.

Nothing at all is visible of Tom's house. She imagines the model houses floating around in it, along with any evidence of his affair with Edith that might still be in the house. She sees herself carefully turning out lights and straightening the dresser drawer, as if anyone would ever see it again. She sees herself caught in the house, unable to escape the wall of advancing water.

Someone touches her arm. She knows as she turns that it will be Harold. She expects to see pain on his face, but his blue-grey eyes seem electric in the dull air, his lips almost red. He looks right into her, as if he knows her through and through. He's like a merman, newly risen from the water below, gleaming in the rain. She thinks how he has touched her inside and is sure he must be thinking of it too.

"I'm sorry about your place," she says.

"Never mind," he says, looking into her eyes. "Donnie and I were getting a bit stuck down there, keeping her alive in our heads. We needed to be moved along."

She watches his face, trying to decide if he really means it.

"Annie, do you think you might want to stay? With Donnie and me, I mean."

She feels drawn to him with such a yearning that it scares her. She can see a life opening up with him in which so many things would be good. His lovemaking, his presence at breakfast eating toast. It would be such a nice life. His body attracts her, the warmth, solidity, and dependability of it. She thinks of his arms around her, his legs against hers.

The more she gives herself to the fantasy, the more it dissolves in front of her eyes. As if this nice life has never really been an option for her. She's almost afraid to find out why. Maybe it's that she can't believe in anything quite that easy. Maybe for Sylvie, maybe for some other woman, but not for her. Or maybe she can't see what she herself would be doing in that life. Her life would be determined by Harold's. She's already let that happen once. Now she has to do something different.

And there's also the baby, still part of her but separate too, already gathering its strength, forming its will. She has to figure out how she and Charles will raise a baby and if they're going to do it together.

It's only two days since she was with Harold, but she feels as if she's turned another corner somewhere. She's watched Tom Bradley dying and driven the car out of the valley. She's received Edith's most intimate secrets. She's fought to save the valley and seen it flooded, despite all anyone could do. And she's finished Eamon's papers. She understands her lineage, her inheritance, more completely than she has ever done. She accepts it.

She has to find out what to do about Charles. Can she accept him too?

Harold watches her face, his eyes demanding an answer. "Charles, my husband, is here," she says. Harold looks disappointed by the word husband. "To cover the flood. But I know he's here to see me too. I have to talk to him. Find out what's happening with us."

"If you want to talk," he says, conceding nothing to Charles's rights, "we're at the store, Donnie and I. There's a small apartment there on the second floor."

"I'm sorry," she says, "I don't know what I'm doing yet."

"Didn't it mean anything?" he asks. His eyes look almost black, demanding, almost angry.

"Of course it did," she says. Harold watches her for a few beats, mouth set, eyes accusing, then walks away down River Road. Watching him go, Annie becomes aware of the three old women turned towards her with a look of understanding or perhaps collusion in their old eyes. Annie feels herself held for a moment by their gaze; then she walks off towards Edith's house.

# CHAPTER TWENTY-FIVE

Edith stands in the doorway of her verandah looking out at the people in the rain-dulled light. Annie eyes her through the window screen. Edith gives no ground. No quarter.

"Harold Borebank again, I see." Edith can do a lot with a raised eyebrow.

"Yes," Annie says. "He's an old friend, you know. Married a friend of mine."

"Old friend, my ass," Edith says coolly.

"So you want me to stick with Charles then? I must say you've had me fooled."

"Really? You'll do what you want, in any case."

"I hope so, Edith. Otherwise, what is the point? I mean, isn't that what you were trying to show me? How you did exactly what you wanted?"

Annie realizes that Edith looks tired today. "I wasn't trying to show you anything. Sometimes you want to

339

tell something, that's all."

"And I just happened to be available?" Annie is enjoying this. Edith's such a bracing adversary.

"No. I wanted to tell you."

"Ah," says Annie. "So you can manipulate me into whatever it is you decide I should do?" She knows as she says it that she's not being fair.

"I suppose I wanted to help you." Edith gives her head a little shake. "Don't ask me why. Either people don't want help or what you have to offer is useless. I've always known that." Edith really does look tired. Or is she just trying to get rid of Annie?

"Are you going to let me in or not?" Annie is suddenly very angry, as certain facts and implications converge in her mind.

"I'd prefer not." Edith holds her body stiff, as if to repel an onslaught Annie may make on her door.

"Let me in, Edith. I mean it." Or I'll make a scene, is the unspoken threat. Does Edith care whether she makes a scene? At any rate, she steps back and opens the door.

Annie follows her in. "How could you leave me down there alone? I didn't even know what was happening. I could have drowned, for godsake."

"You wouldn't have drowned."

"You're not the voice of God, Edith. Do you know, I actually thought of staying there until there was more light? I didn't know the goddamn dike was going out."

"Oh, would you stop fussing," Edith says. "I paid a

taxi driver to go by your house and see if the Cadillac was there. He came back to the hospital to tell me."

"Oh," Annie says, impressed in spite of herself.

"I would rather not have mentioned it," Edith says, "but you do harass a person."

"I was still in danger. I could have gone off the road."

"Oh, pooh. There was never any danger of that."

"Oh, pooh? Is that all you can say? You'd have had fun explaining my death to Charles."

"I'm old," Edith says, "but I haven't lost my nerve yet. I gave you the chance to have a true adventure and what do I hear? A lot of bitching and complaining."

"I didn't ask you for an adventure. If I want an adventure, I'm perfectly capable of getting one on my own."

"Sometimes you get an adventure whether you ask for one or not. Anyway," she says, decisively, "I needed you."

"Really. What as? Chaperone? Or accomplice?"

"Don't be silly." For a moment Edith looks uncomfortable.

"Edith, why didn't you call an ambulance in the first place? They might have been able to save him." Edith doesn't speak. "You didn't want them to save him!"

"No, I didn't," she says angrily. "Not so he could be hooked up to a respirator. I don't call that life."

"You don't know it would have been like that."

"He'd had two heart attacks before. He told me he thought the next one would get him. He said he wouldn't want to go on hooked up to machines, maybe not even aware of being alive." Edith sounds so calm, so reasonable.

"So you decided to make sure. You took your time getting there." Edith doesn't say a word, but she doesn't have to. "You're right," Annie says, "you haven't lost your nerve." She doesn't want to give Edith time to react. "So tell me what I want to know."

"We'll see. Right now I'm hungry," Edith says. "Have you had dinner?" Annie shakes her head; Edith's trying to distract her. Oh well, let her think she's succeeding.

In the kitchen, Edith puts a saucepan of soup on to heat and makes plain tomato sandwiches. Annie makes tea and sets the table. Edith's hands seem shakier than usual, the knuckles more swollen. They sit down in the nook and Edith ladles soup into bowls. Annie finds herself devouring the food as if food has just been invented.

"Have you seen Charles?" Edith asks when Annie is nearly finished her food.

"No, not yet. I'm not ready for him."

"I wouldn't say you've much choice." Edith watches her with amusement.

"Is that so?" Annie says sarcastically. "We'll see about that."

"That's so mature, Annie. I haven't heard those words since Locky was small."

"That spoilt brat." This is good; they've never really talked about Edith's son.

"Yes, well," Edith says smugly, "you liked him well enough at one time."

"If I hadn't needed a date for my high school grad, and if Mother hadn't already got me a dress, it would never have happened. And how did he know I was that desperate?"

"Maisie told me, of course."

"I knew it. But it was you made him do it, or you put him up to it anyway."

"I suggested he consider it," Edith admits. "But when he did consider it, he quite began to like the idea."

"Sure. He was always looking for ways to be mean to me. Did you know that rotten little bugger used to throw snowballs at me with rocks packed in the middle?"

"And you continued to go out with him?"

Annie can't help it, she starts to laugh. Edith's so good at the subtle jab, the sarcastic, the ironic, the sardonic. Annie realizes she's having fun.

"I meant, of course, when we were kids," she says. "Speaking of which, did you know he peed on my shoes once just because they were new and he thought I liked them?"

"Oh dear," Edith says, "That is bad. And did you? Like them?"

"I didn't, actually."

"Be that as it may," Edith says, "he swore he behaved like a gentleman on the night of your graduation."

"Oh, he did. That was the really sneaky bit. Locky

the Louse, Locky the Dirtball, at my house in this white sport coat and spit and polished to his fingernails, and he hands me this purple orchid. Your idea, I'm sure." Edith merely raises her eyebrows.

"And he pins this exotic bloom to the left side of my dress, without seeming the least suggestive, without even a hint that my breasts are mere inches from his hand. I suppose you call that playing fair? Edith, I'd never seen the guy clean before, you know? And he turns out to be a real smooth operator. Species I'd never run across before. In my limited experience. You don't think that's a bit confusing for a girl?"

"You always exaggerate. Allison was just the same."

"I'm not just the same. I exaggerate in my own peculiar way."

"Finish your soup."

"And I'm funnier." Annie tips her bowl to finish the soup.

"Anyone is. Allison was never funny. Sarcastic, mostly. Ironic, sometimes. Funny, never."

"Worst of all," Annie decides to get it all out, "was that he could dance."

"Of course he could. All my children danced."

"Of course they did," Annie mimics. "They probably had their own private dancing master."

"Nonsense," Edith says tartly. "They learned at the church youth club."

"Be that as it may," Annie mocks Edith's phrase, "he waltzed me onto the floor, and for the first time, I saw that a waltz is more than just one-two-three and keeping a diagram of the box step in your head. And that's how the damage was done, Edith."

"Did you sleep with him?" Edith asks. "I just wondered."

"Yes, I slept with him, and he got me pregnant too. And he didn't have any ideas what could be done about it when I told him. I was sure I was going to have to go to Mother, and then I started to bleed." Amazingly, Annie starts to cry. She'd thought she was over this years ago. "He drove me to the hospital, and then he drove away for good. I had to beg the doctor to tell Mother I was having trouble with my periods. So there's your answer, Edith. Just think, your first grandchild, it would have been. You'd have been just thrilled."

"My dear Annie," Edith says firmly, "must you be so histrionic? It was for the best. You'll be a much better mother now."

"You must have been so relieved when he dumped me," Annie says bitterly.

Suddenly Edith is really angry. "Goddamn it, Annie, stop this self-pity. I would have been pleased to have you as a daughter-in-law."

It stops Annie dead. Can Edith really mean this? She struggles to unravel the words.

"I'm only sorry you went from my son directly to my nephew, because there isn't a lot to choose between them."

"Now wait a minute," Annie says indignantly.

"There's quite a lot to choose." Amazing. She's defending Charles.

"Ah, there's a lot to choose, is there? So you will stick with him?"

"I didn't say that." Annie wishes Edith would stop looking so amused. "It's just, he does have a lot more, shall we call it, husband material, than Locky will ever have."

"But less, of course, than Harold Borebank, I take it?" Annie doesn't answer. "Are you sleeping with Harold?"

"None of your damned business!" God, this woman knows how to be annoying.

"So you are."

"I'm not. 'Sleeping with' implies a regular thing."

"Aha!"

"Don't give me that." Suddenly Annie's having fun again. Edith is a good person to tell forbidden things. She's in no position to point fingers.

"All right now," Annie says firmly, "you've had your little *frisson*. Tell me about Allison." Edith gets up and pours more tea. "Tell me, Edith."

"You're ready to hear, are you?"

"I'm ready for anything you can tell me. You know, if the two of you had a lesbian affair, or if she was a secret coke addict, or you were, or whatever."

"I've never actually had a lesbian affair," Edith says. "Sorry to disappoint."

"Tell."

Edith sits across from Annie in the nook, near

enough that they could reach out and touch each other.

"I suppose I've been putting it off, because I wanted to find a simple way to present it. Nothing flashy or sensational. I'm going to tell you about something that happened when Allison was only eleven years old and just beginning to be a woman."

"Cut to the chase."

"All right." Edith sits up very straight and begins to speak, very calmly, making no attempt to embellish or add expression. "One day she went walking on the prairie, early in the morning, before her parents were awake. She was pretending to be a knight in search of adventure. Phillip had been reading her tales of King Arthur and the Round Table, but she didn't want to be the damsel waiting for a knight to come and rescue her. She wanted to make her own adventure.

"She crossed the railway trestle over the valley. She walked across the prairie until the land turned to rolling hills. She looked around her for signs and omens, but aside from a mare with its foal, she found nothing. Then she spied a rock, which somehow had been split in two; and inside one of the pieces she found the fossil of a nautilus shell. You know, the kind that makes a spiral."

"Yes, I know what a nautilus is," Annie says, "But how do you know all this? Did she tell you?"

"In a manner of speaking, yes. Now Allison recognized this fossil as something valuable to her. She picked it up and called it her talisman. It would lead her to her adventure and bring her luck. She walked through the hills till she came to a dried-up creek with an arched stone bridge over it. Beneath the bridge she found a stick of diamond willow. She peeled the bark from it, and called it her sword. While she was doing this, a car went over the bridge. Without questioning why, she knew enough to hide herself."

"I don't understand how you know all this," Annie says. The account seems so detailed. No one could remember all this.

"Be patient," Edith says. "You're just like her that way, so impatient. After the car was gone, she came up from under the bridge. She followed its trail in the dirt road until the tracks left the road into a disused gravel pit gouged into the side of a hill."

Even in the midst of the story, Annie notes Edith's careful use of language. "Disused," not "unused."

"All the best gravel had been taken, for road-building I suppose, and there was nothing much left but boulders and a residue of sand and gravel."

"You've been there, haven't you?" Annie is suddenly sure.

Edith ignores the question. "Against the hillside she found a small mound covered over with some of the remaining gravel. She probed the mound with her willow stick."

"Wait!" Annie says, suddenly uncertain. "Don't go on. Not yet."

"You *said* to cut to the chase."

"I'm not ready," Annie says. "Not yet."

"Never mind, it's a good place for me to stop," Edith

says. "I'll let you hear the rest of it in her own words." She opens a drawer in the nook table and pulls out some papers. She sorts through them until she finds the place she wants. Annie watches, her mind jumping to all sorts of conclusions, wanting to let them bounce around in her mind before she lets Edith confirm any of them.

The writing is Allison's. An account of this story Edith is telling. Why does Edith have it? Allison gave it to her? Or mailed it to her, in a posthumous letter like the one Annie got? No, Edith found it. Where? In the house. Took it away so Annie couldn't read it. Or so she couldn't read it right away? Is that it? She knew Annie would read all the papers. She didn't want her to see Allison's letter until she was ready. Until she was stronger. Until she needed to know. Isn't that the first rule of storytelling? Never give anything away until your audience demands to know. But how did Edith know Annie would ever demand to know? How did she know she'd even stay?

Edith has set her up from the beginning. Set her up to stay. To reclaim the house. To read Eamon's papers. And now to hear this story. Is it all for this? Or is it simply the whole experience she's wanted Annie to have? Why? Why does Edith care about her? Is it because of guilt about the way she treated Allison? Or is it truly affection for herself too? No, she doesn't want that, doesn't want to think about it.

Why is it so hard to accept that Edith might care about her? Even as she formulates the question, she sees the answer. Because her mother is dead. If her mother is dead, nobody else can be her mother. She will be an orphan. No matter how much it hurts. Woe to the person who doesn't accept that. But Edith doesn't accept it. Nor is she afraid of Annie. Edith watches Annie as all these things go through her mind. Annie has the feeling that Edith hears them all as if she were right there in Annie's mind.

Annie snatches the papers from Edith. She reads.

My stick touched something, and I must have known immediately what it was, even though I wouldn't let myself know. But I couldn't stop pushing back the gravel until she was uncovered.

It was a baby, a girl. Stillborn, only I didn't know that word then. Her face and hands were dusty from the gravel and her face was beginning to have small indentations where the gravel had lain on it. But she was clean. Someone had washed her and wrapped her in a flannelette nightgown with the price tag still on the hem. I touched her face, and it was not absolutely cold. But even I who had never seen death understood that she was dead.

I tried to say a prayer for her, bits and pieces of things I'd memorized in Confirmation Class. The more I tried, the less I believed in the words or their power to comfort or help.

Finally there was nothing I could do but cover her up again. Over the head of her grave, I placed my talisman stone with the fossil side facing up. I wished her a good journey or something like that.

I started for home and promptly got lost. I wandered around for hours until I was very hungry and thirsty. I thought of Jesus wandering in the desert. I wondered what was the use of it. At that moment I knew I didn't believe in my religion anymore. Soon after that thought, I was able to find the right direction and make my way home. I told my parents I had gone for a walk and had got lost. I promised them never to do it again.

After that time I was conscious of a dead place inside me. I had trouble believing in people, their professions of interest or affection. I had never been a child for whom anything came easily. But after this time, I think I must have become more prickly and difficult.

All my life I have tried to believe that she was only stillborn and that no one in that car was responsible for her death. I have never spoken of it to anyone. Even now, I feel I shouldn't write this. But it happened, and I must bear witness.

Annie reaches the end. Edith takes the papers from

her hand and puts them on the table. Now three women have borne witness.

"Yes, I have driven out there," Edith says. "But I didn't find any trace of a grave."

Edith touches Annie's hand lightly, then seems to feel a repelling force and takes it away. But her eyes never leave Annie's, staying with her. They sit for a long time, as the last light fades from the sky. Then Edith goes upstairs, leaving Annie alone.

At last Annie gets up and goes into the living room, dark except for the light spilling in from the kitchen. The piano is where it always is. She sits down on the backless bench.

The keys on the extreme left make sounds so deep and low she can hardly perceive them as musical. As she moves up the keyboard, they become recognizable as sounds she could make with her own voice, then they rise until they are once again beyond her range.

The cool keys feel good against her hands; they have a formal beauty, black on white, always in the same arrangement, top to bottom. She knows what an octave is. She plays two bass notes, an octave apart, repeating them endlessly in a driving rhythm until that loses its appeal, and then she plays three high notes in a row, over and over, with the fingers of her right hand, accenting them in different ways, adding bass notes with her left in accordance with some pattern her body has decided upon. She plays single notes, then two or three at a time, some discordant, some harmonious. She plays big clanging chords, with both hands. She strikes the keys with a flat palm.

She plays and plays, her own strange music, making the piano express all the things that she would rather not know. She hears in her mind Eamon's words: *I envied them the things I would rather not have known*. Too late now not to know so many things. She hears her mother's words: *No one is to blame*. Her playing gathers speed and force. She plays her rage and her pain and everything she has seen and learned since she came to her house. She plays for herself and for her mother, Allison, whose presence she can almost feel. Allison, who did love her. Is this how Allison wanted to play? She sobs out loud with the need to get it right, to make the piano do what she wants. She plays until she herself is touched by a kind of beauty in it; until there is nothing more to play.

Outside the rain is still falling, soft music against the window.

Annie sits in an armchair in the dark room. The house is utterly quiet. Water drips in the fireplace chimney. She couldn't move now even if the waters had swollen to scale the cliff, even if they were lapping at Edith's door.

She hears the doorbell ringing as something far away and unconnected with her life. She hears Edith answer the door, hears Charles's voice inquiring after her. And Edith answering that Annie isn't feeling well and is spending the night here in the house. That tomorrow she will see him. That he shouldn't worry. There is a pause as Edith looks for something.

"Annie asked me to give you this key." Edith must be giving him her own key. "You can stay in the house, of course." Incredibly, Charles seems to accept all this without question or objection. She hears him thank Edith and leave.

Edith comes into the living room. Annie closes her eyes so Edith will think she's asleep and will not try to speak to her. But Edith only puts a blanket over Annie and goes out to the kitchen, closing the door after her. Annie sleeps.

CHAPTER TWENTY-SIX

When Annie comes into the kitchen next morning, Edith is sitting in the nook watching a flood bulletin on a television set concealed until now in one of the kitchen cupboards. She stares at the set, apparently unaware of Annie. It's Charles again, speaking over a shot of a drawing of an elaborate three-storey house. Although he's not as filled with emotion as in the previous report, there is still a heightened awareness about him, a sense that this story interests him powerfully.

"This is an architect's rendering of the Harley Newsome residence, built for his great-grandfather, Dr. Gerald Newsome in 1899, the first of River Park's grand houses. And this is it today [shot of a rooftop and chimney and an awful lot of water], as the waters of Spring Creek pound at its porches, parlours, pantries, bedrooms, kitchens, and dining rooms. Harley Newsome was born in the house fifty-two years ago and has never lived anywhere else. Now there is no telling whether he will ever live in it again. His home, along with all the other stately, magnificent, and sometimes downright odd river showpieces [stock footage of the neighbourhood, focusing on some of the strangest houses] may never recover from the devastation of this flood [shots of the flood].

"But not all the valley homes were grand. [Still black-and-white photos of much smaller places.] Some were humbler structures which sheltered people who worked in many jobs around the city. [Shot of Charles standing at the end of River Road, looking faintly military in a belted trenchcoat, a soft drizzle dampening his hair, with the flooded valley in the background.]

"I can't show you what Tom Bradley's place used to look like, although neighbours describe it as a modest frame bungalow, pleasant and well maintained, because its roof is now under water. I can show you, however, what it used to be like inside.

[Shots of the interior of Tom's house, no doubt from the same television item Edith saw several years ago, showing Tom patiently working on the creation of one of his model houses. The Newsome house, as luck would have it.]

"In the last five years of his life, Tom Bradley had found a new and unique art form. He was building replicas of the lovely old park homes. [Close-up views of various model houses around Tom's living room.]

He said he hoped to document not only their beauty but their history. He hoped to do them all before he died. And he did finish almost all of them. Most were purchased by the owners of the homes and given pride of place on mantels and coffee tables. Now Tom Bradley's replicas, lovingly carried from homes just hours before the flood crest struck, may be all that remains of these once vibrant dwellings when the waters recede.

"But the irony doesn't end there, for the man himself is dead, without having had time to complete his work. [Shot of Tom up close, painting trim on a tiny window.] Sunday morning, when the valley was dark and rain-swept, Tom Bradley, aged sixty-six and a lifelong park resident, suffered a heart attack. He had been up late working, apparently unaware of the approaching flood crest.

"Tom had no surviving family, but he did manage to call a friend for help. At 5:02 a.m., he was rushed by ambulance [stock shot of an ambulance speeding up to a hospital emergency entrance] to the Sisters of Providence Hospital [shot of an old brick hospital], where he was pronounced dead later that morning, a few hours after the dike he had helped build gave way. His house and his work in progress [shot of Tom working] are covered in swirling, murky water [shot of debris shooting through dark water, then back to Charles looking over the valley].

"If Tom Bradley had not regained consciousness long enough to make that single phone call, the river would have claimed him along with his work, and along with the houses of River Park.

"In fifty years, a hundred years, this flood may not be much remembered. It will be just another weather statistic from the past. But for thousands of people in Riverbend, especially those who took turns building the dike they hoped would save a vital part of their community, there is little else to think of today. This is a sad day for them, and for the friends of Tom Bradley and those who loved his work. And for this reporter, who, boy and man, camped in the river world's hidden places – which may be forever altered by the river's own awesome forces. For National Report A.M., this is Charles Wilkins in Riverbend."

He gazes for a long three seconds into the camera before someone switches to a commercial. Annie continues to see his face superimposed on the images of take-out hamburgers, continues to hear his words.

Edith gets up and flips off the television. No zapper, no channel surfing for her. Watch what you planned to watch, then get up and turn it bloody well off.

"Yes, it's a sad day," she says, "and also not. Do they have to turn everything into an *item?*" Annie realizes that part of Edith's crankiness is probably from pain in her hands.

"It's his job," Annie says.

"Yes, some job," Edith says scornfully. She waves in the direction of tea and the makings for toast. Today Annie can help herself if she wants anything.

"He's good, isn't he?" It doesn't occur to Annie to think this very often. She's usually bored by the whole thing, and anyway, as an anchor, Charles rarely does reporting anymore. But she can see that he's made a lot of connections, pulled a lot of threads together, in a short time.

"I couldn't say," Edith says. "I know so little about these things."

Annie pours herself tea and starts her toast. "I wonder how much he's actually found out about Tom. He must have talked to the ambulance people. Or a local stringer."

"He probably knows more than he was letting on," Edith says testily. "He's probably saving the rest to blackmail his old aunt with."

"Oh, Charles wouldn't do that," Annie says. "And anyway, what could he possibly want from you?" She puts a slight, insulting emphasis on the "you."

"Don't be rude," Edith says. "There could be lots of things."

Edith rubs her aching hands together, gazing at them as if unsure how they came to be attached to her. Annie immediately feels sorry for needling her, but decides there's no point in saying so. After all, if Edith wanted to spend time with nice, considerate people, she'd hardly have gone to so much trouble over Annie.

The toast pops. Annie butters it with great concentration.

"He called earlier this morning," Edith says, "when

you were still sleeping. He's got himself a rental car."

"Really?" Annie's stalling for time. She's still not ready to see Charles. Not yet.

"Yes, really. He has to file another report, then he's done. He said he could meet you at the house. Your house, I mean."

"No," Annie says, feeling panic like jagged teeth working at her vitals. "I can't meet him there. Anyway, I have to go to work."

"You don't work till the afternoon." Edith is inexorable.

"True," Annie says, trying to recall when she was ever so unguarded as to have told Edith her schedule. "But I have to get my hair cut this morning."

"You don't say." Edith barely suppresses her contempt for this flimsy excuse.

"I do. It hasn't been cut for the whole two months I've been here."

"Looks it too," Edith says.

"Oh, shut up." Annie sees Edith's lips twitch in an embryonic smile. "So where do you recommend I go?"

"Well, I go to Agnes at Miss Rose's, but you'd probably find that a bit tame. Why don't you try Mark's Unisex? That's where I see a lot of the young people going for their inexplicably unbecoming styles."

"Young people," Annie says. "I'm not sure I qualify."

"You do to me," Edith says. "But go where you like. It's always a crap shoot anyway. You want the car?"

Annie thinks of the last time she drove Edith's monster. She wouldn't have thought she'd ever consent to drive it again. But it would be better not to be dependent on Charles for transport, not when they're facing each other for the first time in two months.

"Sure," she says. "That would be a help." Edith tosses her the keys. "Thanks." Absurdly, she feels like a teenager who's scored the car for Saturday night. Just let Charles try to intimidate her when she's got the grey tank to peel off in. Of course, to be fair, he hasn't tried to intimidate her in quite some time. He hasn't tried anything at all.

"In case you don't have to time to stop off home," Edith says, "I left a dress you might like to wear in your old room."

"Oh, thanks," Annie says, "I'll take a look."

Later, Annie comes down in a cobalt blue knit cotton dress, its gathered skirt dropping from an Empire waist; very stylish, but not one of Edith's; Edith has gone out and bought it for her. As Annie heads for the front door, Edith calls out from the kitchen.

"I'm to tell him where to find you, am I?"

"Just as you like," Annie says. "I've no objection."

"Run along then." Edith flaps her hand in dismissal.

"Bye, Edith. And thanks for the dress." As she goes out the door, Annie realizes she's going to miss Edith when it's time to leave Riverbend, if she is leaving.

Or when Edith dies. Surely that won't be for quite a while. But her days are numbered, like everyone else's.

# CHAPTER TWENTY-SEVEN

M ark's Unisex is not a place she would usually enter. It's shiny black everywhere – floor, walls, ceiling – with work stations outlined in strips of bright theatrical make-up lights. Like being inside a huge black garbage bag with a bunch of penlights, Annie thinks.

A tall young woman, dressed in a black leather mini-skirt and red thigh-high boots, peers out of the darkness; "Sh'lisse" says the name badge on her white leather sleeveless top. Sh'lisse's flame-red hair is parted to one side and combed over the top of her head to drape across one eye and cheek. On the other side below the part, her hair is simply gone; she doesn't have any, not even any fuzz. She must use depilatories on it.

Her ensemble is completed by a gold nose stud and nearly black lipstick, along with multiple gold rings stuck through various parts of her unusually convoluted ears.

"I need a haircut," Annie says.

"I guess I could take you," Sh'lisse says, looking doubtfully at Annie's hair. When she speaks, Annie sees that Sh'lisse even has a gold stud piercing her narrow pink tongue. Amazing how well she can still talk.

"What sort of look were you thinking of?" she asks.

"Well, I want something different." Preferably something where even my husband won't recognize me, Annie thinks.

"Good," Sh'lisse encourages, "I would recommend that."

"Although not quite as adventurous as what you've got."

"Oh, no," Sh'lisse says, "I wouldn't give you this. I'm just sort of trying it on. To give the clients an idea of the kinds of things we can do here."

"What I'd like," Annie says, "is quite a bit shorter and sort of soft and fluffy. Sort of layered. A bit more volume. Maybe a bit spiky. But not too spiky. Could you do that?"

"Oh, for sure. No problem. Do you want some colour too? I could layer in some pink and some tangerine, just to give your own colour a little more visual interest, you know?"

"Another time that would be very nice. But I don't think I will today. Because I'm pregnant, and I'm not sure if the dyes might affect the baby."

"Whatever you say," Sh'lisse says, but it's clear it would be a severely frosty Friday in hell before she'd neglect her hair on that account. "Let's get you shampooed then."

She leads Annie to the row of sinks at the back. Too

late Annie notices that her black-painted fingernails stick out nearly an inch beyond her actual fingertips. She's surely going to get her scalp ripped to shreds.

But all is well. Sh'lisse has the most amazing manual dexterity, massaging Annie's scalp to immaculate cleanliness using only the soft pads of her fingertips. As she pats Annie's hair dry with a towel, Annie catches sight of a door with a price list on it for various kinds of body piercing. The rates for navels and nipples are surprisingly reasonable: only $40 each, including both antiseptic and hoop. Nipples are definitely out, but perhaps Charles would like to see her in a tasteful gold navel ring.

Sh'lisse cuts Annie's hair with scissors she says cost three hundred bucks. She prunes away what feels like huge clumps of hair, but in fact she only snips a little at a time and each swatch of hair is tapered meticulously to a tiny point. She mousses up what remains with something called Ice Crystale Eternelle and painstakingly blow-dries it, a little hunk at a time, spraying each hunk individually as soon as she's satisfied with the shape.

Why am I doing this? Annie suddenly wonders, now that it's too late to stop. Is it a) to confuse Charles and gain some kind of (probably unfair) advantage? Is it b) to show him that she's changed? Or c) to show herself that she's changed? Or is it d) to distract herself from the fact that she's going to have to tell Charles she's slept with Harold Borebank?

Probably it's e) all of the above. Although d) would have been quite sufficient.

Sh'lisse is in the home stretch now. All the individual spritzes are dry. She takes a brush and delicately blends the whole thing together, like folding egg whites into cake batter. She considers the effect from every possible angle, brushing a little more here, cutting away a stray hair there. At last she holds up a hand mirror for Annie to see all around.

Her hair looks like a hat of some odd multi-layered fur, say porcupine or hedgehog. Or like a bowl of artfully arranged dark feathers. Or a very interesting and shapely bird's nest. She looks about fifteen, or she looks older and very sophisticated; she's not sure which.

Her eyes wander back to the price list for piercing. Imagine greeting Charles with a tongue stud, his surprise when he kisses her. (Who says he's going to kiss her?) But it's probably too late. You probably need an appointment in advance. She knows in her heart that she'd only have to mention it and Sh'lisse would have her needle out in five seconds flat. But she's not really the type. The type that's willing to put up with that sort of pain.

Annie does let Sh'lisse sell her a lipstick in the same near-black shade she wears herself. When Annie puts it on, it makes her eyes and hair look darker too; it sucks light from everything around it.

"Cool," says Sh'lisse, and she's right if by "cool" you mean "sinister and cruel teenager." Annie savours the moment, resists the urge to wipe the lipstick right off again.

ANNIE WALKS FROM THE CADDY to the front door of Al's, trying to look calm. The air swishes through her puffed-feather hair in a newly intimate way. As she enters the store, Al steps forward, ready to serve her. Then he looks again, takes in the feathery hair.

"Annie, for Christ's sake, you'll scare away the customers!"

"That bad?" She gets a tissue from her purse, scrapes it across her lips. "Better?"

He considers. "Now you look like child labour."

Annie gets out her usual lipstick, an innocuous dusty rose. It slips from her fingers and skitters across the floor. Al gives her an odd look as she dives to the floor to pick it up. He takes in the blue dress, her shaky hands, but doesn't comment. To assure them both that she's completely normal, she flicks on her lipstick without recourse to a mirror.

"That's better. Now you look like the teenage daughter giving the old man a hand in the store."

"Sounds good to me." Annie says. "Responsible, helpful kid. Plucky family enterprise. Come to think of it, I'd have loved this job when I was in high school."

"Please. You're making me feel old. But at least you probably won't scare the gorbies now." Gorbie is Al's term for a certain type of well-heeled customer.

"I don't see any gorbies at the moment."

"Have faith," he says.

Miraculously, as if they have jointly conjured her from the insubstantial air, a woman pulls up in front, a peach of a gorbie in a BMW. She gets out of the car, revealing a chic outfit and hair expensively highlighted in subtly-graded shades of gold. Why not just wear a sign saying, I HAVE MONEY, LOTS OF IT, Annie wonders.

"Good morning," Annie says. "May I help you find something?"

The woman spoons up Annie's sweetness and courtesy like it was honey or maybe cocaine. Annie pours it on, but she isn't pretending; she makes herself want every piece she tries to sell the woman. She even points out tiny dents and scratches, so that everything is above board. She catches Al's eye; he winks. God, she thinks, I could've been an actress.

The woman buys a curved mahogany sideboard (twelve hundred bucks) Al's had kicking around for six months, a pricey glass-topped curio table (five-fifty) that's a genuine something or other, and six leather-seated dining room chairs (fifteen hundred), which Annie personally promises to give a special polish before Al delivers them. She stops just short of saying, My father will see they are delivered safely. But it takes an effort.

When the woman leaves, Al, according to their established custom, pays Annie her commission of six hundred and fifty dollars in cash. She takes a quick tour of the store and makes some snap decisions. She chooses a lawyer's bookcase (four hundred and twenty), which she tells herself will be a present for Charles (or for herself should Charles decide to have nothing further to do with her), and a gorgeous mahogany apothecary's cabinet with dozens of tiny drawers for storing things (five hundred and ninety). This is well above the commission she's earned, even with her twenty-percent discount, but Al agrees to call it an even trade. He loves cash sales above all others.

Annie is thrilled with her finds. The cabinet will come in very handy if she continues to attract lovers. She can then file away each one in his own handy little drawer, the way the apothecary did with his medicines and herbs. She can file Charles under "Wilkinsbane Charlesii" and her more recent adventure under "Haroldwort" or maybe "Borebank's Essence." Her life will never again seem cluttered or out of control.

Really? Who is she kidding. Charles could walk through that door any second. Her hands and feet are like ice; her heart must be sending all the blood to her vital organs. What is it expecting, a fight to the death?

Suddenly she feels terribly worn out. She drops into a burgundy plush armchair and wishes she could stay there until the floodwaters have all dried up and Charles has gone back to the city, or maybe even to L.A., if that's what he wants. Come to think of it, that's probably what'll happen. He must think by now that she doesn't want to see him. He'll probably take the hint and go away. That would be for the best – wouldn't it?

No, it would only be easier. And if that's what she wanted, why did she ask him to read Eamon's papers?

A dark green Taurus parks beside the Caddy. Charles

gets out and looks in the window, looks at Annie without recognition. The hairdo's working, she thinks, giggling nervously. Al gives her a look, wondering what's going on. Charles enters. He still doesn't know her.

Annie wonders what she knows about this man or he about her; wonders how much of what she thinks she knows is true. She's attracted by his looks; she'd almost forgotten she could feel that way. In a moment he'll recognize her, then everything will begin. To change, unravel, she doesn't know what.

He sees her now. He looks glad and then he looks very uncertain.

"Annie?" he says. She makes herself move towards him. He's scared, she can tell.

Annie's scared too, her whole body trembles. Will he embrace her? Will he want to kiss her? She makes a small move in his direction and he opens his arms. They hold each other, both shaking. He feels thinner and for some reason it wrings her heart. Isn't it always the woman's fault if her husband doesn't get enough to eat? But he's not only thinner, he feels stronger. He must be working out. Not starving at all.

CHAPTER TWENTY-EIGHT

"I never knew you cared about houses." Charles looks around the living room. He's working so hard, trying to speak normally; she can feel the effort he puts into it.

They sit in the wing chairs facing the living room window, turning towards each other when they speak. The air in the room feels heavy, as if there's about three times as much gravity as normal. Extra gravity must be caused by having a large number of topics to discuss, all of them possible minefields.

"I felt at home right away," he says. "I never knew you could do this, but when I saw it, I liked it."

Annie can't help but be pleased. She pours tea and wonders where to begin. In the time she's been on her own, she's got used to doing the things she decides on, hasn't had to explain them to anybody. There are many things Charles has the right to know, but she doesn't want to fall back into the rut of explaining and justifying everything while Charles the rational looks on, judges.

Maybe she's been considering things too much from her own point of view, not wanting to go back to being the dependent, emotional, less rational one. Now she has to think of him too. He's not that rational, after all. She can't cede him that territory anymore. Or cut him out of the other.

"You never told me what happened about the L.A. job." This is not the most important thing they have to talk about, but it's a start.

"I didn't get it." He tries not to look crushed. "They gave me an interview, but…." He hesitates, embarrassed. "They said the guy who got it had better reporting skills."

Annie experiences, as she did when Edith criticized Charles, a stab of loyalty. "You have good reporting skills."

A small smile breaks across his face. "I tried to figure out what was behind the words. I think they thought I was a bit of a cold fish."

God, she thinks, they expect a man to behave a certain way and when he does, it's still not good enough.

"I liked your work on the flood," she says. "That didn't seem cold."

He's pleased, but brushes it off. "I'm from here. Who wouldn't feel something? Robin Hill, where I used to sleep out, under twenty feet of water." She hears the love in his voice for that bit of wilderness that was allowed to be part of his childhood.

"I guess I'm sorry you didn't get the job," she says, "if that's what you really wanted."

He sighs. "Maybe it wasn't really. Maybe I even sabotaged myself."

"Why would you do that?"

"Oh, it was all starting to seem so facile." He looks almost ashamed to tell her this. "The usual histrionics over the latest crisis. The Economy in Crisis. Young People in Crisis. Health Care in Crisis. Sometimes we even did our part to manufacture the crisis."

"And everything processed and boiled down into an *item*. Edith was complaining about that, just this morning."

"Really?" he asks. "She's a lot sharper than I thought."

"I know."

"Maybe I knew L.A. was no answer," he says. "Even before you left, I felt like I was coming to the end of something in Toronto. Packaging the news. Endless items flooding past every day. The voice of authority."

As he speaks, his voice seems to relax. She realizes that Charles has always articulated his words much more carefully than other people. When he stops doing it, his face looks softer; younger.

"But Charles," she says, surprised, "I always thought that was what you wanted."

"Oh, I did enjoy it," he admits ruefully. "It's a kind of

power. Part of me would hate to give it up."

"What else could you do?"

"Well, there's this guy at work who's always talking to me about doing independent productions."

"Like what?" she asks, really curious.

"Oh, documentaries and stuff. We'd have to sell it to the networks, but at least we could work on subjects we were really interested in." His face actually seems to light up as he talks.

"Sounds risky."

"Oh, it is. There'd be a lot less money, at first. But I could learn more. I don't only mean facts, this job has filled me with facts. But it's like I still don't know anything. I want to understand how things work."

Annie feels an excitement. She can't remember him talking like this before. About freedom: to think, to interpret. "What kind of things?" she asks.

"All the stuff that never fits into the items. Because it's considered too dull or too disturbing or too complex. You know, things that take too long to explain, so people zap to another channel to keep from getting bored."

"Do you mean things like why a small city is having its industries stripped away one by one? Why it's suddenly cheaper to ship all the beef in North America to Chicago or Winnipeg or whatever, cut it up, and then ship it all out again?" He nods, about to reply, but Annie keeps talking, she's on a roll now. "Or why people's work is being devalued into monotonous, poorly-paid, part-time bondage? Until they have no pride left, and no money to buy all the stuff that gets produced?" It feels good getting these ideas out; she hadn't even realized they were there.

"Those are some pretty good possibilities," he says, a little amused at her vehemence.

"That could be interesting." Annie gets up and walks around the small room. "It could be exciting."

He's surprised by her enthusiasm. "Nothing's decided yet. Rob and I are just talking." But he's pleased too. It's so long since she's been interested in his work.

She stops pacing as a thought strikes her. "Would you have to move to Los Angeles to do it?"

"Oh, no. But we've been thinking about moving to Vancouver. There's lots of production there and experienced crews." She sees the relief in his face. He didn't really want to move to California either.

"Moving to Vancouver," Annie tries out the words. At least she doesn't find them as instantly threatening as the phrase "moving to Los Angeles."

"I want to take some time off to work on a few ideas. I'm interested in doing an interview show about current topics. Something like *Larry King Live* or *Pamela Wallin*. Dig out the viewpoints you don't usually hear. I could pitch it to the network."

"You've been doing a lot of thinking," she says. "Maybe my being away helped."

"Maybe," he says. "It was a catalyst. I've known for a long time I needed a change. Something more substantial, something that might last for a while." She nods. "If I want to do that, I've got to find some time. Take a leave of absence for the summer."

"Will the network give it to you?"

"Oh, sure. Why not? They get someone to fill in for the summer and save a bundle on my contract. Of course, they might start to think they don't need me."

"You're one of their best announcers."

"They forget you pretty quick in this business. Out of sight…out of sight."

"But you'll take the risk?"

He nods. "I found your note yesterday. I stayed up most of the night reading Eamon's papers. I felt like he was taking me over."

"Me too," Annie says. "And the more I read, the more I understood my family." She takes a deep breath. "I understood why my mother couldn't show her love."

"I guess it was important to spend the time here?"

"I had to do it," she says. "Part of me knew it, but it was Edith made me stay."

"Edith?" he says. "You could never stand Edith."

"I thought she was a total bitch," Annie says, "and maybe she is. But she's stuck with me through it all."

"You know," he says, "things weren't working…in Toronto. We'd pretty much stopped talking."

"A couple of icebergs," Annie says. "Nine-tenths underwater."

"Actually," he says, "it's not always exactly nine-tenths, that's a bit of a misconception."

"Charles," she says, "I don't want to hear about an item."

He looks at her, uncertain; then they both start to laugh. Annie feels as if they're in a piece of complex music and have now completed the first movement.

THEY ARE WALKING DOWN ORINOCO STREET. Fresh green leaves have given the street new life and restored some of the charm Annie remembers. She tells Charles about Doreen and the children and shows him their house. She tells him about the tea party.

They wander through streets they've known since childhood, feeling these spaces claiming a kind of loyalty from them. They stop to look at Annie's old school.

"I have to find something else to do too," she says. "I'll never type another goddamn thesis. I'm sick of other people's words."

"I did sometimes wonder how you could stand it," he says. "So what about your own words? I always thought you had a wicked sense of humour."

This can't be Charles speaking. It's like a science fiction fantasy in which people enter an alternate dimension where their lives have developed differently. Annie has entered Riverbend, explored the past. Maybe she's pulled him along with her.

"I thought of writing a book myself," Charles says. "About Eamon Conal."

"Maisie would turn over in her grave," Annie says drily.

"Isn't that the point?" he asks. "We can't go on letting her have her way."

"I think she'd started to realize that herself. It gave her so little in return."

"When I think of writing a book," he says, "I'm terrified. All that research. Sitting in a room, writing. Six months, minimum, I figure."

"What's so awful about that?" Annie is genuinely puzzled.

"I've never spent that long on anything," he admits. "News items, backgrounders, mini-docs, I'd be in and out in a few days or at most a few weeks."

"I like the idea of a book," she says. "Built around Eamon's words. So it wouldn't only be about TB, it would be about the way people thought."

"How we all come to be the way we are," Charles says, and again she feels his excitement. "I could research the whole history of tuberculosis. It's making a comeback, you know. There's cases in North America resistant to all drugs. And it's still a worldwide killer." She looks at him in amazement. "Sorry," he says sheepishly, "I did an item on it."

"It could be really good, couldn't it?" she says. "Eamon's voice anchoring everything. Family pictures. Interviews with Old Crocks."

"And we could turn it into a feature-length documentary too," he says.

Annie makes herself slow down; she has to make sure

what he's saying. "Charles," she says, "you talk as if we might work on this together."

"Well, we could," he says. "It would be a lot more interesting than what either of us did before."

"That's true," she says. "It would be a lot more interesting."

They fall silent, thinking of implications.

THEY STAND ON THE RIVERBANK where the water still streams by at amazing velocity. It can hardly be the same river as when Annie crossed on the ice, the same river they'd casually called "the crick" when she was young. During Annie's stay, the river has assumed an awesome power and the people have been helpless to stop it. Annie and Charles hunker down among chokecherry bushes where the hill, sheltered from wind, radiates heat absorbed from the spring sun. Charles takes Annie's hand, tentatively; she doesn't pull away. They balance there on the bank above the hurtling water; nobody speaks.

BACK IN ANNIE'S LIVING ROOM, they head for the wing chairs. Before Annie can sit down, Charles adjusts the chairs so that they face each other.

"That's better," he says.

"I suppose you did an item on feng shui," she says.

"No," he says, "I just want to see you."

"Speaking of items," she says. "Dust mites." God,

she's changing the subject; trying to postpone what's coming.

"What?"

"I sat here and watched you do an item on dust mites." She makes her voice sound authoritative. "The hidden danger that may lurk in *your* home."

He laughs. "Dust mites are so gross. Made my skin crawl for a week."

"You had me convinced there were millions of them in my house, fanning out across rugs and mattresses looking for little flakes of my skin. Every flake a week's groceries. I could almost see them piled up in heaps in the corner of the room."

"Annie," he says, "there aren't any dust mites here."

"There aren't?"

"It's too dry. They need a certain amount of humidity to survive. It was in the story, how did you miss it?" He thinks about what he's just said. "I guess you must have turned me off." She doesn't answer. "Can't say I blame you. I was starting to sound a bit pompous, even to myself."

"A bit?" she asks, and Charles laughs.

"Did you see my report on Tom Bradley?" he asks. Annie nods.

"When I saw the model of Aunt Edith's house on your table, I didn't know what it meant. The next day, I talked to the ambulance drivers and found out she'd been with him, and the only way I could make sense of it was so fantastic, but it wouldn't go away until I'd extrapolated a whole new side to her life from it."

"Did you ask her about it?"

"Yeah, but I could see she was nervous. Something else she was afraid of me knowing. More than just that she'd had an affair. And then everything clicked. Like I must have always known there was something about Tira."

"Tira doesn't know."

"No," he says, "I didn't think so."

"Edith says I could tell her, but I'd have to be sure I wasn't doing it just to hurt her."

"Why would you want to hurt her?" Charles looks bewildered.

"Because I've always been jealous of her."

"Of Tira? Why?" Can he really not know this?

"Because she's beautiful, or hadn't you noticed?" Annie feels foolish and petty, admitting her jealousy.

"Tira?" He sounds genuinely amazed. "She's good looking, of course, but you're more – I don't know why – more interesting to me."

"That's only because she's your cousin."

"No, it isn't." He sounds very definite.

Somehow this creates a small wave of good will that seems to flow through the room. It allows them to realize they're ravenous. Annie makes canned salmon sandwiches and Charles throws together a green salad. Annie lights candles and turns off the overhead light and they sit down to their meal. She feels the air getting heavy again. The little wave carries them through the meal. But the stuff they've talked about so far is the easy stuff.

THEY SIT IN THE LIVING ROOM, dark except for the candles casting amber light on their faces and dripping wax in fantastic patterns like frozen waterfalls. Charles is getting ready to speak, Annie can almost see the words hanging in the air.

"Annie," he asks, "did you sleep with anyone?" His voice is soft, the announcer sound patterns totally abandoned. Once again it strikes her how young his face looks. How undefended.

"Yes. Once." She wishes she didn't have to say it.

"Harold Borebank," he says, a statement, not a question. She nods. "He's the only man you ever mentioned." Charles tries to make it matter-of-fact, but of course it isn't. It's his way of letting the words sink in. Words he must have expected to hear.

"Why did you do it?" he asks, trying to keep his voice from accusing.

"I've been trying to work it out," she says. "It seemed like things were sort of on hold between us. I didn't know if we could get back together."

"If you felt that way, I guess that's how it was for you." He tries not to show how hurt he is, but it's there in the careful, still way he holds his face, as if movement will destroy his control.

"You think I betrayed you," she says.

"I wish it hadn't happened," he says. "But it has, and it doesn't have to be the end of everything. Not if we can find out how to get on with things again."

Annie would like to seize that possibility, but it's too easy. What she's going to say scares her.

"I wouldn't want to, if it was going to be like before."

He nods, looking very serious. "No. It couldn't be like before. But what would it be like?"

"I don't know," Annie says. "I don't know what I want yet. Do you?"

"Not in any detail. Maybe like we've been today. That was better, wasn't it? Better than before?"

"Yes," Annie agrees, "it was much better than before."

"I like being here with you," he says eagerly. "Just talking. And I like being in this house. I didn't think I would, but I find it beautiful. We had better stuff in our apartment, but it wasn't beautiful, was it?"

"No," she says, "it wasn't." Is he saying he loves her?

"I didn't know I needed that."

"I didn't know either," she says. "I had to find it out."

"With Harold," he says, trying not to break down, "maybe you were making sure we couldn't go back…to the way it was."

Annie reaches across the table and takes his hand in hers. "I'm sorry I hurt you." When he can't keep back his tears, she goes to him, holds his head against her breasts. "I'm sorry, Charles," she says.

THE CANDLES HAVE ALMOST BURNED DOWN in the dark room. Annie has totally lost track of the time. It feels like she's run a ten-kilometre race. They have been sitting a long time in the big wing chairs.

"I know about the baby," Charles says, finally.

"How?" Annie asks, wondering if he's pleased.

"I know the feel of your body," he says. "You were pregnant before the funeral, of course."

"Yes, but I didn't know."

"How far along are you?"

"About three and a half months."

"Annie, whatever happens with us, I'm happy about the baby." Annie feels an immense relief. He wants the baby, of course he does. "Are you glad?" he asks.

"Yes," she says, and he smiles a little. "But I'm scared too."

"Scared of what?"

"Killer bees."

"Killer bees? Didn't I do a report on them? But they're far away from here yet."

"But they're coming, aren't they?"

"Well, they might be. Or they might not. Nobody knows."

"Right. They might not be. Or they might."

"They probably wouldn't survive the winters. Wasn't that in the report?"

"Charles, a boy tried to rob me last week. On the street, in broad daylight, as they say. He hurt my breast, and he called me a whore."

"Annie, did you see a doctor? Are you okay?"

"Yes, I'm okay. Listen to me. He was just a teenager with pimples on his face and no education, and he thought he hated me. He did hate me."

"I see them all the time in the city. I guess they're here now too."

"They're everywhere. Cold winters aren't enough to stop them. Charles, what if the baby's a boy?"

"Do you think it's a boy? Annie?"

"I don't know. But if it is, how can we make sure he isn't like the boy who hurt me? How, Charles?"

"We could spend time with him, help him learn."

"They're not all from bad homes, you know."

"Listen, I can't promise you everything will go right. But why would we start out thinking we're going to lose?" Annie looks uncertain. "Annie, we can do it."

She takes a careful breath. "We might not be together."

"Then we would each do our part separately," he says firmly. "Whether we're together or apart, I'm going to be this kid's father."

"That's good." He's right, she doesn't have to be in this all alone.

"I know you get scared. Everybody does. I do."

"If only I'd known that," she says. "You never said so before."

"I've never been a father before."

"You really did want to be, didn't you?"

"Of course," he says, almost angry. "What did you think?"

"I guess I thought it was, oh, to prove your masculinity or something."

"Annie, for Christ's sake, I wanted a child. I didn't think I needed reasons. Do you need reasons?"

Why couldn't they have talked like this before? Now, looking at him, she understands that there's something in him that wants to look after their child. Maybe he wouldn't always do it that well, but it's part of his nature that he wants to.

"I used to think I needed reasons," she says. "I don't seem to anymore."

"You're pregnant with our child. You can't stop me from being happy about it."

"I don't want to stop you."

"Can I touch your stomach?"

"It doesn't kick or anything. That doesn't come for a while yet."

"I want to feel."

She takes his hand and holds it over her belly. A slow smile spreads over his face.

"See," she says, "there isn't anything to feel."

"There is so," he says.

## CHAPTER TWENTY-NINE

The room is just as before. Two neatly made beds, two dressers, two gauze-covered metal cups on two bedside tables. Charles has his notebook in hand and scribbles away furiously. He draws a quick but functional sketch of the room, complete to the black-striped grey blankets and the round clay pigs. Trying to absorb the room, make it part of his mental space. Annie is surprised at how evocative the sketch is. Another of the things she didn't know he could do.

She's prepared for the emotion this time and finds it less overwhelming. She wonders if Charles feels it. He runs his hand over the rough blankets, checks in the empty drawers. He points to the left-hand bed. "That's where I see Eamon. Jimmy on the other side."

He moves out into the long porch with its row of beds, each with a wicker visitor's chair. He goes to the screen windows and gazes out. Again he sketches, first the porch and then the view through the screen of hills and sky. Far up on the hill he puts in two figures, almost too small to be anything at all, but still suggestive of children climbing.

Sensing her watching, Charles helps Annie to one of the chairs and gently propels her into it, without taking attention away from his notebook. Like something that belongs to him which he has to look out for. Annie considers stopping him, pointing out that she's a woman four months pregnant, not an invalid, but she's too fascinated. She can't quite remember if he was always like this.

When he comes to the bed and moves to stretch out on it – no doubt to see what Eamon would have seen – her arm goes out to prevent him.

"No, Charles, don't do that," she says sharply.

"I just want to see all this from his point of view," he says, surprised.

"I don't want you to lie there."

"I didn't think you were superstitious." But he makes no further move towards the bed.

"I'm not. I was going to do the same thing myself. But the woman who was here stopped me. She used to be a patient here, and she said I shouldn't lie where Eamon lay."

"Oh, all right." He begins sketching the doorway to the bedroom. "A patient, eh? I'd love to talk to her."

"I'm sure she'll be glad to help. She's full of information and only too pleased to find anybody interested. I think she's trying to make sure people don't forget."

"We're her man, then." The doorway takes shape on the paper, with the shadowy outline of a woman, Maude it must be, in the opening. "Could we give her a call?"

"I suppose so. I thought she'd be here, but they must have different volunteers on different days."

Charles works in silence, the figure growing uncannily like the way Annie imagines Maude. She wonders how his vision can be so similar, until she recalls showing him the photos of Eamon and Maude.

The floorboards creak. "Oh, hello," a woman's voice says, "I didn't know anyone had come in."

The woman is about fifty, dark-eyed and slender, with a name tag reading, "Maryna Lezak, Volunteer."

"Is this your first time at our museum?" she asks.

"No, it's my second," Annie says, "but my husband's first."

"There's a lot to see, isn't there?"

"There certainly is," Charles says, although there isn't all that much.

Maryna Lezak looks at Charles's notebook. "Oh, what a nice drawing."

"I was hoping we might run into Vi Tripps," Annie says. "She gave me a lot of information about the days when she was a patient here. I was hoping she could talk to my husband too – we're thinking about writing a book about the San."

"I'm afraid that's not possible," the woman says.

"I could call her at home, I suppose."

"I'm sorry, but Vi passed away. A couple of weeks ago."

"What?" Annie says, thinking the woman's made a mistake, or, as she's often thought in such situations, that she's misheard or somehow misunderstood. Is there some innocuous, everyday meaning for the term "passed away"? "She can't have died. I never saw anyone so healthy in my life."

"Well, you know what it was like for the Old Crocks. They never knew when they might break down again. She always fought it off before, but I guess this time she hadn't the strength. And of course, losing Billy – her husband – last year. Poor old duck. We're going to miss her here. She was really the spirit of the place."

Annie can't help it, she starts to cry. Charles drops his notebook on the bed and scoots over to her, putting his arm protectively on her shoulder.

"I'm sorry," the volunteer says, "I didn't realize you knew her well."

"She was very kind to me. I looked forward to seeing her again."

"She was truly a wonderful woman. Always so cheer-ful. She did her regular shift here at the museum the day she died, and then that night she began to cough the way they do, and she threw a terrible haemorrhage. She called for help, but by the time they got to her –"

"Annie, would you like to come outside for a breath of air," Charles is saying, "it's a little stuffy in here. Excuse us, please." He gets her past the woman's offered ministrations and apologies.

Coming out the main door into air and sunshine, Annie feels a tremendous release. Nothing will ever induce her to enter that building again. Vi Tripps did so all the time, going in and out of the house of death until it was as familiar as her own face. Until the one time when the trick was no longer possible.

Charles finds them a warm flat rock in the sun. He holds her. "It's all right. Just breathe deeply. I shouldn't have taken you there. I shouldn't have let her babble on."

Annie lets him hold her. It feels good.

Charles spots a drink machine on an outside wall of the building. He goes over to it, and at first it keeps spitting back his money, but after several more tries he makes it give him a can of ginger ale. He offers this to Annie with the air of a mother bird about to pop a worm down her nestling's throat. She gives a little sob, half weeping, half laughing. The soft drink is delicious; sweeter than she'd like, but the ginger gives it a clean astringent quality, as if the drink really must be made from the genuine spring water mentioned on the side of the can. Pure, clean water, if such a thing exists anymore.

They sit side by side, shoulder wedged against shoulder, sipping the drink in turn. When Charles gets up to return the can to a recycling bin, Annie looks to the northwest, to the hills Eamon watched from his windows. She imagines, superimposed on their outlines, the small black shapes Charles drew to represent the children.

Charles returns, still looking concerned. No doubt trying to think up additional first aid procedures to try on her.

"I'm much better now," she says, to forestall him. And she is. An idea slides into her mind. "Charles, I need to climb the hill. The one the children climbed."

THE RISE BEGINS VERY GRADUALLY, almost invisibly. Annie manages easily, breathing deeply and feeling strength flowing back into her arms and legs. Charles keeps an eye out for big rocks, gopher holes, and cacti, steering her out of the way of these hazards. Touched by his concern, she's not offended by the slight officiousness he can't keep from creeping into his manner.

The sun is hot for early June, but the breeze keeps it comfortable. Annie is pleased she decided to wear Edith's flowered dress. It allows the air to swirl around her legs in a way she finds delightful. The grass is hummocky and very thick, washed with a delicate tinge of green after the wet spring. Clumps of wildflowers Annie has no names for bloom along the way, visited by hovering non-killer bees. And the prickly-pear cactus, its fleshy leaves holding the water that will keep it alive in seasons when there is no rain.

The hill is much higher than she imagined. They climb a steep rise that looks like the top of the hill, because nothing can be seen beyond it. As they reach the top, the perspective changes, showing a brief drop in front of them and then a second higher rise beyond.

At the top of the second rise they turn and look into the valley – and the arm of the valley that shelters the San. The buildings looked diminished, flat, their detail smoothed away by the distance; the lake is a glassy sheet, placid waves indicated by what looks like rows of squiggly pen marks.

At the third and final rise, they remember Eamon's description of the hills. They aren't really hills rising above a plain. The valley is the deviation, a minor abyss carved into the earth below the plain.

Ahead of them on the prairie is a fence and an ordinary wheat field showing the first green blades. The wind, stronger up here, vibrates the wire fence to make a deep humming drone that grounds the whole spectrum of sound. A meadowlark sits on a fencepost and sings elaborately. Annie strains to catch and remember the pattern of the song, but can't. Do that again, she mentally challenges it; and the bird does it again, but the mystery remains, ungraspable, at least by her. She wishes she had a tape recorder, not in the end to unravel the song, but only to be able to hear it again later to recall this place.

A small grove of stunted poplar stands improbably at the top of the hill. Charles leads her by the hand into its coolness, past sturdy wind-hardened trees with scarred initials of lovers branded in the bark of their narrow trunks. In the centre in a small grassy clearing, the sun shines through. The lake is still visible, but the curve of the hill cuts off the view of the San. Charles sits them down on the grass and fishes in his pocket until he finds a roll of English toffees. He peels the paper from one and offers it to her. The sweetness of it and the sucking are pleasant. He takes one himself and they sit companionably. The meadowlark sings again, very close.

"I can't believe Vi's gone."

"What happened with her?"

"She took me to her house to rest." Annie speaks through tears. "She did some kind of healing for me. Moving her hands over my body, but not touching. I felt the most amazing warmth and energy flow into me. There's no way someone like that could die."

"That woman said she lost her husband last year. Maybe she decided she'd gone on long enough." Annie looks unconvinced. "Whatever she did for you, it was her choice."

"She was worried about me being on my own, but she was relieved when I told her Edith was looking out for me."

"Is that what Edith's been doing?"

"In her own peculiar way. Charles, I think I'm getting more like her. Maybe what I need is Edith's bloody-mindedness and Vi's sanity. But then where will I be?"

"You'll still be Annie, only more so."

"You're just buttering me up because I'm having your baby."

"That's right. I have to keep you happy."

They sit listening to the birds, the wind. Luckily there are few mosquitoes at this hour. A robin lands close by and hops around fearlessly, as if they're part of the grass. A breeze slips by them, soft as a moth's wing. If only Eamon could have seen this place. If only he could have come here with Maude.

Charles is absolutely still, but his whole body is a question. Eloquent pleas and arguments flow soundlessly between them. Things that would sound foolish if they were said aloud. Annie feels calm here and, for the moment, safe. Grief has receded, allowing room for desire, or maybe it's part of the desire.

Charles is hardly breathing. She touches his face. It feels more intimate than any previous touch between them. They unfold themselves backwards onto the grass, lying face to face, holding each other. They kiss, and the warmth astonishes Annie. She pulls him close, against her breasts, her belly. One or the other of them lifts her skirt, eases away her underpants. When Charles enters her, he shakes all over. He feels her tighten around him and begins to move. Each movement is like a question or a petition for acceptance; each takes him deeper. And creates such strong feeling in her it makes her gasp for breath. Dr. Summers has told her there is more potential for sensation during pregnancy because the body grows a new and more efficient network of blood vessels around the womb and vulva, the better to carry out its work. Dr. Summers has not exaggerated the truth. But there's more to it. She recognizes Charles in some new way that is beyond the previous history between them. She understands that there are many more things to be known about them both.

## CHAPTER THIRTY

*I*n the paddock with the pony. Night air warm and thick, gritty like the dregs of Greek coffee. Moon and stars like bright rough crystals on midnight blue cloth. Charlie nuzzles her; she strokes his face, fingers electric, crackling. He nudges her shoulder. What does he want? To give her a ride? She's never ridden by herself.

The pony moves to the paddock fence. She climbs to the second rail and slides onto his back. Feels his solid round-barrelled body, the rough short coat prickly against her legs, against the soft skin of vulva and inner thigh.

Charlie walks. She feels his muscles move, feels his warmth and his sharp sweat soak into her skin. He breaks into a trot. Too bouncy, no reins to hold onto. Hold onto my mane, she hears a voice say in her head, though Charlie's never talked before. She sinks her fingers into the long silky stuff as he breaks into a gallop, a lovely, light, rocking gallop. She's never done galloping before; it turns out to be easy.

Charlie swings in a wide loop at the centre of the paddock and, picking up speed, heads straight for the fence. My God, he'll smash them both. But his muscles tense and gather power and, as she instinctively flattens her body against him, he sails over the fence.

They run hard across the river flats; Charlie's hooves beat like drums on the soft earth. Other horses come out of the dark to run with them, their hoofbeats echo around the valley like thunder. Old horses, spirited young horses, in an array of colours visible in the starlight. A big bay hunter keeps trying to get ahead, as three powerful Arabian mares, dappled greys, run to one side of Charlie with effortless delicacy.

Out of the night a pearly grey mare with deeper grey spots surges forward, mane and tail streaming behind, an envelope of glowing light, the moon transformed to an animal. They all run together, leaping and then falling back to earth, galloping that's almost flying, like a carousel loosed from its moorings and set in unending motion. The grey mare takes the lead now, stronger than any of them, lighting their way.

Straight to the river they run, its waters no longer in full flood, but still swelling over the banks. She feels the old fear rise in her belly, but they all plunge into the river together, legs stroking water warm and thick as blood. Into the deep currents they plunge, the river eddies and swirls around them, fear dissolves in the water. She is not drowning, she can breathe in this water. The other mares surround her, their bodies brush against her, as do ranks of strangely orderly minnows that nip and tickle and dart away, and tiny insects that flick her skin, and eerie threadlike grasses that trail across her legs, her arms, her face. All these things she is aware of, and of the dark, reedy odour of the river.

Then the moon's falling into the river, exploding into millions of silver bubbles. Charlie swims for the silver, straight for the moon's radiance, plunging upward, his breath and hers streaming into the water like drops of mercury, as they strain now for the light.

They break through into sweet air that strips the water from their bodies and fills their lungs. Nearby the three greys rise into the light and together they climb the riverbank. No more horses emerge. They remain behind in the water. She won't see them anymore. Annie feels tears on her face for the glowing moon horse.

And then one more horse does surface, not one of the mares, but a foal's head breaking the water, its spindly legs stroking for the bank. She watches it with great interest, not sure if it's a filly or a colt, as it takes the air for what might be the first time. It finds its feet and runs towards her, a graceful Appaloosa with galaxies of white spots on its blue-black rump. Charlie starts to run, and the foal follows after them, keeping up easily.

She turns to look and without warning the foal streaks ahead, leading the way now with Charlie and the Arabians working hard to keep the little horse in sight. Until they are only following a trail of light racing under the full moon riding high in the night. The shiny trail grows more and more distant until Charlie slows and lets it go.

CHAPTER THIRTY-ONE

Edith swirls brandy in a bell-shaped glass and drinks. Charles lifts his a moment later. Annie sips tea, lying propped up with pillows on Edith's chaise longue. A citronella mosquito coil drifts smoke into the air to mingle with the sweetness of roses and the surging heavy fragrance of peonies.

Annie's arms and legs have reached that perfect state of warmth where winter can be forgotten for a time, here in the dark summerhouse where the air's still fluid and easy although it's close to midnight. A few minutes ago she claimed to see some last rays of light in the west and neither Charles nor Edith bothered to say it was just her imagination.

She has been living this month in a trance, a sunspell cast by the waxing light. She has become aware of her own mass and gravity, her own complex arrangements with the solar system; her daily dance with moon and sun.

Today is the summer solstice; the sun has pushed back the night as far as it will go. Tomorrow the balance will turn back towards night and dark. But the earth is warm now as Edith's garden passes from spring into full summer. Annie sees the younger Edith and Tom on just such a night here in the summerhouse, as real as the people now around her. Blanket on the floor, clothes cast aside, moonlight silvering their skin, their hair, their eyes. She wonders if the other two see the same vision. Perhaps Edith is never here without seeing it.

Below the river runs swiftly, once more contained between its banks.

SOMETHING FLIES THROUGH THE SUMMERHOUSE, an intimate flapping of wings and rushing air close to Annie's face.

"Bats," Edith says.

"I never knew we had bats here," Charles says.

"They come out at night along the river," Edith answers. "Lots of people don't know they're here. Most would rather not know."

Annie leans against the back of the chaise longue. She wears a bright yellow stretchy dress that comes almost to her knees. It fits, soft and smooth, over the heap of wheat. On which her hands are interlaced.

A movement registers deep inside her and everything's transformed again, just as when she first acknowledged she was pregnant.

"Charles. Edith. I think it moved."

"Very likely," Edith says. "It's getting to be about that time."

Charles edges his chair closer and rests his hand on her belly, still pleased as a child to be granted this privilege.

ANNIE RISES FROM THE CHAISE, still awkward from her new centre of gravity, and picks up an unglazed clay urn. She looks to Edith and Edith nods slightly. She walks out behind the summerhouse to a small stand of birch and poplar, moves into the trees to a small grassy clearing; she touches the bark, rough but soft, of a poplar. Tipping the urn, she watches the unexpectedly heavy and gritty contents fall to the grass, brightened by moonlight. She gives the urn a shake; a few more bits fall to the grass. The night flows softly around her, the trees a companionable circle. She smells moist earth and the river, hears the waters race. Every part of her is warm. Annie returns to the others.

ARCHING OVER THE SUMMERHOUSE, a mountain ash in full leaf has begun to flower. Later in the summer it will yield its crop of gorgeous scarlet berries. This tree is the most magnificent example of a mountain ash Annie has ever seen, four large trunks growing out of a single place in the earth, each one as thick as her own waist. It was probably planted, decades ago, by Eamon, when he tended the garden for Edith's parents.

Charles has explained that the mountain ash is from the same family as the rowan. In the winter, the birds will feed once again on the sweet, frozen berries. Maybe Annie will be here to see them or maybe she'll be far away. Edith will be here. In the cold season when Annie's baby will be born.

A cool breeze touches her face, raises the hairs on her arms. Not so far from the summerhouse, a small chunk of the earth crumbles away and tumbles almost noiselessly down the bank.

## ABOUT THE AUTHOR

BARBARA SAPERGIA writes fiction and drama for stage, radio, television, and film. Her previous fiction includes: *South Hill Girls* (Fifth House 1992), adapted by her and broadcast on radio in Canada and Australia; and the best-selling Coteau novel, *Foreigners* (1984), which she is currently adapting for film for Saskatchewan's Minds Eye Pictures.

Sapergia has had seven plays professionally produced and her numerous radio plays include appearances on CBC'S Morningside, Vanishing Point, and Stereodrama. Her television credits include working as a writer/producer on the *Prairie Berry Pie* children's series.

Barbara Sapergia is a graduate of the Universities of Saskatchewan and Manitoba. She has lived in many cities in Canada and England and currently lives in Saskatoon with her husband, writer and editor Geoffrey Ursell.

ACKNOWLEDGEMENTS

I WISH TO THANK:

Jack Hodgins, for being a wonderfully thoughtful, thorough, and sympathetic editor;

The Saskatchewan Arts Board for a grant that provided some of the time needed to work on this novel;

The Leighton Artists Colony, Banff, where some of the novel was written, for providing an excellent working space and kindly and helpful staff;

Edna Alford, Bonnie Burnard, Bob Currie, Jennifer Glossop, Don Kerr, Wenda McArthur, and Janice Ursell for their helpful comments at various stages of writing;

Karen Steadman, Nik Burton, and Duncan Campbell for their skilled and dedicated work producing this book;

Margaret Hryniuk, Betty Lou Trimmer, Paul and Sis Trimmer, and Veronica Eddy Brock, all of whom helped me understand the strong spirits of the Old Crocks;

Geoffrey Ursell for his insightful comments at all stages of writing and for his continuing love and support.